BETTY BURTON

Betty Burton is the author of *Jude, Jaen, Women of No Account, Hard Loves, Easy Riches, The Consequences of War, Goodbye Piccadilly, Rose Quinlan* as well as the acclaimed collection of short stories *Women Are Bloody Marvellous!* She has written for both television and radio and won the Chichester Festival Theatre Award. She is currently working on a new novel.

Born in Romsey, Hampshire, she now lives in Southsea with her husband, Russ.

BETTY BURTON

Long, Hot Summer

HarperCollins*Publishers*

HarperCollins*Publishers*
77–85 Fulham Palace Road,
Hammersmith, London w6 8jb

This paperback edition 1994
1 3 5 7 9 8 6 4 2

First published in Great Britain by
HarperCollins*Publishers* 1993

ISBN 0 00 647635 X

Set in Linotron Sabon by
Rowland Phototypesetting Ltd
Bury St Edmunds, Suffolk

Printed in Great Britain by
HarperCollinsManufacturing Glasgow

For my new granddaughter

Grace Elanor Burton

Elanor means 'The Golden Flower' –
how appropriate to this book

Thanks to my son Simon Burton for his generosity in making his papers on crop symbols, barrows and 'dragon veins' freely available to me. Also for raising my awareness of the practice of *feng-shui* and acting as guide to some spectacular pictograms.

AUTHOR'S NOTE

On a summer evening in late June 1990, I saw my first real-life pictogram in a wheatfield at Cheesefoot Head near Winchester.

Although I had been interested in the phenomenon since I first heard of it, had read whatever I could find and looked at dozens of photographs and diagrams, and although many of these occurrences were appearing in the area where I had set my earlier novels – virtually in my own backyard – I had not until then visited any of the sites.

In the mid-seventies the formations appeared as small, simple circles, then they began appearing larger and in groups of circles arranged like spots on dominoes. Over the years larger and larger and ever more complicated arrangements of rings and circles emerged, until today vast and beautiful pictograms are appearing.

Although the formations are best viewed from above, on this particular evening, even from the vantage point at the top of a rise, I could see well enough the impressive size of the dumb-bell figure formed in the Cheesefoot Head field.

I went down to take a closer look at how the corn was laid down. Having played in hayfields and cornfields throughout my childhood I had often seen windblown patches and trampled play 'nests', but could not see how the stalks of this configuration could have been bent in the way they were without breaking.

Standing around inside the figure was a satisfying, calming experience – a bit like being in a quiet country churchyard on a sunny day. I began to wonder how it must feel to wake up one morning to find that a circlemaker had come close to your home during the night and left a 300-foot 'engraving'.

Whilst speculating, this novel came to mind. I claim nothing for any mystical influence, I can only say that, whilst standing around in the flattened corn, *Long, Hot Summer* came to mind almost complete, by the time I reached home that evening I knew the whole story, and by the next day I had got the first 6000 words written.

A year has passed and the novel was completed months ago. Throughout 1991 hoaxes were perpetrated, while new explanations and old theories have been contorted to fit each new development in the on-going 'Corn Circle' story. I don't think we have heard the last of it. Hoaxes have been demonstrated, but the hoaxers have left as many questions unanswered as they have answered. Whatever the outcome, there can't be many people who have seen the real thing who have been untouched by the scale and beauty of these ephemeral creations.

BETTY BURTON
SEPTEMBER 1991

LIST OF CHARACTERS

The Hampshire Tallentires

Nat	Creator of the Sunbarrow Farms complex
Myrr	Married to Nat
Daisy	Their eldest child, an editor of children's books
Rin	Daisy's twin brother, with a successful career in advertising
Jake	The younger son and Sunbarrow Farms manager
Poppy	Youngest child, ready for university
Mary	Rin's wife, an entertainer with 'The Hotheads'

The New York Yins

Dr Kuan-Yin	Analytical psychologist and 'phenomenon' researcher
'Lady' Yin	Founder of the Blossom Park restaurant chain
George	Eldest of the three brothers who run the Blossom Parks and Kuan-Yin's father
June	George's wife and Kuan-Yin's mother

Lenny and Burt	Second and third of the Blossom Park sons
Louis and Henry	Kuan-Yin's cousins and the third Blossom Park generation
Heavenly	Louis' wife

Hong Kong

| Lee Han | 'Lady' Yin's eldest son |

The Petherbridges

Roz	Myrr Tallentire's friend
Duncan	Her husband, one-time vicar of Childencombe
Ian and Malcolm	Their twin sons

Childencombe villagers

Lizz Taylor	A painter and Jake's occasional lover
Grandpa Cole	Village elder
Granny Cole	His wife, member of an old Hampshire family connected with the Tallentires
Mrs Pack	Their daughter
Chrissie	Her eldest child, Poppy's friend
Susie and Rich	The younger Pack children
Jez and Phil Carter	Owners of the village shop
Mimm and Emma	Their son and daughter
Rex Farenbach	Proprietor of the Green Man pub and its up-market restaurant
Tom	His son

Mike Alexander	Analytical psychologist with a Harley Street practice
Martin Lilie	Film-maker and corn circle enthusiast
Young Sid Postlethwaite	Childencombe's barber
Matt Pridhoe	Schoolfriend of Poppy, Tom and Emma, son of one of the 'newcomelatelys'
Bishop Rupert	Duncan Petherbridge's old school chum: 'The Great Roo'
Teddy	An old flame of Roz Petherbridge
Maurice Cockrill	The Tallentires' solicitor
Addie Haffenfleish	Kuan-Yin's secretary in New York

ONE

Here is a place of disaffection
Time before and time after . . .

T. S. ELIOT, Four Quartets

Time was, long, long ago and the land was still dreaming, when the spirits of women and men were free to wander, following the spirit of Gaea, the Earth Mother.

Then women and men stopped wandering and the dream passed, and they began to lose touch with the Earth Spirit which, for a while, continued to roam free.

The Spirit was wonderful and powerful. As well as being the creator and provider, it could move the firmament, crack the sky with lightning, make fire, flood plains, spew molten rock from the earth or whip up a tornado. The energy that, in the wandering days, people had held in awe yet understood, now changed to fear and ignorance. Now there arose warrior castes who desired to have the energy of the Spirit pinned down for their use. So they began to devise methods of capture and searched for points on the known paths along which the Earth Spirit flowed in its wanderings.

The Ancient Greeks had their god Zeus send out eagles east and west, and where their paths crossed they waylaid and impaled the Spirit. Soon that was the way of things in other lands.

HAMPSHIRE, ENGLAND, LATE SPRING, 1990

Jake Tallentire, as blond, handsome and physically perfect as many a Hollywood romantic lead, misses the tack and hits the base of his thumb.

'Sod it!' He thrusts the hammer into the torn back pocket

of his shorts, a pair of cut-off washed-out denims, and sucks the damage.

The cardboard notice didn't warrant four tacks anyhow. It would probably be gone by tomorrow.

> KEEP OUT.
> BE WARNED.
> THIS FIELD HAS BEEN SPRAYED
> WITH INSECTICIDE.

Jake's Old Man had made the notice, you could almost hear his short fuse fizzing:

'I don't care what you say, it's still trespass, and if I had my health and strength I'd get out there with a twelve-bore. You're too bloody free and easy, Jake, you let them treat Sunbarrow like it was a safari park. I sweated blood for this land.'

Jake knows that.

Sunbarrow Farm has not come easily to its present size and profitability. And the cost has been to more people than his Old Man, and higher than sweated blood.

Jake knows too that the Old Man's health and strength isn't the problem – it is the fact of total achievement. Jake's Old Man is like a collector who has achieved a complete set – he has collected Sunbarrow Farm, and there are no pieces left to desire.

HONG KONG, LATE SPRING, 1990

Dr Kuan-Yin's slim ankles and knees emerge from her Uncle Lee Han's long, dark-blue limousine after it has slid silently to a halt at the entrance to Hong Kong airport. The young and smartly-turned-out chauffeur's body pulsates in every minute muscle. Every day for the last six weeks she

18

has been doing this to him. Every day she has invaded his daydreams and every night he has been disturbed by lust. He doesn't know what Jungian analytical psychologists do or what her books are about or why she appears on American TV chat-shows. He is not interested in her mind, for she is beautiful, desirable, and she touches people when she speaks to them. When she is speaking to him he is not a mere chauffeur, he is not mere at all.

She calls him Honey. He can't bear it that her six-week visit with her uncle is over.

She has this effect on men.

HAMPSHIRE

Myrr Tallentire, trapped in the chaos and mess which is choking the old Winchester bypass, sits in a long line of cone-guided traffic. She has a faint smile on her face and she relaxes into the unfamiliar but comfortable shape of the bucket-seat of her new car. She feels like whooping with the sheer exhilaration of her satisfying day, but Myrr is a mature woman and has long since learned how to savour pleasures. It has taken her many years to fulfil today's particular fantasy.

Feeling her way into the powerful engine with the short gear-stick, she inches forward. The rampant sound which comes from the exhaust, Myrr finds very satisfying. As the traffic moves slowly along between the closely-lined cones, she passes on her off-side a group of barrows which mark one of the boundaries of Sunbarrow.

All the land from here to a village five miles distant is Tallentire land.

Nat Tallentire comes away from the window from where he has been watching for Myrr's return for the last hour, goes to the kitchen and opens the cabinet where his pills are kept. A moment's hesitation, then he slams the door on the little brown bottles which remind him that Nat Tallentire is no longer master of Sunbarrow Farm, but that Sunbarrow has mastered Nat Tallentire.

'Ah, bugger it!' he says to the cat. 'I'll take bloody pills when I say I'll take bloody pills! Where the hell is she, Tib? She goes off in the morning, saying she thinks she'll have a run over to the auction at Salisbury, and then she's gone all day.' The cat cupboard-loves until Nat gives in with half a cold bacon sandwich Jake has left. 'She could have phoned, couldn't she? And there's nothing on the television except that bloody Irishman.' But the cat has wolfed the sandwich and has gone.

HONG KONG

At the airport, neglected by his smitten chauffeur, Kuan-Yin's Uncle Lee Han emerges from his beautiful limousine and asks his niece, 'You have *lo p'an* safe, Kuan-Yin?'

'Don't change the subject, Uncle Han: I said that you must come to New York to visit your mother. Lady Yin is in good health, but she is very old.'

'I hope that you be lucky to find Custom officer who will agree that *lo p'an* is scientific instrument, not smuggle antique.'

The young chauffeur offers his helpful hand to the beautiful Dr Yin and respectfully watches the way she swings her knees sideways from her seat. His heart breaks a little. She is leaving, flying out to her home in New York. Last night he imagined himself running up the aircraft steps and falling at her feet. He has dreamed up a wealthier version of himself, visualized entering her office in Park Avenue. On seeing him, she would clutch her throat with emotion. He is sure that she likes much younger men, and that he has not misinterpreted the way she has looked at him, touched his arm when complimenting him on his driving skill.

He loves the way she manages to be small, quietly-spoken, and at the same time have people, without understanding why, step aside for her. Even her name is exotic – Kuan-Yin.

The chauffeur is right. Kuan-Yin has something – presence, mystique, charisma, sex-appeal? Whatever it is, it works to make people follow her with their eyes.

Women are captured by her striking style.

Men by the way her neat ass moves within a soft, kingfisher-blue skirt.

Europeans guess that she must be some movie star.

Americans remember having seen her on TV chat-shows.

Chinese might guess that they read the signs – ardour and elegance – indicating that she was born in a Year of the Horse, but she is slightly older than that. She was born in the Year of the Tiger – short-paced, up-front, quick mind and the only partner suited to mate with the Dragon.

'This way.' She points to an indicator with an enamel-tipped finger. Uncle and chauffeur follow her direction.

Today she wears her hair up, decorated and padded in a version of a traditional geisha style. Her face too has been made up to emphasize the racial features of her almond-shaped eyes, small mouth, ivory skin-tone and black lashes and brows.

It is only in appearance that there is any suggestion of geisha. Kuan-Yin, wearing large tortoiseshell-framed glasses and carrying a leather document case, strides as confidently as her high heels will allow.

She wags an admonishing finger at her Uncle Han. 'Lady Yin is very old, Uncle Han. You should visit New York before it is too late.'

Uncle Han too is not a person to go unnoticed. He is tall and looks almost too much like Charlie Chan to be true. Perhaps, on seeing some old movies, he understood the advantage of fostering this resemblance and has slipped into the role. At least it does Lee Han no harm to have the enigmatic eyes, stretch smile and dignified manner of the old Hollywood detective.

Several people here recognize him as Lee Han, Hong Kong's most prestigious *hsein-sheng*, master of the art of *feng-shui*. They bow a little or nod respectfully as he makes his progress along the concourse. Years ago his name was Lee Han Yin, but since he left mainland China for Hong Kong, his family name has been let go.

He is the foremost *feng-shui* consultant: no new prestigious building in Hong Kong is ever contemplated without its architect engaging Lee Han to consider whether the effects of earth configurations and the flow of living energy – the *ch'i* – is favourable. Most Hong Kong Chinese like to think themselves *feng-shui* experts, but only the likes of Lee Han have merchant banks and multinational companies as clients. On their way about Hong Kong these last weeks, he has pointed out to Kuan-Yin impressive buildings which have been built in this or that particular location and of this or that particular shape on Lee Han's advice.

'Look through window this side. See new premises of bank. It was necessary to have architect alter position of entrance . . .

'See office-block on corner. New House of Finance, once planned on site under most malicious influence of Wanchai, the Bad Woman rock. It was necessary to re-site position and alter design.' He had stretched his lips in a self-satisfied smile. 'For the fee I take a new automobile each year for ten years. Daimler is first payment. What does your father drive – Cadillac? Aah. Tell George he should buy more dignify auto, maybe German-built, maybe English. Client like to see success, also they are impress by dignity. European autos have dignity. Queen go only in English auto. Very dignify.'

A flash of amusement across Kuan-Yin's expression at

the thought of her father's red Mustang, yellow Cadillac, and custom-built English Morgan, each bearing the cherry-tree logo of the Yin family's Blossom Park restaurant chain.

Rich and renowned as he is, Lee Han is happy to follow in the path now swathed by his niece through the passengers.

They have reached the departure desk and stand in line. Lee Han's suffering chauffeur deposits Kuan-Yin's baggage; she rewards him with a word and a sweet smile. 'We could do with drivers like you in New York. The package on the back seat is for you . . . it's a silk shirt, I hope that you like it.' He is overwhelmed. He thanks her with restraint and respect. He salutes, keeping his eyes upon her just too long for correctness, and leaves to soothe his cracked heart with the shirt and the gleaming body of Lee Han's new Daimler.

'Goodbye, Uncle Han, and thank you for . . . oh, for everything, honey! Specially the *lo p'an*.'

'I hope you will not be tempt to use it for serious *feng-shui*. Is not suited to female spirit.'

She gives his hand a reassuring squeeze not backed up with words.

He wags his head in admonition. 'All China people like try *feng-shui*.'

'I promise that if I ever build a house, then I shall engage Lee Han to arrange the most propitious situation.'

'Please send copy of Dr Yin book. Sign for Uncle Han.'

'Sure I will. Better still, I'll dedicate the book to you.'

He gave a little Charlie Chan bow with lowered eyelids.

Waving, Kuan-Yin went through into the Departure area.

Until he could see her no more, he stood watching. She had swooped into his life six weeks ago, cast her spell upon him, drawn secrets from him, written notes and made tapes and videos of his work, and now he felt like a child who has had a wonderful treat unexpectedly cut short.

Kuan-Yin was the only member of the Yin family he had seen in a very long time. Lee Han had been born in the Year of the Snake, whose attribute was wisdom – but he had probably not been snake-like in telling such an inquisitive and forceful woman so much of the practice of *feng-shui*?

If Lee Han did not feel snake-like, he did feel most happy to have been visited by his only Yin niece and not only because she was very beautiful. The fact that she was an analytical psychologist with rich New York clients had impressed him greatly.

At some point in prehistoric Britain, people with engineering skills and knowledge of astronomy had gone in organized groups to one of the high points of the southern downlands. There on a ridge where the softly undulating contours fell away, they started work excavating a pit.

It is possible that they had come from the area beside the clear springs four or five miles to the west. Equally possibly, they may have come from the south, where they were settlers by the stream in a valley. Whoever they were, taking their tools and under the guidance of those members of their group who were the repository of knowledge, they climbed the Downs to this particular site and there they excavated the pit.

The location wasn't random, but chosen because it was close to a river and lay directly in line with other high points and tumuli and the great henge of blue stone. At the base of the pit they built a cyst – a chamber of stone. They covered the chamber with alternate mineral and organic layers – burnt flints, earth, gravel, turves – until the cyst was covered and became a mound. The covering layer, being of chalk, added a certain dramatic and quite awesome touch when lit by the last rays of the setting sun.

As time passed their descendants built other layer-covered cysts, each in alignment with the great circle of stones. Centuries later, because of the significance of this powerful location, some of the cysts were used to hold the bodily remains of important members of a community from where their spirits could travel the boundaries of the land. Other cysts stayed sealed through four millennia. In time the barrows, now scattered liberally across the face of the southern counties, grew surface layers with grasses, toadflax, squinancywort, fairyflax and thyme.

And today on the Hampshire Downs the tumuli still stand, marked or encircled by ash or yew trees, close to the path of ancient lines of power, aligned with henges and cathedral spires.

Here there are farms which have names like Sunbarrow, Millbarrow, Stoney Hard and Honeyman; where Downs are named Cheesefoot, Gallops, Gander and Hazeley; where an ordnance map shows sites of Saxon churches, Roman villas, medieval castles and farms; and places with derivative names: Owlesbury, Happersnapper, Nob's Crook and Piddles Plantation. But, on the skyline, in a much-used landscape, the untouched enigmatic barrows still stand. Now, in AD 1990, they are mysterious, familiar landmarks, still where the last rays of late sun touch them.

By the seventeenth century – following in the original tracks of the barrow-builders walking over the curves of the Downs – a raike had been worn by sheep, cattle and travellers on foot. Horse-riders, wagons and carts deepened and widened it. By the nineteenth century the raike had become a good road leading to and from Winchester.

In the thirties, the road became a dual carriageway.

Now, in 1990, approaching from the south and running very close to the barrows and developing very quickly, there is coming an eight-lane highway. These latest road-makers have no concern about the configurations of the landscape, or the people who live in it. Their concern is for those of us who feel compelled to speed through this most beautiful of English landscapes. They slash directly into the feminine curves of the downlands, gash the thin skin, and expose the meagre flesh so as to hack the white chalk skeleton of the soft and gentle Hampshire Downs at Childencombe where Myrr Tallentire inches her way home.

Along the roadside boundary there have always been ancient hedges, mostly hawthorn or may. Every year for as long as Myrr has lived on Sunbarrow, the hedge has bloomed profusely with white may blossom. She realizes that it has bloomed this year without being noticed in the greater whiteness. Every living thing around is white. Every tree, leaf, blade of grass, every panicle of guelder rose and may blossom is covered with chalk-dust, as are labourers' boots, caterpillar tractors, road-signs and traffic cones.

Her mind wanders to the cornfield just beyond where a gang of men is working. In spite of the fields containing very little moisture, they were looking good. Bone-dry corn at harvest meant less weight and so less income. Myrr knew farmers who added moisture after harvest, but not on Sunbarrow, certainly not Myrr's husband Nat, nor her son Jake.

A little less income? Sand Fairy Anne!

Myrr had been sixteen before she learned that her mother's philosophical attitude had nothing to do with fairies. But a Sand Fairy had sounded gentler than the alternative – 'What Can't be Cured must be Endured'.

If there was less income from this year's corn, it wouldn't hurt them: the Tallentires of Sunbarrow were sitting pretty these days. Nat's farming skill, now handed on to Jake, had turned Sunbarrow into a tidy business, and in recent years, as a result of going into Europe, they had seemed to come in for every grant that was going. Now, on top of that, Myrr had recently inherited a little more from a

Jeavons great-aunt. It was from this that she had bought her lovely new car. Impractical, and untypical of a farmer's wife. But for Myrr, it was *the* car.

The road forked and she left the coned lane, went up through the gears and sped along the Childencombe road on whose signpost had been tacked Mimm Carter's temporary sign: 'Strawbery's and creame 50 yds. on left', and so on home to Sunbarrow. Myrr smiled. Mimm knew well enough how to spell, and he knew a lot about attracting custom.

PARK AVENUE, NEW YORK, 1990

It was hot, hot, hot on the streets of New York. Addie Haffenfleish, Dr Yin's secretary, protected by being thirty air-conditioned floors above the sizzle, put the faxed newspaper cutting in a folder marked 'Crop Circles – UK' and placed it at the top of an accumulated pile ready for Dr Yin.

Dr Yin would love this piece about the circulating hedgehogs.

Working for Dr Yin was the most interesting job Addie had ever had.

Dr Huband put his head around the door. 'Dr Yin due in today?'

'That's right.'

'Tell her about Mrs Shamalla being back again.'

'What happened?'

'She won't see me. Mrs Shamalla won't see anybody but Dr Yin.'

'She'll be lucky.'

'I know. Ask Dr Yin to see me, anyhow.'

'You'll be lucky.'

Dr Huband grinned. 'I know, I know. We can but try to focus her attention on this practice when there are dragons to be chased.'

'It's not only dragons. Dr Yin is into any kind of unexplained phenomenon.'

Dr Huband put up a hand. 'Stop right there, Addie. Look, my ear is bent double from hearing about it.'

'You should listen, Dr Huband, it's great. Wouldn't you just give your front teeth to be able to fly off round the world looking for the place where dragons and tigers mate?'

'Tut, tut, Addie. Do I hear ever so slight scepticism?'

'No, you don't, Dr Huband. It's not so long since your profession was sceptical of acupuncture. Her dragon lairs aren't so different.'

'Pow!' He shot her with his fingers. 'Don't forget Mrs Shamalla – that is if Dr Yin is still practising analytical psychology.'

'She's a terrific lady, Dr Huband.'

'If there's any justice, such loyalty in a secretary will not go unrewarded, Addie.'

He went, and Addie, laughing, called after him, 'I know you love her too, Dr Huband.'

She went to check the water-cooler and flowers in Dr Yin's office. Dr Yin was a terrific lady.

The children of Childencombe have a stream and a wood which is virtually theirs. Known as Goose Grass, it must be owned by somebody – perhaps the Church, which owns quite a lot of land in the Winchester area. Few adults ever go to Goose Grass unless it is a straying hiker who is soon coldly stared out. There, until they become sixth-formers or bikers cluttering up the bus shelter, Childencombe kids just mess around . . . they muck about . . . they idle to their heart's content, not knowing how lucky they are to have a place like Goose Grass.

Childencombe children have, as well, a school from which they are ejected at age eleven, Zippo's Circus once a year, Molly's Sweetshop, and Dan's Mobile Chips on Tuesday evenings and Saturday dinner-time.

For the youngest of Myrr Tallentire's four children – Poppy, almost eighteen and awaiting A-level results – Goose Grass is a place of past but happy memory. She is away, back-packing in Greece in an organized group along with Emma Carter and Tom Farenbach, who are from old Childencombe families, and Matt Pridhoe, whose family has lived here for only fifteen years, and thus are not villagers but belong to the newcomelatelys who can afford to buy up picturesque farm labourers' cottages.

For their pleasure and convenience, Childencombe adults have a pub, the Green Man, and a restaurant, also the Green Man, the Rec. shared with the children, Carter's general shop, delicatessen and off-licence, Anstey's Tea Rooms, Breary's Ironmongery, Rose's Ladies' Hair Salon, Sid Postlethwaite – Barber, Southern Electrical Goods & Hardware, Eve's Drapery and Gupta Singh's Chemists & Dispensary – still known as Treece's, just as it has been since great-grandfather's day.

Childencombe's Victorian church has Saxon foundations and a saint's name, but is always known as The Church. Catholics must, at some inconvenience, rendezvous with their Maker outside this parish. Other denominations, who are lumped together by the rest under the generic title of The 'Vangelists, worship in front rooms and various other make-do places.

Carter's was still open but empty of customers when Myrr stopped to pick up a jar of instant coffee and some fruit. Although the building was old-fashioned and much as it had been when Myrr was a girl, the interior of the shop had been stripped out, modernized and stocked with thirty varieties of cheese and the kind of delicacies, wines and up-market brand names that the newcomelately villagers expected and true villagers had jolly soon got a taste for. Jez Carter went to the window and exclaimed as though at a Page Three girl: 'Fhaw . . . what's all this then, Myrr?'

'Like it, Jez? I've just bought it. Did part exchange on my old one.'

'Fhaw, I bet you don't half fancy your chance. That's a nice bit of car you got there, though. What do ole Nat say to it?'

'Ah well, old Nat doesn't know yet.'

Jez Carter massaged the palms of his hands. 'Better see he takes his beta-blockers before you land it on him. And what about your Jake then, he a be wanten to have a borrow of it – soon draw the birds in a jalopy like that.'

The automatic shop-door swung open for Myrr. 'Thanks, Jez. I shall have to see to it that Jake sticks to his Range Rover. He draws enough women as it is.'

Jez slavered slightly and rubbed his hands together. 'He's always been a bugger for the girls has your Jake. Where does he get that side of him from, eh?' He jerked his elbow nudging the air, and watched as she slid into the seat, her narrow skirt riding up way above her knees, then gave the dashboard and wire wheels a close inspection. 'Ve-ry nice indeed, Myrr. If you need a co-pilot any time, you know where to come.'

Myrr was aware that a low bucket-seat and tight skirt were not the thing when Jez Carter was about. 'Thanks, Jez, I'll remember.' She started the engine by way of indicating that he'd better move. 'By the way, have you heard from your Emma?'

'Not a lot. She phoned once. They all seem to be having a good time and the organizers seem to be responsible enough. What about your Poppy?'

'Well, you know Poppy, she gets so full of what's going on, she probably hasn't given us two thoughts since she's been there. We've had a couple of postcards, just said they'd been swimming a lot.'

'Times have changed, Myrr. Going for a swim up Goose

Grass was about all we dreamed about for a summer holiday.'

'We enjoyed it at the time, though.' She took off the handbrake, the car rolled forward and Jez let it slide away from beneath his hand.

He wouldn't mind a slick job like that, but he'd never get Phil to get a car that didn't have a good solid roof and adjustable arm-rests. Ah . . . Myrr Jeavons had always been tasty, right back to the days when they were all kids together mucking about at Goose Grass. Nat Tallentire was a lucky bugger all round – well, except for his heart, of course, but then nobody could have everything.

'Tell Phil I asked how she was.'

He saluted acknowledgement and watched the white MG with its tasty driver, until it disappeared from sight.

As Myrr Tallentire's spinning tyres sprayed the gravel of the back lane, her son Jake – older than Poppy but younger than Daisy and Rin who were twins – was on the main road at the other side of the farm having just finished with the Old Man's warning notice.

He looked down at himself, brushed off a bit of the dust of the day, felt his chin, and decided that he wasn't too scruffy to walk down to the Green Man. He fancied a game of darts and a pint. He wondered briefly whether he should go back to the house and see if the Old Man wanted to come, but decided against it in favour of a quiet half-hour.

Although Jake was extraordinarily like his father in looks, he had quite a different nature. In embryo, he had gathered to himself a great quantity of his mother's good-natured Jeavons genes, and it was those Jeavons genes which kept him out of trouble, as when boots and skulls met on the rugby field:

All right, mate?

And Jake, who was seldom shorter than any other player, would ruffle the opponent's dented head and give a sympathetic wink to show that there had been no animosity in his size twelve studded boot. And, as did Myrr, Jake let the Old Man's storms swirl around him with a kind of lofty geniality. But that was not what struck you first about Jake – or Nat or Poppy or Rin – what struck you was their long-legged height and very good looks. Although Daisy was Rin's twin, it was only she, of the four Tallentire children, who had not inherited the Tallentire stature and beauty. Daisy, like Myrr, was pretty.

In red biro, Jake added to the Old Man's notice: 'This warning is for your own sakes as the insecticide is still on the surface of the corn'. You would need to get close to read it, but there was no way to get into the field except through the swing gate. It looked like a bit of graffito, and people would always read graffiti.

The cornfield was separated from the main road by an ancient hedge and a grass verge. Jake leaned on the gate and watched the speeding traffic. There was a bad bend and too many of them took it at too fast a lick. Snaking black marks on the road were evidence that occasionally one of the sheep in the field opposite would somehow get through the barbed wire to graze the verge and put the wind up an unsuspecting salesman burning Michelin as he took the bend.

Unlike most farmers – who, when leaning on a gate usually look inwards at their crops, animals, investment, profit – Jake Tallentire always looked away. Jake knew that the Old Man thought that an interest in botany, albeit a casual one, was a more suitable interest for a schoolboy than for a grown man, but that didn't bother Jake. Jake had always had a great curiosity about what grew in his native bit of earth, and in the way the whole great mass had come to arrange itself with greater delicacy than any landscape designer. Interest in indigenous flora and playing rugby union fullback are not necessarily mutually exclusive.

The driver of a white Escort cabriolet which had drawn up on the opposite side of the road, could have spent all day and not guessed what thoughts were going on behind the tanned face of the big labouring type in ragged denim shorts and T-shirt who leaned on the gate gazing along the line of the hedgerow. Jake had seen this young man before in the evenings, and guessed that he was not a casual sight-seer, but was doing a bit of research in his spare time. Jake remembered him because the white convertible was exactly like Myrr's car, which reminded him that she had gone off today to a car sale the other side of Salisbury. His mother got a real buzz from cars and car sales, and knew better than most what was what under the bonnet and over the chassis.

Seeing nothing new, the young man drove on and stopped again further along at the crest of the rise where he once more scanned the rape and corn growing on Sunbarrow's undulating downland fields.

Then a Sierra, with typical salesman's clutter in the back, stopped. The driver hauled himself up on to the roof of his car and squatted precariously as he too scanned the cornfield through binoculars.

Jake crossed the road. 'Bit of a bad bend there. You want to draw into the opening a bit.'

'Think it's all right?'

'As long as you don't set fire to the corn or anything.'

'Christ no! That'd be criminal. Wants shooting, anybody who'd go in there with a cigarette.'

Jake re-crossed and once more leaned against the gate. The man parked his car off the road, peeled off the jacket of his business suit, rolled back the sleeves of his white shirt and slung a camera about his neck.

'What's the notice say? Damn! Spraying. Everywhere's the same these days. Can't move for chemicals.'

Jake gave his half-wink and half-nod that gave strangers a kind of assurance that this bloak wasn't just a hunk in shorts. 'A lot more farmers going organic these days, though.'

'I was hoping to get a picture. Got some from a distance, but my daughter wants me to get her a close-up – she's doing a project at school. All projects these days. Global warming project. Kids these days have to start worrying about things before they're hardly out of nappies.'

Jake nodded to the tractor lanes in the wheat. 'If you keep to the tramlines where the tractor's been, you'll be all right.'

'You think so? I shouldn't like to breathe in any muck that might make me dopey and send me off the road. I've got to make Liverpool tonight.'

'You'll be OK.'

'You think so?'

'Sure. I sprayed it myself – its bark is worse than its bite.'

'Oh well, thanks, then.'

Jake opened the gate, let the man through and watched him as he walked in the waist-high half-ripe corn, took half a dozen photos from all angles, and then walked back again, keeping strictly to the tramlines.

'Fantastic. Fan-bloody-tastic. My little girl will be made up with these.'

For a minute the men leaned on the gate and gazed along the tramlines, then the salesman heaved a sigh. 'Fan-bloody-tastic, isn't it?'

Jake nodded.

'Any ideas how they get there?' the salesman asked, reluctantly getting back into his car.

Jake said, 'No, and I'm not sure that I want to. It's nice having a bit of a mystery.'

'That's what I told my daughter. Somebody or something's doing it to give us a bit of fun . . . a bit of magic.' He nodded to himself as he clipped in his seat belt. 'Nice that. Wish I didn't have to get along.'

'Maybe next time you're passing,' Jake said.

'Thanks, mate.' He started the engine and manoeuvred ready to draw out on to the sticky tar of the road, then asked, 'You must live round here then?'

Jake, watching for oncoming traffic, nodded in a vaguely southerly direction. 'A bit further down.'

'Lucky you.'

Jake nodded as he waved the man out into the road.

I know. I know. Who'd drive to Liverpool on a summer evening? A lot of poor buggers. Lucky old Jake. He kept telling himself that: bloaks like that one wouldn't mind half a mile walk to the pub.

As he walked down towards Childencombe he reflected on the people who came, stopped, took pictures and stayed looking, often looking for a long time – 'I never thought it would be like that, you can't tell from the telly, can you?' They aren't the invading hordes like the Old Man reckons, most of them are just decent and ordinary. Some thing unexplained was happening. Some thing strange and mysterious. They just want to be in on it, to tell their friends: the crop circles? 'Oh yeah . . . I've seen them, they're fan-bloody-tastic. Nah, of course they're not hoaxes . . . could you make a thing like that in the pitch dark?'

It's what they were – absolutely fan-bloody-tastic.

Back at Sunbarrow Farm, Nat Tallentire was fidgety. Seven o'clock. He still hadn't taken his propanalol. Jeff Daniels had said, 'It's just one of the beta-blocker-type drugs, Nat. It's a kind of chemical ticker. A couple of them a day and you'll be fine.'

Chemical ticker! Why the hell could quacks never treat their patients as equals?

Nat had handled enough chemicals in his time; he knew their properties and their generic names. Did they think it was too difficult for a farmer to understand that propanalol was a pulse regulatory drug? Was it easier for the quack or for the patient to say that it was a 'ticker', and not a heart, that was playing up? Nat Tallentire had had pains in his chest and then what was supposed to be a mild heart attack. After all these years as the Tallentires' doctor, Jeff Daniels ought to know not to come out with guff like 'chemical ticker'.

Jake had to duck as he went into the Green Man. Sixteenth-century, bulging walls, timbering, broad stacks with numerous chimney-pots and a cat-slide roof, the Green Man was just the sort of pub and restaurant the English Tourist Board and the up-market magazines loved for their illustrations.

Until the fifties it had been much like any other pub, but then its landlord, Rex Farenbach, with native shrewdness had bought adjoining property and had made himself into Mine Host by taking management courses and reclaiming the right to 'talk broad', which had been ridiculed out of him in secondary school. Nowadays, the Green Man was able to cater for well-off out-of-town diners and tourists in Rex's restaurant as well as for his village regulars and friends in his pub. Rex, who still preferred to serve in the bar and so delegated the management of the restaurant, drew a tankard of real ale for Jake.

Jake joined a group of darts players. 'I've just been talking to a chap who had come off the Isle of Wight ferry and was on his way home for his supper in Liverpool.'

'Liverpool?' said Fred Carter. 'Bugger that for a game on a day like this.'

'You an't seen nothin' yet,' said Sid Postlethwaite. 'This summer's going to be the hottest on record, you mark my words.'

Rex ducked under the bar and came to join them. 'Got to go some to beat last year. I heard you got another circle

36

in that field by the road – you should be charging admission to the sightseers, Jake.'

'Bloody menace.' Mort Harding also, last year, had had a field beset by the appearance of several small corn circles in neat formation.

'Ah, go on, Mort,' Jake said. 'You're just like my Old Man, you've got no soul.'

'Soul my left foot! Last August there wasn't a day went by but what there wasn't some townee or other tramping over my land asking questions. One of them asked if we wasn't doing it all ourselves just to get our name in the paper. Christ! Can you imagine . . . going out after dark to roll down your own crop just to have a bunch of *Daily Mail* reporters come and make you out to be a fool or something?'

'You might have done it to get on the box,' Sid said.

'Yeah, I was sure to do that instead of down here supping a pint a Rex's best. Thanks, Jake, just a half then.'

With the exception of Sid Postlethwaite, these men were of a generation older than Jake. He thought that he understood them as he thought he understood his father. Whatever they grew, be it crops or animals, the purpose was to make a bit of cash and to pay off a bit more of the bank loan. If a cow dropped a calf with two heads they were not likely to think of it as a wonder, and if circles and symbols appeared in their fields, that didn't put up the price of corn. They never saw the pleasure and interest in such things.

Jez Carter came in and Rex drew his ale. 'Cheers.' He downed half of it and sucked his lips appreciatively. 'Well then, Jakey boy, what do you think of your mum's new car then?'

'I didn't know she had a new car. I knew she was going to the car sales today. Has she got a new one?'

Jez turned to the others. 'Has she got one! Has Myrr Tallentire got a car or has she got a car?'

Jake was intrigued and amused as always by the innuendo and crumb-dropping dissemination of gossip that was the technique of Childencombe villagers.

'You mean you haven't seen it then, Jakey boy?'

'What's she got then, Jez?' That was Jez's brother Fred. 'Myrr been and bought a Roller? I did hear tell she was left a tidy bit by old lady Jeavons.'

Sid Postlethwaite said, 'That was a turn-up for the book. You'd have never thought old Mrs Jeavons had two pennies to rub together. Is that right, Jake, she left it all to your mum?'

He laughed and held up his glass to Rex for a refill. 'Not all, and not enough for a Rolls-Royce, Fred.'

'I tell you what,' Jez said. 'I'd swap a Rolls for this one any day. I'll tell you.'

'Christ a'mighty, our Jez,' Fred said, 'you don't half know how to hang it out. Go on, what's Myrr got now?'

'She been and bought herself a spanking sports job. A classic MG.'

'MG?' Jake said. 'What model?'

'A "C". Beautiful job. Wire wheels, old-style bumper, chrome AA badge.'

'Any roll bar?' Jake wanted to know. 'They're deadly without a roll bar.'

'I never noticed, but I heard the engine. Vrrmmm. You should have heard her go.' He skimmed his hand along the bar surface.

'I don't know what it's all coming to,' Mort said. 'My missis been getting leaflets on swimming-pools. It's all since Myrr Tallentire got that there pool up at Sunbarrow, I asked her: when do you think anybody here's got time for swimming? Oh, I'll find time all right, she says. I tell you, Jake, your mum's a bit of a bloody menace with her alterations. She's setting everybody off.'

'You'll be all right now, Mort,' Jake laughed. 'I reckon now she's got her MG, there isn't much left for her to buy.'

'Good luck to her,' Rex Farenbach said.

Mort changed his tune: 'Ah . . . fair enough. And good luck to us all. They was hard times in this village till recent years, we all know that.'

Fred said, 'Still is for a good many. I heered you're putting in an ice-cream plant up at Sunbarrow.' Fred lived in a rented cottage on state retirement pension. 'Make a fortune if these summers keep coming.'

'That's old Nat's idea,' Jez said. 'They reckon Sunbarrow's profits is down by a million or so this year . . . an't that right, Jake?'

Jez had never yet succeeded in getting Jake to take his bait.

Putting on a good field accent like Mort's, Jake said, ''Tis true, Jez, just look at these rag-arse ole jeans . . . it wouldn't surprise me if we only cleared three or four million this year. Too much competition.'

They liked that. Jez, with the only supermarket store, had no competitors and charged tip-top prices.

'It's a queer sort of car for a woman to want, if you asks me,' Mort said.

'I reckon a MG-C is a man's car. Too big and powerful for a woman,' Jez said.

'Isn't it what they all wants to be these days?' Mort said.

Sid laughed. 'What? Something big and powerful like you, Mort?'

'It was never the same after they let them in at the Boys' Grammar,' said Fred.

The older men nodded into their tankards, and Jake, who had enjoyed his time at the newly feminized Boys' Grammar, set off for home smiling. Myrr would be on tenterhooks waiting for him to look at and approve her new acquisition. The Old Man would never enthuse enough for Myrr, who appreciated words of approval such as Terrific! Smashing! Absolutely Great! One thing was sure, he didn't begrudge his mother one penny of the fun she'd had spending her legacy and her share of Sunbarrow Farms' profit. But he didn't go straight home; he called in on Lizz – and stayed.

Nat switched on the wireless in time to get the new episode of 'The Archers' and was gratified to hear that small farmer still crabbing on about the way the big farmers were coining it in. There was a time, and not that long ago either, when Nat felt empathy with the struggling non-conforming Grundy family of the soap opera; but now, since Sunbarrow was thriving, he felt that he had reneged on them and joined the side of the self-satisfied Archer family. For sure this was the most comfortable side, but all the old challenge and gamble was gone. Sunbarrow was successful and Nat had grown rich.

Twenty past seven and the programme ended. He switched off in time to catch the sound of a car coming up the back lane. He didn't recognize the engine sound. It wouldn't be Myrr, who always used the front farm-gate, and hardly anybody except Jake in his Range Rover came by the back lane now that they were on the main sewer and the cesspool lorry had stopped coming. He went through into Myrr's conservatory to see who would turn into the yard.

Myrr's conservatory – as it was Myrr's bathroom, Myrr's kitchen, Myrr's swimming-pool – everything they had acquired in the last few years was down to Myrr. Nat only wished that he could find something that pleased himself half as much as buying things pleased Myrr. He was pleased for her, though. She'd had to put up with too much over the years.

The car came very fast up the long, narrow lane, roaring exhaust, spurting gravel and sending up dust clouds. Bloody speed merchant, whoever he was. A flash of white passed a gap in the hedge, quickly followed by the entire length of the car as it braked to a halt in the old cattle yard.

Christ, what would she do next?

He went out to meet her.

'Like it?' she said, dusting off the long bonnet with a huge sheepskin polishing mitt. 'My God, Nat, it was an absolute snip. Only two previous owners. Been up on blocks for years, beautifully restored. The owner was a collector. Poor chap went bust in some insurance scam and had to start selling up. Just think, if I hadn't taken it into my head to go over to Salisbury today . . . I dread to think that some yuppy merchant might have got his paws on it.' She polished away the thought of such paw prints.

Nat had circumnavigated the immaculate MG-C. 'He should have had it done racing green.'

'Rubbish, it's beautiful. Get in, I'll give you a ride.'

'I'm not getting in that thing.'

'There's more leg room than you think.'

Nat looked pointedly at the only two seats. 'All bloody leg room, by the look of it. I thought you were getting into this ecologically-sound stuff . . . this thing must drink petrol by the gallon.'

'Well, I thought about that, and I came to the conclusion that as I use trains for long journeys and only do short ones by car, it would even itself out, and it might be possible to put in a catalytic converter.'

'You're kidding yourself, Myrr. That thing's a guzzler and you know it.'

She opened her mouth to refute that, stopped, then changed her mind, put her arm through his, and said, 'I know. I'll probably feel guilty about that, but I couldn't resist it. Oh, Nat, it is so beautiful, something I've always dreamed of driving. It was as though I had been sent there to find it. I just longed for it, absolutely desired it, Nat. Do you know what it's like to feel like that?'

She had been Myrtle Jeavons still in her teens when they had got married. He still fancied her.

Stretching out his long legs under the dashboard, he said, 'Come on then, give us a run down the lane.'

PARK AVENUE, NEW YORK

Dr Kuan-Yin whirled in and kissed her secretary's cheek. 'Addie, Addie, say, it's great to be back. Are you OK? Fine. It was wonderful! I must have a dozen tapes for you to type up. You have no idea what China is like. Be sweet and find me some spring water. See that yellow bag, the things in it are for you. Something from China and a few things from the duty-free. That perfume is exquisite, from Hong Kong. Try it – it will suit you. And the shawl, it's hand worked, every stitch. Unbelievable. I watched it being done. Women and girls. They get a pittance. Cost almost nothing in dollars. I got so mad. But it's no use is it? They need the foreign exchange. So pin it on the wall and be thankful. Oh, lovely! Thanks, Addie, nothing like the water one is used to.'

'No need to ask if you had a good trip, Dr Yin?'

'Oh terrific, terrific! I feel absolutely buzzing with energy. Met my Uncle Han. Is he something!'

'Did he demonstrate this *feng-shui* stuff for you?'

'Absolutely! He gave me the whole works. Wait till there's time and I'll tell you how it goes. What's new?'

'Dr Huband said Mrs Shamalla insists on seeing you.'

'The last time Mrs Shamalla came to America on a shopping trip I told her what the score was. I said: Mrs Shamalla, the only thing wrong with you is that you are Mr Shamalla's Number Two Wife and you are intensely jealous of Mr Shamalla's Number One Wife.'

'Must be hard,' Addie said.

'What about wives Number Three and Four? He's loaded, is Mr Shamalla.'

'What shall I tell Dr Huband?'

'That I think Mr Shamalla's Number Two Wife needs a good sex therapist. Write recommending her one. She likes to go back from a New York shopping spree with a new treatment. What she should really do is to buy herself a pearl-handled gun and make herself Number One Wife by using it.'

'Oh, Dr Yin!'

Kuan-Yin laughed, showing no sign that her recent hours of travelling had in any way incommoded her. Whilst she had been talking, she had been sorting through the piles of papers Addie had prepared for her, and finished up with four piles of her own assortment. 'Dispose of those, please, Addie. File these. Answer that lot yourself. And these are mine.'

The rest of the day was spent with patients. Then she wrote up notes for her book, made several telephone calls and went along to see her associates to break the news to them that she was taking no new patients for the present because she would be taking a summer vacation abroad starting after the weekend.

Addie's spirits dropped. Dr Yin would be off again, taking the colour and fizz away from the office. Time was when Dr Yin had a pretty conventional engagements book, but over the last couple of years she spent less and less time on her practice and more time doing research for her book. Now she had at last achieved an empty diary until well into 1991.

'What's that look for, Addie?'

Addie shook her head. 'You going away so soon. I like it when you're here.'

'Next time I go to Hong Kong, I'll take you with me if you like.'

'Yes, Ma'm! I'd like.'

Kuan-Yin laughed her media-famous, porcelain-toothed laugh. Millions only knew it from their screens, Addie was privileged to have it beamed upon her whenever her boss was in the office.

British people were expecting this summer to be a re-run of the famous English summers of '76 and '89, which were of long, hot days with cloudless skies and dry air. In '76 and '89, generous Mediterranean weather allowed the British to go sleeveless for weeks on end, to smoke out their neighbours with barbecue fires, to saunter without purpose and still be in their gardens at midnight. Those years had been good for the British soul.

Yesterday had been fine, but until then there hadn't been too many consecutive hot days. Even so, at dawn Jake hopefully pulled on his shorts, a ragged relic of last summer. Sunday . . . maybe the weather would perk up and behave like last summer again. Four-thirty, and the sky was an uninviting hazy fawn colour. He went to push open further one of the three dormer windows that lighted his room and, as his gaze wandered up and over the fields that rolled away from the back of the house, it fixed upon the facing slope.

His heart leaped at what he thought he saw in the faint early-morning light. Grabbing his binoculars, he focused upon a dark mark in a cornfield. Bloody hell! He gave a low whistle. Bloo-dy hell!

Taking sweater and socks he went quietly in long strides across the landing where he heard the Teasmade hissing and slurping in his parents' room. Sod it! He wanted to get out to Clump Field without being heard. The Old Man was supposed to be taking it easy after his heart attack, but he still kept to his old morning ritual – he couldn't bear to let the day start without him.

His mother had the Old Man taped all right: Your father likes to drive the day himself, don't you, Nat?

Drive it? Drive it? What d'you mean, drive it?

You know perfectly well . . . you like to be in the driver's seat, making it go the way it suits you. Like when the contract harvesters come in, and the day gets going without your say-so . . . you can't abide anything going its own way.

You do talk some rot, woman. It's no wonder our kids have got such queer ideas.

Not rising to the bait, in her wise and cheerful way, Myrr Tallentire would pick up something to hand and empty it, dispose of it, dust or wash it – whatever was appropriate – to avoid being tempted into the wrangle about Young People Today and their own sons and daughters in particular.

Jake had planned to go down the back stairs rather than pick his way through the minefield of creaking boards that gave away his presence to the Old Man, but the running of the shower had already given him away and the door to his parents' bedroom stood unlatched.

'Jake? Is that you?'

'Of course it is, Dad. Who else do you think it is coming out of my room at four-thirty in the morning?'

'Knowing you, lad, it might be anybody.'

That story had been running for years. Ever since he was seventeen and had taken a notebook from his pocket and an empty condom packet had fallen out, Jake had, according to his father, led a life filled with sex and affairs with women.

This was not entirely true. Jake had other interests.

Propping the door open with a bare toe and combing his hair to indicate that he was having to do things on the trot, Jake nodded a greeting at his father, who was already in his dressing-gown and standing at the open window pouring tea.

'Isn't it today that film lot is coming?'

'You know it is, Dad, we went all through that yesterday. It's just Martin and the helicopter.'

'Well don't think I shan't be watching what they're up to. I don't want them crawling all over the fields.'

Myrr's voice, from the bed behind the door, was as pretty and clear as her face. 'And don't think I shan't be watching what you're up to, too, Nat Tallentire . . . you've been told to take it easy and if you've got any sense you'll stop interfering with Jake and let him do what he's got to do.'

'Hello, Mum.' Jake peered round the door. 'I take it the white job in the yard is yours? Will you be taking it up to the Silverstone track?'

She gave him a funny, smug smile. 'No, it's just my little shopping run-about to go down to Carter's for the groceries.'

Nat moved slowly when he carried her tea across the large room, momentarily crushing Jake with sadness at the change in his father. For years as master here, Nat Tallentire had had Sunbarrow by the scruff of its neck and shaken it into shape. Even before he was twenty years old and cattle, stampeded by warble-fly, had sent his father, Nathaniel senior, into an early grave, Nat Tallentire had been master here in every old-fashioned sense of the word.

When that tragedy had happened, the responsibility of Sunbarrow and of his two sisters, both younger than himself, settled heavily on the young Nat's shoulders. Pride, inherited obstinacy and belligerence, and a determination never to be bested by anything, or anybody.

Neither man, woman nor beast crossed Nat Tallentire.

Except for young Myrtle Jeavons, who had married him when she was only a few years out of school and pregnant, and he, not much older, responsible for her condition. Myrr had learned – and later taught their four children – how to live with him, value his formidability as one values a good foundation: The thing about him, you see, is that body and soul he's a good man, and there's not too many of them in this world. Happy-go-lucky bad ones are ten a penny. A good person has to be paid for.

'Want some tea, Jake?' Myrr asked. 'Is there still some in the pot, Nat?'

'No cup.'

'It's OK, I'll make myself a cup of instant downstairs.'

She smiled and Jake smiled back, knowing that, without her glasses or contact lenses, she could only see a blurred face. The contact lenses were new: he had still not got used to seeing her about the house without her glasses. She looked somehow vulnerable, as she did now with the permanent indentations on the bridge of her nose caused by a lifetime of the pressure of frames; and the tissue-paper-like skin beneath her eyes which were clear and noticeable without their usual protection behind lenses. But Jake knew that his mother was the tougher of his parents.

The Old Man snapped his cup into its saucer. 'Aren't you going to work today, then?'

Facetiously tugging his forelock, Jake said, 'Why, look at the time, 'tis dawn already. Just waiting for orders, Master.'

His father pulled at the ends of his dressing-gown cord, tightening it around a waist that was scarcely thicker than it had been thirty years ago. 'You know what wants doing, so get on and do it.'

As he went downstairs, Jake heard Myrr say, 'You shouldn't talk to Jacob like that, Nat. He's not a boy any longer.'

'I know how old my own son is, Myrr. I do know that.'

Jake's instinct was to dash straight up to Clump Field, but before doing so he thrust four slices into the toaster and put a cup of water and instant coffee into the microwave. In any case, what he thought he had seen could be just a trick of the light.

Restraining himself, he went on to make his coffee. He could have chosen to take coffee beans, grind them either by box-grinder or electric blender, then make the coffee by filter or Cona, or steam, or, as of last week, in a new cappuccino machine. Myrr Tallentire disliked chores and loved domestic machines, and would buy any gadget that promised anything.

The kitchen was Smallbone in quality and up-to-date in design and materials. Myrr had no time for the grottiness of fashionable farmhouse kitchens, all Agas and copper pots and rails hung with useless ladles, wickerwork steamers, with dusty flavourless dried herbs, and with corn-dollies – whose fertility spell, had they known of it, would have shocked many a wax-jacketed newcomelately couple.

In a Guernsey pullover that reached almost to the fray of his shorts, two toast slices sandwiched with Marmite and two with marmalade in one hand and mug of milky coffee in the other, Jake at last let himself out of the back door. The morning was deteriorating. The earlier haze was fast turning to lumps of cloud. The phone rang.

Jake guessed that it was Martin Lilie. Sod it! Jake should have rung him, but had thought he had enough time to skip up to Clump Field first.

'Jakey, hi.'

'Martin. I was about to ring you.'

''Salright, Jake. What's new? How's the weather?'

'Clouding up.'

'Oh, fuck!'

'I should think you'll be OK until midday.'

'We don't get the 'copter till half-ten.'

'Couple of hours should do you, shouldn't it?'

'Don't depend on it. Never does to depend in this business.'

'How soon can you get over here?'

'Time we've loaded the equipment? . . . Half-eight?'

'Half past eight! Good God, Martin, it's not yet half past

48

four, and it's not more than twenty minutes' drive. Move your arse and get over here – now.'

The freelance photographer laughed. 'Jake, it's the weekend. Even as I speak my lady is rolling over to this side of the bed.'

'Martin. If what I can see from the house is true then you might want to leave that for later. Get . . . over . . . here p.d.q.'

Another moment of silence. 'Oh . . . oh . . . oh! You don't mean . . . a new one?' Martin, who was compiling a book of photographs, was being cagey, probably because his lady was new to him.

'I do.'

'How big?'

'Big, but you know what they say, size isn't everything. Just get over here.'

'Is it a change of form?'

'Exactly. Vast, complicated and very, very beautiful. A really perfect symbol this time.'

'Jesus! You haven't told anyone?'

'Of course not.'

'What about noddy patrols?'

'It's Clump Field: nobody can see it from the road.'

'I'm there! Thirty minutes max. See you.' And the phone clicked off and buzzed.

Above the kitchen, Jake heard his father's slow tread as he went into the master bathroom that Myrr's ever-ready interior decorator had designed.

Nat, now that there was no shortage of money, letting Myrr go her own way with domestic matters as he had always done, had accepted the pine cabin of the sauna, and the whiteness and green jungly plants of the bathroom:

Well, woman, if that's what you get for thirty thousand quid, I reckon I'm in the wrong business.

But he was not averse to fifteen minutes in the jacuzzi or an hour stretched out on the pine bench with the sauna rocks nice and warm but not hot enough to upset his dodgy circulation.

It would be half an hour before the Old Man got down to the kitchen, by which time Myrr would probably be there to pour oil on the troubled waters of the news of what Jake had seen in Clump Field.

Sunbarrow was set quite high on the Downs. The tan-coloured loam was shallow but fertile and showed lumps of chalk when turned over and white tracks where tractors made tramlines. And on the Downs, where the Sunbarrow flocks grazed, there too chalky outcrops showed through.

On most mornings when the weather wasn't wet, Jake spent ten minutes over his toast-sandwiches and coffee sitting on the veranda listening to the sheep on the Downs and thinking of nothing much except perhaps yesterday's rugby game if it was a Sunday, or an occasional NFU meeting, or as often as not about Lizz.

Called Lizz because her name was Taylor – Lizz, who was small and soft. Lizz, who had the same dry sense of humour as Myrr. Lizz, who everyone – excluding Jake and Lizz themselves – thought would make a couple with Jake. In the language of the eighties, Jake and Lizz were an item.

This morning he could restrain himself no longer but headed off up the slope of Clump Field and on up to the top of the ridge where he could look down into the field.

The mark in the corn was huge, but as he had told Martin, it was not its size that was extraordinary, it was its complexity. Over the last few years, these marks that kept appearing in cornfields around the area had developed from small, simple circles, to triple sets and quintuples, all patterned like dice, and then dumb-bell patterns. But this . . . by no stretch of the imagination could this have been caused by any whirlwind in Jake's experience. This was a definite pattern. A symbol configuration impressed into the field of growing cereal.

This was quite extraordinary. Until now, he had been

generous in allowing sightseers into Sunbarrow to look and to photograph, but this one he felt he wanted to keep to himself for a while.

Basically it was the beautifully executed but gigantic dumb-bell pattern he had seen before, except that here one of the circles had a halo and a hanging fringe. He almost wished that he had not been so hasty in telling Martin, but had enjoyed it alone for a while.

Squatting on the ridge, he ate his toast and used up a reel of film. Usually the researchers liked to have measurements, but he felt that, whatever answer there might be, it wouldn't be found in dimensions, only in the things themselves. And, although he didn't mind Martin recording them on video and film, or people like the young man in the white coupé and the salesman looking, he wasn't too happy about the scientists. These things were beautiful; there was something crass and small-minded about measuring them. It was like trying to know something about a sculpture like 'The Kiss' from the size and nature of the stone Rodin used.

He climbed on up and went to sit on one of the barrows to wait for Martin.

When Martin arrived he rubbed his hands gleefully and slapped Jake on the back. 'Well, Jakey m'boy, what have we got here?'

'Come up to the top and take a look. It's . . . it's . . .' He fell silent, unable to explain his emotions about the thing. 'I could do with a cigarette.'

'You don't smoke.'

'I know.'

It tasted pretty foul, but it was what was needed to settle the hairs on his arms and legs.

When Jake had left the house, Nat went to stand in Daisy's old room and watched as he easily climbed the slope of

Clump Field and remembered how it felt to have long, solid legs that could carry your body without trying.

It'd make a bit of sense if it was in our make-up to appreciate our youth when we had it. You think that your digestion will always be able to take chillies and strong cheese and spirits, and your eyes will always be able to read small print, and that you'll always wake in the morning knowing that you're a man. But Nat, who was by Western standards nowhere near the age 'the Old Man' suggests, thought that he felt something snapping at his heels.

If people could see him there, watching Jake, a replica of himself at the same age, they might think he was envious. Of course, it would be daft to say that he wouldn't want to feel like that again, but he wasn't envious, he was glad that Jake was as he was. Jake never seemed to let the world sit on his shoulders. But then Jake's world had never been very heavy – at least it hadn't been till last year when his heart had played up like that.

It was a bit different now. Jake had everything to do with the farm on his plate and Nat had to admit that, since he had handed over, he hadn't found anything that he could take too much exception to. Except that Jake still courted the notion that you could go back to the old methods. The proof that the soil responded to replacing the chemicals taken out by intensive production, was to be seen in the yields. Soil responded to feeding and tilling. Horse dung and worms might work for an acre or two, but never on the hundreds of acres that Sunbarrow had grown to.

Nat wished that he'd been able to say something to him, to tell him that he thought he'd done a good job and that he had no fears that Sunbarrow would falter now, after centuries in Tallentire hands. But he couldn't do it. Never had been able to do that kind of thing. He wasn't too bad with Daisy and Poppy, he'd been able to take them on his knee and give them a shilling for a good exam result, but he had never known how to treat the boys. He had never learned how from his own father.

When Rin was at school he worked like a little Trojan to keep up. And he had succeeded. But how can a man . . . a man like Nat, who didn't know how to go about it . . . what can he do or say to a lad? No father can take a lad on to his knee, or give him a hug.

All any man can do is to try to let them see in other ways. Tell them you know that they're better than the other boys in their class. Show them how to shoot straighter, to fish better, to kill an animal more humanely than the next man. Show them that you think they're as good as their forebears and be proud.

Daisy was the only one with any Tallentire in her. Rin and Jake and Poppy might look like them, but they were pure Jeavons. Not that that mattered. Myrr was as good a person as ever stepped foot in a pair of shoes.

But how can a man tell his sons: I'm glad you've took after your mother, and I love you for it?

He could still make out Jake half-way up the slope of Clump where he had stopped. Nat peered, pulled his distance glasses from his pocket and focused upon Jake in Clump Field. That looked like another bloody circle. He hurried into Jake's room where he knew he would find binoculars. They were gone. He rummaged in the landing cupboard and found his own.

He focused. It was another one! A bit different from the first ones ten years ago. A group of little circles along the road a bit, a crop of them in the Punchbowl. But this was nothing like – nothing like at all.

He heard Myrr coming along the landing, talking to him before she ever reached the door.

'Aren't you going to get dressed this morning? I've got some grilled bacon and tomatoes. Green bacon, not much fat.'

'And you still call it bacon?'

She came into Jake's room. 'Would you rather have muesli and grapefruit, then? I can soon finish off a plate of bacon and tomatoes – no trouble. So I'll put out the muesli jar?'

Nat wrinkled his nose in disgust.

Picking up Jake's discarded shirt and underclothes as she went, Myrr came to stand and look out. Nat waited for her reaction. She wasn't wearing her glasses, but he could tell from the sure way she walked that she was wearing her contact lenses.

Astonishment caught her breath. 'Oh, Nat! Have you seen that? Here, give me the binoculars.'

He watched her, her lips apart as she re-adjusted the eye-pieces and fiddled with the focus.

'Have you seen that?'

'Of course I've seen it. It's why I got them out of the cupboard.'

'It's enormous! Isn't it lovely?'

He came and stood behind her, pulling her firm, fit body to his, and folded his arms gently across her. Their age gap seem greater to him now than it had when he was in his twenties. Perhaps she'd always be youthful like this, the Jeavonses were all long-livers, a tenacious lot they were, hang on to life like grim death and live to their nineties.

'Nat?'

'What?'

'All sorts of people are going to want to see that thing, and I don't want you to start getting upset.'

'When do I ever get upset?'

'All the time.'

'I don't want people tramping over my land.'

'That's always been the thing hardest for me to swallow about farmers. They don't own the land, nobody owns land.' Myrr seldom let a chance go by to make it clear that she wasn't part of the farming fraternity. Past Jeavonses had long memories of being turned from their jobs and tied cottages by landowners and farmers.

'Till God comes down and tells me otherwise – I own Sunbarrow. I don't owe the banks hardly a penny piece.'

'I don't mean possess. The Tallentires happen to have arrived here and are farming it for a few generations. A thousand years ago, who knows who was living here? In another thousand years somebody else will be. There's nobody should own what's God-given.'

'It's been Tallentire land as long as anyone can remember.'

'Don't be obtuse, Nat. You know what I'm saying, that people have got no more right to own bits of the earth than they have the air or the sky, and when something like this happens on it, then I don't think we have any right to tell people they can't come and look. What would you do if Jesus Christ appeared out there? Tell people: Go on, clear off, he belongs to me?'

'People are vandals. Look at Stonehenge, the hippies . . .'

'Who are mostly reverential and decent people. It was the police who did the vandalizing, they broke up homes and vans . . .'

'You can't have the invading hordes . . .'

'That's just what people said about giving over The Centre Youth Hall to kids to run: They'll vandalize it in five minutes, they said. But they didn't. Once the kids had a stake in the place and they felt that things were a bit fairer, there wasn't any need for the law and there hasn't been so much as a pane of glass broken or any new graffiti.'

'The Jeavonses always were a bolshie lot of radicals. It isn't hard to see where Jake gets his ideas from.'

'Jake's got a mind of his own, he doesn't need any supplement from mine. And it'd be damned hard for this branch of the Jeavonses to be radical these days – we're a lot of fat cats, Nat. So don't you start laying down the law if Jake says a few people can come in and take photos.'

'You mix with too many social workers and feminists these days.'

'Too many for my conscience to be easy, anyway – I won't argue with you there.'

YIN'S NUMBER ONE HOUSE, NEW YORK

Blossom Park Chinese Restaurant Number One was downtown New York, but not down-market. Tourists and diners who wanted the whole authentic show booked and waited and paid through-the-roof prices at one of the glossier Blossom Parks. Authentic Chinese families preferred this old Yin's Number One House, as did Western aficionados of faithful ethnic dishes. And the Yin family ate there all the time, running family and business affairs at the Yins' table in the Yins' alcove.

This evening – as the only daughter of the family had safely returned from visiting mainland China as well as stopping over in Hong Kong – her father, her mother, Uncle Lenny, Uncle Burt and her grandmother, known as Lady Yin, sat at a round side table chattering in a mixture of American English and a dialect for Lady Yin's benefit.

Kuan-Yin was on time for the family meal, although the family was there before her. Young, slim waiters in white shirts and black waistcoats were already writing up orders and nodding agreement with every choice.

'Alison is here. Here is Alison.' June Yin pointed out her daughter's entrance to Lady Yin. Alison was Kuan-Yin's given name, and her family seldom acknowledged that she had any other.

June Yin's mother-in-law, Lady Yin, seldom spoke in company. The word was that she understood English perfectly but chose not to speak it, because that gave her an advantage – she only understood what she wished to understand. Although it was these three of her four sons who ran the Blossom Park chain, the inspiration for the oriental eating-houses had sprung entirely from Lady Yin's cooking skills, and the recipes she had carried with her in her head, when they arrived here in the fifties. Now she looked up and nodded as she watched her granddaughter enter. Lady Yin's family said that they could read her nodding. This one was a slow deliberate nod – almost a bow – which George interpreted as approval of the first order.

Heads turned as Kuan-Yin, taking small steps on high heels, followed the head waiter through the restaurant to the family table in the alcove. Her hair was dressed and decorated with long wooden pins and ribbons as she had worn it in Hong Kong. She had forsaken her usual expert Western make-up for classic oriental rose-bud lips and pale powder. She wore a black gown embroidered liberally and encrusted at neck and hem with things which glittered. She looked stunning and was quite aware of the attention she drew.

At the table she lowered her head to each of her elders in turn, then seated herself between her mother and grandmother placing a be-ribboned package before each of them.

'Hi, honey.' Kuan-Yin kissed her mother and then her grandmother. 'And how's my Lady Yin?'

The old lady answered long in her own language.

George Yin was always his mother's mouthpiece whether necessary or not. 'Lady Yin says she like your dress.'

'Hong Kong Chinese, Grandmother.'

Lady Yin nodded and touched the silk approvingly.

'Well, Alison,' Lenny Yin said. 'You now ready to start work?'

'She will have jet-lag still,' Burt said.

Lenny said, 'Not jet-lag from Hong Kong, Burt.'

'Because of difference in time,' George explained.

Burt lifted his shoulders with a continental shrug. 'Difference in time is both ways.'

'No, uncles, I don't have jet-lag. I slept on the plane and have done a day's work.'

June Yin fingered her package and Kuan-Yin said, 'Open, open, Mother.'

The contents of the packages were identical except for the materials used: earrings carved in the shape of a double spiral with facets etched into a complicated pattern, one pair made from solid pieces of jade, the other from ivory.

June Yin had the jade and at once fixed them in her ears. 'Do they look good, Alison? George?' She wagged her head so that they swung.

Lady Yin held hers on the palm of her hand and fingered them gently, touching them as though reading Braille. She smiled and bowed her head in Kuan-Yin's direction, then put them back into the box which she re-wrapped as it had been when given to her.

'Lady Yin likes the gift,' June Yin said.

'I know that, Mother. I keep telling you, it's not necessary to interpret. I can see what she says. In any case, she could tell me herself if she wanted. Isn't that so, Grandmother?' She kissed her grandmother's sunken, wrinkled face from which her very round eyeballs looked out from small straight eyelids.

Food arrived in many dishes which took every available space on the table. The eating did not stop them talking. People sitting outside the favoured circle smiled at the family of three generations, the grandmother eating quickly, holding the dish close to her mouth, the sons with sleek hair, grey business suits, dark ties and white shirts with gold links and thin Rolexes on their wrists; June – in features but not manner an older edition of her beautiful and striking daughter – watching them all, their food, their expressions, with quick bird-like movements. And her daughter, so exotic, so sophisticated, yet clearly the lowest in the order of status at table, was entirely doted upon by the rest.

'Now, Alison, you tell all about China. They do not eat

like here?' Uncle Burt speared and held up a choice piece of pork.

'Uncle Burt, there is some truly wonderful food in China. Nothing like in Yin's Number One, but small places, street stalls, very good eating.'

'Chinese people always know good ways with food. Historically,' Lenny stated.

June said, 'It is why Yin's Blossom Parks are famous.' She made a little head bow to the old lady. 'Lady Yin's recipes.'

'Of course, of course.' None of her three sons wanted to be seen not giving credit where credit was due. 'Lady Yin is backbone of Blossom Park.' They drank a little sake to her honour.

'I went to the Great Wall.'

Lady Yin leaned forward closer to Kuan-Yin, who repeated, 'Great Wall, sweetheart.'

The old lady became very animated and chattered quickly. George said in English, 'That must have been seventy years ago. Lady Yin went there as a child.'

Uncle Lenny said in a low voice, 'I wish Lady Yin try to use English, all this interpreting.'

'You don't get exasperated with me for not learning your language, Uncle Lenny.'

'Our lan-wage American, Alison.'

'English,' said Burt.

George said, 'She understand, don't you, Lady Yin? You understand English as good as family understand.'

She had unwrapped her package again and was caressing the ivory spirals, smiling.

'Father, uncles, I must say something. You sit here talking about your mother as though she was a ghost or a child, and yet at the same time you are chiding her for not taking part in the conversation. You don't mean to be unkind, but you should know why Grandmother does not speak English.'

The three men looked at one another. Out there she might be an expensive Fifth Avenue doctor, and she might be on Ed Sullivan and Oprah Winfrey, but here, where America hadn't quite seeped in, she was daughter of the house.

'Alison. You should not speak to your uncles in that tone of voice.'

'Mother, you surely can understand. I think, Lady Yin, that your language and your recipes are the only things left that are yours. I've always noticed that you eat only dishes from your original recipes, Grandmother, the later additions you never choose. I think, maybe, you're still hanging on to China.'

'She is an American,' Burt said.

Then they all looked at their plates and furtively out of the corners of their eyes. Suddenly Kuan-Yin realized that her explanation was probably quite wrong.

The prerequisite for an immigrant was the ability to read, write and speak American. Even if Lady Yin was able to speak the language, she certainly could not read or write it. It dawned upon her that Lady Yin might be an illegal immigrant. And she realized too that this was the reason for the brothers' irritation at their mother's apparent obstinacy in sticking to her old tongue. How stupid not to have understood. Her sons were always a little afraid for her.

In a low voice, she said, 'Father, the immigration authorities do not send eighty-year-old ladies away from their families.'

Nobody acknowledged her. Instead, her father signalled to a waiter, swirled his finger around the table and said, 'Lychee. Fresh lychee all round.'

Whilst the small piles of lychees and dishes were being placed, Lady Yin gave Kuan-Yin the ivory spirals and held out her ear lobe for the insertion of the wire hooks. Kuan-Yin stood up and fitted them and offered her grandmother a small hand mirror. Lady Yin grinned widely and shook her head to move the spirals.

'Thank you, Arison. Snake.'

Her family gaped as though the old lady had uttered something shocking.

'Grandmother!' Kuan-Yin exclaimed.

Grinning, the old lady wiggled one of the earrings, then spiralled a forefinger. 'Snake, Arison,' and patted her own chest.

'Your birth sign is the Snake?'

Lady Yin grinned and nodded. 'Wis-dom.'

'Goodness!' said Kuan-Yin. 'Grandmother is a Snake, that means that you are . . .' she counted her fingers.

Lady Yin nodded. 'Year of Snake.'

George, Lenny and Burt absently cracked and peeled the large juicy fruits, popping them whole into their mouths and ejecting the stones into their dishes. The utterance of these few halting words must have been as amazing to them as once their own first words had been to Lady Yin.

'Well, I'm darned,' said Kuan-Yin. 'I was sure that Uncle Han must have been wrong about Lady Yin's age.'

For a moment, except for Kuan-Yin, nobody made the slightest move or sound, they were a Pompeii tableau caught in the act of eating dessert. Diners at the tables closest to the Yins, themselves closed down momentarily at the sudden descent of silence upon the chattering family – more than mere quiet, it almost had scent and taste.

Then Lady Yin said, 'Han?'

Kuan-Yin inspected one of her long red fingernails before she answered. 'I was saving that news for later. Yes, I tracked down Uncle Han, and I spent time with him.'

There was a man in her bed, a warm hump against her back, but for a moment Daisy Tallentire could not remember who was making it. It wasn't that she took so many men into her bed, or ever had so much to drink that she couldn't remember: no, it was a simple matter of her memory playing her tricks first thing. Although she had been living in London for several years, whenever a bird sang close to her window before she opened her eyes, she was fazed into thinking that she was still living at home and if she opened them it would be to the sloping ceiling and the leaded lights of the dormer windows of her old room at Sunbarrow.

She wasn't at Sunbarrow, but in her own cherished mortgage investment in the 081 phone region of London. Bill. Of course, who else? And it was Saturday, the one day of the week she cherished as her own to do as she pleased, dress as she liked and live for the day as she thought fit. And she had gone and blown it by not making him exit last night. He was a nice guy and not a bad lover, which, now that it was Saturday morning, was the trouble. He would want to buy her lunch in return for breakfast and before she knew where she was he would probably make her feel randy again and the weekend would be over.

From the kitchen of the reclaimed Edwardian terraced house, she saw all the garden jobs she had saved and savoured for a week. She decided to go on with her gardening, not to do anything about breakfast and hope that Bill would find the garden chores boring and go back to his flat. He probably wouldn't, for the same reason that Daisy had let him stay: his flat was utilitarian, in a road that was scruffy and an area where there was 'trouble'. But Bill was a polytechnic lecturer on a salary far smaller than that which bought Daisy her house and garden.

She filled the pockets of her canvas apron with bits and

pieces she would need and went first to tie in a passion flower which, in its present state, was her favourite of the month. Her eyes smiled with satisfaction as she worked. She liked the personality of this plant which, whilst in its pot and trained around wires, had been so neat and controlled, but as soon as it had been set free had gone exuberantly wild. It was the sort of job that suited Daisy's nature: take something that had got out of hand and impose a little order. Particularly something that had the prospect of being beautiful or satisfying once order was imposed.

It was inherent in her work — she was chief editor of children's books with a seat on the board, in a large publishing house. She weeded and pruned and dug for the ideas she suspected a particular writer or illustrator was capable of producing.

Since she had owned her own house, gardening had become Daisy's passion. On seeing the pretty, thoughtful garden and comparing it with their own, friends would say, 'Well you'd expect Daisy's garden to grow better than ours, she's been brought up to it.' 'I expect her father probably gives her all sorts of fertilizer stuff that we ordinary people can't get hold of.'

And, because English roses, campsis and clematis frolicked together up the brick walls, euphorbias burst like green and yellow fireworks from odd corners and cranesbill poured over the sides of pots, she wasn't believed when she said that at home nobody had ever been able to persuade her near things that sprouted from soil.

'Aren't you sorry now that you didn't go to horticultural college instead of university?' Rin had once asked her.

'Oh, Rin, you just don't understand, do you? There's no connection. Sunbarrow's a factory ... just an open-air factory churning out sacks of wheat and legs of lamb — this is almost an art form, you take living things of different colours, shapes, textures, and you work at mixing them until you get a satisfying picture.'

She stood back and admired the new arrangement of its vines, and the scores of complicated flowers that were visible, now that the passion flower's green trails were under control. She thought she heard the chink of cups from the kitchen and hoped that Bill was up and dressed and maybe ready to leave her alone to tend her conservatory plants. The phone rang.

Peeling off her gloves, she went into the tiny conservatory which had been built at the same time as the house.

'Hello. Daisy Tallentire.'

'I didn't get you out of bed?'

It was Rin.

'How are you . . . things . . . ?'

She could almost hear the shrug in his voice. 'Oh well, you know.'

'Still in a mess then.'

'Sort of.'

Getting anything out of Rin was like trying to squeeze toothpaste out of an empty tube. Particularly anything that he didn't want to be reminded of or face up to. The world's greatest prevaricator . . . unless he was in the throes of an enthusiasm; then he went like the Starship Enterprise going into hyperspace.

'Look, Daze . . .'

She did a rottweiler snap into the mouthpiece.

'Sorry . . . Daisy. I thought about going down to Childencombe tomorrow and wondered if you wanted to come too. It's ages since I went to see the Old Man. It makes me feel a bit guilty . . . you know, everybody flocking round when he was in hospital, then once he's back home . . . You know?'

'Oh, Lor'. I want to go . . . you know . . . but I hadn't really planned . . .'

'It wouldn't take us long. Less than couple of hours' run,

have lunch with them, a couple of hours back. Be home early evening. Time enough for you to get up to whatever it is you get up to with your friends.'

'I don't get up to much, you can be sure of that.'

'You mean that you're all on your ownio on a Saturday morning?'

She didn't reply.

'Aha!'

'Well, are you? On your own, I mean?'

'Of course I'm on my own. Whatever else I might be, I don't play around when Mary's away in New York getting laid by anybody in trousers or skirts.'

'You sound bitter . . . and you've every right to be, but if you'd only get yourself sorted out, then you might not be on your ownio and sounding crabbed on Saturday mornings.'

'And you'll come down with me tomorrow, Daze?'

'OK, seeing that you're trying so hard to be nice. Pick me up at about nine . . . Aneurin.'

'That wasn't bitterness.'

'No?'

'I'm glad for her, Daisy. Honestly. Life hasn't been a bundle of fun for a long time. 'Bye.'

She stood gazing at the handset for several seconds before she returned it to its cradle.

She wondered why Rin and Mary didn't put an end to it, admit it had all gone wrong and maybe start again with somebody else. Rin needed someone permanent to share his kitchen and his bed. Not so Daisy, she knew that she would never stand the hassle and complications of sharing.

As he retracted the phone aerial, a little flurry of tooth-edged pieces of paper scattered across the table. With tweezers he picked up a piece that looked like a luminescent fish-scale, touched it with glue and held it in place on the back of a papier-mâché model, then continued gluing in other pieces until the bare patch was covered. With a fine brush he painted scarlet inside the gaping mouth around the wide smiling lips of a nine-inch model of the kind of dragon which, at Chinese New Year, wriggled through the streets where he lived.

'There!' Gingerly, he picked it up and inspected it. 'Let anybody call you Puff and I'll thump them.' He turned the dragon head-on. The dragon grinned widely at Rin. Rin smiled back. 'I wonder if you can make the Old Man smile?' The dragon grinned. Rin was pleased.

One stroke, one mark in the wrong place and models could look appallingly vengeful. Children knew this about toys and, Rin believed, they would purposely lose any that were not benign. If one found a doll or soft toy on a bus or a park bench, it frequently had a maniacal stare like a ventriloquist's doll, or the wild leer of Mr Punch. Its owner had probably seized the chance of being rid of it. He snatched his thoughts back from toys and children.

With a swoop of his arm he swept all the left-over bits and pieces into the waste basket and took it through into the kitchen. It was a friendly room, and reminded him of home – not this home, but Sunbarrow, the home in which he had spent the greater part of his life so far. It was exactly as he liked it: biscuits in the biscuit jar, spice-jars in the spice rack, no limp or mouldy vegetables in the bin and no crumbs in the door seal of the fridge.

Mary said that he was pernickety, but Rin didn't see how liking a simple, clean orderliness that made life easier, could be pernickety. But he was easy-going so, as Mary liked to use the kitchen more than any of the other rooms, they had it her way until she went on tour and then it became Rin's once more. More and ever more Rin's since she had become a Hothead.

The Hotheads – a kind of actors' co-op who worked community theatres, pub nights and the fringe circuit. Since they had got a couple of awards and mentions in the national dailies, a little fame and money they really weren't desperately seeking came their way. In America, apparently, there was a growing interest in the kind of drama the Hotheads specialized in – raunchy, punchy, irreverent and political.

'This is the biggie, Rin.'

'You stand in danger of becoming a cult, Mary.'

'I know, I know.' She had been gleeful. Rin hadn't expected that; he had expected a denial. 'We'll go down a treat there. You don't mind, Rin? I mean, if we get the tour extended.'

What if I do?

'No, go for it,' he said. 'If it's going to happen, it's as likely to happen in the States as anywhere.'

She had looked up from the paella she was stirring, and quizzed him as though she suspected he was saying something.

'If the Hotheads' success is going to happen.'

'Success in that way is not the name of the game for us, Rin.'

'I know. But you would be pleased.' Rin knew that *pleased* was hardly the word. She could deny it, but the Hotheads wanted a bit of fame and fortune.

'Well, gratified. We've been hauling our wagon for ten years, it'd be nice to get a horse.'

Rin thought that sounded like Sandi's phrase. Maybe not. Maybe Mary talked like that now – how would Rin know? They kept out of one another's way pretty well. Arm's-length discussions about their respective careers such as the one about the American tour. When they were together in the flat the sleeping arrangements were usually settled by Rin having work to do that would keep him up till two in the morning, or Mary would have a late gig and wouldn't want to disturb him.

So, amicably, they had their separate bedrooms. Not

only to sleep luxuriously in their own space, as people with plenty of bedrooms do, but for the purpose of being separate and celibate and safe from the mingling of guilt and grief they had succeeded in burying when they were out of sight of one another.

As doomed marriages go, it worked pretty well – in that they didn't actually fight now – but both knew that it was only a matter of time. It was just that Rin didn't want to be the one to broach it and Mary was never at home long enough to start anything. There was always The Drill Hall, or The Hornpipe, or The Warehouse, or Chichester or Glasgow Mayfest or Edinburgh. It was easier to leave things as they were until something happened.

Rin took the dragon through so as to put it on the pine sideboard to dry. He thought he'd get Myrr something from the National Gallery this afternoon. Not that she was the sort to look for something just because Rin had made the Old Man the model – he liked to give her things. He liked to give things generally.

As he placed the model his hand caught the leaf of an art nouveau picture frame and knocked it to the floor.

For a moment, Rin stood looking at it, then squatting with knees spread he picked up the picture from beneath the star-shattered glass. A fat anonymous baby. It was a typical studio portrait looking as every baby looks in its first months. In another six months the moon face would have changed to the point where not even a portrait photographer could have made the baby look like anybody but himself.

But this one, this small Nathan Tallentire had not got that far: he had gone to sleep contented and full, and had not woken up. The baby in the shattered frame had become one of the number that had swelled the sudden inexplicable deaths statistics. The shock and grief of it had cut a ring around the bark of the marriage tree which Rin and Mary had been trying to grow, the sap had been unable to flow and the tree had shrivelled. All that was needed now was a clean bonfire.

They hadn't gone in for recriminations, but recriminations were there . . . they were there. Recriminations and guilt.

We thought he had slept round for the first time.

How could I have known . . .

You never think it will happen to you.

We thought he had slept round.

If only we had . . .

Thousands of unwanted babies in the world and yet . . . Why?

And so on. Longing desperately to step back to the time just before it happened and do everything over again, and this time do it right. Not expect anything of her. Not think that he's the one who should have done something. This time, do everything yourself. Everything. Trust no one but yourself.

But we both thought that he had slept round.

It was so bloody awful.

Rin took the photograph out of the frame and slipped it between books on the shelf, threw the glass away, shoved the frame in the glory hole and heaved a great relieving sigh. They should have done that ages ago. Neither of them ever really looked at the picture, but it had stood there, a wasp-gall on their dead marriage.

If I get a chance tomorrow, I'll have a talk to Jake. Jake listens.

Cheered at the thought of driving down with Daisy, seeing Myrr, talking to Jake and giving the Old Man the dragon, telling him its significance, Rin rang the Community Law Office and asked for an appointment. One of them had to start the ball rolling.

* * *

The new cappuccino coffee-maker hissed satisfyingly as the process completed. Myrr poured two cups, sprinkled chocolate powder over the foamy drinks and passed one to Nat, who frowned at it.

'What you got this time, Myrr?'

'What does it look like?'

'Shaving soap with chocolate.'

'Oh get on and drink it. I thought you'd like it, you always used to like it when we were young.'

He drank the coffee through the froth.

'Well?'

'It's a drink. Queer drinking it at breakfast time, though.'

They were seated in Myrr's Victorian conservatory which was the best that the salesman could offer to build on to a 400-year-old house. The house took the change in its stride as it had taken half a dozen major alterations and adaptations since it was first built as a single hall with a couple of doorless chambers under its roof. From it they could see Martin Lilie's car parked at a distance, and he and Jake standing in the new corn circle.

'Martin Lilie's going to be green as grass when he sees my lovely MG.' Myrr smiled cream as she anticipated the moment when her white tiger performed before another sports-car owner.

'You'll be able to compare how much of the world's oil you can get through between you before it runs out.'

'I'll be only using the share I should have had over the thirty years when I went everywhere on a bike.'

Their chivvying of one another meant nothing, it was their way. They knew one another inside and out. Nat's tuneless, quiet whistling between his teeth when things were on an even keel, his sulky silence when they were not. Myrr's good-humoured chat and gossip, and her days of tearful moodiness. They each played the other's moods according to their own.

Today no hobgoblin sat on their roof, but then neither

did a good fairy. Myrr was going to do her stint as a counsellor and Nat had Martin's helicopter to keep an eye on.

'You out today?' he asked.

'It's Saturday.'

'I know it's Saturday.'

'Well, then . . . it's my Community Centre day.'

'What about our dinners?'

'In the larder.'

'I didn't like that corned beef.'

'Well you'll have another chance not to like it, because it's corned beef and salad rolls.'

'The film people will be . . .'

'I know. There's plenty and a bread pudding. If anybody wants any more they'll have to go down to Rex's and have a bar meal.'

'I don't see why we have to feed them.'

'We don't have to. We just do. It's how we Jeavonses were brought up. Good manners. I'm going upstairs.'

'Jake's on his way up.'

'I can see him. They'll be ready for a drink. You can make them some cappuccino.'

He looked at her with drawn brows. 'If they get anything, it'll be tea. In a decent-sized mug.' He held up the new wide, shallow coffee cup, holding the handle between thumb and finger.

'You do just that, Nat. That's the Tallentire way.'

There were times when Roz Petherbridge would sell her soul to be back in Childencombe. There, they had lived in the old vicarage which had been as small and manageable as Duncan's congregation. There, they had known everyone, joined in everything, had gone to supper with ordinary people and had them back for drinks after Sunday morning service. Their years at Childencombe sat in the middle of

Roz Petherbridge's later chilly life as a patch of warmth. Duncan was a winner in the ecclesiastical rat-race. His prize had been life (as Roz put it) closer to God's head office, and a beautiful old house that they could not afford to maintain or heat.

In the city, Roz seemed to have no function; nothing she did appeared to matter to anyone, not in the way that it had mattered in Childencombe. These days, only her work with the Rape Crisis Line at the Centre mattered. There, anonymity was what was wanted. There her calm, dis-embodied voice was often a hurt woman's first help over the hurdle of saying it aloud.

Since moving here from Childencombe, her only link with the past was Myrr Tallentire. The thought of meeting Myrr started Roz humming as she powdered herself with talcum. She glimpsed herself in the misted mirror, her heavy copper hair curling from the steam as she ran her hands down her body. Flat and slender and bony but with well-cupped breasts, she had not gained or lost an inch in years.

Hands on hips, legs straddled, she arched her back and thrust her rib-cage forward seductively. 'What a waste, Mrs Petherbridge.'

Her reflection, with a resigned expression, exhaled heavily.

Before Myrr changed into her counsellor's clothes, she tended her bathroom. A squirt of polish for the white sur-faces, a spray of water for the ferns and air plants, a rub for the many taps and the mirrors, a drink for the ever-thirsty spider plant and a step on the scales for Myrr's own peace of mind. The needle showed the same extra ten pounds that she had been taking off or putting on since she was thirty. She had once estimated that she had dealt with something like two hundred pounds of body-fat over that period of time.

Now, as the women's health books advised, she stood before the long mirror and tried to look objectively at her unclothed body. Her soft flesh sagged a little, her hard fat dimpled. Her body hair was becoming sparser, leg hair coarser, head hair coloured by the hairdresser. One breast was slightly larger than the other, always had been – it didn't notice.

Objectively? How can a woman look objectively at her own body? Having worn this same plumpish flesh since her teens, she stands before its reflection with definite subjectivity. She knows what it feels like to be inside it, to make allowances for it, to be exasperated by it, to love and hate it simultaneously and to know how it has felt being loved and penetrated and nuzzled and caressed by others. And how it has felt when it was being distorted and cut and split and torn. And how it feels now as day by day it slowly deteriorates.

Objectively, it is the torso of a mother. Convex belly, crinkled stretch-marks. Objectively, it is a mature woman's body. It has a very old appendix scar and a new long sickle-shaped scar. The fine line left by a sterilization operation is invisible, the work of a very good surgeon – a very rare man, a sympathetic male gynaecologist. 'I'll hide it in your bikini line.' Myrr had nodded gratefully, even though, at the time, she did not much care if the scar were to leave a wide red pucker; just so long as she did not have to go through any more miscarriages or another nine months of a pregnancy only to have a still-born baby.

She had not handed on her incompatible blood to any of her surviving children – although Poppy had been affected by antibodies, and it had been touch and go with her. But, in a way, Myrr had gone through that trauma again, with Rin and Mary's baby. In many ways that time it had been worse than her own still-births and miscarriages, because that baby had a name, Nathan, and a status, grandson, and she could do nothing to make it better for

Rin and Mary. Startled at meeting her own gaze, she snapped the shutters down on that particular episode.

Dressing for her role as counsellor wasn't easy for a woman of Myrr's age. The young volunteers mostly wore jeans, but Myrr had never decided how some of the clients saw her or even if they really saw her at all. One thing she did not want was to appear to be a middle-class, middle-brow, do-gooding lady. Actually, Myrr thought that doing good was the most civilized and humanitarian act, but too many people had fallen for the scoffing. Of course it was actually true that it was usually one class imposing their sort of good. Myrr had set out from the beginning to keep reminding herself of her own roots and of her and Nat's hard times and how easy it is for any marriage to blow apart.

She decided to wear a fuchsia skirt and pink top with sandals, and cheap, pretty dangly earrings with her hair hooked up off her neck.

She had learned how to let her children go. Now she and Nat had security, money to spend on the house, money to spare, money to give away.

Farmers moaned, usually the ones with least to moan about, always wanting things better than they were, always looking over their shoulders for subsidies, grants, government money, EC money. But suggest to one of them the idea of a coal mountain, or subsidies for house-building and they looked at you as though you were a traitor to your kind. Well, Myrr didn't mind. She'd come from rural stock, and married a poor farmer but a damned good one. The Jeavonses had been carters and carriers for as long back as anyone could remember. Nobody had ever given them a grant or a subsidy to not carry something or to stop doing something. Look at brother Fred, driving himself into the ground trying to run a decent removals firm when the world was full of cowboys with no insurance, and vans held together with string and chewing gum, who got council contracts because their dodginess came cheap.

She smiled at her frowning reflection. With the luck of the draw, Myrr, having found that she has won a prize in a competition she never entered, enjoys to the last penny the money that has dropped into their laps after the years of hard work and hardship.

Quite often she found herself in a mood of reflection, but guessed that most people thought of her as happy-go-lucky and a fluff-head. She had the face and figure for it – not like Roz Petherbridge, whose spare leggy body and bony face appeared to be serious and intellectual.

Good, lunchtime with Roz. That was always something to look forward to.

She could hardly wait to get into the MG.

Smiling to herself, she drove through the old cattle yard and slowly past the house where she could see Jake, Nat and Martin. It was an impressive-sounding horn. She saw every nuance of expression on Martin Lilie's face as he came close to the window. She revved up – unnecessary but satisfying.

The road, for once, was clear, so she put her foot down and shot out of the farm-gate and then towards Winchester. What would people in her old village have said if they could have seen Carter Jeavons' little maid in her white drop-head auto?

Filtering into Winchester's one-way system, she forced herself to give all her attention to the Saturday morning traffic and, as always, thought to herself: I shouldn't mind living here. If I was ever left a widow, that's what I should do. Live in a town where there's always lights, and the important things people want as they get older – libraries, health centres, good pavements, easy shopping, trains and buses. I would be twenty minutes from Jake and not much more than an hour from Daisy and Rin.

Roz Petherbridge was manoeuvring into one of the only two empty spaces left as she drove in. 'Just in time, Myrr.

Hey, Myrr, look at you! I'm green with envy.' She came over to smooth the shining bodywork.

'Better to be born lucky than rich.'

'It's lovely, but I've got to dash. We're meeting as usual midday?'

'We'll go to that place along Jewry Street.'

'I'd have thought you'd want to whizz off out of town in that thing.'

Myrr smiled. 'I don't have to drive it, it's enough to know that it's mine.'

Roz nodded and whisked herself off to her stint in the Rape Crisis office. Myrr press-studded the tonneau cover and locked up. As she walked through the building – hardly changed at all from its role as a Victorian junior school – she saw how crowded the place was getting.

There had been a time ten years back when there were classrooms to spare and used for storing chairs, but now every cupboard and cubby-hole had either a title or a set of letters on its door. Roz called them the Alternative Social Services – the ASSes.

It was in places like this that Myrr felt shamefaced about the Sunbarrow affluence.

Myrr looked into the crèche where two men of about Jake's age and a woman of about her own were organizing finger-painting, sand and water play and paper-cutting. Chaz, Pete and Edith. They greeted Myrr. Chaz said, 'I've got somebody wants to see you, particularly you . . . well . . .' he grinned and made a moue '. . . wants to see somebody older . . . well, more mature like.'

'Watch it, Chaz,' Pete said. 'You're digging yourself a big hole.'

'I know. Ageist pig that I am. Myrr knows what I mean, don't you, Myrr?'

Edith, tying a plastic apron around a small boy, said, 'He means they want to see somebody with her head screwed on the right way, no arty-farty beards and jeans.'

'Couldn't have put it better myself,' Chaz said.

Myrr felt at home with people like these. Graduates without a job, many of them, and it had been being in their company these last years working at the Centre, that had started her brain functioning again after it had become clogged with boredom and fatigue.

The room used for counselling was in the quiet, more private end of the building. The volunteers had tried to make the most of it. Myrr had brought in her old sitting-room carpet and a couple of armchairs. Myrr's work here was a small step in the right direction so far as marriages tottering on the brink of divorce were concerned. Trained volunteers whose job it was to try to keep the animosity out of a break-up in the hope that the kids would come out with parents instead of warring factions. Having grown up in a large family in a closely-knit village, Myrr had, when she had first started as a volunteer, been shocked to discover how little people seemed to know about getting any family relationship to work. So many thought that it just did. You simply popped a marriage seed into the ground and up came a thriving plant. Many of them never gave a thought to watering, feeding and weeding it.

As usual the morning passed quickly. When she arrived at the little restaurant, Roz Petherbridge was already there, leaning sideways over the back of her chair gesticulating with her elegant arms which were clad in flowing bat-wing sleeves. She was laughing flirtatiously with a man at the next table. She was being Roz. Deep copper hair that Myrr envied, and a long face and hollow eyes which she did not. She waved and patted the empty seat as though Myrr didn't know that it was available for her. 'Say hello to an old flame, Myrr.'

'Hello, Old Flame,' Myrr said, in a sharpened voice not unlike Roz's.

The man laughed and flung up a hand as though hailing a passing ship. 'And hello, Myrr.' Myrr wondered why the flame had gone out: on the face of it, he and Roz appeared eminently suited.

'He's Teddy; isn't he lovely, Myrr?' Roz said.

Teddy sandwiched Myrr's hand tightly between his own. 'Ah, Myrr, lovely name, lovely lady. I always said the South had all the prettiest women.'

'Now, Teddy, put her down. Myrr won't fall for your old lines, she's already got a gorgeous man who looks like Paul Newman.'

Myrr laughed, enjoying being flirted with by a man who probably saw himself as the wine, women and song type. He was actually quite attractive. A bookie? Estate agent? He looked affluent. 'Well,' she said, 'Nat is somewhere in the same age group as Paul Newman.'

'Shame on you, Myrr, you've got too used to that wonderful face.'

Myrr said archly, 'Perhaps I need a change.'

Teddy said in a mock whisper, 'Think I stand a chance there, Roz?'

'You haven't changed a scrap, you old reprobate.'

'Not so much of the old.'

'What then . . . maturity?'

He rubbed a forefinger along her arm. 'Maturity is good, Roz – in fact on some people maturity is fantastic.' It was a very direct look that he gave her.

'Still the same randy bugger, Teddy,' she said in a throaty voice.

'Still doing things to me, Roz?'

Slightly flushed, Roz said, 'Myrr, this man is getting overheated: get some cold water to throw over him. Now that's enough, Teddy, I'm going to turn my attention to Myrr and we are going to order, and you are going to sit up straight like a good boy and wait for your lady wife.'

Teddy laughed and gave her shoulder a long squeeze before relinquishing her. 'Good times eh, Roz?'

'Oh yes, Teddy, very good times.'

His wink at Myrr said it all. 'She was a goer, our Roz.'

And Roz looked like the cat that got the cream.

They ordered, jacket potatoes and green salad. The menu declared: 'All veg. organically grown in local fields'.

Roz, obviously trying to keep her mind from the presence at the next table, said, 'Has Nat thought any more about going organic? I mean, for a start can you imagine a better name for a logo than "Sunbarrow" – it practically sounds organic.'

'Bone of contention. I keep out of it. Jake wants to make the change, but Nat is all for maximum yields and spotless produce. He has conceded one field, but it will take about another three years before Jake can get it officially recognized.'

'It's a start.'

'Not really, not unless Nat agrees for Jake to take over that whole area; it's easy for contamination to occur.'

Roz, like Myrr, led this secret life. In it she liked to be called Roz and to use the street language of the Centre. When Duncan Petherbridge had been Childencombe's vicar, Roz had been Rosamund, the vicar's wife, whom Myrr had thought rather uninteresting. But since they had been working at the Centre, Roz had begun to change, and in her Roz persona, with her masses of hair fixed so that it looked about to come tumbling down, her slightly eccentric clothes and massed necklaces, Myrr had grown to like her more and more.

It had crossed Myrr's mind more than once that perhaps as Rosamund she had never been dull, just blunted. Perhaps it was the old domestic thing. Hadn't Myrr herself been like that? Or perhaps the fault lay in Duncan. Perhaps he had married a Roz and turned her into a Rosamund, Vicar's Wife. Quite obviously she had once been Roz, years ago when Teddy was her flame – Teddy's eyes had been all over her, really quite hungrily. What had happened?

What happens to all of us, Myrr?

Men don't want their wives to remain the raunchy girls they panted for, ran after, competed for. Men want good common sense and a damper on raunch anywhere but in the master bedroom.

'You're smiling, Myrr.'

'Am I? Roz, what does Duncan know about the ASS side of you?'

'Quite a bit. It's part of his job to know the various voluntary bodies.'

'I don't mean what you do at the Centre, I suppose I mean does he know this side of you . . . of us, really. I can't quite explain, but Nat would be quite shocked if he knew that I sit and listen to people talking to me about the problems they have in their sex lives. And Jake and Poppy . . . I don't suppose it occurs to them that I deal with people to whom incest and rape are a fact of life? My family only know the Myrr they want to know – an ordinary mum.'

'Come on, nobody could exactly call a lady with a car like yours an ordinary mum.'

'Well then . . . a bit of an odd-ball ordinary mum. I've sometimes wondered what Daisy would have to say if she realized that her mother could easily get hold of crack. And how would Rin react if he could heard me talking to some girl in the four-letter language she feels at home with?'

'Perhaps it's better if our kids keep their illusions about us.'

'ASS is ASS, and Sunbarrow is Sunbarrow, and never the twain . . . etcetera, etcetera?'

'Something like that.' She lit a cigarette, pointing the packet at Myrr. 'I know it's no good asking you.'

'Why not? It's years since I did.'

'Actually, it tastes bloody awful, but I like the after-glow. Actually, Duncan hardly knows the woman he married, let alone this Roz. I imagine as long as his old Bish didn't find out, I could take Old Flame there and have a bit of how's-your-father.'

'Roz, be-have.'

Roz drew on her cigarette and stubbed it out. It was obvious that part of her mind was still on the table that was just out of her line of sight. 'It used to taste so much better having a drag and blowing the smoke out of the bedroom window. What's she like?'

Myrr had seen Teddy's wife come in. 'Just what you would expect: long legs, slim, long face, coppery hair.'

Roz smiled wryly. 'A Roz substitute?'

'Definitely a poor copy.'

'Age?'

'Maybe older than the original.'

'Sexy?'

'Not as . . .'

'The bugger shouldn't have gone off as he did.'

Myrr thought that she meant that. Poor Roz, poor Teddy. And for all Myrr knew – poor lady.

'Ready?' Roz said.

'My turn to pay.'

'The wife of the church mouse will not argue with a Euro-grant money-bags.'

There was something so satisfying about this bit of her life that Myrr kept for Myrr. She had wondered if this was the feeling one would have if one had a secret love life.

'Roz? Have you ever cheated on Duncan?'

On the short drive from the city centre out to the Saint Cross area of Winchester, where she and Duncan lived, Roz Petherbridge thought about Myrr and about Teddy. Thinking about Teddy turned her on. God, what wouldn't she give for a night or two with a guy who knew what it was all about. And wouldn't Teddy just about appreciate a night or two . . . Teddy's only trouble had been that he was inclined to put it about, and in some extraordinary places too . . . but didn't we all at the time?

Good times, Roz.

Good times, Teddy.

The thought of looking for them at the bottom of the sherry bottle this evening depressed her. Maybe Duncan would be in the mood. It could still be good for them when they got it right. Trouble was, getting it right these days too often involved smashed mugs, scratches and bruises, Roz giving as good as she got. She longed for a something languorous and extended, light-hearted and fun, something lasting for three or four hours and then another three or four . . . somewhere hot, by the sea . . . Greece . . . Cape Cod . . . A young bloak maybe . . . maybe she wouldn't even know his name . . .

A horn beeped loudly – the lights were green. The indignant driver glared as he accelerated, overtaking to prove his need of the five seconds she had stolen from him after the lights changed. As he drew level, she plunged her stiff forefinger between her lips, then waggled her tongue at him and winked.

God only knew how she had got to be a vicar's wife. It would be funny if he turned out to be a sidesman or in the choir or something. Or a copper . . . or was it Filth? . . . Pig was out . . . Noddy absolutely out . . . There was a story in there somewhere. The accused made an obscene gesture, your worship. What kind of gesture, sergeant? What one might say was a suggestive gesture, sir. Vicar's Wife in vice scandal! Rev's Redhead Roz gave him the green light!

That was the kind of ridiculous nonsense Teddy would respond to, getting more and more outrageous – and funny.

Great times, Roz.

When she and Myrr had left the restaurant, the Old Flame that he had been before his wife joined him had dimmed. Elinor. They had been briefly introduced. Roz

82

had never met Teddy's mother, but wondered whether she too had been a bony, round-eyed woman with good tits and coppery hair. Weren't men supposed to do that, marry their mothers? She could have named half a dozen men who proved the theory, and a lot who didn't, one such being Duncan. The Hon. Enid Petherbridge and Roz were most un-alike. Duncan must have married the Hon. Enid's opposite out of spite.

Perhaps that's what has gone wrong. Things are bad between us from way back. Marrying Duncan because Teddy went off to make a quick buck in the Rhodesian copper mines wasn't very bright. No more bright than Duncan marrying me because of the aggro with Enid about kaftans and long hair.

It was hard now to believe that Duncan was ever hip . . . what a fossilized word, hip. Was the fun being hip, or was it untroubled youth? Being reminded of his flower days image embarrassed Duncan. If she wanted to be really wounding in one of their many wrangles, she only had to shout: You were a decent type when you had long hair – for him to slam out of the room and sulk angrily for days.

Their entire lives these days seemed to be a series of sulks. Roz hated the thought of returning to it. Whilst Ian and Malcolm were still living at home, there had always been so much going on that she and Duncan were able to fool themselves that they had a good solid marriage, a little dull maybe, not much room for a lot of sex, holding hands, that kind of thing, but lasting. That was the image that suited their situation.

It hadn't been true. In one fell swoop when the boys accepted the offer by Duncan's childless brother to put them through college in Los Angeles, Ridge House lost its heart and voice. Even their noisy dog had been run over. Roz didn't know what she would do without her two lifelines – her work in the Rape Crisis network, and meeting Myrr Tallentire twice a week.

Roz would have supped with the Devil to have succeeded as Myrr had done. But then Myrr had started out on the right foot, she had fallen for the right man. Roz wondered whether the death of Myrr's baby grandson and the heart attack of her Nat had been the only dark clouds in that family. Myrr didn't give the impression that there had been others.

As she drew into the gravel drive she saw a car already there and recognized its sleek lines at once. A Bish's car. Not their own Bishop, but a Bish of some sort. Before she went indoors, she took off her earrings and beads and put a plain blue jacket over her blouse, becoming – except for her tumbling hair which she tucked behind her ears – something like a Vicar's Wife.

Cigar smoke and whisky fumes had seeped into the hallway. At four-thirty on a Saturday afternoon? Roz could not imagine anything less likely in Ridge House. She jingled her keys and clattered her heels a bit to warn Duncan that she had come home. Almost at once, Duncan flung open the door to the big sitting-room in which the gas fire and table lamps were expensively burning. As she glimpsed it now, looking alive and warm, she thought how pleasant this room was.

'Darling.' He kissed her lightly on the cheek. A genuine kiss, he looked as warm and alive as the sitting-room. 'We have a visitor.'

'Yes, darling, I did notice the car.'

Holding her hand, he led her into the sitting-room. 'Come and meet Rupert, an old school chum of mine.'

Roz caught the flash of magenta as the chum rose from the depths of an armchair.

Smiling at Rupert as Duncan guided her towards him, she said, 'A school chum, how nice for you, darling.'

'Rupert, meet Rosamund.'

He was . . . he was . . . well, just the kind of man she might have had in mind on her drive home had she not had Teddy and a young bloak in there already. He was really much too handsome to be a Bish. Although he could only be Duncan's age his short curly hair was white but not ageing, for his face was very tanned and unlined except for character creases about the lips and eyes. His eyes were very blue and his eyelashes and brows very dark.

Welsh ancestry, Roz guessed, and if it wasn't for his dog-collar and purple dicky you'd take him for a randy sort of a bastard. Actually, he looked a randy sort of a bastard anyway. Roz whipped his clothes off. Nice. Plenty of him. Nice and extravagant round the belly. Roz was a woman who liked a man who was not fat but had a soft swelling belly, a man without too much restraint, self-indulgent enough to satisfy his appetites. Roz thought that it would be great if women were as open about their preferences as men were: Nice buns, but just look at that smashing belly!

'My dear,' his voice sounded like an actor's, trained to produce resonance. 'I've waited years for this pleasure.' Cream flowing over satin. She had his measure in one. He was great at the old malarky. His eyes were everywhere.

She shook hands, inclining her head slightly, deferring to one of Duncan's superiors and allowing her hair to tumble out from behind her ears. 'Duncan's talked a lot about his schooldays. Your reputation goes before you as they say, and we have always admired your taste in Christmas cards . . . quite Dickensian.'

'Ah, you like them? A thing of mine – do sit down, please – wherever I happen to be in the world, I always send to England for my cards, in June.' He laughed.

Roz thought how ludicrous it was for a Bishop of the Church of England to write home from Africa, South America or wherever he might be doing whatever it was he did, and to place an order in midsummer for so many dozen boxes of ebullient winter scenes.

'How organized you must be. I'm afraid I am often still delivering mine by hand on Christmas Eve.'

'But nicer for your friends. I should like that, a hand-delivered card on Christmas Eve.'

Not if you were cooking for the entire population of Winchester's Skid Row. Bet you're not married. She smiled her wide smile.

Duncan, who now claimed the cigar that had been smouldering on an ashtray on the opposite side of the fire from the chair in which Rupert had been seated, indicated that he would pour her a glass of sherry.

'Really, darling, not now.' She would have loved some of the whisky from the bottle on the hearth.

'Give the lady some of the single malt, old man. A fine brand, Rosamund. Very fine.'

Recognizing the label, she said smiling, ' "Bowman"? What luxury. You've twisted my arm, and then I'll leave you in peace and get on with the supper.' She raised a questioning eyebrow at Duncan.

'You'll take a bite with us, Rupert?' Duncan asked.

He looked at his Rolex.

'I sent my man down into the town and he'll be back in . . . Well, why not, he can sit in the car and play the radio for an hour. Do you know what, Rosamund, I haven't seen Dunk since our hippy days. Lord alive, did we swing, Dunk, or did we swing? Hair, kaftans, hash. You should have seen us.'

And Roz remembered — Roo. Rupert. The Great Roo who had just left for the hash trail when she and Duncan had crashed into one another's lives. It had always been a wonder that Duncan had metamorphosed from hippy student to ordination. But from hippy student who hit the hash trail to a Bishopric . . . ? That was something!

'Do eat with us.' She knew that he would. 'It's only cold on Saturday, but it's my own baked pie,' she explained.

'Nice salad stuff, though – we have an organic shop in town.'

Rupert laughed, his eyes on the deep vee of her blouse. 'It's not what's on the plate, it's who's at the table.'

'I was just thinking that very thing on my way home. I eat a snack lunch with a friend on Saturdays, only a potato but it's the most enjoyable meal of the week.'

'Rosamund is a great one for parish work,' said Duncan, ignoring her disloyalty.

Yes, thought Roz, I suppose Rape Crisis Line is parish work. But a long way from the kind I did in Childencombe.

Sitting perched on the arm of a chair, she sipped the whisky, momentarily closing her eyes and allowing its ripe fumes to drift into her nostrils.

'I say, Dunk, you've got yourself a lass who likes her single malt, eh?'

'Gorgeous peaty stuff: I'd forgotten this lovely smell,' she said.

'Just a wee dram more before you go and toss your salad.' He was obviously a man who did not take refusals and a good measure was in her glass before she could have placed her hand over it even had she wanted to. 'Well, man. Aren't you going to tell her?'

Duncan had been sitting there looking like a cat with nine tails, which Roz had put down to the empty space in the bottle of Bowman. But there was, apparently, more.

'Darling. Rupert has made me an offer.'

'An offer he can't refuse, I sincerely hope.'

Duncan smiled sheepishly at Roz, but avoided her eyes.

'Yes,' he said. 'A chance to head up an organization that Rupert's about to launch.'

'It's a chance to work for a charity,' Rupert said.

Roz said, 'Sorry?'

'A charity. Like Oxfam, Save the Children, RSPB, RSPCA.'

'Oh, you mean a *charity*. I thought you meant a charity . . .

you mean it's a charity, with your actual money.'

For a brief moment a look of panic swept Duncan, but he recovered marvellously. 'Right, darling. And Rupert thinks I'm the man to administer it.'

An administrator of a charity? For the moment she held on to the shirt-tails of the Vicar's Wife so as not to get too carried away. Those jobs carried big salaries. 'Why Rupert, what an absolutely wonderful chance. However did you know that Duncan is exactly the right man for the job?' She leaned forward and touched his knee with her fore-finger. 'He'll be so good at it.'

Bishop Roo laughed. He was the most attractive cleric since Richard Chamberlain in the *Thorn Birds* film. Raising one eyebrow and pursing his lips in mock archness, he said, 'I have a little black book of names.'

Roz responded, smiling straight into his eyes: 'I'm sure you have.'

He laughed again. 'Seriously, Rosamund, we must have a Winchester man heading up the board. The first major funds (well into seven figures) are being put up by a Winchester man. I foresee other Winchester men taking a personal interest.'

He meant, of course, not Winchester the city, but Winchester the public school where Roo and Dunk had been chums.

'Do you know, Rupert, I'll let you into a secret, I've never thought that my husband was best cut out to be a vicar. Of course he does his work punctiliously.' This last word came out with a syllable too many, but Bishop Rupert was too mellow and too much under the influence of tum-bling copper hair and a slightly gaping cross-over to notice.

'I'm sure that St John's has never had better. You'll be missed, Dunk old man.'

Duncan knocked back a good half-inch of neat whisky.

Roz got up, leaned over and kissed his forehead. 'Dar-ling, I am so pleased for you.'

Rupert washed the palms of his hands like a market trader. 'Does that mean that we've got a deal?'

Duncan offered his hand to the Bishop.

'We've got a deal, Roo.'

Rupert laughed.

When Roz offered her cheek she knew that he would take her lips and that a hand would linger warmly on her back and his fingers linger a little in the friendly squeeze. Except for Richard Chamberlain, she had never actually used a fantasy Bishop.

'Do you like Thai food, Rupert?'

He washed his palms again. 'Love it!'

'Good, then we'll skip the pie and salad and eat Thai as a celebration. Don't worry about your man, I'll see he finds somewhere decent to wait for you.'

'She's a marvel, your wife.'

Roz slipped off her jacket as she left the room and allowed her soft bat-wings to catch the air, and as she walked she knew that, although he was a true boobs man, he was also a man who would appreciate a woman who knew how to move her bum when she walked. He would be pleased that he had selected old Dunk from his notebook.

In the hall she went to the phone and splurged a fortnight's housekeeping money, and then some, on a delivered-to-the-door Thai celebration dinner.

At midnight he crashed out in the back of his limo, lovely and mellow from some pretty great wine he happened to be carrying in the car boot, and one or two joints: For old times' sake, eh Dunk?

Great times, Roo.

Great times.

NEW YORK

In Yin's Number One House, waiters hovered behind trellis waiting to be told to bring tea, but Mr Yin did not call them. It was obvious to them that something unusual was going on at the family table where they usually talked over one another non-stop.

'I didn't tell you before I left that I would try to see Uncle Han because . . . Hell, Pop, you know the fuss there would have been, and if it hadn't worked out, what would have been the point?'

'Han?' said Lady Yin. 'Tell Mai Yin of eldest son.'

'Grandmother, he's great. He is very fit. During the cultural revolution he worked on farms, but that suited him very well. People in the villages were pleased to have a geomancer living in their midst.'

It seemed that now she had broken her language barrier, there was no stopping her. 'Is *hsein-sheng*?'

'He is. Very respected and very wealthy. He's got himself quite an impressive clientele in Hong Kong.'

Burt Yin signalled for tea to be brought, and the scent of warm jasmine pervaded the table. They sipped from the delicate cups, allowing the perfumed steam to drift about their lips and nostrils. The pale liquid had a calming effect.

In a sad, low voice, George Yin said, 'You should not have gone, Arison.'

'At least you should have consulted family, Arison.' June Yin's tone supported her husband's sadness.

'It is not the thing to do, to go without telling first. Louis and Henry might have said their thoughts,' Lenny said.

'Uncle Lenny, Louis and Henry wouldn't have said any thoughts, they'd have said: It's your affair, Kuan-Yin, you are entitled to go see your own uncle.'

None of them responded to this truth.

'You know what, Father? You really should listen to yourselves some time. You won't be heard speaking anything but English, and you and Uncle Lenny sent us children away to school, you saw that everything we did was American as apple pie. You even gave yourselves Western names. OK, you could be excused for calling me Alison and my cousins Louis and Henry, but you, Father, do you really think that you look anything like a George, and who is Uncle Burt copied from – Burt Lancaster, Burt Reynolds?'

'It was necessary in the way of business.'

'Maybe you're right, but you can't have it both ways. The point I'm making is that you wanted American children for show . . . but you never wanted us to behave like Americans within the family – for goodness' sake, look where we eat. New York's most authentic Chinese restaurant. Look at me, didn't your faces light up when I came in looking more oriental than American? Uncle Lenny, you've all done your best to make me grow up as an all-American woman: well, all-American women make up their own minds. I did just that. It was very American of me to go find my own uncle when I'm in his country.'

Burt Yin looked at his brothers and gave his shrug that was almost Jewish. 'We learn something every day.'

George said, 'Arison is a Jungian analytical psychologist,' as though that explained everything. He signalled the waiter, who brought glasses and a bottle of French brandy.

'Do you want me to tell you about your brother?'

Lady Yin, nodding, said, 'Speak of Han, Arison.'

CHILDENCOMBE

Sunday morning and the sun had reached the window on the wide wall. That meant that it was about eight o'clock. Lizz Taylor remembered vaguely Jake getting up and letting himself out; he had kissed her somewhere in the region of her ear, grunting quietly as he pushed himself up from the squatting position it was necessary for him to take because Lizz slept on a low futon.

Even as a girl she had realized that Betty was not the kind of name to hang on to if one wanted to see it in lights.

Like the Barbaras, Beryls, Ritas and Junes in her year at art school, she soon found something more suited to fame.

Raising herself on one elbow she felt the cup of tea she knew he would have put on the low stool beside her. She didn't mind cold tea and drank it leaning back against the padded wall-hanging she used instead of a headboard. The wall-hanging was the work of a woman Lizz greatly admired. Using any material – from broken car windscreens to ravelled cocoons of silk – to produce the effect she desired, this artist created landscapes of dream and nightmare. Although Lizz had other lovers who leaned against the textured hanging, she did not usually care, on the morning after, to see its imprint on any bare back other than Jake's – it was as though they had borrowed Jake's razor. He had such a wide, fine-skinned back on which she had once traced round the imprinted landscape with felt-tips and it had become transferred to his shirt.

'I don't know what Myrr will think,' Jake had said.

'She'll think: Hello, hello, he's been 'avin' it off with that artist woman again.'

'She'd be wrong then, wouldn't she?'

That's what was so nice about Jake. He'd be willing to scatter aromatic oils on her and use his large, tough-skinned hands to caress her – sometimes chastely, sometimes not; or spend the night with his arms around her. But when they loved, they loved. Sometimes quietly, sometimes wildly; sometimes dramatically. Sitting or standing, in his Range Rover or on her mattress, they enjoyed themselves greatly.

She finished the tea and went into the tiny shower cubicle whose shower-head missed the top few inches of Jake. Usually, she was up and painting long before this, but today she had decided to be leisurely. In her engagement diary, 'Sunday. Day off – Summer pudding at Sunbarrow' in Jake's small, controlled handwriting.

When he had asked her to come to the farm because,

with luck, it would be the occasion of the first of Myrr's berry crop, he had not known that it would be a family occasion.

'Daisy and Rin are coming down tomorrow. Will you mind?'

'Why should I? I've liked Daisy and Rin when I've met them.'

'It's just that ... well, you know how the Old Man can be and he always seems to be worse when we are all together.'

'He's always all right with me.'

'You are a calming influence.'

'Have you told him that I'd like him to sit for me?'

'I mentioned it, I think he's flattered. He saw that review of your one-woman show in the *Guardian* and cut it out. He has one standard to denote fame – a photo in the *Guardian* or *Times*.'

'I should like to have him with a kind of pre-Raphaelite flavour, the barrows in the background to suggest the great stability of his family, with perhaps some spirals and double-helix motifs in the foreground.'

'You're beyond me ... he's a dirt farmer, Lizz.'

'No, he is not. He's chief of the Tallentire tribe. You said yourself that he had traced the family back to the fourteenth century?'

'Tallentires have been living around here for a long time.'

'So he's an important figure.'

She would have liked to use Jake as a model, but knew that she would find it difficult. They went back a long way. She knew him too well. It was something she discovered quite early on in her career when she had tried to paint her parents. Her father's face had shown the lechery she had tried to disguise, and from behind her mother's hard-faced mask had peered terrified eyes. She had sketched them over and over again, but they still appeared as oppressor and victim.

When she had told Jake, he'd said: 'Is that why you've never wanted me as a model? What do you think you'll discover?'

What indeed? Stodginess? Conventionality?

She passed the long mirror she used to get a better perspective of her work and give herself a more critical viewpoint, but she did not even glance at her own reflection. She had accepted that what she had been given at birth she could not change, so unless she needed to appraise herself dressed in something she had not worn before, she seldom inspected Lizz Taylor.

It was as well that she had been given such good material at birth.

Good bones, healthy hair, good teeth and fine skin. That wasn't bad for a start. As she grew up, the DNA that destined her femaleness triggered off firm rounded breasts held apart and high on a strong rib-cage, high buttocks, a womanly pelvis. Both her ancestry and her mother's insistence on a good plain diet for children, had given her a healthy and robust constitution. Her defects were a neck too short for beauty, some crooked toes, and a thickening of some of her leg veins from long hours of standing at her easel.

She had a great sense of humour and a healthy heterosexual appetite.

Her home was a long, long roof-space over a converted bakery. A large skylight, like a stage-set, gave her good daylight. Her work-space took up a good half of the area, her sleeping space half of the rest. There was a small kitchen, tiny lobby, lavatory and shower. The whole place was well insulated, well lighted and warm. She loved living here.

Dressed in olive-green culottes, black top and flat Roman sandals, and with her long black hair dressed in a complicated weave of plaits, she looked as she wanted to, interesting and a touch eccentric.

Jake had said: 'Come when you're ready – about eleven. Daisy and Rin will have got their effusions over by then.'

There was a bit of a hefty wind, but it would be behind her, so she decided to cycle. She arrived darkly spotted with raindrops.

Jake's father was seated alone in the conservatory. 'Hello, all right if I come in, Mr Tallentire?'

'Ah. Come in, my girl.'

'Rain, Mr Tallentire, I got here just in time.'

'Looks as though they're going to get wet.' He nodded to where Jake and his brother and sister were wading through Clump cornfield.

'Good Lord! Is that the new corn-mark?'

He nodded enigmatically.

'It's wonderful!'

From where she stood, to the side and just behind him, she had a good view of his profile. It was splendid. As on other occasions, she was fleetingly reminded of some of the early plates illustrating profiles of North American Indians. His features were clean and beautifully distributed in proportion to his large, thickly covered head. He had a fine, high forehead and deep-set eyes with a well-defined ridge of eyebrows. His nose was straight, with fine, flaring nostrils. With his well-drawn mouth set like that, Lizz had a glimpse of Jake in the next century. Jake looked very like him, but had a long way to go before his good looks developed the degree of handsomeness of his father.

As she studied him, Lizz thought that there must be many a man who would sin for a head like that, and most women could get excited by the perfect shape of his mouth and his clear blue serious eyes. But, Lizz guessed, he was not the man to respond to any such excitation. From what Jake had told her of him, his father was an old-fashioned Nonconformist with a personal moral code that took some living up to. His opinion of Jake and Daisy were that they were sexually unprincipled. Lizz wondered whether he was one of these moralists who had never known temptation.

Now the rain was coming heavily; Jake and his brother and sister ran into the conservatory.

Daisy Tallentire noticed Jake wink at his girlfriend, who responded with a brief mock kiss across the room. She wondered how serious their relationship was. It appeared to have stability – they had been going around together for ages – yet they didn't seem to live in one another's pockets. She knew for certain that Jake had other women in his life. She had met some of them. When there was a special rugby game at Twickenham, Jake would usually invite Daisy and her partner to supper at some nice Mayfair hotel where he was spending a weekend with a girlfriend, and it was not always Lizz.

Rin noticed, too, and wished that he had something as on-going as Jake and Lizz appeared to have. One of the things he missed about Mary was the good love life they had once had together. He was no good at one-night stands, it made him feel depressed to be discarded the following day. Daisy seemed to prefer it that way. The wham, bam, thank you Sam, practical love life she led made Rin feel sorry for her. But Jake, the lucky bastard, had the best of all worlds. It was no wonder he shrugged his shoulders if anyone twitted him about still living at home.

'What do you make of this new circle then, Dad?' Daisy asked.

'I don't make anything of it. I just wish they'd go away and let us get on with our lives.'

'I should have thought that they were part of your lives now,' Rin said. 'If it was me who had to pack up work, I should be pleased to have something as intriguing as that to study.'

'What makes you think I've packed up? And don't write me off. It'll be a good few years yet before Jake gets to take over Sunbarrow.'

Jake was used to the Old Man; he put his feet up

amongst Myrr's plants on the windowsill and bit into an apple.

Myrr came in. 'Get your feet down, Jake. And don't spoil your appetite eating before dinner. And I'll tell you what it looks like in here, it looks like that advert for one of the Sunday papers where the whole family's sitting round reading the various sections, whilst Mother is smiling away seeing to the roast. But I'll tell you this for nothing – Myrr Tallentire's got a sight more sense than that. So come on, Jake, you open up a drop of wine; you, Rin, set the table.'

Lizz rose from the rattan easy chair. 'What shall I do?'

'Nothing. You're a guest.' She winked. 'In any case that's men's work. Go on, Nat, you can start carving whilst we have five minutes to talk about you behind your back.'

He walked heavily through to the kitchen. The three women watched him go.

'How is he, Myrr?' Daisy asked.

Myrr looked quickly to see that Nat was gone.

'Well, he isn't ever going to get back out there, that's for definite.'

'He thinks he's going to.'

'He doesn't, that's whistling in the wind.'

Daisy gave a little frown.

'Oh don't worry, if he takes care of himself, he could outlive us all . . . on the other hand . . . ?'

'Other hand what, Mother?'

'You don't want me to spell it out, do you? Gin and tonic all right for you two? On the other hand . . .' she dropped her voice '. . . what happened last year was a warning.'

'And he knows the score?'

'Of course he knows.' She included Lizz, handing her a drink. 'You wouldn't get Nat Tallentire sitting around here if he didn't.'

Lizz asked, 'Jake says that these circles really upset him because of people wandering into the fields.'

'He wouldn't be a Tallentire if he didn't make an argument about everything, but underneath I think he's really interested. No way would he have let a film crew into the fields if it didn't suit Nat Tallentire.'

Daisy took out a cigarette.

Myrr nodded at it. 'That won't exactly extend his life, will it?'

'Sorry.'

'Won't do you a lot of good, either.'

Daisy shrugged, indicating that it was hopeless, but put the cigarettes away and nestled lower in the big armchair. 'I'm glad Rin made me come. Oh God, that sounds awful. Not made me, but made me get up off my ass and come. Is it like that with you, Lizz? Friday evening you intend to do such a lot, and suddenly you're gathering things up for work on Monday. You say to yourself: Now I've got all the bits and pieces out of the way, next weekend I'll do so-and-so. Come next Friday there's grass got a mile high and hedges growing over everything or the freezer is all iced up.'

Myrr laughed aloud. 'Oh you poor old thing, sounds to me you could do with a wife.'

'If I was a man, I could send away for a mail-order Filipino girl. I'll swear half the lone rangers in my road have got some poor girl tucked away – it's a kind of dreadful fashion, "my little Filipino thing".'

'Is that true?' Lizz asked.

'It's true. Men have no conscience when it comes to their own comfort.'

'Not all men, Daisy,' Myrr said.

'Well I'll bet Jake hasn't started doing his own washing yet?'

'Oh, come on. I have the washing machine going, it doesn't make any difference if his things go in at the same time.'

'But he changes his own sheets, of course.' Daisy flicked

a look at Lizz as much to say: Listen to this, he might be yours one day.

'It's not as though he can't do it, but he's got the farm to run.'

'And I've got a department to run. Nobody says: Daisy's been in the rush hour traffic, dashed around the office all day and often all evening, poor old Daisy, she needs somebody to change her sheets . . .'

'I'd have changed them for you if you hadn't wanted to go and work in London.'

'Oh, Myrr! That's not what I'm saying.'

'I know what you're saying all right, you're saying men expect to have it a damned sight easier than women and women don't tell them to get lost.'

'Right!' Daisy said.

'Well?'

'That's my point.'

Myrr said, 'I thought you had something new to say. I've known about men all my life. They're the pits, Daisy, the absolute bloody pits. Now tell me something new about them that you young women have discovered.'

Lizz and Daisy's burst of laughter coincided with a similar burst from the direction of the kitchen.

'There!' said Daisy. 'Exactly my point. You can't even trust them to do a simple job like lay up the table.' She hauled herself to her feet. 'I'll soon sort them out.'

But before she could go, Jake came to the door. 'You'd better come, the wine is breathed and the beef is sliced.' He stretched his arms about all three women. 'And I've put the vegetables in their proper dishes and without being told.'

'Oh, Mother,' Daisy put on a silly sentimental tone. 'Isn't he a really good boy. Jakey, you're a good boy.'

He tugged at one of her curls.

'Rat!' She pummelled him playfully as they went in to arrange themselves around the long table.

Lizz, from her seat on one side next to Rin and opposite Jake, watched as they handed and helped one another to the makings of a traditional English Sunday lunch. She had been here a fair number of times, and had met Daisy and Rin on various occasions, but this was the first time she had been included in a Tallentire family gathering. She supposed it was another stage in her relationship with Jake.

These are nice people.

They should be set in aspic and displayed, just to prove that it isn't all mixed doubles with the children shared around at the weekend, or single parent families, or girls with lovers like me and Daisy. She turned to Nat. 'How is it done, Mr Tallentire?'

'Done?'

She pointed down the table. They were all animated and loudly enjoying themselves and a little better for plentiful fruity wine. 'How do you make happy families?'

Nat, genial at the head of the table, looked at Lizz for a long moment, then nodded as though she had made a discovery of something that had been there all the time. 'Myrr and a bit of luck, I suppose.'

The last few words fell into a moment of silence.

'Luck!' said Rin. 'That reminds me, I left something in the car.'

He came back with the boxes he had carefully stowed on the back seat. 'One for Myrr, and one for Dad.'

Nat took out Rin's dragon and set it carefully on the palm of one hand level with his eyes, holding it so that they could all get a view. Rin was standing between Jake and his father and opposite Lizz so that she could observe the eagerness in his eyes as he watched Nat turn the glistening, colourful creature this way and that. Rin needed his father's approval.

'It's a dragon,' Nat said.

A wry cheer went up from his family. 'Give the man a coconut,' Daisy said.

Rin held himself tight. Jake's eyes were fixed upon his father's face, willing him to like Rin's gift.

These are nice people. They care about one another.

'Did you make it?' Nat Tallentire asked.

'Yes. It's papier mâché.'

'Oh, Nat,' Myrr said. 'Isn't that lovely?'

'Lovely, woman? Lovely? This is a bloody work of art.' Nat nodded at Rin. 'Thanks, lad.'

Lizz saw Jake flick a look at his brother, and Rin, gratified that he had pleased his father, returned to his place.

'Anyone guess the explanation?' Rin asked. 'Can't you, Daze? You work in the field of magic and dragons. Do you want me to tell you?'

'No, no,' said Daisy. 'Lizz, what about you? I'll bet Lizz knows.'

'I can think of one thing it might be.'

'Well, go on then,' prompted Jake.

'Your father was born in the Chinese Year of the Dragon?'

Rin gave two claps. 'She's too bright for this family, Jake.'

And Lizz again noticed Jake flick a look at Rin.

'Be quiet. Be quiet a minute,' Nat said. 'I want to hear about this dragon.'

Rin said, 'The Chinese follow a twelve-year cycle of animal years. And the Dragon is the best of all creatures — dragon people are lucky.'

'How did you get to know all this stuff?' Nat asked.

'Living in Soho, and I've got a Chinese neighbour. They take their signs a lot more seriously than we do.'

'There could be something in it,' Nat said. 'Taking all-in-all, I suppose you could say I've had a fair bit of luck one way and another.'

From the way they all looked at him, Lizz guessed that it was a rare moment when the head of this household let emotion show.

With his finger he gently smoothed the iridescent scales of the little dragon, Lizz guessed to cover his embarrassment. She felt that she was being given a brief glimpse at the emotions of a very private man. If he did agree to sit for her she wondered how he would react to her exposure of his vulnerability – she would not be able to conceal it, any more than she had been able to disguise her father's lechery or her mother's fear of him.

Daisy and Rin went back to London early in the evening. Jake and Lizz cleared away and loaded the dishwasher. Myrr went to relax in the sauna and Nat took notice of Myrr and went to put his feet up on the bed and read the Sunday papers.

The house was silent when Jake sat slumped down into a soft sofa with Lizz's legs across his lap, massaging her bare feet. He liked the feel of the knobby bones of her toes, the indentations made by the sandals, the curve of the arch and the smooth flow of curves from toes to ankle. She liked him to dry her feet after a shower. He knew what the flicker of his tongue between her soft toes could do to her.

He was easy and content enough to be sitting with her, touching her, listening to her body living and breathing close to his own, allowing his mind to drift along a stream whose source was a bunch of grapes they had just fed one another. All day they had lived as one organism. They had eaten meat from the same animal, shared wine from the same bottle, had Sunbarrow fruit from the same bushes, breathed the same air.

'Jake?'

His warm fingers slid from her ankles and into the soft tunnel of her culottes. 'I like these things.'

'I think you have a smashing family.'

He pulled her on to his lap and gently bear-hugged her. As always, in comparison to his own hard muscle, her softness came almost as a surprise to him. She was wholly curved and supple, and as always the female delicacy of her shoulders, breasts, hips, made him aware of his own heavy muscles, the square hardness of his torso and the roughness of hair on his arms and chest. 'I'm glad you like us.'

'I like your father. There's a lot of him in Daisy. I think they both have this hard shell that is protecting a soft centre. And Rin's nice. I'd never really met them properly before. I think that he's soft inside and out.'

'And you like Myrr?'

She put her arms about his neck and kissed him in a friendly way. 'Well you know that. She's a lady who one day is going to surprise you all.'

'So you liked us as a bunch then.'

'Yes . . . I liked the Tallentires en masse.'

'What about the young one?'

'Poppy?'

'No, the youngest son?'

'Oh, you mean that hunk with the slim hips and wide shoulders? Fairish hair?'

'Right, the super-hero type.'

'I thought he wasn't half bad.'

'You fancy him then?'

'Doesn't "fancy" date you a bit?'

'Do you fancy a walk up to the barrows?'

'I've got a bicycle ride yet.'

'We could take a walk up to the tumps and then put your bike in the back of the Land Rover.'

'The grass will be wet.'

'I'll wear my riding mac and you can wear your cycle cape.'

'No shoes.'

'Go barefoot and I'll dry them for you.'

'I like it here.'

Each time he answered a protest, he kissed her, sensing

103

her blithesome mood change to excitement. Sudden rain threw itself against the windows.

'Well, hunk, there goes the hump on the tump.'

'Lizz Taylor, did you think that humping, as you so elegantly put it, was my intention?'

She laughed at his mock indignation. 'Can't take me anywhere, can you?'

'I could take you home?'

'A Land Rover parked outside my place two nights in a row! What about my reputation?'

'You could always marry me.'

There was not enough light for Lizz to see from his expression whether he was serious or not – she preferred to decide he was not.

'And spoil a perfectly good affair?'

GREECE

Poppy Tallentire, although she occasionally missed Myrr and Dad, wanted this summer never to end. It had all been romantic and thrilling. The days had been slow and fast, they seemed to have been here in Greece for ever, yet almost half their time was already gone.

They had seen olive groves burgeoning on parched earth and had breakfasted upon warm bread rubbed with garlic and dipped in heavy, green olive oil. They had tramped hills and country roads and bathed in a warm sea. One night, not having reached the expected destination, they had camped out 'under the stars' and Poppy had slept almost chastely in the arms of Tom Farenbach.

Poppy, whose best subject was literature, had been captured by the images of warmth and light and emotions in the descriptions by Laurie Lee, Forster, Lampedusa and Thomas Mann of travels in sun-heavy landscapes. She formed a vision of Italy, Sicily and Spain as one sun-drenched romantic whole along with legendary Greece.

Dust-dry earth, terracotta pots spilling with geraniums, groves of gnarled olive trees, warm rocks and dells filled with violets, stark sunlight and fluttering curtains, cool purple-shadowed churches, and hardy peasants. Landscapes of adventure and romance.

She had just written to her mum and dad to say that she would phone home as soon as they reached a favourable place. It was, of course, not much more difficult to make a phone call in Greece than elsewhere, but the truth was that here Poppy could easily go for a couple of days without remembering home at all. The whole group seemed aware that they were living through the halcyon days of their youth. Soon they would be at the bottom of the work-scramble escalator which, once they were on, it was virtually impossible to get off, and even if one did take a leap one was hampered by the baggage acquired en route.

Poppy's travelling companions were young, white and from – however liberal and aware they might consider themselves to be – families who were in a privileged situation. Rin thought that Poppy was old before her time.

'Not old, Rin, just realistic. My generation is the product of Thatcher; we have to take what's going while we can. Your generation were lotus-eaters.'

'Come on, Poppy.' She looked up from her writing to see Tom Farenbach already strapping on his back-pack and the others gathering ready to go to the assembly point for the next leg of their trek. Responding to his outstretched hand, Poppy wondered whether, when they returned to Childencombe, the new, sophisticated Tom would still shine through, or would he slide back into the skin of the publican's son she had known all her life and with whom she had played at Goose Grass with all the other kids of their age.

Half a mile down the road from where Jake Tallentire and Lizz Taylor were provoking one another into a familiar light-hearted lustfulness, Duncan Petherbridge sat in the car park overlooking the Punchbowl. When he had still been vicar here in Childencombe, before he had got the Winchester preferment and before he had sorted himself out, he used to come here. Looking for his lost faith.

Exhaling heavily, he flicked the wiper-switch and watched the rain sweep in from over Gander Down to spatter itself in great gobbets over the car. Where at one time he had come here to commiserate with himself, Duncan had this evening come to sit and gloat over his good luck. Whatever happened now, he was on the up and up. Imagine . . . having enough money. If it had only come before the rot had set in.

No one could accuse Rosamund of actually drinking as such, but when she did, she did so secretly: it was as though she was playing at having a drinking problem.

It pained Duncan that she treated him in that manner. He was a counsellor, trained to comfort people with problems, he was a professional who did voluntary work at the prison, one who could get a recidivist to open up to him . . . even get a young tearaway to confide his frustrations and inadequacies.

But he could get nothing from Rosamund.

'If you loved me – or even had an ounce of respect for me – you would talk to me.'

'Talk to you?' That look of hers could slash like a razor.

'Then you shouldn't have married me . . . you should have shacked up with one of your lefty lovers.'

'It's exactly what I did do, if you remember – or doesn't this count as marriage?'

'You married me on the rebound from some love affair.'

'You don't listen. You don't listen.'

'You don't want anyone to listen,' Duncan had snapped. 'You're afraid you might get to know the truth about yourself.'

'The truth about me is that I fell for you, and believed

what you said about changing things. You had ideals, I believed in your altruism.'

'Altruism is for kids and only the naïve can afford ideals.'

But goading and prodding merely pushed her further behind the mask of the Vicar's Wife until she would only respond in that bland, controlled way she had adopted.

'Don't be ridiculous, darling. I married you because we fell in love and wanted to do good to people.'

Each time she said that, or something akin to it, he was cut by the sarcasm he knew lay behind 'doing good to people'. What cut deeper was the self-knowledge that since he had been ordained, he doubted that he had ever done one speck of real good to anyone.

'At least I'm honest enough to admit to myself that high ideals can crash.'

There's never been enough time to do anything much for anyone, never enough money, never enough peace of mind.

The twins, coming too soon after getting married, had been a nightmare of cots and clothes. She had never forgiven him for that. Neither had he forgiven himself once he knew that he'd made her pregnant.

She had gone berserk when she had felt him lose control: I trusted you! I bloody trusted you! And again when she had discovered that those ten seconds of indulgence had made her pregnant: What do you mean, it was just that once? One sperm is all it bloody takes!

But there had been two.

Yet she had adored the early stages of motherhood . . . he was sure that she had. She seemed to. Always bare-breasted and suckling them, one under each arm whenever he had come into the house. Those early years when the boys had been babies had probably been the best of their entire marriage.

The real trouble came almost as soon as she had weaned them. They had begun to be expensive. He hadn't wanted his sons' childhood to be any less privileged than his own. In a very short time-span he had gone from having only himself to fend for to having four mouths to feed, four people to clothe and house. Even though there had been money from Grandfather Petherbridge to help with the school fees, there had been all the clothing and gear, and later when he had been given the Winchester preferment there had been Ridge House with its great garden which had been laid out in the days of gardeners. What a relief Patrick's offer had been to give the boys a couple of years with him in America.

He stretched luxuriously. But that was all over. Not the marital problems, but the money worries, the worries that make a man feel anger and envy and vindictiveness.

And perhaps their marriage wasn't irretrievable; perhaps all it needed was a good feed of cash at its roots. Holidays. Dinners in restaurants, plays and concerts – it must be twenty years since he and Rosamund had listened live to something grand like *Belshazzar's Feast*. Rupert had said that Duncan needed to have a decent car: Make it something about 20–25K, decent bodywork, and upholstery, but not flash. 25K!

Perhaps he and Rosamund could try one out and go for a weekend somewhere. A BMW? A Saab? Ah . . . a Saab convertible. It wasn't so much the actual car that excited Duncan, but the future that was represented by the image of solid chrome and bodywork unblemished by some panel-beater.

A weekend in France. The notion grew. He fired the ignition and drove slowly through the huge pools that had gathered on the pot-holed surface of clay and hoggin of the car park. As he drove away out, a Land Rover passed, a corn-sheaf logo and 'Sunbarrow Farms' painted on its side. He waved when he recognized the driver as young Jake Tallentire. Jake used to sing in the choir when Duncan was vicar of Childencombe. Young Jake? Seeing choirboys grow into men brought it home to you that time was short and you needed to grasp at anything to make up for lost time.

This wasn't a rehearsal. You got only the one shot at it . . .

At Ridge House, the sudden storm that had hit Duncan had a bit earlier spurted down through the breaks in the roof-guttering and hammered flat the soft-stemmed nicotiana just as they were about to flower. At any other time Roz would have cut up some old nylon tights and tried to resuscitate the poor things. Not this time. This time she hunched her shoulders at them as, withdrawn into herself, she went out, down the warm, steaming drive and along the already drying pavements towards Winchester city.

If only time could have stopped still somewhere in the late sixties. Sex had been easy, wholesome, freely given and accepted. They had lived their student days with a sense that the world was waking up to the fact that it wasn't necessary to consume or to fight. Make Love, Not War had been the future.

Music and love had seemed at the time to be the bed-rock of human goodness. It was the best time in all history to be young. Duncan had worn his hair long and played classical guitar; they rocked, danced naked at festivals, painted one another's bodies, smoked a few joints, shared the experience of LSD. Then, dedicated to peace and love, he had gone into the Church. But the days of flowers and grass had turned out to be a fantasy, a psychedelic, hash-high trip. And so had his faith.

Duncan's faith. His great, much-vaunted Faith went, taking his idealism with it.

Once those were gone, it seemed that they could do nothing except hang on in there. Cling on with their fingernails. But for years they had been losing their grip, slipping back down. Too many responsibilities had attached themselves to their lives for them to change direction. Too old and too many children . . . only two, but too many.

They had grown up in the swinging sixties, that decade of the young and idealistic; the next decade had turned out to be the sober seventies, when the young and ruthless reigned. The eighties turned out to be the decade of the young and ruthless and greedy. Perhaps in this decade the pendulum would start to swing back – already flared jeans were back on the streets. Roz smiled in spite of herself, remembering the extreme loons she had bought in Carnaby Street when she was still a schoolgirl.

When Duncan had found himself to be an atheist trapped inside the Church, he put the time spent on his knees to some use – meditating on a strategy to succeed within the only organization he knew. If her husband was anything, he was clever and ambitious. In industry or commerce, he would have trodden on necks and cut opponents' feet from under them and achieved the very highest position. In the Church he had not been able to climb very far; perhaps because there was even more neck-treading and foot-cutting than in industry or commerce.

His strategy had been to volunteer himself for committees, to accept chairmanships, to speak up at conferences and speak out at Synod – but not too controversially. And it had paid off. Hadn't it? Not with the purple shirt that Rupert had achieved, but with one of the other prizes. Administrator and a real salary, starting almost immediately, and – as the Great Roo had said: A salary with a plethora of noughts.

When the Reverend Duncan Petherbridge returned home from his hour or so of contemplation in the Childencombe car park, it was late. Rosamund's church-going, if any, took place early in the day and, in recent years, very irregularly. Because he felt let down by her lack of concern at least for appearances, they would, from time to time, have one of their rages that took them slamming back and forth through the house, until it all ended in tears. Promises on her part, guilt on his. Amid debris of hurled cartons, packets, cushions, clothes – never anything hard or break-able because of the cost – they would make love as they had not done since the last time they fought, when she would promise that she would renew her attempt to keep up appearances and be a good wife for the Church.

Duncan knew that, even though she professed to dislike sherry, Rosamund nevertheless bought cheap stuff from time to time to top up the Harvey's bottle supposedly kept for visitors. Duncan Petherbridge, failed cleric, father of two absent sons, husband of a wife who was drowning, not waving, arrived at his home minus his dog-collar, the symbol of all that he had been for twenty-five years.

He had hung the collar on the fence when he had leaned over it pondering this year's corn circles in the Punchbowl. Having read a little psychology he supposed that there was nothing accidental about his having left the collar there. It amused him to wonder what people might think, finding a dog-collar in such a well-known lovers' place. When he arrived at Ridge House, he wanted nothing more than to take off the rest of his dark clothes and make love just there, anywhere he might find Rosamund. They used to do it like that before the twins. Perhaps they could start again. They weren't old.

But she had gone.

Propped in front of the electric kettle:

Dear Duncan, I've gone away for a short while – to think things over as they say. Don't worry. I'll phone you in a day or two. I have taken the housekeeping and the emergency money from your drawer. You can tell people I've gone to nurse a sick aunt.

Sorry, Duncan. It was now or never.
Roz

It was past midnight when Myrr got up to answer the landing phone.

'Did I get you out of bed, Myrr?'

'It's all right, Roz, wasn't asleep.'

'I wouldn't have done it . . . only I've left.'

'Left? Where?'

'Duncan. Left home. Run away, I suppose you'd call it.'

'Good Lord.'

'I know. That's a bit how I'm feeling at the moment.'

'Where are you?'

'Oh, I'm all right. It is all a bit crazy . . . not thought out . . . I just went to the station and got on the train that was standing there. Got off at Southampton.'

'Do you know anyone in Southampton?'

'I've got a few friends from when I used to work here years ago, but I'm staying in a small private hotel close to the Avenue. It's quite nice, really.' She giggled. 'I feel terribly thrilled, in fact. Enjoying it, really, now that I know that Duncan will have got my note. I felt a bit dicey before.'

'I don't know what to say, Roz. I had no idea. I always thought that you and Duncan were OK.'

'I know . . . one always does unless there's an obvious bust-up going on. I've always taken it for granted that you and Nat were happy, but nobody really knows what goes on inside other people's relationships. If anyone knows that, then it's you.'

'Actually, Nat and I are fine.'

'Good. But you know . . . on Saturday, what you said . . . ?'

'About what?'

'You asked if I had ever cheated on Duncan?'

'Good Lord, Roz, I didn't really mean it seriously. I was

just wondering what it felt like to have a secret of that importance.'

'And haven't you got one?'

'Only what goes on at the Centre. It was that I was thinking about. The family not knowing the same Myrr Tallentire you know.'

'Odd. She's the only one that I do know. I drink sherry secretly.'

'Much?'

'Very little, actually. I don't like it. It doesn't do anything for me. Well it does . . . it makes me feel that I'm putting two fingers up at all those pricks Duncan has to kow-tow to.'

'What about Duncan? He won't go to pieces or anything?'

'Duncan? No. Anyway, I told him I'd soon ring him and that I was only away for a short while.'

'Right.'

'But I'm not. I've really left him. I shan't go back. We must have reached one of those points that palmists point out as breaks in the love line.'

'I'm sorry, Roz. I wish there was something I could do or say. I always think it's bad when people have to face crises alone.'

'It doesn't feel like a crisis, and I'm not alone.'

'Oh . . .'

'I meant you. I'm not alone because you're being a real friend, letting me go wittering on like this, at midnight.'

'What are you going to do now? What about money?'

'I took what I could find. It's enough. I'll apply for Social Security.'

'Oh, Roz, will you really?'

'Duncan won't see me starve, but I think I want to go it alone. By the way, Duncan is going to be administrator to a new charity – it's a chance in a lifetime for him. Huge salary, posh car.'

'That's not the kind of news usually makes marriages break down.'

'It seems to me to be the best of all possible times. Whilst we were church mice it would have been the absolute pits splitting up, but now I feel free to go. Duncan will have secretaries and people around him.'

Myrr heard the bedstead creak and then Nat's footsteps. He called out. 'You all right, Myrr? Who's that on the phone?'

Roz said, 'I thought I heard a voice. Is there somebody else on the line?'

'It's Nat . . . just a moment. Nat, it's all right, go back to bed, it's just Roz Petherbridge.'

Myrr couldn't hear his actual words of reply.

'Sorry, Myrr, I'll ring off now. It's just that I wanted somebody to know where I was and that I'm OK. I'll ring Rape Crisis and tell them they'll have to find somebody else for a bit.'

'Well, if you're sure that you're OK. We've got spare rooms here you know, four of them.'

'That's really nice of you, Myrr. I might just take you up on it.'

'I mean it.'

'I know.'

'Any time.'

'Right.'

'I'll say goodnight, then.'

''Bye, Myrr. Just before you go . . . I've written a play, for radio – actually I think it's quite good. It's about the wife of a vicar who comes out and goes to live with her lesbian lover.'

There was a moment's pause before Myrr said, 'Are you saying something, Roz?'

Roz laughed quietly. 'Not really. Goodnight, Myrr.'

'Call me soon, Roz.'

'Will do.'

Myrr found it depressing. Two or three times a week, she sat and listened to people whose relationships were breaking up. There was always some public figure or other laying down the law about the advantages of making it more difficult to marry. If it could stop some of the pain she saw then that might be an argument, but it had very little to do with making vows or commitments. In her experience it made little difference whether couples had known one another for two weeks or two years, whether it was a common-law, secular or religious agreement; it was the daily rubbing against one another that wore marriages out to destruction. There was no way of knowing whether it was going to work until you were in it up to your necks.

Roz and Duncan were probably totally different people from when they were twenty. Most of us are. She had often thought what a good idea it would be if marriage agreements ran only for a limited time – renewable if both parties agreed. There might not be so much taking for granted.

It was depressing, having your best friend go through a break-up. You couldn't become involved, neither could you stand to one side. Either way you were on to a loser. Not many friendships survived in their original state.

TWO

If you came this way,
Taking any route, starting from anywhere,
At any time or at any season,
It would always be the same: you would have to put off
Sense and notion.

<small>T. S. ELIOT</small>, Four Quartets

Disinformation, like propaganda is as old as Adam. Give a dog a bad name, mud sticks, and all that. So the Earth Spirit was given bad names – Python, Dragon, Serpent, Nidhoggr – and a fearsome reputation. Thus it became A Good Thing for heroes to go questing and seek to pin down the energy of the Spirit in known and marked places.

Apollo, St George, Beowulf and Siegfried all set forth to quell their special dragons. All triumphed and, wherever lances, arrows or rods struck, the spot of the capture was marked by an important stone, pillar or tree. Aha, they cried, the Dragon shall not go wandering again but shall become a source of exceptional energy, a potent force under the control of men.

In Delphi a carved stone rested on the head of Python. In Delhi, an iron pillar rested on the head of Vasuki. In Madagascar, the One-Able-to-Answer was trapped in a cave at Andringitra. Of course, the Spirit tried constantly to get free. Nidhoggr, for instance, gnawed at the roots of the tree which had been planted over it.

Nidhoggr still gnaws.

Kuan-Yin went to look for an antique *lo p'an* in a specialist shop in London where, Uncle Han had told her, she might find an antique Heaven Pool as a guest gift for Mike at whose house she would arrive later that same morning.

As a host Mike had a lot going for him. He, like Kuan-Yin, was an analytical psychologist. Male, good-looking and great in bed, he had sounded delighted when she had said that she would be in England for the summer. Also going for him was that he lived in a village in which there were ancient dragon veins and where recently there was a great amount of crop circle activity.

She knew Mike Alexander from an unforgettable three days in Washington, when they had let the conference go hang and pleasured one another wonderfully. Mike was a guy with two attributes she liked in a man, sensitivity and a great sense of humour. As a bonus, he was good-looking.

She always took care with her make-up and today she took extra time in applying it, taking dark kohl well beyond her normal eye-line, adding extra individual lashes, blending deep colours on her lids, so that, when finished, she had eyes as exotic and striking as the Nefertiti mask. If she liked drama in her life, she also liked drama in her appearance, as when she had arrived at the family dinner wearing traditional dress.

Today, because she knew that it would please Mike, she again emphasized her oriental appearance, wearing straight, narrow trousers with a soft brief top and a long, straight silk coat, the hem of which floated somewhere around her ankles. Black hair and ivory skin. The jade green of her earrings and hairpins was heightened by the black tussore-silk clothes. As she walked along Piccadilly and Shaftesbury Avenue to Soho with the panels of her coat flying she looked as though she might be modelling the cover of a fantasy novel.

In the small, deceptively seedy-looking shop, the proprietor brought out a few beautifully ornamented *lo pa'ns*. The place was an Aladdin's cave of oriental curios and artistic objects. She had been in other such places in Bangkok, Sydney and New York, and had always felt very aware of her ancestry and of the gulf between occidental and oriental cultures. There was so often something fine about even the most warlike of Eastern antiquities and for a few minutes she walked around touching basket-weave warriors' helmets, enamel-handled swords, pieces of netsuke and ivory, feeling nostalgia for what she had never known. Very aware that she was of the variety Chinensis cultivated in unnatural soil.

Excited at her finds, she bought two very costly *lo pa'ns*.

When she returned from Soho, a black Jaguar of a similar model to her New York car had been delivered to the street outside her hotel. Here there was no waiting, so she had to dash out and was soon crawling away from London at five miles an hour, in the skeins of traffic which created the most un-charming and un-quaint feature of the capital city.

It took an hour to escape London, but once on the road south the car sucked up the miles. Driving at speed exhilarated her, and in this country where 70 mph was legal and 90 only a little over the limit, she swished along in the outside lane. Back home a cop booking you for speeding made you feel about two foot high, but in her experience of driving in England, there were hardly any speed-cops lurking. Speeding through their small country, any Manhattan penthouse dweller might, as she did, feel warm towards the British, with their friendly cops, tiny fields, old stone and flint, and people, such as Mike Alexander, who could trace ancestors almost as far back as could the Yins.

Taking the exit Mike had indicated, she turned off the Winchester highway on to the Childencombe road, and eventually in at the gate of Mike's house, Loxwood.

Bordered by a wood on the boundary of the village, Loxwood stood serenely apart, very expensive, very picturesque, and typically English fourteenth-to-sixteenth-century. It was midday, the day was sunny. The rambling garden in which Loxwood was set gave the impression of having been there for as long as the house itself. All cream and pale pink against the flint and brick walls, climbing roses, hollyhocks, clematis and lacy petiolaris hydrangeas leaned and climbed around the leaded lights and up over mellow roof-tiles. Mike himself, in faded blue shorts and old tennis shoes, was edging up the lawn.

She greeted him with arms wide, the panels of her coat undulating on the warm air. 'Mike, honey. With this house you should be wearing full sleeves and a neck-cloth.'

He hugged her warmly. 'Well, Dr Yin ah do declah. The lady who has obviously discovered the reverse-ageing process.' For all his attempt at Deep South, his tone was expensively English-made. 'Three years has made you more beautiful.' For a moment, he looked uncertain and then made up his mind and gave her a plenitudinous kiss.

'I thought you'd be working,' she said.

'What do you think this is?'

'I was thinking more of fee-earning work. Cutting grass is for pleasure. Is this a vacation?'

'A couple of days off – special occasion.'

'National holiday?'

'Private visit of a well-known American Jungian practitioner – I am to make myself available for her.' Tucking her arm under his, he guided her into the house.

'Working visit, I'm afraid, honey.'

He handed her from the sunshine into a cool, shaded hallway where they kissed one another as though satisfying a hunger – which is what it was.

'Ah . . . all work and no play . . .'

Kuan-Yin had had many lovers before and several lovers since Washington. The time spent with Mike had been rich, leaving her with memories and desire for more. Memories of sugar melodies of the hotel muzak; of flavours, light sparkling wines, crème brûlée, whitebait; of smells, ylang-ylang oil in the shower, and Mike's own body smelling like warm bread on the two mornings when they should have been listening to lectures. But on the third she had begun to feel that her life might be about to be taken over. Mike had plans. Seeing him now, that feeling was forgotten, she was again hungry to experience time with him.

'Lovely room.'

'Not to my credit, it's as it was when Ilse and I split.' He had told her about his and Ilse's fairly amicable divorce which had taken place just before Washington. She guessed that there was not another live-in woman seriously in his life; had there been, then Ilse's furnishings would have been changed.

'She has good taste, for a German furnishing in English period style.'

Like the house, the room was low and oblong; timber framing, plaster walls and a beamed ceiling; small diamond-paned windows contemporary with the house, and sympathetically inserted glazed doors to the garden that must have been added this century. A low, yew-wood table between two long sofas piled with cushions, four armchairs and some inlaid Queen Anne chairs standing against the walls looking elegant, small plain chests on which there were bowls of flowers. Furnishings were unbleached linen and ivory silk, two Aubusson rugs, a gilt-framed convex mirror, a very modern tapestry, some framed water-colours, two oils and a pine-shelved wall of assorted books.

Kuan-Yin was drawn to the oils. One large, beautiful painting of Loxwood seen from the gate looking misty and mysterious like some minor Manderley, and the other a back view of a male nude, legs straddled, fists on hips, perhaps wondering whether the river by which he stood was too cold for diving – or was it that he was waiting for Ophelia to float by? 'Are these to your ex-wife's choice?'

'No, those are down to me.'

'Nice.'

'I'll make you a present of one.'

'I couldn't take it, the room would not be complete. But if I were to be such a vandal, then I should take the house. I carry my own picture of him.'

He laughed. 'It's called *Man in Nature*.'

'*Naturellement*. I remember that butt.' Briefly running

her hand over the very butt. 'I think the artist is talented — and also very fortunate.' She patted him.

Before they went to bed they ate lunch outside, each, from time to time, looking up and catching the smiling eye of the other. He re-learning the contours of her flexible ivory body of which only her bare arms were at present visible; she letting her inward eye travel upwards from the cuff of his shorts to the open neck of his tennis shirt.

He was a lean man, with the hard muscles of a ball-games player; of average height, dark thick hair laced with grey, skin that appeared to be suntanned but was not and dark-brown eyes. As a lover he was unexpectedly languid and generous, unexpectedly because, in Kuan-Yin's experience, most athletic types were *pistolas*.

In the afternoon she talked about the reason for her visit. 'Two things. I have done a little work on the effects of high-power electricity towers, and that led me on to other forms of energy, *ch'i*, earth energy, leys . . . you know? The Chinese call them dragon veins, energy running across the earth.'

'Aren't they supposed to be like acupuncture channels?'

'Right. I'd like to check it out in an active area where the circles are appearing. I want to take a close look at whether there is any effect on people living close.'

'I read a couple of papers. Are you with this international team that's setting up close to here?'

'The Blackbird Project? No. I guess I could've, but I like to do my own thing. It's interesting, but I can't say that it has stuck its foot in my door.'

'Interesting! I'd have thought that you would have more than interest — collective unconscious, and whatever attaches to the human psyche.'

He raised his eyebrows. 'Are you working on the collective unconscious area?'

'From all accounts something is going on.'

'Practical jokers?'

'OK, but how and why? Leave aside anything else, I find it interesting. These things seem to appear overnight in the middle of some dark field, for Christ's sake – that indicates something more than a bunch of students on a high taking the piss and there are scores of the darned things. I just don't understand how you can just take it or leave it?'

'OK, so what do you plan to do?'

'I'd sure like to know something about people who farm land close by. How do they react? How are they affected? I don't want to go in as a researcher, that's why I wouldn't want to join the "Operation Blackbird" thing, I want to be around the people who live with this phenomenon, to see how they function, to live close at hand for a while. My charts show your village as being at the centre of a lot of the activity. I thought I would put up in the village.'

'You could stay here.'

'You're sweet, but I'd rather come visit here. I'm not such a good house-guest when I'm working. But you could help if you know people who have crop circles on their land, or point me in the direction of local barrows.'

'I do, actually. They have circles and barrows. We play squash.'

'Oh Mike, perfect. Could you arrange a kinda casual meeting as a visiting friend of yours?'

'Only one snag.'

'We will overcome it, honey.'

He stopped her pacing, pinning her arms to her sides. 'Difficult. He's very tall, very fair and very handsome, he's got a reputation with women and I'm selfish.'

'Mike, honey, he's safe. What would I do with two handsome men?'

He gave her a crooked smile. 'I could have a pretty good shot at guessing.'

That evening, Mike Alexander and Kuan-Yin walked into the village to the Green Man pub, where he said they would probably find Jake Tallentire whose farm had seen crop circle activity over several years.

'And you say the guy is a hunk?'

'He plays not a bad game of squash. But he's big and heavy, not quite speedy enough to beat me often.'

Kuan-Yin wanted to sit in the garden of the pub and, the evening being warm and not too midge-ridden, they did so.

'Oh Mike, honey, I must have pork scratches . . . you don't have pretzels and peanuts, but I do love pork scratches.' And she was up and away into the bar where darts seemed to pause in flight, bar-billiards balls halt on the rim of pockets, and drinkers' lips hover an inch away from the glass. In reply to her 'Hi, there', she received nothing but the satisfaction of seeing the effect she had on regulars in an English country pub.

When she returned to the garden Mike was offering a chair to a very pretty black-haired girl and, unmistakably, the farmer. She hung back a little. Tall, blond and handsome? Well yes, she thought, exactly. They're a pretty good-looking pair. Mike was stroking the girl's sunburnt shoulders sympathetically. Kuan-Yin had an urge to stroke them herself, the reddened skin looked so tender. No matter how stimulating and exciting a man's body might be, it could not, in Kuan-Yin's estimation, compare for sensuousness with a woman's curves and softness. On the whole she preferred to sleep with men, but she liked women of this type.

'Ah here's Kuan-Yin. Come and sit down and meet Lizz . . . Lizz meet Kuan-Yin . . . and this is Jake. Jake lives up the road a bit and Lizz has a place here in the village.'

They exchanged handshakes and commonplace greetings.

'Can I get you a drink?' Jake asked.

'I should love a beer. Is it OK if I come in with you, then I can see what beers they have?'

He held his hands apart as she passed in front of him as though guarding her from breakages.

In the bar, the men who had previously stared at her cheerfully greeted Jake as one of themselves.

'Is this your regular pub?' she asked.

'Mmm, practically the centre of my universe.' His voice was good, different from Mike's, less of the Englishy accent, more of his own locality, a soft huskiness. Kuan-Yin made judgements on voices; if only more men realized what a turn-on a good voice was to a woman. His was relaxed and confident, no stress, and there was humour there – the vital ingredient in the kind of sexual partner Kuan-Yin liked. She guessed that this bar was not the centre of his universe, nor was he the uncomplicated farmer that his open shirt and veldskoen gave an image of.

He bought the beers and they joined Mike and the dark girl, Lizz.

'Guinnesses all round?' Jake said, handing out the foam-lidded glasses. 'And four packets of the lady's scratches.'

'We were wondering,' Mike said, 'how pretzels would go down in an English pub.'

Jake made a sour face. 'Myrr bought some, but we all thought they were tasteless – except for the salt.'

'I guess that's the point,' Kuan-Yin said.

And they went on talking in a friendly way about bars in America, where Jake had never been, and telling anecdotes about countries they each had visited.

'Mike says this is a working holiday for you,' Lizz said. 'What's the working part?'

'Oh . . . well I have some meetings. I'm in the same field as Mike. Work is boring. But it won't stop me from asking about you. What do you do?'

'I paint . . . pictures.'

'Of course . . . those in Mike's room? I loved them. You have real talent. I mean it. Or does that sound patronizing? You must have been told by greater experts than me that you're good.' She wondered what the relationship had been between her and Mike during the painting of *Man in Nature*.

'I'm egoist enough to not tire of hearing it from anyone else who likes to tell me.'

'Oh, good! Talented people who are modest are such bores. Would you let me see some more of your stuff?'

'Of course. You could just drop in any time. I'm sure to be there working.'

'Say, that's really great.'

'Is this your first visit?' Jake asked.

'Not to England, but to Hampshire.'

'Best county in Great Britain.'

'You are a farmer?'

'You probably passed some of our fields when you came from Mike's.'

'It's large, then?'

He laughed. 'Not by prairie standards in the States. Mostly cereals and we run cattle and sheep.'

'And it is in this area that there have been some of the corn circles. Have you any idea how they come about?'

Jake hesitated.

'We've been finding circles in Sunbarrow fields for years, but we're not any nearer discovering how they get there.'

'Say, is that so?'

Jake nodded. 'There's an international research project about to start, but I don't think they're going to get answers.'

Kuan-Yin had guessed right, he was more than just a hunky farmer.

'Every time somebody makes a statement saying that they know, everything changes. New things happen. Just this week something totally new happened.'

She saw that behind the smile in his long-lashed blue eyes was a watchful shrewdness.

'It's quite impressive. Like this.' He drew a diagram on the table in spilled beer.

Controlling her instinct to exclaim, she said, 'That certainly blows any theories about whirlwinds, don't you think?'

'Most of the circles are ellipses anyway.'

Lizz said, 'It's Gaea.'

Kuan-Yin felt excited that she should have discovered so quickly people who were intelligent and open-minded. She said, 'I expect you get pretty sick of people asking . . . but would you let me see it?'

'No problem,' Jake said.

'Say, would you really?'

'Why don't you come to the farm in the morning. Myrr and the Old Man will be there. Myrr would be chuffed to meet you: she's always saying she's going to take a holiday in America, maybe you can give her some ideas.'

'Who is Myrr?'

'My mother.'

'She's nice,' Lizz said. 'So's his father. Likes people to think he's a bear, but he's a really, really nice man.'

'Can I bring a camera? I should like to take some shots home with me.'

They left the pub at closing time, Kuan-Yin renewing her promise to go to Lizz's studio. When she and Mike got back to his house there was a message on his answering machine from his ex-wife.

'Damn Ilse! She never thinks. She's made a sudden decision that I can start my spell with Jack tomorrow. She could have told me before this. She just never damned well thinks . . . not about anyone else anyway.'

'Who's Jack?'

'My little boy, my son.'

'I didn't know you had children.'

'Just the one.'

'But of course you must see him, honey. I'm sure you

don't see enough of one another if you have only limited access.'

'They live in Yorkshire. I'll have to drive up and fetch him. Darling, I am sorry, I could murder Ilse, but she does that, she knows that I won't let a chance to have Jack pass. You are welcome to stay here.'

'No, honey, that's nice of you, but I'll be fine. Your little boy won't want to share his Poppa with some strange woman. I'll go to Jake's farm, then maybe I'll call in on Lizz.' She linked her arms about his neck. 'Tell you what, I'll book in at the place we've just been to. It looks a nice place to stay.'

When she awoke next morning in the high bed, with Mike and sheets and herself entwined, she wondered for a fleeting moment what it would be like to wake every morning in a bed like this, in a room like this, with a man like Mike.

Probably pretty damn boring after the first month or so, she supposed.

Then, resting on her elbows, she took a good long look at the body that had suited her own so well last night. Light brown skin dressed with only fine hair until a line below the navel; spare, fat-free rib-cage, a fit youthful torso, good-looking face that revealed a serious, sensuous disposition.

Hell, who cared about boredom ... for now it was pretty damn good. She decided to drop anchor for a while in the village, and maybe spend some time with him.

Mike had suggested that they go to church on the Sunday morning. 'People here do,' he said; 'you'll probably enjoy it. You've seen Childencombe drinking, so come and see them praying. I can't get Jack until this afternoon, so there'll be time before I have to leave.'

'You don't need to sell it to me, Mike, I just love to go to church sometimes: it's a great place to relax.'

'I'd quite like to give them an eye-opener. Childencombe doesn't get to see that many oriental beauties.'

It is also, she thought as she made her way to St Mark's on the hot Sunday morning, a great place to take a look at people. They had secured Kuan-Yin a room at the Green Man and they left her bags and car there.

She seldom attended church back home except when visiting some friends who lived in New England, where the women had worn hats. She didn't have a hat here, so she dressed her hair in a large bun and chose a grey belt-less silk take-you-anywhere shift she had bought in Hong Kong, knowing that she was dressing to appear vulnerable. Not exactly Little Orphan Annie, but a slightly tender flower who would not intimidate a soul.

'It's a pretty place, but why does such a dynamic man as you choose to live in a rural village and travel back and forth to London to see your clients?'

'If you live in a village like this, you belong somewhere . . . pubs, cricket teams, tennis partners, and when you collect your paper from the shop somebody asks how you are.'

Kuan-Yin thought: If a quiet life is what you want, then this is probably a good place to choose. 'It's really great, honey, a regular tourist-brochure village.'

'My God, don't say that aloud.' He indicated the houses set around an open square. 'Those cottages are Tudor, the doctor's and the solicitor's are Regency, down Mill Lane there are Victorian and Edwardian terraces. And St Mark's is built upon stone foundations that were put down by the Saxons.'

'Maybe if the American Indians had used stone instead of wood and hide, America might be able to claim some history.'

'What about your own people? The Chinese had a civilization when the rest of us were dressed in skins.'

'You put your ancestors down, they were engineers long before anybody. And really, I don't think of the Chinese as my people, Mike. When Lady Yin – that's my grandmother – brought her sons to the West she was determined to make them into good Americans. So I have a grandmother who communicates only in her old language, and parents who worship America. What do you think that makes me and my cousins? Would you believe, my uncles have changed their names to Burt and Lenny, and my father is George . . . after Washington.'

Mike laughed. 'Good old Chinese names. At least they had the grace not to name you Myra or Patsy.'

'You shouldn't bet on that. My name's Alison.'

Mike tucked her arm in his and smiled. 'Ah, poor baby.'

'I renamed myself for my favourite goddess, Kuan-Yin. But Kuan-Yin Yin was way over the top, so I dropped a Yin.'

'I'm sure you were never an Alison.'

She laughed. 'You shouldn't bet on that either. At home I'm never anything less. Second-generation, all-American-made, the Yin brothers will have nothing less than one hundred per cent Uncle Sam. Except that they make a living importing oriental goods and selling Chinese food.'

The air smelled green and nice, the sun didn't shine through oil-haze and petro-carbons and there was a gentle traffickless quiet, just the tolling of a bell and somewhere small birds fighting. Kuan-Yin thought: I could stand this pace for a week or two. Tomorrow, she decided, she would ring her office and tell Addie not to make any engagements until after August and then phone home and tell them that she was taking a holiday. There was enough going on here to fill a lifetime of research – dragon veins, barrows and crop circles. Was it possible for people to live here without being affected? Were they perhaps affected as people living close to high-voltage towers were affected? Certainly Jake Tallentire appeared healthy and normal.

The church, set on a rise on the edge of the village, was tiny, flint-faced with a small bell tower. As they joined the trickle of people heading up the path between old gravestones and iron markers, Kuan-Yin caught their curious glances.

'I'm afraid I don't have a family pew,' Mike said. 'We shall have to sit with the hoi polloi.'

When they were settled, she was surprised to find that the church was already fairly full. 'You're right, it does seem to be the place to go on a Sunday morning.'

'It's OK on a bright sunny morning like this, a bit of a different story in winter. I usually only come Easter and Christmas.'

Kuan-Yin felt relaxed and happy and she looked forward to the prospect of Mike and the chance of looking into the possibility that there was a connection between dragon veins and the circle phenomena and people. Sun streaming through small windows on the eastern side spotlighted each group or family as they entered, many of them flicking a glance in the direction of herself and Mike.

Mike whispered, 'People love it when there's a stranger in camp. Poor old vicar, he's got to compete with having a beautiful pagan in his congregation.'

'I'm a fully paid-up Protestant. I was baptized.'

'I know . . . and they named you Alison.'

She smiled. Mike was nice, the village was peaceful, and life was great. 'They named me Arison.'

The tentative sound of organ notes sounded and meandered through the tiny church. The vicar and a small choir entered solemnly and the congregation stood. At once, Kuan-Yin's attention was drawn to two figures on the other side of the aisle in a pew towards the front. She nudged Mike and whispered, 'Bet you that's Jake's father?'

'No prizes for that. He's the clan chieftain.'

The two men stood side by side, head and shoulders above the rest of the congregation. Both with the same head and profile, except that the father wore a full beard and, whereas Jake's hair was shoulder-length, his father's was less sun-bleached and cut so short that washing had made it spiky above his ears – probably combed without aid of a mirror. They had the same clearly defined features, and the kind of bone structure that a sculptor would have no difficulty in modelling.

She had thought Jake handsome, but the profile of the older man had a kind of symmetry that Westerners considered to be the ideal of male beauty, and for all her ancestry, Kuan-Yin had been brought up on Robert Redford and Richard Gere. You saw profiles like that on the screen but it wasn't often that you saw them in everyday life. There were Jake types about, handsome, splendid young men – but the dour, intelligent faces such as Jake's father had, were rare.

It was a long time since Kuan-Yin had seen a stranger who interested her more. His stance, and how he held his head. He was not singing, just standing looking straight ahead. He was aloof from what was going on. She thought that although he probably wasn't as arrogant as he appeared, he knew himself to be superior. She guessed that he was a loner.

And it was on his land that more crop-mark activity had occurred than in any place else. Now that was really, really interesting.

When the service ended, she made him her target.

'Jake, hello, nice to meet up with you again.' She held out her hand so that his parents too had no choice but to stop.

Jake smiled. 'Not bored with country life yet?'

'I've only had one day.'

'It's enough for some people. Myrr, this is Dr Yin – this is my mother, Myrr Tallentire.'

The woman who took her hand was probably in her late forties, had wide-set grey eyes, a small shapely nose, broad forehead and full lips with good even teeth which showed extensively when she smiled. Kuan-Yin judged that she was a woman who used her smile to hide behind: there was the same shrewd look she had detected in Jake. So she, with her crisply-curling reddish-tinted hair is the wife of the clan chieftain. Her hand was warm and dry.

'Jake told me that he'd met you,' she said. 'Here for a holiday?'

'Working holiday. I hope to see Avebury and Stonehenge and Silbury ... this is a really interesting corner of the world.' As she spoke she looked up and caught the penetrating, almost fierce, look of the man.

'This is my husband, Nat.'

Nathaniel Tallentire. A splendid name. Tallentire. It sounded like a title.

He took her hand in his large strong one and shook it once. 'Hello.' Short and clipped. 'They won't let you near Stonehenge these days and Avebury's nothing but a theme park.' His voice was not loud, as one might have expected coming from such a large frame, but husky, in the way that Jake's was, but Tallentire's was deeper and with no attempt to put into it any of the false enthusiasm usually reserved for first greetings.

'I'm more interested in things that don't make the tourist brochures.'

Jake said, 'I invited Dr Yin up to take a look at the barrows on Clump Hill.'

She noticed the relaxation of a tiny muscle which had been holding Jake's father's frown in place.

He said, 'You're interested in barrows?'

'Ancient burial sites. These are very often situated where there are dragon's veins. I was just in Kowloon ... oh, you know, just poking around. I guess we Americans are just nosey.'

They had begun to move as a group back towards the village, Mrs Tallentire talking to a couple of women she had met, which gave Kuan-Yin the opportunity to walk with her interesting husband, leaving Jake and Mike to go on ahead discussing squash games and cricket fixtures.

'What's a dragon's vein, then?' His voice, bass but soft; he was obviously not at ease with small-talk.

'It's what you would call ley-lines?'

'I see,' he said non-committally.

'I have an uncle who is a diviner – a *feng-shui* expert.'

'Can he earn a living doing that?'

'He can in Hong Kong. He's loaded.'

'A diviner?'

'I suppose you could call him that. He's a *hsein-sheng* . . . a kinda Grand Master at the top of his profession.'

'It's a profession?'

'It is in China and Hong Kong. I have just returned from there.'

She saw him rise, his interest hooked, and guessed that she had hit upon a subject that interested him.

'Hong Kong? Do they go in for this sort of thing there?'

'In a big way. None of the big corporations puts up a new building without consulting the *hsein-sheng*.'

'Is that so?' Still non-committally, although from his response and tone of voice, Kuan-Yin judged that he probably knew more than he was admitting.

She knew his type. Dour and prickly as a defence. The type who has problems admitting an interest in anything that might not fit in with his image of himself. And what was that? A plain kinda guy – no messin'.

What luck, she thought.

She looked up to find him frowning down at her. She was not intimidated, for she saw through the machismo to his sensitive core.

They walked in silence in the trail of Sunday worshippers until they reached the car park in the village, when he said,

'You could do worse than have a walk up to the barrows at the top of our field.'

Ah. Kuan-Yin was careful to restrain her delight. 'That's real nice of you. Maybe I'll take you up on it.'

'Whenever you like. I don't go far.'

Later, Mike said, 'You made a hit with Old Man Tallentire, didn't you?'

'What's all this Old? Even Jake called him the Old Man. He's not.'

Mike considered. 'Well no . . . but he's always called the Old Man – Old Man Tallentire. I guess it's a kind of title: I expect that every Tallentire who has been head of the house at Sunbarrow has been known as the Old Man. Interesting.'

'Would Jake be the next Old Man?'

Mike grinned. 'I don't know. Somehow I just don't see it.'

'Probably not. Jake hasn't got the same Captain Ahab streak.'

Mike raised his eyebrows and nodded. 'Spot on. Old Man Tallentire has got a touch of the Ahabs. Farmland has been his great white whale.'

After Mike had left for Yorkshire, Kuan-Yin walked the village, going round and round like a cat settling. When she felt comfortable she called at Jake Tallentire's girlfriend's studio.

'You said to drop by. You don't mind Sunday callers?'

'Wonderful!' Lizz said. 'I didn't think you'd take me up on it. Come up, I'm only preparing some canvases.'

'Ah . . . this is a great room.' Kuan-Yin stood looking, appearing to take in every detail. 'Such atmosphere. Wonderful light. Very good *ch'i*. It is no wonder that you produce such strong, feminine portraits.'

Lizz looked at her visitor with curiosity. 'That's interesting. You think that my fellas show the feminine touch?'

'Oh yeah. You paint a nice butt.'

Lizz grinned at her. 'I do, don't I?'

'That painting of Mike . . . a very feminine feel about it.' She exploded with gleeful laughter. 'Perhaps *feel* is not the most appropriate word, but you know what I mean.'

'What would Freud say?'

Kuan-Yin held up her hands in mock horror. 'Not in my presence – I am a Jungian. I think we cope better with the female psyche: a little better than old Fraud.'

Lizz liked her visitor's lack of coyness, and laughed with her, inviting her to where some low chairs and cushions represented what in a more conventional flat would be the area for socializing.

'Feel is a good word though, I can feel shape . . . form, with my eyes. It was great having Mike model, he has a terrific body.' Lizz admired the grace with which Kuan-Yin, dressed now in wide, pleated-crepe white pants and soft blouse, arranged herself in the leather-seated African birth-chair. Lizz sat on an enormous duvet-like feather cushion. 'I hope you don't mind. Mike's an old friend.'

'Mike's not my property. He strips for whomever he chooses. Was he a good model?'

'Perfect, actually. He's quite a raconteur which always helps – it saves me having to talk.'

'I brought you something.' Kuan-Yin smiled.

'Why, thank you.'

'I buy when I find something interesting. The right person always comes along.' She handed Lizz a tiny package. 'I found this in London. Yesterday evening, in the Green Man, I knew that you were the one who should have this.'

Lizz opened out the nest of tissue. 'Netsuke! It's a wonderful piece. My goodness, just look at her, the shameless hussy.'

'You like her?'

'I do. Thank you, I absolutely love her.' She held the tiny squatting figure in the palm of her hand. A benign female with exaggerated pudenda, belly and breasts, but with delicate hands and small feet. 'A thelytokous fertility figure. Is that right?'

Kuan-Yin pressed her hands together with satisfaction. 'Right! you answered the 64,000-dollar question. The lady produces only female offspring. In oriental cultures women must have sons, but this little sweetheart – she's a real rebel.'

Lizz ran her fingers over the delicate carvings of the nooks and crannies of the appealing little woman, and Kuan-Yin watched her with obvious enjoyment. 'She's happy being a woman,' said Kuan-Yin. 'She's content with what she is . . . see that wide grin. I'm pretty sure only a woman could have carved her.'

'Oh yes.' Lizz had a strange and satisfying sense of having known this Dr Yin all her life. 'D'you like beer? Or I could make coffee?'

'I'd just love a beer.'

Lizz fetched cool bottles and heavy glasses and, as she handed Kuan-Yin hers, she realized she was being scrutinized.

Kuan-Yin said, 'I feel that I know you so well. It's as though we have met before.'

'I certainly don't feel that you are a stranger.' Lizz laughed. 'But let's face it, with you it just has to be "once seen, never forgotten". I'm sure that nobody ever forgets having met you.'

'In the States, a lot of people think they know me because I do a lot of guesting on TV shows.'

'You do that?'

'Oh yes. I'm a great show-off, and I love to talk. When I am interested in a subject I get real enthusiastic, so it's great to be on Joan Rivers or the Oprah show because people from all over will write in and tell you something they've found or observed. There are some great people out there. Do you do any TV coverage?'

'Good Lord, no ... at least nothing like those shows. I've done three or four small appearances on the local network – it seems to help with the commissions.'

'It sure does. Have you thought of getting yourself an agent?'

'What, pay somebody to get me on the telly?'

'You pay a gallery to show your work, don't you? An agent is only part of the scheme to get John Doe to part with cents and dollars.'

'I might end up getting commissions from company directors who fancy having their egos painted by somebody who appeared on television?'

'If they're that kind of prick, then you put up your fees. It's the dollar-pricks of this world that free you up to do the things you like best.'

Lizz, her head held to one side, pondering, raised her eyebrows as though to say: You reckon?

'Listen, honey, I have what I call my Pricks-Practice on Park Avenue. Not many of those clients have any real problems, except being too rich and not caring much about anybody but themselves. They just love to talk about themselves. Unfortunately, so do their rich friends, which means there's no one to listen except me – and I make them pay.'

'You mean that all they get from you is time?'

'Not all. They get a slice of all the other stuff that has cost me ... years in college, conferences ... and all the experience I've ever had. They come thinking I'm going to tell them what to do, but I don't do that, they have to make their own decisions. If a woman's got a man treats her like a pet canary, she's the only one who can say, "OK, if I don't want the bastard to do that to me, then I don't have to let him."'

'Trouble with us is, our training is in handing over our

rights. We've been at a disadvantage for too many generations . . .'

'Right, but if a society woman with a million-dollar man wants me to spend time showing her how to stand up for herself, then she needs to part with a very large cheque or she won't believe that I'm the real McCoy.'

'Is it only rich women who come to you?'

'No, but they're the ones who provide most of the potatoes I need to work in my down-town clinic. There the women do have problems . . . boy, do some of them have problems?'

'I suppose the difference with me is that I'm not so sure that I need that much more income.'

'D'you mean that you never want to say the hell with it – and be off at a minute's notice to satisfy your curiosity about something? I wanted to see things here for myself, so I came. To do that kind of thing you need to be pretty rich . . . and independent. And I'm both.'

Kuan-Yin drank beer and gave Lizz a thumbs-up sign.

Lizz was intrigued by the woman's candour. Many Americans she had met were proud to tell you what their income was, but Kuan-Yin wasn't boasting about being rich, she merely stated it as a fact as she would if saying: You need to have large hands and be pretty strong to lift a sack of flour.

Lizz looked down at the tiny netsuke figure. 'You said you knew when we met that you had found the right person to give her to?'

'On the mundane level I'm a psychologist, which helps. I guess I saw that you are a woman who is contented with who she is. You kind of enjoy being a girl?'

'But not for the reasons in that song. You're right . . . I like myself.'

'Good. Then I wasn't wrong.'

'Another beer?'

'Why not, if you don't mind my being around.'

'Stay as long as you like,' Lizz said. 'If you don't mind me working.'

'I'd like to watch: you never know, there might come a day when I shall need to know about preparing canvases.'

Lizz got on with stretching, priming and putting a wash on her canvases whilst Kuan-Yin wandered about. When she had finished, Lizz picked up a bundle of pencils and a large sketch-pad. 'Do you mind if I make some sketch notes?'

'Of me?'

'Yes. I feel desperate to get you down on paper.' She began to make long, quick movements over the paper. 'Is it all right? Against the wall, please.'

'Of course.'

And for the next hour, Kuan-Yin sat against the scarlet wall and drank beer whilst Lizz, entirely absorbed, observed and sketched Kuan-Yin. At last she let go the bunch of pencils she had held on to as she worked. 'I think I've got it!'

'Is it permitted for the model to look?'

'Usually not a chance, but this I think you should see. Say whatever you like about them, it doesn't matter what you say. That's it! I have every brush-stroke in my head.' She held her arms aloft like a footballer who has scored a spectacular goal. 'Terrific! Now let me get you something to eat.'

Kuan-Yin sat in a half-lotus and placed Lizz's beautifully executed sketches in a semi-circle around her whilst Lizz, in her little galley, assembled a dish of hard goat cheese with a bowl of endive, peppers and mushrooms dressed with dark balsamic vinegar and lots of coarsely chopped garlic and nuts. As usual with Lizz's meals, it was done in five minutes including pulling apart a loaf and opening some wine that was almost as colourless as water.

'Well?' she asked, setting the tray on the floor between them.

'I feel . . . let me think. Flattered for one thing . . . kind of pleased that's how you see me. I guess that's how I see myself, but I doubt that I could have . . . encapsulated, I think that's the word, I don't think that I could have encapsulated my own essence so neatly.'

'Will you mind if I decide to use them for a full painting for my exhibition?'

'I should absolutely love it.'

Eating hungrily, they sat as close and as uninhibited as friends of years' standing do and talked with great animation about what Lizz said she planned to do.

'I have two more pictures to do for my one-woman show. It's my biggest yet – in London. There's a kind of hole in my work and I've been fratcheting about it. I need a slightly enigmatic piece. I knew pretty much the kind of thing but not the thing itself – until now.'

'If you do this, then what about the other?'

'Oh . . . I know who I want for my model, but he's not the easiest of men to persuade.'

'Are there men who aren't flattered by being asked to sit?'

'I feel it's rather like asking one of the Ayatollahs. Actually, it's Jake's dad I want to sit for me.'

Kuan-Yin let out a knowing, 'Aah. I understand, I met him – he's quite a guy. Does he ever let his hair down?'

Lizz raised her eyebrows. 'I can't imagine it, but if he ever did then I'd like to be there to see it.'

Nodding thoughtfully, Kuan-Yin said, 'So would I . . . yeah, I sure as hell would.'

'He's a complex and interesting man, which is why I want to paint him. Also, he's got that wonderful face.'

'He's beautiful.'

'And he's totally unaware of it. That terrific profile, everything arranged just so and hanging on a perfect skull. Still quite young, you know, in spite of having a son as big as the side of a house – well, two actually. Rin, the elder one, he's another of the beautiful Tallentires.'

'Beautiful . . . yes. That's how I would have described him.'

'A great body, too. I have dozens of sketches of him.'

'You mean Jake?'

'No, Jake hasn't really got there yet, Jake's just common or garden stunningly handsome, but his father . . . he has the most wonderful presence. Austere.'

'Tell me about them.'

'Mrs Tallentire, she's a lovely lady. Uninhibited, likes flash things and doesn't mind who knows. Always has time for people. She was quite devastated when Mr Tallentire had his heart attack.'

'He's had a coronary?'

'A mild one, but enough to be advised to hand over the running of Sunbarrow to Jake. He – Mr Tallentire – resents it, but Jake's like his mother, not easily ruffled. She's one of those people who hide their hurt under a smile.'

'Whilst her husband hides any smiles under a frown?'

'They all underestimate her. I get the feeling that one day she'll surprise them all.'

'How they suffer, those smiling women,' Kuan-Yin said.

'There's a girl, younger than Jake – has the family legs that go right up to her bottom. She drives the local boys wild, but until now she's appeared as unconscious of her figure as Mr Tallentire is of his profile. Rin? His marriage is in the process of blowing apart. And there's Daisy, Rin's twin. She's looks like her mother and she's got brains.'

'And are they all on the farm?'

'Lord, no. Daisy and Rin have been in London for years. Jake reckons that Rin is a one-woman-at-a-time man, but Daisy bounces men around much as she pleases.'

'Not your average dirt farmers.'

Lizz considered. 'They think they are, on the face of it they do seem to be . . . and yet they really are not. There's some sort of hidden (or maybe it's repressed, I don't know), a kind of suppressed unconventionality about them all. I'd never be surprised to hear that Mrs Tallentire had decided to sail round the world, or that Daisy had discovered a talent for playing a church organ or an ocarina.' She laughed. 'It sounds daft, but I don't know how else to describe this . . . this seemingly ordinary farming family who are all simmering away inside.'

'You know them pretty well.'

'They intrigue me. They talk about Sunbarrow as though it's a couple of fields and a flock of sheep. But it's really a huge operation. I believe when they were first married, they were absolutely dirt poor.'

'Mike says that they have bought up a lot of land around here.'

'Everything. According to Jake, they've been in debt to the bank all their lives. As soon as they began to get out of the red, another bit of land would come on to the market, and Mr Tallentire would have to have it, and then another and another. Jake reckons that his father is obsessive.'

'About?'

'His farm . . . his land. It's true, he does seem to think more of Sunbarrow than anything or anybody. People round here will tell you that they are worth millions.'

'Your Jake is rich, then.'

'He's not my Jake, but yes, that family isn't short of a bit of cash.'

'But Jake's not a wound waiting to be stung by vinegar like his father?'

'Jake is the most sociable person in the world.'

'No protective shell like his father wears?'

'Is that the professional psychologist speaking?'

'No, just a woman who walked with him for ten minutes.'

'Jake's shell isn't like Mr Tallentire's. Jake wears a thick, soft, rubbery armour of niceness from which people rebound when they get too close.'

'An excellent form of protection. But what is he protecting?'

'Now you answer me the 64,000-dollar question,' Lizz said.

'Privacy – like his father? Inadequacy? Being found out?'

'Probably not. I believe that Jake has dreams in there. Perhaps he's a secret poet or something, perhaps he's a thwarted musician. I don't know. I wish I did.'

'But he is a good lover.'

Lizz, her eyes smiling, pursed her lips. 'What do you think?'

Kuan-Yin smiled. 'Professionally speaking? I'd say a good many women would change places with you.'

When Poppy returned from Greece quite a few things had changed.

'Gosh, Mum, you look terrific, I've been telling you for ages you should lighten your hair.'

When there stepped off the train a tall, tanned young woman with long, shaggy, sun-bleached hair, who wore espadrilles, shorts and a top cropped so short that she must have revealed the lower part of two perfect young breasts when she reached up to retrieve her bag from the luggage-rack, Myrr felt, momentarily, that she was here to meet a visitor. Emma Carter, Matt Pridhoe and Tom Farenbach were there too, looking changed by their Greek experience – something animated in their gestures and a confident look in their eyes. Eighteen years of experience as children of Childencombe village had been overlaid in a matter of weeks with their first coat of cosmopolitan sophistication. Myrr, who would have felt herself to be a stranger in a strange land roaming Greek islands, was a touch envious of them.

'Poppy love, you look pretty terrific yourself, and Emma . . . you're so tanned.'

'So do you, Mum. Your hair is triffic.'

'You like this blondey sort of colour?'

'It's great.'

'And it's not too short?'

'Short hair on you is great. We had ours done in Athens, didn't we, Emm?'

Emma, who had always been a solemn and anxious child, giggled. 'It cost an arm and a leg, but it was worth it. Oh, Mrs Tallentire, you should go to Greece, it's absolute heaven.'

Myrr inspected the Athenian treatment. 'It looks massive, as though it's grown a foot since you left.'

'We had it permed to bulk it out.'

Myrr, before she had gone through the late eighties with a teenage daughter, might have thought that their perms had gone wrong, but she had come to accept the great matted lion-mane fashion and wished that she was young enough to wear her own hair like that.

Tom, quite out of the girls' gushing chatter, pushed the trolley with all the bags which, Myrr noticed, Poppy had airily left him to see to.

'Gosh,' Myrr said, 'when I offered to collect you all I didn't know you'd be like a tribe of Bedouin.'

'It'll go on the roof-rack all right,' Poppy said.

'It won't, there isn't a roof-rack.'

'Crumbs!' said Poppy when Myrr unfastened the tonneau and began to organize them.

'Wow!' said Tom. 'You mean that this is all yours, Mrs Tallentire?'

Myrr heard envy mixed with incredulity that a woman who was as old as his dad should be let loose in such a beauty of a car.

'You don't have to worry that it'll run away with me. I'll drive slowly, but you'll have to carry some of your bags

147

on your laps. I bought it more for show than taking a calf to market.'

By the time they arrived back in Childencombe, Myrr knew that she had gone up a notch or two in the estimation of some of the youth of the village.

Having dropped Emma off at Carter's shop and Tom at the Green Man, Myrr turned the car towards Sunbarrow.

Poppy had noticed that Tom had hesitated to show his new-found sophistication in front of her mother, so she took the initiative and kissed him on both cheeks: 'Ciao, Tomas. Ring me.'

She knew that her father would be hovering around waiting for them to arrive, pretending that he wasn't. He was in the old cattle yard sweeping the already swept concrete. She flung her arms around him and buried her face in his chest. 'Oh, Dad, thank you for letting me go. It was lovely, lovely, lovely.'

She felt his large, warm hand ruffling her hair as she had felt it as far back as her memory went. She knew that she was his favourite, accepting it but seldom consciously playing upon it, as she might easily have done, to get her own way. It was unnecessary: he would have given her the moon.

With her arm about his waist and his about her shoulder they followed Myrr into the house.

These days he broke her heart, even his smell was different. For sixteen of her years he had been calloused-handed, hard and weathered, and when he had ruffled her hair he had given off confidence and protectiveness into the air. Sometimes cows or hay, sometimes the tarry smell of chemical sprays or sheep-dip, sometimes damp sacks — always overlaid with his own sweat-damp shirt.

Then overnight he had altered.

In hospital she had been pained by the scented soap and orange-juice replacing farming sweat. Before last year, she had never imagined that her dad could have soft white hands, and that he would come down to breakfast with his hair damp from the shower. She became fascinated by these stranger's hands with their clean, unbroken nails. And now, as she gave him another brief hug, she only got from him the neutral odour of bathed skin, clean cotton and expensive after-shave.

'I got a bit of tea ready, Myrr.' He indicated the wicker table in the conservatory, laid with cups and saucers and a covered plate of cakes and sandwiches.

'That's nice, Nat. You talk to Poppy and I'll make the tea.'

Again Poppy was stabbed with the pain of affection for them and this new relationship where they seemed to tread around one another's feelings as though on egg-shells.

Four or five years back, there had been times when they made her want to scream. It was at a time when she had begun to read feminist books and magazines, and at every turn she saw the arguments played out before her. Her mother, locked into the male-dominated world where the old title, Master, still meant something. Her father, ignoring Myrr's needs and satisfying his own ambition to be the best of all the Tallentires, expecting his wife to anticipate his needs. He never went into a shop except for his own clothes, he expected meals but couldn't cook, he expected clean clothes but didn't know how to wash soiled ones, he used the bathroom but never thought that polishing the seat or taps was anything to do with him. There had been a period when Poppy had fumed at his chauvinism and at her mother's compliance.

Those feelings were still there, but not so spiky and sharp-edged. Now, when she saw small signs of role-reversal, where her mother made all the domestic decisions and her father laid up a tea-table with cakes and best china, she was cut to the quick. What would happen if his damaged heart made him retreat until he shuffled around like some of the old Childencombe farm labourers who she could remember tossing about bales of hay and driving great harvesting machines fourteen or more hours at a stretch? In their retirement, without a pig or a cow or a tractor to drive, they were fishes out of water.

Myrr came in with the teapot and poured.

Nat said, 'Well? Come on, tell us what you've been up to.'

As she told them the bits she knew that they wanted to hear – of the un-touristy countryside they had traipsed, of how marvellous mature goat's-milk cheese tasted, and rare olive oils peculiar only to some small village, and of the blueness of sky and sea – Poppy felt the first sliding away of her few weeks of lotus-eating. She was telling of something in the past, and wanted to be with Emma and Tom again to keep the memory green.

What she did not tell them was how it felt sleeping with Tom Farenbach's body curled around hers; and how they had once caressed one another to their first wonderful mutual climax; and how adult they had been in their discussion about safe sex and the problems and delights of continuing their affair if they obtained places at universities situated very far apart. Nor did she say anything about the freedom she found to talk to Tom about how her father had changed, and how they had discussed preparing oneself for the death of one's parents. At a distance she had realized that her life was pulling away from theirs now. She would leave home and, like Daisy and Rin, there would be a huge part of her life that would have nothing to do with them. Sometimes that thought made her panic, sometimes it warmed her.

In their discussion on death, Poppy had said confidently that her dad's heart attack had already prepared her for his death; she would grieve but she would cope. In her heart of hearts, she guessed that this was just whistling in the wind. If Dad died she felt that she would be desolate and that her whole future would be blighted.

'What's this, Mum?' She whistled through her teeth, put down the tray that she was taking through to the kitchen and held up a cream and white silk bomber jacket that had been hanging up. 'It's great! Where did you get it? It must have cost an arm and a leg.'

'It probably did, knowing where it came from ... it's not mine. It belongs to some American woman who has been haunting us lately.'

Poppy rolled her eyes exaggeratedly. 'Who has Jake got in tow now?'

'Not Jake, it's your father she's after.'

'Dad? The old dark horse.'

Myrr said, 'Her name's Yin, and she's a doctor ... not the GP sort – an American ... well Chinese, but born in America.'

Poppy tried on the jacket. 'Do you think she's coming back for it?'

Myrr, picking up the tray and taking it through to the kitchen, half-looked back and said wryly, 'Don't you worry, she'll be back all right. Now you go on and unpack and we'll get your stuff in the washing machine out of the way. Then go back and sit with Nat, he'll tell you all about the famous doctor.'

Poppy was quite shocked to detect the bitchy edge to her mother's voice. She couldn't imagine her father so much as looking at a woman in a way that would make her mother jealous.

But Myrr's mind was scattered with pricking images. She felt ashamed of herself for feeling so mean-minded, but they lodged there, like so many tiny splinters – the latching on to Nat coming out of church, the casual way she dropped in at Sunbarrow, Nat's eagerness to please, and the way his mood lightened when she came. Myrr knew she should be pleased that Nat had found someone who was interested in his old barrows and ley-lines. A pretty young woman. Jake was of course quite smitten, Lizz liked her, Rex Farenbach and Jez Carter . . . even Mrs Pack who came to clean had come under her spell. No doubt, now, so would Poppy.

On the day of Kuan-Yin's first visit to Sunbarrow, Myrr had driven Nat for his hospital check-up in Winchester. Lizz had rung Jake to say that Kuan-Yin was on her way up there. 'I hope your mother won't mind, Jake, but I told Kuan-Yin to bring a swimsuit with her. She says she's dying for a swim, but I don't think she'd like to ask. So be sweet and invite her.'

'Of course she can swim. Hardly anybody uses the pool this time of day. Why not come too?'

'It'd be lovely but I've found my subject for the big portrait, and I'm longing to get to work on it.'

'You're going to use her.'

'How did you guess?'

'She's got everything that would appeal to you.'

'Well you're absolutely right. I'll be working all hours. Now all I need is for your father to agree to sit for me, and I'll have my collection ready on time.'

'I can't see him sitting for you. He'd think it was being pushy and vain. Does it have to be the Old Man?'

'Yes. I've got enough young males. Besides, he has as perfect a head as I've seen. And I want to see those eyes boring into whoever looks into them.'

'OK. I'll ask Myrr to work on him.'

Jake, who had come to the house to get something quick to eat, had watched the Jag come slowly and carefully down the front drive, and park well into the hedge. Going to greet her, he called, 'If you've got your swimming things, bring them with you.'

She waved acknowledgement with a small plastic bag.

Shaking hands, he said, 'Welcome to Sunbarrow. I'm glad you decided to come. Lizz said you wanted a swim. Feel free, it needs using.' He indicated the undisturbed surface of the pool.

'Say, that looks real good. But maybe I should go out in the fields first?'

'All right, I'll take you.'

'No, no. You have your farm to run, just point me in the right direction.'

Taking her cumbersome camera bags he said, grinning, 'Give me any excuse to skive off. And in those shoes you'll probably come a cropper and want rescuing. In any case I'm entitled to a dinner-break.'

She took off her sandals, threw them in through the open window of the car and slipped on some stout moccasins. 'OK, lead on.'

He held open the small wicket gate on to the path that ran beside Clump Field and up to the barrows. 'I'll take you to the best point to take photos, and then we'll go down through the field. Have you seen crop-marks before?'

'Not big ones. I was touring around Glastonbury a few years back. That's how I first became interested. Of course, the early ones were quite small, weren't they?'

'Not now.'

'That's what's so interesting. It is almost as though, each year, whatever it is causes these marks takes up where it left off.'

They had reached the stile at the end of the footpath. Jake leaped over, but as she made to step up he jokingly barred her way, grinning. 'Come clean, Dr Yin. You've got more than a passing interest.'

'Oh dear, found out.' She mounted the stile and sat atop it looking down at him. Then she tapped his forearm gently. 'If I confess, will you keep my secret?'

Jake, looking upwards, was drawn from the delicacy of her lovely jaw-line down her lovely throat and lower to the lovely shape of her breasts as he watched their slightly panting rise and fall caused by climbing the upward incline of the pathway.

'You aren't listening.' She tweaked his hair.

'Oh dear, found out,' he said, gently mocking. 'This way.' She followed him along a cart track of bare dry chalk.

'I'll come clean. I am interested in unexplained phenomena.'

Jake wondered whether this was the whole story, but didn't push it. People only told you what they wanted you to know. He knew that she was a psychologist, which made him a bit wary as well as curious.

It was early afternoon and the hottest part of a hot day. Jake had been truthful when he said he liked an excuse to skive off. Like Nat, Jake too felt so good on a hot day like this that he couldn't bear to think that in a few months at the most it would be over and autumn would be around. Often during his lunch-break he would come along this path, climb over the field-fence and sit, or stalk the hedge-row looking at what new thing might be growing there. Often he came home with his neck-cloth full of edible fungus that English people rarely eat, and Myrr was at one time loath to cook until she came to accept Jake's expertise.

'I'm afraid there's no shade along here.'

'Don't apologize for this exquisite view, it is wonderful. Tell me what I am looking at.'

Standing slightly behind and towering above her, he pointed out living villages and the sites of others long deserted and dead; racing stables; where the source of the River Itchen lay, and the site of a Roman villa. 'And, of course there are tumuli wherever you look.'

'Where?'

'You'd be better with binoculars; if you'll come up again some time, I'll point them out. I assure you the place is littered with them – long barrows, round barrows, saucer barrows, tumps of all kinds.'

'And the local ones?'

'You are interested in barrows too?'

She smiled at him, showing even, porcelain teeth that

made him wonder what it would be like to have them bite you seductively. In a caricature of a B-movie Chinese, she said: 'She who is not intalested in ancient ballow is not intalested in life – Ancient Chinese ploverb.'

'How my father would love you. He'd have liked us to have been interested but none of us was, and he's not the man to talk much to anyone outside the family.'

'We talked a little on our way back from church. I guess the new highway must disturb him.'

'He's always had this sense of the earth being some kind of living thing. Yet he can't see that his farming methods are like force-feeding. We've always fallen out about that . . .' He grinned. 'When we were kids he tried to instil into us his ideas about the magic of the earth, but we preferred Superman. My sister Daisy used to whistle "Tell Me the Old, Old Story" under her breath.'

'Shame on you. We know almost nothing about this planet. My fear is that I shall not live long enough to discover something about it.'

'We all have something that turns us on.'

'What turns you on, Jake?'

Ignoring the question, his attention suddenly captured, he stopped and bent down. 'Well I'm damned, will you just look at this.' Delicately with one finger he raised one of the florets of a spike of flowers. 'I've never seen one around here. There's hope for the planet yet.'

Kuan-Yin bent down beside him. 'What is it?'

'Orchis. Not yet under threat, but scarce. *Coeloglossum viride*.'

'How does that translate? Um . . . green belly . . . and tongue? Throat? My Latin was never good.'

'I'd call it a Frog Orchid. See? Little froglets. What else could it be called?' Joining finger and thumb into a ring, he ran the spike through it with a caressing movement. 'Beautiful.' He appeared for the moment to be lost in the little orchid.

Then, seeming to have made a decision, he picked up her bags and began to stride along the track that ran along the top of Clump Field. 'Come on, this way. It's a walk, but I promise you a reward. What turns me on? I'll show you what turns me on.'

Just below the barrows, he halted, dumped the bags and stood, hands in pockets, looking across to where the land rose again behind the farmhouse. In the hollow, Sunbarrow house was laid out like a model. Shaped like an angular letter C, the flint and brick house settled easily into its surroundings, reddish grey surrounded by acre upon acre of ripening wheat and barley. The only harsh note was the bright blue oblong of the swimming-pool.

To the north a field of peas, and next to it a wide expanse of yellow rape; the whole of the rest was green corn.

He watched for her reaction.

A sharp intake of breath. Wonderment. Her hands stretched, her arms apart as though about to bless the corn-field which resembled a green blanket with spectacular blazonry embroidered upon it.

'Hell.' She paused, allowing the spectacle to sink in. 'Will you just look at that!'

Without thinking, he took her hand and squeezed it in a kind of salute. 'That turns me on.'

The symbol engraved in the field must have been at least a hundred and fifty feet in length. It was enigmatic and beautiful. From here its outline was so exact and finely drawn that it gave the appearance of having been stitched with a fine needle. In form it was a bar with a huge disc at either end, and crowning one disc was a precisely balanced three-tier halo.

It was long minutes before either of them spoke or moved as they took in the blazonry of that Sunbarrow field. Eventually, Kuan-Yin said: 'Vajra. Weird, but it is Vajra.'

Jake looked sideways at her, only then realizing that he

still held her hand which he now released. 'What's Vajra?'
He squatted down and she beside him.

'And no one else has seen it?'

'No. What did you mean, Vajra?'

'It's a really-really ancient symbol. Buddhists use it. It
represents the spiritual and the physical worlds.'

'And it looks like that?'

'Yes, it looks very like that.'

'But how . . . ? How could it?'

'Wouldn't we all just like to know?'

Jake sat down, knees spread, elbows on knees gazing
at the beautiful pictogram. 'Beats me why people are
afraid.'

'Fear of the unknown.'

'Some of the tabloids are paying people to create hoax
circles.'

'It is inevitable that they would,' she said.

'They pay people to create hoax circles, then write
articles saying that circles are created by hoaxers.'

'Do you care, Jake?'

He gazed at her thoughtfully for long seconds, then said
cheerfully, 'No, I don't. They can't make any difference in
the long run. Something is going on, and it's going on here,
and it's like nothing we've ever seen before. I don't care
about the tabloids, so long as I can come out here and find
something like this.' He looked at his watch. 'I'm afraid
I'll have to get back, I have to see some reps this afternoon,
but you're welcome to stay.'

'Would you mind if I went to have a closer look?'

'Of course. If you don't need all this gear, I'll take it
back and leave it in the house.'

'Thanks, I was hoping you'd say that. Will your father
be there?'

'Oh, sure to be. He doesn't go far.'

'Is he sick?'

Jake shrugged. 'At heart maybe . . . literally. He's got a

heart condition and has been advised to stop work. He can't bear seeing me doing what he's always done.'

'Poor him.'

'Yeah. He could do more, but he's an all or nothing man. If he can't give the orders, he doesn't want to see the men and women who work for Sunbarrow. He knows that I have to run the place, but he hates the fact that I do.'

'That's understandable, he isn't an old man.'

'No, he's not. But he needs something to grab him and drag him out of his apathy.'

YIN'S NUMBER ONE HOUSE, NEW YORK

On New York's Lower East Side, in Yin's Number One House, George Yin is relating in every small detail the telephone call that Alison made from an old village in England, a call not to himself but to June – not that this stops him hijacking it. June sits opposite, nodding agreement and confirmation. Except for daughter Kuan-Yin (daughter Alison because this is the family), almost the entire Yin family is seated in their usual alcove to celebrate the official announcement by Lenny Yin of his son Louis' forthcoming marriage. Louis is there with his long-time Live-in Lady who is daintily Chinese and obviously pregnant.

'Alison is staying on for a few more weeks. Her friend's house goes way back to ancient times of Henry the Eighth or some guy like that.'

June Yin nods her pride. 'And her friend is a famous doctor.'

'But is this one a He doctor, or a She doctor, Aunt June?' Louis asks, smiling at his lady.

'Arison has only said that it is Dr Alexander.'

'Knowing Allie, I'll bet you ten cents he's a He,' Louis says.

George looks down his nose. 'It is not courteous to speak

of your cousin lightly, Louis. I wonder what you will make of Blossom Parks when we're gone.'

'You don't want t'worry, Uncle George. Allie's tough as a boot, and the Blossom Parks will still be going strong when junior here's ready to take over.' He pats the small mound at his lady's middle.

Lady Yin's round eyeballs swivel from one to another behind their fine slitted openings. She misses nothing, and gives nothing away.

Her eye is suddenly caught by something at the far side of the room by the entrance. Letting the family chipping and gossiping go on around her, tuning in only to any bits that seem to be worthy of listening to, she watches as a waiter and a customer have some discussion. The waiter signals to the head waiter who comes to sort things out.

Suddenly Lady Yin rises, drops her starched serviette on to her plate of half-eaten fish and is out of her seat before the agile waiter can rush to assist the queen of the empire that pays his wages. 'Lee Han,' she says quietly, threading her way between tables. 'Lee Han, son.'

Before the head waiter can do anything, she has reached the small foyer by the cash desk, and the tall Charlie Chan-like man.

In the dialect of their old village, he says humbly, 'I am Lee Han Yin.'

Replying in the same, she clutches his hands, kisses his knuckles. 'Do you think that a mother does not know her own firstborn son?'

'Kuan-Yin said that I must come.'

'That is exactly the character of my granddaughter.' Lady Yin smiles proudly. 'She gives instructions to everyone. My mother was like that.'

Now he kisses the palms of her hands. 'My mother also.'

'Better for children to have a strong mother.'

'You are not old.'

'In my family ninety years is not old. You could have waited twenty more years and still found me well.'

'Ah . . . but perhaps it is I who have not inherited tendency to long life as in your family.'

She smiles up at him. 'You have chosen good ancestors.'

He was the finest of all her sons. Tall and imposing, with the same round eyes as her own. He was the first, coming when she was young, when she had thick red blood and strong milk. When the others came she was older, more work-worn and had less of herself to give. They had grown to be men each one successively a little less tall and with a little less brain than firstborn Lee Han.

The Blossom Park chain had grown rich, not with their brains, but with her questions:

First: Why do we not start a second eating place?

Then: Why do we not open more eating places and train men in our ways to work in them?

Then: Why do we not open Blossom Parks in best side of town where the rich people eat?

To which George, Lenny and Burt had replied: We shall do that.

And without shame they had thought that they were the ones with the ideas from which the Blossom Park chain had grown.

But Lee Han. He – the firstborn son who had suckled all his brains and strength of character from her – he had stayed on in their home village where, as a boy apprentice, he had been learning the secrets of *feng-shui*. He had worked in the rice-fields during the bad years, and, because of his ancient knowledge, had not been harmed by the cultural revolution; and now here he was, a man of mature years, rich and famous among his own kind.

She led him by the hand along the waiters' lanes between the tables to the alcove where, by now, George, Lenny, Burt, Louis and Henry were all standing showing expressions of indecision and puzzlement. Louis' lady looked as though she might have second thoughts about legally becoming one of the Yins.

Lady Yin held her hands apart. To the Blossom Parks she said, 'Firstborn son – Lee Han.' To Lee Han the famous Hong Kong adviser to multinationals on the placing of their prestigious buildings, she said, 'Lee Han – little brothers, George, Lenny and Burt.'

Lee Han bowed his Charlie Chan bow and took the seat offered him at the head of the table. 'Kuan-Yin said ... no, she *commanded* I should visit family.' He smiled his wide smile at them.

Louis leaned over and poured wine into his Uncle Han's glass whilst George gave orders left right and centre to the head waiter. 'Well,' Louis said, 'she sure does try to put the world in order, does our Allie.'

'She has special qualities to make one obey.' Lee Han raised his glass and drank to them. 'Also, she is very beautiful niece. And she thinks now that I should make a tourist of myself and visit England.'

Nat Tallentire turned his attention from the weather forecast – which was for temperatures in the South in the high eighties – to the bit of garden that bordered the swimming-pool. He could hear Myrr and Poppy's voices drifting through the fuchsia and polled eucalyptus border, as they did their morning lengths. Right from when he was a boy he had enjoyed heatwave weather. He loved to feel the sun hot on his back, to drip with perspiration and feel his body's cooling mechanism at work. Even when a shortage of diesel during an oil crisis had driven them to hand-harvesting, he had gone out into the sun-drenched fields and worked hard. It was no good complaining about bad weather, it was a fact of life, but, so long as there was enough rain to keep things growing, Nat loved a really settled, hot summer.

Now – he felt a surge of frustration go through him – he was supposed to take things easy and sit in the shade. Although he had just done a few lengths of the pool, he already felt clammy again. Whilst somewhere out there, Jake was doing the rounds, taking off an ear of corn here, thumbing a seed there and biting into it to check its progress. A mile further on, women employees of Sunbarrow Farms would be milking ewes whilst others were preparing the milk, making yogurt, potting and packing. In the farm office, the foremen would be checking order-forms, or telephoning to suppliers, or chivvying up a mechanic. All the various units that went to making up Sunbarrow Farms were ticking over on the wheels that Nat had put in place, worked and oiled.

But now he wasn't part of it.

And if he was no longer Master of Sunbarrow, then who the hell was he?

Equilibrium. The heart man at the hospital had advised: You're going to have to avoid stress and anxiety, Mr Tallentire. Give up the farm, let your son take it on. With a condition like yours, nothing's worth the hassle. Learn to take life as it comes and you'll live to be a hundred.

The bloody man hadn't a clue. He gives his patients the run-around by booking them all in at the same time, to suit himself, and then advises them to take a more relaxed attitude to life. He'd do a lot better to turn up on time and not rush his Health Service patients through his sausage machine.

Nat would have liked-to open up a dialogue with him: How do you think somebody like me can take a relaxed attitude? If a field of corn gets struck down, that don't sit in a waiting-room patiently waiting for attention. You chaps are all right, you get paid whether your patients live or die. If my crops get struck down, nobody pays me. So don't you talk to me about stress and anxiety.

And it was all very well for Poppy and Myrr to talk

about equality and equal opportunities: they were the ones who were getting something out of any changes that might take place. Men got nothing, and no thanks for handing over what had always been theirs.

I've been brought up in a world where men and women had their place and knew it. Men were brought up to make the decisions and if there was a war it was men who went to fight in it.

Poppy, of course, all vegetarian, whales and Greenpeace, argued: If it wasn't for men there wouldn't be any wars.

But he'd taken her to task over that: I suppose the Prime Minister isn't a woman then? Because I've yet to come across anybody who likes a good war better than her.'

Poppy had said: She's in the men's game using men's tactics. So for the purposes of my argument, she *is* a man.

Myrr, who was the one who put these ideas into Poppy's head, had said: Don't get your father worked up. But being treated like that had worked him up even worse. Those kind of arguments were beyond Nat. All he knew was that the women in his family were light-years away from his mother and sisters, and that he felt diminished when Myrr went out and left him to make his own sandwiches. He'd rather make do with a few biscuits or a packet of crisps than start ferreting about in the bread bin.

His arms were stiff with the tension he had wound up in himself. All this idling about did him no good.

Even so, when he heard them getting out of the swimming-pool, he put on the kettle – something he'd never done before Jake took over.

A car came down the front driveway. At once and with a flutter of anticipation, he recognized the posh purr of the Dragon Lady's Jag. He had been listening to the news in his towelling robe but there was no way he was going to let her see him half-dressed.

From his bedroom he watched as she got out of the car, unaware that the thighs of her elegant legs were revealed to him. She was a bloody attractive woman. In the shower he felt his body suddenly surge with sexual life.

He remembered when he had first shaken her hand, how firm it was, yet how soft and light, and how small and delicate it had appeared in his own large fist.

Her voice was, like her hand, firm, soft and light. He felt overwhelmed by her. She was lovely. Her forehead and jaw were made with beautiful curves, her eyes were almond-shaped and wide apart, the arc of her eyebrows echoed the curve of her brow; small nose, a beautiful mouth and her dark hair was heavy and shining. He didn't think that he had ever come across anyone as fascinating. Strange . . . but beautiful.

He continued to watch as he dressed until she disappeared into the house below.

Myrr came into the bedroom as he was about to leave. 'Hello, dressed yourself up for your Dragon Lady?'

Nat tried to look as though he had picked out by chance a new blue sports-shirt and cream linen trousers. 'Can't let the side down. She makes me feel like a clodhopper. She's not *my* Dragon Lady.'

'Well she certainly isn't mine.' Myrr smiled, falsely sweet. 'She don't call me *Mistress* of Sunbarrow. I've just introduced Poppy to her and left them to it whilst I get dressed. That shirt looks good with those trousers, suits you. I told you it would, it's a nice colour. I've put the coffee perk on, you can pour it out for her.' Myrr was determined to conquer her base feelings. Who did it hurt if the woman flirted a bit with Nat? It had all seemed so charming when she had seen Roz and Teddy doing it. Harmless.

As she went past him to hang her swimsuit in the bathroom he reached out and took hold of her, letting his hands run down the familiar lines of her cool body. 'Would you like me to put some sun-lotion on your back?'

'Not with the Dragon Lady down below. Look, you're

creasing your nice new shirt. Go and give her some coffee. She says she wants to talk to you.'

Since he had heard the Jag come down the drive, he had felt an unusual thrill of interest in the prospect of being out and about. It was true what Myrr said, he did get quite a kick out of it when she called him Tallentire, or even Master of Sunbarrow. There was no wryness in her use of the title, neither did it seem over the top in the way that she used it. But, he assured himself, his interest was not so small-minded as Myrr suggested: the American woman, with her interest in things he knew something about, lifted his spirit.

She was in the conservatory, where Poppy, in a bikini, was squeezing her new hairstyle under some drying contraption and wailing, 'I'll simply have to put a brave face on it and wear a bathing cap.'

'Pile it on top and learn to swim with your head out of the water like Joan Collins,' the Dragon Lady said. 'Watch American TV soaps and you'll see the way it's done in Bel Air. Oh, here is Tallentire himself.' She came to Nat as though they were old friends and, leaning somewhat towards him, kissed him on both cheeks. 'Tallentire of Sunbarrow . . . don't you think that is a terrific title?'

'Oh, lovely,' Poppy said.

Nat felt a flush of embarrassment at Poppy's pert look coupled with pleasure in the attention of the woman Myrr insisted on calling the Dragon Lady.

Poppy noticed.

Smiling as she teased her hair back into a lion's mane, she said, 'What does that make me? The Poppet of Sunbarrow?'

As she went through into the kitchen to fetch the coffee, Nat saw what he had tried to avoid seeing for a long time, that from the chrysalis of his bonny daughter had emerged a fully-fledged butterfly. It was but a split second of revelation, yet in it he saw Greece and olive groves and black-haired macho men ogling her long, suntanned legs. And there was nothing he could do, nothing he would ever be able to do.

She had been his for nearly eighteen years, and now she was becoming detached from him as, a few years back, Daisy had done. At that time he had thought that Daisy was like a liner pulling away from the secure berth of Sunbarrow, gradually snapping the paper streamers, their final connections. Now for ninety-nine per cent of the time Daisy and Sunbarrow were connected only by the electrical impulses of a telephone.

He felt himself flush again when he noticed the Dragon Lady observing him, and felt compelled to say something. 'It seems only yesterday that she was a toddler.'

'She's a real sweetie. She's going to become a very lovely woman.'

Her voice was an intriguing mixture of laid-back American slur and, he presumed, traces of the formal broken English of her parents.

'She was lovely to me even when she was a blob in a woolly bonnet. We nearly lost her when she was born.'

That was out without him realizing why he had said it, particularly why he should have put into words something that he had not mentioned to anyone in seventeen years, and to say it to practically a stranger. Confused, he leaped up saying, 'I'll see where the coffee's got to.'

In the kitchen Poppy, absorbed in gazing out of the window, had momentarily forgotten what she was there for. She started at her father's footsteps. 'I was miles away. It's ready. I'm going to get dressed. Tom's dad has to go to Winchester so we're hitching a ride.'

'You've only just got home.'

'So?'

So ... So, nothing, Nat supposed. Why shouldn't she want to be with young people like herself? The

Greek episode had been the crossing of the Rubicon into independence.

'Are you all right for money?'

She smiled, remembering his admonition never to run out of money in a strange place. 'I remembered what you said . . . I didn't come back broke.'

Reaching in his back pocket he took out a twenty-pound note and put it on the kitchen counter.

'Better take this, just to be on the safe side.'

'You spoil me.'

'I know. Now let me take this in or it will be cold.'

'Careful, Pop, she fancies you.'

He frowned fiercely at her.

'She does.'

'Suddenly you are an authority on such matters, and in . . . what was it, two minutes of being in her company?'

'That's all it takes. Is she after Jake, too?'

'Now, that's enough, I don't like all this kind of talk that goes on nowadays. Dr Yin is here because she's interested in ley-lines and barrows.'

'And anything that's male and moves.'

'Is that the kind of thing you've picked up since you've been away? Well I don't like it.'

'I'm just saying she likes men . . . there's nothing wrong in that, is there? Pop, it's sixth-form college that I've just left, not junior school.'

'All the more reason that you should know how to behave.'

She came to him and picked up the money which she tucked into her bikini bra, then she hugged him. 'Darling Pop, you are so starchy and proper that you are a positive temptation to tease. But listen to me . . . your Dragon Lady is a man-eater, and she fancies you.'

For a brief moment, Nat Tallentire felt an unfamiliar flush of pleasure.

When he returned to the conservatory, Kuan-Yin was

standing at the door panning her video camera across the skyline, taking in the clump of trees and the barrows. She was, as usual, dressed in silky fabrics of unusual colour that moved in even the faintest breath of air. Today she wore her hair hanging loose but with half a dozen, apparently randomly arranged, thin plaits. Nat felt good, better than he had felt for months. The heart man had said that there was no reason why he should not lead the normal life of any man in middle years.

'Your daughter is charming.'

'She thinks she's one of the international jet set since she's been to Greece.'

'It is wonderful to be young.'

'To me, young is when they still take notice of their parents.'

'We all have to grow up . . . grow away.'

'It's not so easy with the youngest.'

'An intimation of the parent's mortality. Ah . . . coffee,' she said. 'You are all so kind to make such a fuss of me.' As she moved, a perfume like nothing he had ever smelled on Myrr or Daisy wafted across the room. He wondered if that was what was meant by heady perfume.

'Not at all.'

'There you go being polite. I am a pushy American and I descended upon you out of the blue and you didn't bat an eyelid but were perfectly English in your courtesy. We're not used to that in New York.'

'I've always understood that New Yorkers are overly friendly.'

'I'm not saying that we're not warm-hearted, but just don't stop us on the sidewalk and spend the time of day.'

'That seems reasonable.'

'I came to ask if you would give me an interview.'

He looked momentarily perplexed.

She smiled disarmingly and laid a hand over his. 'I promise it will be painless.'

Her hand was still on his when Myrr came through.

Myrr said, 'Sorry you caught us on the hop like that, but it was such a lovely morning I stayed in the pool longer than usual.'

With a pat, Kuan-Yin let Nat's hand go free. 'I was just wooing your husband to get him to tell me about barrows.'

Myrr smiled at her and helped herself to coffee. 'You've no need to woo Nat, I'm sure he'll be only too pleased to have somebody to tell all those old tales to.'

'Dr Yin don't want to hear all that. She's a scientist.'

Kuan-Yin smiled eagerly. 'Not true, that's exactly what I do want to hear.'

'Well,' Myrr said, 'if you don't mind, I must go . . . I have to meet a friend in Southampton.'

Nat looked up sharply. She was always going off somewhere these days.

'I'm meeting Roz Petherbridge for lunch. I didn't think you'd want to come, Nat.'

'No, thanks!'

'Well listen . . . instead of me leaving you sandwiches, Nat, why don't you have a wander down to the Green Man and get yourself some lunch from Rex Farenbach's nice carvery? You could take Dr Yin with you if she's still here at lunchtime. You like English pubs, don't you, Kuan-Yin?' To atone for her earlier pique, Myrr offered Nat generously.

'Love them, especially the Green Man. Let's do that, Tallentire. Tell you what, you give me my interview and I'll buy lunch.'

For a moment, Nat's eyes held a trapped look. They were doing it again. A different two, but doing the same thing. Women taking over, making arrangements to suit themselves. In the hospital it had been the nurses or Myrr and the nurses, then Myrr and Poppy, Myrr and Daisy and now Myrr and the Dragon Lady.

When Myrr and Poppy had gone, she took the lounger

he offered beneath a fluttering yellow robinia tree. 'This is nice. Very nice.' She inhaled deeply, then breathed out slowly. She stretched, unfolding, uncoiling. She smiled, close-lipped and amused eyes.

And again came the perplexing will o' the wisp flutter of excitement, inciting him to action, as it used to come when there was still the prospect of adding to Sunbarrow.

Sitting opposite her, Nat watched her face with pleasure as she let her eyes wander over his land. Over the undulating fields where heat shimmered above the growing corn and a breeze moved the billion ears as wind moves the surface of water. Over the long, ancient hedgerow and the clump of old yews on the ridge. Over the chalky paths beside ditches. Over the invisible ley-lines whose routes Nat held in his head. He wondered just how sensitive she was.

He could have sat just where he was now and without his chart indicated the ley-lines that crossed Sunbarrow. Of course, there was nothing to see, nothing to hear, nothing one could say was truly felt – except with hazel wands. In the hands of a person with Nat's sense, the whippy switches would move as irresistibly as iron to a magnet, or silk to a static electrical field, whenever one of the invisible lines was crossed. Carrying a hazel rod, he had walked every acre of his own land until he had fixed the course of the lines and knew them as well as he knew the course of footpaths, overhead power lines and sheep raikes that traversed Sunbarrow.

'Thank you.' She accepted the glass of lemonade Nat offered. 'Are those the barrows?' She pointed. 'Those three humps on the skyline?' When Jake had pointed out the barrows she had noticed that he had none of the same interest that she had observed in Tallentire when they had walked from the church. She wanted to draw him out.

'There are four. You can't see the fourth from here, it's collapsed. Would you like to walk up there?' He noticed her moment of hesitation and, standing up, thrust his fists into his trouser pockets. 'It's all right: I shan't drop dead on you, if that's what they've told you.'

'Nobody told me anything.'

He turned and looked down at her.

She looked up, languidly smiling. 'Tallentire, honey, you'd do better with a longer fuse.'

Honey! Christ Almighty! But he was polite. 'I'm sorry, but I can't stand people fussing.'

'I was only going to ask whether you would tell me if you knew anything about the dragon veins around these parts – you know what I mean . . . the ley-lines?'

Till the day I die I shall never forget this moment. They come seldom enough in a lifetime. If I was Jake I'd be able to say it, reel it off, tell you about other moments. The annexation of new land to Sunbarrow; of Poppy at no more than half an hour old; a night at Ship Fair when Jake and Rin pulled the rope-ring with me. And then, about ten years ago, that first sighting of that first queer dice-pattern in the Punchbowl. Rare moments when the world seemed to stop gyrating for a second before it moved on, ever so slightly changed. 'A still moment at the turning of the world.' Wasn't that something to do with Dervishes whirling?

He thought to himself as he had thought at those other moments: I shall remember this. When things are bad I shall remember. All the while knowing that when things were bad that would be impossible. One can never take a pinch of a good moment to leaven the slab-heavy rest of it.

She was interested in ley-lines. The dragon veins of Sunbarrow: he savoured the phrase.

'Just a minute,' he said.

She watched him go. Alive and eager, he returned with a rolled paper which he spread on the ground before them, weighting down the four corners, then watched as her eyes flicked from the lines and marks on the plan to the contours of the landscape and then back again, following the lines with her long red lacquered fingernail.

She's no fool.

After a while of silent concentration she sat back with her knees raised and her arms clasped about them. Her eyes were closed almost to slits. She rocked gently back and forth.

'And you have traced . . . divined, all these? Of course you have, of course.'

He felt strangely elated, out of all proportion to what was sensible.

Mrs Pack, who had come in to clean the house, was surprised to hear the rumble of his voice going on and on. It was Her again. Mrs Pack had seen her in church, seen her at the Green Man, seen her all over the shop as well as up here at Sunbarrow. Before she started on the floors, Mrs Pack had taken them a jug of her own home-made lemonade, but Nat Tallentire had scarcely noticed: that little Madam Butterfly had got him so that he couldn't hardly take his eyes off of her. Well, she was a pretty thing, you had to give her that. No flies on her, though. Wasn't a man in the village didn't get a bit . . . you know . . . when they started on about her. Started on . . . ? They never hardly stopped.

He'd been telling her about that old Cunning Man as used to be in the Tallentire family. Mrs Pack had good healing hands herself and what with the Cole side of the family being related to the Tallentires, she knew about that old Cunning Man. It wasn't only the length of a man's backbone or the colour of his hair that could be handed on, but senses and intuition could be passed on too.

She sprayed polish on Myrr's wood-block floor.

Not many, these days, knew about bone-cracking and healing and dowsing. Mrs Pack ran Myrr's electric polisher along the hall, bringing up the grain lovely. There had been a television programme about a bone-cracker in Ireland, or was it Scotland? According to Mrs Pack's mum, who was one of the Cole family, when her great-gran was a girl in Childencombe there had been a Cole who was the village Wise Woman and a Tallentire who was a Cunning Man. They had gotten married and that was how the Coles and the Tallentires were related.

Electric polishers were all very well, but there was nothing like hands and kneesing to finish off properly. It didn't do your weight no harm, either.

It was probably how the Tallentires had always been looked upon as being somebody special. Quite probably how Nat got called the Old Man when he took over from his father. Nat Tallentire might like to keep quiet about the dowsing, but she had seen him out there with a hazel rod this many a time. Mrs Pack knew that Nat Tallentire was a diviner: Coles and Tallentires all had powers and knowledge of the old ways. Mrs Pack, herself a Cole with bred in the bone healing hands, had recognized what was on that map Nat Tallentire was showing the Dragon Lady.

The thing is . . . why is he showing her where the earth energy was?

She obviously knew what he was on about.

Perhaps it was true what Grandpa Cole always said, yellow-skinned people did still have some of the old powers.

Eventually Nat talked himself out until he was sitting still leaning forward but with his hands now at rest. 'You let me ramble on . . . you should ha' stopped me.'

'But why? I've been fascinated.'

He made a dismissive gesture. 'My grandfather believed all that stuff. I doubt anybody wants to hear it these days.'

'But they do . . . I do.'

Suddenly, Nat was assaulted by such desire for her that he felt panic. She was only an arm's length away, and he could have easily have made a move. Her soft, translucent skin was within touching distance, her beautiful throat and lovely breasts were in the next chair. For long moments he was aware of nothing except her exotic, overwhelmingly desirable presence. He longed to put his arms about her, saw himself touch and feel how warm and soft she was, smelled the exotic scent of her hair, her skin and the perfume she wore . . .

The sound of Jake's Range Rover braking to a halt in the yard yanked him back. He recovered so that he was able to say with some degree of normality, 'That's Jake; would you like to go down to Rex's with us?'

'I'd like to walk.'

Jake went ahead and Nat and Kuan-Yin went down to the Green Man by the field paths. Nat, still a little shaken from his sudden plunge into desire for such a young, such a very foreign sort of a woman, forced himself back into his usual restraint. Outside the pub, Jake was already sitting on the terrace having a ploughman's and a pint. 'Well this is great, like old times, Dad.'

'Not quite.' Nat's soft rumbling tale-telling voice of earlier had sharpened and reset the teeth of its brusqueness. 'In old times I used to come in a working shirt.'

'Don't look a gift horse in the mouth.' He winked at Kuan-Yin. 'You wouldn't get to escort a classy lady like Dr Yin if you were in your farm gear.'

Kuan-Yin trained her gaze on his veldskoen and rolled it past his heavy knee-socks and ragged shorts to his eyes. 'Jake honey, you obviously don't know how much I like to be with a man in work things.'

Giving her as good as he got, he said, 'A bit of rough?'

Nat's rebuke was sharp. 'That'll do, Jake.'

Jake smiled and drank up. 'I have to get back, they're coming to test some new fruit flavours at the creamery. I said I'd be there.' He waved, climbed into his Land Rover and was off.

Nat was surprised at how easy it was to sit outside Rex's

with a woman he hadn't even seen until a week or so ago. She was so different from anything he had ever experienced that she might have come from Mars. He had never much liked the American accent, yet even though she said that hers was pure New York, he thought her voice lovely. And as for Chinese women . . . he hadn't really ever given it a second thought as to whether they were attractive. In fact, if he ever thought much of it at all, he would probably have said that it was only natural that a white man would be attracted by a white woman. And yet . . . She was so bloody attractive. And attractive was a bloody useless word, but he could find none that fitted.

Now in control of his thoughts, he allowed himself to look at her as she leaned over Rex's ornamental bridge feeding some ducklings.

She was alien, yet she interested him like no woman had ever done in his whole life. He had fallen for Myrr, and never really wanted any other woman. Never in thirty-five years had he felt anything so overwhelming. Desire. What he had felt then was a longing for her so strong that he understood how men and women came to make fools of themselves. And yet . . . it wasn't folly: the emotion he had experienced then was lucid and clear-headed. A most natural emotion. He longed to be able to let himself go to feel again such a pure and wonderful sensation. But he was Nat Tallentire.

Suddenly she turned and smiled at him. 'Oh, Tallentire, I do so love it here. I think I have found my spiritual home.'

He smiled tightly, not giving her – or himself – any encouragement.

'Let's have some of Rex's lovely white wine.'

Rex brought them a misty bottle and poured two glasses. 'Nice to see you looking so good, Nat. I left our two kids mooning over one another in Winchester.'

For a moment, Nat's mood was tugged at, but Kuan-Yin came and sat beside him facing the stream and he felt a kind of deep sigh run through his body. He felt almost reckless.

'Would it be all right with you if I smoked?' she asked. 'I noticed that your house is a smoke-free zone.'

'Feel free. That's Poppy, she's a fanatic about health. You can understand it, she's seen what twenty a day has done to me.'

'Oh, she's right to be. But it is just that there are moments when one of the old vices seems to be seductive. If you are sure it won't make you want one.'

'I'm over all that.'

'Did you never smoke grass or anything like that?'

His usual reaction would have been scathing condemnation of a silly suggestion. He said, 'I might have done if someone had offered me.' He smiled wryly. 'I don't think it's too easily available around here.'

She touched his arm, amused. 'I assure you . . . it's available, I'm sure you've only to ask Rex in there. Back in the States most everything's available right on the sidewalk. But I don't do drugs. If you've got a mind that works you don't need it.' She smiled and raised her perfectly arched eyebrows. 'I can get high on my work.'

Taking her cigarette-lighter from her he leaned across the table and applied the flame to the end of her cigarette. Years of youthful Saturday evenings spent watching Hollywood movies had left in Nat's mind the idea that this was one of the most intimate acts, more so even than kissing. It was a long, long time since he had done this for a woman. He cut the flame but for long seconds he did not take his eyes away from the white tube held in her full, lipsticked mouth.

With her wine glass in one dangling hand, tapping her cigarette with the other, she exuded sexuality. He was nostalgic for his youth and freedom. He handed back the lighter and for a second she grasped his finger-tips. 'Thank you, Tallentire,' she said, smiling as she blew a long stream of smoke skywards. 'I had no intention of monopolizing you for so long, but it has been so stimulating.'

He said, 'It's a long time since I enjoyed myself so much. You can stop in a rut too long.'

She stretched languorously, tapping the cigarette ash into a shrub with her long scarlet-tipped fingers, exaggeratedly assertive and American. 'Not me. Sure as hell, I can't live without something happening. If things aren't bustin' out all around me, then I make them.' Then she changed. 'My family think that I am beyond redemption. Except my grandmother. I'd like you to meet Lady Yin, Tallentire, you'd like her.' She laughed. 'Oh, they don't know the half. But I'm no longer a child, so I live my life as I wish.'

'I hardly know anything about you.'

'My name is Alison. Will that do?'

Nat shook his head. 'I'll tell you a secret. In this family, your name is Dragon Lady.'

She laughed. 'I like it, I like it.'

Nat said, 'Tell me about New York.'

'We could save that for another time.'

'You're trying to wriggle out of it now it's my turn to ask.'

'No . . . just giving myself another excuse to visit Sunbarrow.' She held his eyes, flirting with him in a way that was second nature to her, but quite alien to Nat.

'You don't need an excuse.'

'It was on my schedule to go to Kingley Vale to see the barrows there.'

His spirits dropped at the thought of her going elsewhere. 'Kingley Vale? Do you know about the yews there?'

'No, are they important?'

'You should take a dowsing rod and find out for yourself.'

'Would you come?'

Pleasure flooded him. He said carefully, 'If you like.'

THREE

. . . you would have to put off
Sense and notion.

T. S. ELIOT, Four Quartets

It became *de rigueur* for every king, mogul, emperor and priest to capture his own particular dragon or serpent and keep it under his control.

Priest-king Ludd of England (whose subjects were terrorized by two dragons which screamed from every hearth in the land) used scientific methods. He measured his kingdom, its length and breadth, calculating that its true centre was at Oxford and that it was there that the force must be confronted. He got the dragons to fight to exhaustion, made them drunk on mead and then buried them in a stone box.

In such ways did the Earth Spirit come under the control of new masculine religions, and their High Commands united to keep control. In a cunning move, the High Command sanctified many of the places where the Spirit was kept, and built temples, mosques and cathedrals over them. Quite often the markers themselves became invested with power and, forgetting that the original purpose of the stones and poles was to mark the place where the power had been subdued, these were often seized upon and used as symbols of potency and sanctity. So seized upon were the Omphalos of Delphi, the Stone of Destiny and cruciform symbols.

SOUTHAMPTON

The first thing Myrr noticed when Roz greeted her in Southampton was the warm glow that her complexion seemed to have acquired in the couple of weeks or so since that last lunch together in Winchester.

Until now, their relationship had been such that they had never needed to greet one another with any kind of salutation other than Ah, there you are, or Sorry I'm late. They had recently had one or two short conversations over the telephone in which Roz had said: I'd rather not talk about Duncan yet a while. He's all right. I've phoned him a couple of times. I will talk to you . . . but not just yet, I'm still not straight in my mind about it.

So, not knowing quite what to do in this situation where things had changed, and the event that had changed them was unmentionable, Myrr settled for squeezing Roz's hand and giving her a bunch of cornflowers she had bought impulsively at the car-park exit.

'Well what about you! My God, I never thought the farmer's wife could look so sexy. What does Nat say to the hair?'

Myrr shrugged and smiled. 'Poppy likes it. Anyway, never mind me: there I was worrying about you, and here you are looking a million dollars.'

Which was true. Roz laughed and plunged her hands into the side pockets of her skirt with a pleased and cocky gesture. 'Thanks. It's as well the weather's so hot – a cotton skirt and espadrilles aren't just cheap and cheerful, they seem to be *de rigueur* in Southampton parks.' She held out her palms indicating the young women wheeling buggies in the leafy park in the city centre, where she and Myrr had arranged to meet.

'You didn't mind not meeting me at my lodgings? It's not that I'd have minded you seeing them, but there really isn't anywhere . . . The proprietors like your space better than your company.'

'Of course I don't mind. This is lovely.'

They began strolling, Myrr with the fingers of one hand

just hooked in the bend of Roz's arm and Roz with the cornflowers cradled in the crook of her elbow.

'It's no great loss. Wait till next week and you'll be able to visit me in my own place.'

'My God, you've moved quickly.'

'Well, I had to. And I've got a job.'

'A paid job? What as?'

'Nothing marvellous and the pay's not all that hot, but I shall have earned it myself by the sweat of my brow.' She laughed light-heartedly. 'Don't laugh . . . an in-store demonstrator . . . can't you just see me?' Laughing again.

The morning was bright and preparing to be hot, and as the two women meandered beneath the canopy of tall, arching trees the sun came glittery and dappled through the ever-moving leaves. Roz's mood was infectious and Myrr felt pleased to be dressed up and out walking with her, enjoying herself in the heart of a city where she could see more people with a single glance than came to Sunbarrow in a week. From the park they went beyond the old walls of the town and on along the wide road in the direction of the sea.

'Well, yes, I *can* just see you, actually.'

Each infected the other with the gaiety of their mood.

'I say!' Roz said. 'Do you remember that awful evening with the Naughty Knickers demonstrator?'

Myrr remembered.

'Don't remind me. What ever made me order all that stuff?'

'Didn't Nat approve?'

'It's still in its box at the back of my wardrobe. It arrived just after Nat went into hospital.'

'Would you have worn it?'

'God, no!'

'She was a good demonstrator, wasn't she, Mrs Naughty Knickers?'

'You aren't kidding. I spent a bomb. I don't know what

to do with it now. I keep wondering what would happen if I should drop dead. Can you imagine Daisy or Poppy clearing out my things and finding all that?'

'You should wear it.'

'He'd die laughing at black lace with openings. I'll have to get rid of it, but it seems a shame to put it in the Aga and I can hardly take it to Oxfam or the WI jumble sale.' They leaned upon one another like teenage girls laughing.

'I say . . . you're not doing that sort of selling in houses?'

'No. It's hyping a new cheese. Something blue and strong thought up by marketing men to get rid of all the surplus milk people like you produce. I say, Myrr, I saw a letter in the local paper suggesting that surplus milk be turned into cattle feed. It was signed J.T. of Childencombe. I thought about what your Jake once said about doing away with milk lakes by turning it into cattle feed . . . in one end and out the other and so on ad infinitum.'

'Of course it was Jake. His sense of humour.'

'It's a neat idea, though. They feed chickens their own shit, why not feed cows their own milk?'

'Nat got niggly, thinks you shouldn't joke about things like farming. He also thinks Jake should have something better to do with his time in the office.'

'How is he . . . are they?'

'Fine. They're all so absorbed in themselves I'm pretty surplus.' She added casually, 'And of course we have our Dragon Lady.'

'Oh dear, poor Nat, he won't like that.'

'Poor Nat? Poor Nat is in his element. She wants to know all about his old barrows. I wish you could see her. She's quite something.' And as they walked along past the gates and solid walls, behind which the old Queen liners used to berth, towards a new, much flimsier seafront, Myrr told Roz a facetious version of how Kuan-Yin had infiltrated Sunbarrow.

'. . . anyway, in church the other Sunday, there was

Mike Alexander with this Dr Yin . . . well, I don't know how to describe her . . . this film star type . . .'

They went into the Meccano-style marina village and bought drinks which they carried to sit where they could overlook the comings and goings of boats.

'And?' Roz said.

'Well, just that really. Jake had been having us on, saying Mike had some doctor staying there. She's not just any old doctor. She's apparently some sort of shrink who's got a practice in a skyscraper overlooking Central Park in New York. She's just been to China, no less, then stopped off in Hong Kong for a visit, then when she gets home she decides that she wants to come and have a look at the ancient Brits. So Jake invited her up and there she discovers Nat, who is just what she's looking for to tell her all about ley-lines and barrows and all that stuff he loves. She's writing a book about it all.'

Roz looked over her coffee cup and raised her eyebrows at Myrr. 'Before I tell you that it's not like you to be bitchy, I'm going to satisfy that lustful cigarette machine that's been giving me the come on for the last five minutes.'

When she returned and had lit up, Myrr said, 'Did I really sound bitchy? It was supposed to sound like wry humour.'

'Maybe, but I'm willing to bet that the men hang round her like bees round mulberries.'

'They do. Nat, Jake and the entire village by the seem of it. When I said that she's an American, it was to give you a stereotypical picture, but this one's Chinese/American, a real Madam Butterfly who exudes female hormones whenever there are men around.'

'Pheromones.'

'Whatever. She exudes them and they home in.'

'And she's staying with Mike Alexander?'

'She was, but Ilse apparently dumped Jack on him and I don't think the Dragon Lady was too keen on sharing Mike with his boy. She's now stopping at Rex Farenbach's.'

Roz smiled. 'Rex will submit to anyone's pheromones.'

She drove like Myrr, fast and assertively, concentrating on the road, her chin just a little thrust out in the same way as Myrr. Musing as he watched her hands, loose and confident on the wheel, it occurred to him that their respective cars reflected aspects of them – Myrr's engine roaring and racing and showing off, Dragon Lady's powerful and purring and showing off.

Aggressive. No, with women it was assertive. They all were these days. The Sunbarrow farmworkers' union representative was five foot nothing and all ginger curls and came to work on a motor-bike: no waffle with her. Daisy too. He had often thought that he wouldn't like to take on Daisy. Poppy would be the same, though not with her fists up like Daisy – she didn't need to, she had taken the changes for granted. He guessed that his mother had never taken a decision in her entire life. It had never occurred to his father to expect her to have a point of view, and it had irritated him to see her complicity in the assumption that what her husband said went and no argument.

He watched the confident way Kuan-Yin swung the car round, running the wheel through her small hands – he couldn't imagine any area of her life over which she did not have full control. He couldn't stand women like his mother.

How beautiful Kingley Vale was: he had forgotten. As he sat on the slope of the South Downs overlooking the valley, he felt a contentment such as he had rarely known. Everywhere there seemed to be hawkbit flashing yellow, deep pink pyramid orchids, there were clouds of butterflies and shrilling larks. He had forgotten. It had been a very long time since he had felt himself to be so much part and parcel of the countryside.

Where the Downs rolled away the matrix of the overlying form could be seen, hills, hollows, ridges running into a plain. Areas of different shades as when clouds pass over the landscape, but this patchwork had been caused by the history in the loam; here a dark patch where a tree has composted and the soil is rich, there a pale starved bit where nutrients have leached away, here south-facing slopes with sparse pale grasses and dark junipers, there a moist hollow where the turf is bright green. Nat knows how thin the top layer of loam is on such downland and yet how productive when it is managed and put under the plough. He knows its feel, its vagaries, its smell. Here, vegetation clings to the thin loam for dear life, and the loam, battling with every cloudburst, rabbit, mole and human, clings to the white elemental chalk skeleton.

He watched as she moved here and there, snapping and snapping away with her camera, and thought what a strange combination of energy and calm there was about her. Myrr, too, was always full of life and energy, always doing something, but Myrr could be exhausting, she was like a blackbird turning over leaf after leaf looking and looking for something . . . anything.

She came back and lay beside him staring up at the clear sky. 'Tallentire, this was landscaped in heaven. I told you that I believe I've found my spiritual home – I doubt if I shall ever leave.'

'Then don't. But heaven didn't make it: people like me and mine did.'

'Something this beautiful? It's just one fantastic work of art.'

'If sheep didn't run on these Downs, it wouldn't be long before the scrub started to grow and then the trees would take over. In ten years the flowers would be gone. And the butterflies, and a lot of the birds. No larks will sing here if the trees take over.'

She smiled up at him, took his hand and briefly kissed his knuckles. 'Well, honey, we do have a lot to thank nice farmers for.' She had kicked off her sandals; her feet were small with bright red nails, and looked as soft and unused as a child's. Her thin, pale-skinned legs were crossed at the ankles.

The word elegant came to his mind. Yes, she was really elegant. And graceful.

She was like nothing, nothing at all in his previous experience. She must have still been a child at the time when he and Myrr were starting out together, and all that time she had been growing up, getting educated, learning to be a doctor, flitting about the world, and he hadn't even known of her existence. She had been in Childencombe only weeks and he suddenly couldn't bear to think of a time when she would not be here. *I doubt if I shall ever leave*. He couldn't bear to think of a day when she would be going up the steps of an aircraft bound for New York, so he turned the painful thought away.

When she closed her eyes he allowed himself to look down at her. Her shoulders, bare except for a single bootlace strap, were narrow and spare but strong from the warrior exercises she apparently practised every day. The soft stuff of her dress had fallen like tinted snow over the landscape of her body which drew his gaze and imagination: to hill and hollow, cave and ravine, to velvet down and bushy combe, and as she dozed he became as privy to hers as he was to the curvaceous landscape of his native Hampshire on whose breast they lay at ease in the shimmering heat of the afternoon.

When newspaper proprietors began to rely on ice-cubed female nipples to boost sales, he had put his foot down and stopped those tabloids being brought into the house, nor would he tolerate titillating calendars in any of his farm factories, or posters in the offices. Now, he wondered at himself.

She was not much different in age from Daisy.

The thought momentarily shamed him – and, like Daisy, she was probably more experienced in satisfying her needs and desires than many men of his own age. It occurred to him that it was as though he had unconsciously switched off somewhen in the late fifties, when women were either respectable or loose, and had switched back on recently to discover that both attributes had withered.

He longed to know what her fit, spare body felt like, not only to be under his hands but to be held close and to hold, to entwine, to know its bones, its butterfly weight on his own solid carcase. He ached for a tender coupling, desired to be locked in an erotic relentless unsubmissive exchange with her. Thirty years ago he would have been pleased to express that in the short Saxon words that long generations of rural workers had used, but their plain language had been filched by the mob – used as fucking adjectives – leaving not a single untarnished word for the profound experience. 'Making love' didn't express the half of it.

Things were getting out of hand.

Yet isn't that what this is all about? If not, then why am I here? Why, when I feel guilty and embarrassed at myself because I can't stop thinking of her, do I keep arranging situations where I am likely to have her to myself? Anything in trousers, Poppy said. Jake would have made his move and not thought twice about it. But Jake's move would have its end in its beginning, Jake's vocabulary would suit Jake's move – a quick screw. He forced himself to look away into the heat-haze that shimmered over the beautiful valley.

I want you. I desire you. I long for you with more passion than I've ever known. More ever than with Myrr, more than any longing for land to feed Sunbarrow. But not the quick screw. For you there should be ceremony. I should be Fire Tongue, Old God, Corn King and all the rest from Jove to Dis. I could write all that, but not speak it, yet be embarrassed that it would read like a sixpenny love-story, then mortified at the thought of you reading and mistaking it for something less than it is.

Suddenly he found himself looking into her wide-awake eyes which startled him with guilt at what the analyst in her might have seen. 'We should go because of the commuter traffic.'

As she slid into the seat of her car she kissed him lightly on the lips and said, 'Thank you, Tallentire. You are such a restful man to be with.' He was both glad that he had not spoiled it by succumbing to the temptation to caress her, and sorry that he had not in the least bit satisfied his curiosity and longing.

On the drive home they hardly exchanged a word until they reached the chalk-white hedges not far from Childen-combe where there were men, machines and trucks cutting into that part of the South Downs. 'Isn't there any way to stop them?' she said.

He shook his head. 'Transport ministries wouldn't know a work of art or a piece of ancient Britain if it turned round and bit them.'

'And what about your ancestors who built the barrows and the ones whose sheep made Kingley Vale?'

'They've gone.' He spoke quite seriously. 'They went when the diggers came in. There's nothing anybody can do about that now.'

He noticed that her knuckles had whitened on the steering-wheel, and when he glanced at her face he saw that tears had welled in her eyes. He looked away, out of the window at the hundreds and hundreds of new cones on the roadsides like fluorescent pantomime crocodile teeth.

'I really am so sorry, Tallentire.'

*　　*　　*

At the marina village where Roz and Myrr had come to rest, the noon sun rebounded vividly from the primary colours of the new buildings, and blindingly from the sea which, as it evaporated, gave up atoms of fish, seaweed, diesel oil and refuse. 'Ah, lovely,' Myrr said, 'the sea, the sea, there's nothing like it.'

'Well, actually, I think this is the mouth of the Itchen, isn't it?'

'Don't be so unromantic, Roz.'

They leaned on the rails and admired the beautiful lines of a barque. 'How'd you like to live on that?' Roz asked.

'Rats, probably.'

'There you go again. Go on . . . so this creature is now staying at the Green Man.'

'She seems hooked on our place. She spends hours wandering around photographing, videoing, poking about on Clump Hill and the barrows. Sometimes she takes off in her XJ6 . . .'

'Oh ho! So there's competition in the swish car field as well, is there?'

'Good Lord, no. I've never wanted a Jag. I'd sell my little finger for a Bel Air Cadillac, but a stodgy old Jaguar . . . ?'

'And even old Nat's smitten, then?'

'I don't know about smitten, but he certainly perks up when she's around. He even puts on a new shirt, something I've been trying to get him to do for ages.'

'It'll do him good.'

'You're probably right. I sometimes wonder if Jake hasn't got the idea. I think couples can be together too much. You get too bogged down. When Nat was in hospital I felt quite differently about him and I began to think about what had happened to us over this last thirty years. Nat and Myrr got lost somewhere. Oh God, Roz, I'm sorry, going on about us when you . . .'

Roz looked half-sideways, not quite reaching her friend's

eyes with her own gaze. 'It's all right. I understand. We're all different people at forty from the ones we were at twenty. Duncan and I suited one another at twenty, but not at forty. We didn't keep pace. Our old selves get lost.'

'I'm going to have a go at finding the old Myrr Jeavons. It's probably too late, but . . .'

'Probably she is worth going back to look for.' After a pause, she continued, 'That's not really true, what I said about me and Duncan . . .'

Myrr didn't prompt, but turned her attention to a man who went aboard the barque and fixed up a notice-board advertising the fact that the vessel was for hire to private parties. For a moment or two she arranged a wedding reception aboard for Daisy . . . or maybe Jake . . . the faces of any spouses were blank, but she saw the champagne, and billowing dresses and the billowing tan sails . . .

'. . . I didn't get lost. Roz was always there and she never changed. The trouble with us was that once we had decided to make a go of it together, it was Duncan who changed . . . not just changed, he metamorphosed into an entirely different species from the person with the long hair and ideals in his heart.'

She lit up another cigarette, dragging deeply, suggesting to Myrr that it was no longer the occasional fag on a Saturday, but a drop back probably into a packet a day. She'd need her job as a demonstrator.

'The only point of contact between me and Duncan was an occasional foray between the sheets. The Petherbridge marriage is a bloody mess, Myrr.'

'I'm sorry. I wish I could help.'

'You do. You don't judge. You accept people as they are.'

'I wasn't very nice about the Dragon Lady.'

'You don't have to be nice to accept people. And you have accepted her. From all accounts she comes and goes at Sunbarrow and you don't sound as though you really mind very much. Her only fault where you're concerned is that she's got terrific looks and you wouldn't mind being her.'

Myrr rubbed her thumbnail between her teeth and pondered. 'Perhaps you're right. You know me pretty well, don't you, Roz Petherbridge? Or is it that I'm transparent?'

'You? You're those still waters that run deep. People think you are totally safe waters . . . I think you've got a dangerous undercurrent.'

Myrr smiled, 'Use your psychology to sell your cheese.'

RIDING WHITE WATER

Three people, surrounded by piles of scripts, have punch-drunk looks which relax into thankfulness as they accept generous glasses of wine from a fourth.

'Right then,' says one; 'here's to it.'

'Cheers.'

'Thank Christ!'

The one who has come in with the wine asks, 'Which one have you decided on, the lesbian one?'

'For first prize, yes.'

'Nothing comes near.'

'It was the runners-up that were the problem.'

'Same old story. One cherry in an awful lot of pie.' She indicates piles of assorted manuscripts, typescripts and printouts.

'Which of you would like to ring and tell her the good news?'

'Her?'

'Well . . . I assumed . . . The nom-de-plume is Juno . . . somebody find the envelope with the name.'

A bottle of wine later it is found.

'Still no wiser. Just R. Petherbridge, a Winchester

address. You live round there somewhere, don't you, Nichol? One of your students?'

'No, I only know one Petherbridge: he's a he and wears a dog-collar. Let's see the address. Yeah … Saint Cross, he does live round there somewhere.'

'Could be his wife … or daughter?'

'A vicar's wife? That'd be interesting.'

'Depends on the vicar, depends on the wife.'

'Anyway, it looks like you're the one to ring and tell whoever it is that they're two thousand pounds in pocket and a contract.'

'I'll go and phone, then.'

The wine goes its rounds again.

Later. 'I got the vicar, but it's not his play.'

'His wife?'

'He flannelled a bit. I don't think he knows.'

'That's not surprising, if it's a piece based on personal experience.'

'I reckon he was banjaxed when I asked if *Riding White Water* was his play.'

' "Seems you've got the wrong Petherbridge," he said.

'So I said, "Right address, though." And he didn't say anything right away.

' "Could be my wife," he said.

'So I asked him if she wrote TV plays.

' "Not to my knowledge," he said, "perhaps it's one of my sons."

' "Can I speak to them?" I said. He said that they were in America. So I said it wasn't likely to be them, then. I asked what his wife's name was and when he said Rosamund I asked if I could speak to her. He seemed a bit spooked, and said she was away from home just now. So I asked him when? I said, it's good news about a play by an R. Petherbridge.

'He said, "Ring back tomorrow, I'll try to get a number where you can call my wife." '

'Ah well, it's a pity we can't tell her now, it's the bit that makes all the rest worth while.'

'Shall I draft a press release?'

'Why not? *Riding White Water* . . . nice title.'

Myrr had got back from Southampton later than she had anticipated, having gone with Roz to look at the houseboat she had been offered for a ridiculously small rent just to keep it occupied while its owners were in Dubai on a three-year contract.

A note in Nat's hand said: 'Ring this number – Petherbridge. Gone on to bed.'

It was almost eleven-thirty when the telephone in Duncan Petherbridge's sitting-room rang. This was the high days and holidays room in which Roz had met Roo. Now that he was fending for himself, Duncan used it every day so that, what with a few books, old newspapers and dead wine bottles around, the room was beginning to look more comfortable.

'Petherbridge.'

'Duncan? Sorry if this is too late, but I thought . . . It's Myrtle Tallentire.'

'Yes, yes . . . oh, yes. Nice of you to ring. I . . . ah . . . don't suppose . . .'

'. . . I know where Roz is?'

'Yes.' She could almost feel him relax because he didn't have to make any explanations.

'Look, Duncan, I know about you and Roz. I'm sorry it's happening. I've been to see her today . . .'

'How is she?'

'Well, blooming, actually.'

'That's probably a very good word to use – she used to bloom twenty years ago.'

'I was going to say . . . she has told me that she and you

are living apart for a while, but that's all she's told me.'

'Is that all there is to know?'

'I have no idea, and honestly – I don't want to know. I'm there for Roz if she wants me, but I don't want to get involved in the affairs of friends . . . if you know what I mean.'

'But you are involved now.'

'I mean that I won't take sides. Roz and I have been friends for years, so it's natural that we should meet. But I haven't any intention of taking sides. These things have a nasty habit of spoiling a friendship, anyhow.'

'Thanks. Perhaps you wouldn't mind being a kind of intermediary. There are bound to be things . . .'

'That's my job at the Centre, you know.'

'I did wonder if that place had anything to do with . . .'

'Absolutely not. But I'm not going to let you draw me, Duncan. I know of old how persuasive you can be. By the way, congratulations on your new appointment.'

'It's about to be made official, so it's all right if you tell Jez Carter's bush telegraph.'

'A great opportunity. Why did you ask me to call?'

'Oh . . . actually . . . Did you know that Rosamund dabbled in writing?'

'Only recently.'

'Mmm. Well, it appears that she's won some sort of prize for a play?'

'She has? That's great!'

'Did you know about the competition?'

'No, I told you . . . I knew nothing about anything until just a few days ago.'

'She must be good. Came first out of two thousand entries.'

'First? I'm pleased for her.'

'She doesn't know.'

'No, I don't suppose she does.'

'I should like to have phoned her but . . .'

'No, Duncan. Don't ask me. I'll tell you what, why don't I ask her to ring you?'

'Right. I need to ask her about things . . . this house . . . the twins . . . you know.'

'Give her another week or two before you advance too far on that front.'

'Ah, of course: nice that you're a professional in these matters.'

He could be a supercilious pig sometimes. 'I simply mean that you shouldn't start getting your hopes up: that's the sort of thing anybody would say.'

Now that she had seen her, Myrr felt sure that Roz was resigning her position as wife and homemaker.

CHILDREN IN APPLE-TREES

Jake awoke at first light, and was surprised to discover that he had spent the night on Lizz's futon. He had intended to go home, but what with the tennis and the beer and . . . well . . . and Lizz . . .

He reached over to her side of the bed. The sheets were cold. She was already up. He heard the scraping of charcoal on paper. Raising himself on one elbow he saw her seated in the embrasure of the east-facing window in a pool of Anglepoise light. Wearing only a long T-shirt and with her knees drawn up and her black hair waterfalling over her shoulders, she was engrossed in drawing. She looked as Jake remembered her ten years ago when she was in art school. There were times, like now, when he wondered whether what he felt for her was love.

How could you be sure?

Most of the time he was content to be with her. They teased one another, they shared jokes and friends that went back to the time when she was at college and he was in the Young Farmers'. And he never got tired of looking at her. She was lovely.

When he first saw her she had been young, pretty and vivacious. The Students' Union and the YF had done a joint carol singing for charity and they had met in the Union bar when she had knocked his elbow and his beer had spilled on her. All she had done was say, 'Whoops!' and insist that he come into her circle of friends who, as he discovered, were better company and had a better attitude than the people he had gone there with.

After graduation she had gone for a spell in Bristol, then London. They had kept their relationship easy-going. It was Jake who had told her about the art and craft co-op that was being set up in the Old Mill. It had come at the time of her first successful show, and she was ready to give up her job illustrating for a free newspaper and try going it alone. When she had come to live in Childencombe, they had already been casual lovers for two or three years.

'If I come to Childencombe, it will be love and let love, Jake. You understand? I shall still be my own woman; this isn't a commitment. Just coincidence that we will both live in the same village.'

He had held up his hands, palms facing. 'Absolutely. No strings.'

Lately, though, he had found his other girlfriends less enticing than in the past.

From time to time, on principle almost, he had a short fling. Usually a weekend somewhere. Usually after Lizz had been on some trip to a continental gallery, or exhibiting in one of the northern cities where her work was becoming appreciated. It wasn't that he was jealous when he saw a portfolio of sketches that had been created elsewhere and often, as he deduced, with another man. It was then that he needed to remind himself that Lizz and Jake had this understanding – Love and let love.

He got up and went over to her.

She shut her sketch-pad and offered her face briefly for a kiss. 'You were snoring.'

He gathered her hair and loosely plaited it. 'I do. That's why no woman will have me. They kick me out when they have had their way with me. Why didn't you kick me out?'

'I wasn't sure that I had quite finished with you. Anyway, you only snored gently . . . like a contented old dog.'

'That's what I am.'

She sat back, clasping her knees, and looked at him. She looked as fresh and wholesome as a wild daffodil. Not a sign of the leopardess of a few hours ago. The crown of the sun came over the horizon and at once the air at the open window seemed to rise.

'Mmm, night-scented stocks and honeysuckle.' She pushed the window further open.

'Another day, another heatwave,' Jake said.

The Mediterranean weather-pattern had settled in over England. Today the stream that ran through Goose Grass would become a little drier, the Dur reservoir would shrink, the turf on the high Downs would show itself parched, wildflowers would hasten to seed and the wayside grass would appear to be too dead ever to recover.

'Jake? You always do appear contented. Are you?'

As they looked out at the dawn arriving on their particular part of the Downs, clear sunlight ran across the rooftops of the village and beyond to Sunbarrow land, and further on towards the West Country. Jake put his arms about her and pressed his unshaven cheek to hers. 'Contented? I never think about it. Do you suppose that means that I am?'

'I don't know. I'm asking you. I've known you for ages and I don't think that I ever saw you . . . ? I don't know . . . dissatisfied . . . aggrieved.'

'God, I wish that were true! As soon as I open a newspaper I'm bloody aggrieved.'

'I'm not talking about the state of the world, I'm talking about Jake Tallentire in Jake Tallentire's own world. Are you content to be a farmer, or do you just accept it? Are you contented to stay in Childencombe or do you secretly long for the outback, or the prairies, or the South Pole?'

His finger-tips moved outwards from her breastbone, across her ribs, up her vertebrae, over her shoulders and down to lock with her fingers, reflecting that there were parts of her body that were more familiar to him than parts of his own.

Contented? There were things he sometimes quite longed for. It had come to him consciously only in the last months and he had felt almost embarrassed when he examined those recurring images of a new kind of desire – a boy on a tractor, a little girl learning to ride a pony, a bunch of kids in the back of the Range Rover on their way to Wickham Fair. And children climbing apple-trees.

A woman might call herself broody: there was no equivalent term for a man unless it was in intimations of mortality and the belief that future generations needed his particular genes in the pool. He reflected that if Rin's baby hadn't died, perhaps Jake himself would not have felt quite so much the pointlessness of his own existence without descendants. Even if they hadn't split up, Rin and Mary would be too afraid to ever have another child. And who could blame them? If Jake still hadn't been able to cope with that tragedy for himself, how could parents ever settle it? Daisy probably meant it when she said that this was no kind of a world to bring a child into. That left only Poppy and himself. Only Poppy really. Lizz's career fulfilled her, he had never known her broody. But he could never quite visualize another woman in the Range Rover going to Wickham Fair with himself and the kids.

Children climbing apple-trees. There used to be an apple-tree at Sunbarrow, where Rin, Daisy and himself had built a rickety tree-house. It used to grow just outside the old scullery, but had been sacrificed to Myrr's swimming-pool. As soon as it was spring, the Old Man used to put up a long rope with two towing hooks on the ends. When there were just the three of them, the tree used to flower, and when the infertile apples made their June drop, they used to have long battles with the hard, stinging missiles. The crop was usually sparse, but occasionally there was a year, probably when there were no blossom frosts, when the tree would be laden. In Jake's dream-past-dream-future, there were hot little fires with apples dripping and sizzling on sticks. But most of all, he saw children climbing, Daisy always on the top branch, Rin on the safest. These were the only times when a child could be king of the world, because only children climbed trees.

If he said to Lizz: What I'd really like is a family of my own kids, she would suppose that he meant his and hers and she'd run a mile.

Her work, her art, her career. He couldn't imagine a maternal Lizz, with her lovely belly bulging, engaged in breast-feeding, or pushing a buggy. There was nothing domesticated about Lizz, and in many ways it was her independence and Bohemian style that attracted him. The way she lived in this studio where, except for the shower room, no part of everyday living and loving was segregated. Her table, her easel, her bed, coffee-maker, refrigerator, accessible and arranged so that she could move from one to the other without going through a door. Totally different from the new Sunbarrow house that Myrr had made.

Lizz could produce an exciting meal, but it was almost always 'discovered', perhaps in some distant little shop that sold a hundred different cheeses, or alpine strawberries got from a specialist, or rare fungi collected by himself; or from guests who, knowing her tastes, always turned up with something they knew she would exclaim over: lox, thin pastrami, sugar peas, Good King Henry. If it was bright red chard she might tear it into a salad, simmer it in butter, or put it in a vase as the mood took her. He couldn't imagine her opening jars of baby food.

He let her go and pulled on his jeans and shirt. 'I suppose

I'd quite like to see the South Pole, but I'll wait for the organized tour.'

'Do you know something, Jake Tallentire? There are times when you are so laid-back that I could scream.'

He winked at her. 'That's a contented old dog for you.'

She stripped off her T-shirt and went to the shower cubicle. Jake noticed that she put her sketch-pad in a drawer, which meant major work that she didn't want anyone to see. He was ready to go now. She put her arm round the door. 'Give me my bathrobe.'

'Please.'

'Oh, for Christ's sake, just give it.'

Ignoring her, he slipped on his wristwatch and put his wallet and money back into his pockets. 'I'm off. Shall I see you later?'

For an answer she hurled her wet sponge at him, shouted, 'Pig!' and dashed out to get her bathrobe herself. Grinning, he fielded the sponge and threw it back. 'All you had to do was to say "please". Ring me if you decide to come to the bowls game.' And he left her alone as he knew she wanted to be.

He recognized the signs of the start of some new work. It would be something important, probably a portrait: she never got stressed up with ordinary commercial commissions, only when her own ideas had gestated and were ready.

He had seen it happen a good many times, her urgency for gratification, her sudden use of physical strength and need to be the dominant partner, getting up to work in the small hours and working with such absorption that her sitter often had to remind her how much time had passed. Sometimes there were days of withdrawal and rejection of people followed by a period when she was gregarious. To be with her at the start of a new work was dicey, she was unpredictable, she could be a prude one minute and an exhibitionist the next. It was part of her enigma. Part of what made her exciting, and what kept him going.

On the way back to Sunbarrow, he noticed as he passed Mike Alexander's that the Dragon Lady's car was parked in his drive. Now there was another exciting lady. And it looked as though Mike was back in favour again. Maybe Mike would bring her to the bowls match at the Green Man. Jake thought that was OK – if Lizz was in purdah, then he might just see how things were with Kuan-Yin.

Myrr came down to the kitchen at seven o'clock and discovered Poppy and Nat already in the pool. Walls, stones and air were still warm from yesterday's residue. It had been a still and hot night and the long-term weather forecast was that, with the area of high pressure stationary, the heatwave and drought would continue. Jake, by the look and smell of things, had been in and fried himself a breakfast.

Myrr felt irritated by the bespattered stove and pan. She had been trying since he was eight to get him to clear up his own mess. Nat always said she made far too much of a thing about it, but then it wasn't Nat who had to clear up. He'd say: If it was my job, I'd arrange things different. Which made Myrr fume. It's easy to say that when you make damned sure that housework isn't your job.

She banged around the kitchen thinking about Jake always having been the same. When he was little she thought she had the answer and would throw all his abandoned belongings into a box under the stairs. The theory was that when he wanted his football gear or his new jeans and found them in a box of rubbish, he would learn the lesson. But not Jake: he would philosophically make do with his mucky gear and wear his old jeans. If necessary he would purloin Rin's or Daisy's things, then there would be blazing rows out of which would come hand-on-heart promises from Jake to turn over a new leaf.

By the time he was twenty he had improved, and these days he at least put his plates in the dishwasher – not with care, but at least in – and quite often he even managed to take his changes of clothes into the laundry room. There had been times when he had frustrated her desire for order and cleanliness to the point of tears. But she loved him. Not as she loved Rin and Daisy for being her children or Poppy for being her late surprise baby, but because of all the people in the world she knew Jake better than any. She recognized Myrtle Jeavons in him. Beneath all her irritation at his casualness and under her threats to make him find his own place to live, there had always been that bond that was unique to Jake.

You'd let him get away with murder.

He can twist you round his little finger.

You spoil that boy.

It was true.

Even so, she slammed the dishwasher door on his plates and sprayed the ceramic hob heavily.

Nat came in with his hair still damp. Playfully he rubbed her neck with his beard.

'What's all this for?'

'I feel good.'

'You look good.'

He sat at his end of the kitchen table and poured himself some of the tea she had made. Myrr sat at her end with a glass of orange juice and a dish of grapes.

'It's going to be scorching hot again,' she said.

'We could have a ride out to Bere Forest, if you like.'

Myrr was something more than surprised. A ride out? He had never wanted to go on the kind of expeditions or picnics that she enjoyed, and he had always had a reasonable excuse for not being able to go with her:

I've got work to do. I can't leave the silage. The new machine is coming in.

Alone she had taken the children to the zoo, to visit museums, to air displays and tattoos. She had gone on package tours without him, she had taken the children when they were little to the Isle of Wight, and in later years to Spain and Switzerland. But Nat could never go with them. It was always ploughing time, sowing time or harvest time. Ewes were always coming on heat or needing dipping, or there were heifers needing insemination, or antibiotic jabs. Reasonably, he'd say:

I'm not stopping you, Myrr. Why not get Phil Carter or somebody to go with you?

Now she was taken unawares by his sudden offer to drive out to Bere Forest. 'Well . . . I was going to the freezer centre to stock up, but . . . I could put it off.'

'Yes, you can go there another day. I thought we could go down to eat in Wickham – there's that nice place we went to for Daisy's twenty-first.'

'All right,' Myrr said, her irritation at Jake entirely dissipated. 'But we go in my car, OK?'

'With the lid down?'

'You're on.'

He picked up the paper and scanned the sports pages. He hadn't done that since she couldn't remember when. His hair dried as it always did, flat and spiky around his face, adding to his brooding expression. There was a touch of white around his ears, yet some ways he looked younger than before his illness, less lined. His legs were as sinewy and hard-muscled as they'd ever been, and although he was beginning to get the same tell-tale soft underarm as herself, his biceps and shoulders were youthful:

Nat Tallentire, you've still got a body and a half and you'll never be anything but handsome if you live to be ninety.

He pushed the paper away in disgust. 'I'll go down to

Sid Postlethwaite's and see if he can give me a bit of a trim. You get your glad rags on and we'll get off nice and early while the air's still fresh.'

'Don't you want any breakfast?'

'I've had it. Jake made me egg and tomatoes.'

'And you went swimming on top of a fried breakfast?'

'I've finished with all the molly-coddling.'

'Just don't go mad.'

He picked up his towel and went up the back stairs, halting half-way up. 'Damn it, I forgot I promised Jake I'd see to the stove and that.'

'It's done.'

'Sorry.'

As he whistled his way upstairs, Myrr thought how fantastic modern medicine was, and how lucky they were to have been born in the twentieth century where a few pink pills could give a person a new lease of life. 'Nat?' she called up to him. 'Don't let Young Sid give you another short back and sides. Longer hair suits you.' She waited for the expostulation of scorn but there was none. Perhaps he hadn't heard her.

As he waited for Young Sid to finish two or three other customers, Nat sat in the next chair half-listening to Sid and looking at his own reflection in the mirror. For a moment last night, just before he dropped off to sleep, he had wondered how he would feel in the morning.

He had made love to Kuan-Yin. Whichever way you looked at it, it was adultery. Unfaithfulness to the woman I vowed faithfulness to. Is she the same woman? Am I the same man . . . ?

He had made love with Kuan-Yin. Whichever way you looked at it, he'd had casual sex with a comparative stranger. For the first time in nearly forty years he had been with another woman, he had handled another woman's body and had submitted willingly to her hands and mouth. And he couldn't even claim that it was just a sudden uncontrollable moment of foolishness: he had been thinking about it for days.

They had made love. Made love. It had not been a quick screw or a leg over. It had been an extraordinary, almost spiritual experience. It had been wonderful. Liberating. By rights he should feel guilt. But in Young Sid's mirror his guilt-free gaze reflected back at him. No anguish about what he had done to Myrr: nothing to harm her, just the opposite. This morning, when he had sat in the kitchen looking at Myrr, he had felt that he loved her more than for ages – even desired her. He looked into the reflection of his own eyes. He had reached a crossroads. Not a crisis, a crossroads. And it wasn't unpleasant to contemplate taking a new direction.

Looking at Sid's copy of the *Telegraph*, Nat saw only a replay of yesterday evening.

The house had been empty. On the telephone answering machine Myrr's voice saying that she was going to take Roz out to dinner and it might be midnight before she got back, and another from Poppy saying that she was going to stop the night with Chrissie Pack.

Unselfconsciously he had made tinned salmon sandwiches, found one of Mrs Pack's cakes whilst Kuan-Yin made tea. 'By the pool?'

She nodded, seeming to Nat to be absorbed in something. He didn't mind her quietness, nor did he feel that she expected him to make conversation. They drank tea but ate scarcely anything. Poppy's cat came scrounging. The sun began to go down, bringing out dancing clouds of midges, and Nat brought out glasses of icy Pimm's into which she put blue borage heads and sprigs of lemon balm.

He had felt light-hearted . . . really carefree. The soft quality of the light, the hum of traffic on the main road muffled by the ridge, sounding no different from the foraging bees, the strong evening scent of nicotiana and philadelphus, the lushness of Myrr's prolific hanging baskets and the crisp sparkle of the blue pool freshening the air.

'I'd like to swim,' she said.

'Go ahead, give the pool a treat.'

She gave him a long quizzical look. 'I'm not one of your natural mermaids, Tallentire.'

'You've got better legs.' He'd been pretty astonished at himself, talking to her like that. She made a funny face indicating her own mild surprise. 'I think I must take after Jake, he's a bugger for women.'

'And Master of Tallentire is not I suppose.' Her suggestion being that the truth must be quite different. That suggestion, for some reason, had pleased him. He had been telling her about the old god-kings and the tribal chieftains, and maybe he had felt a bit like one.

She'd made him feel big, in a way he wasn't used to. Not the way that some snotty little interviewer making a farming programme might try to butter him up. Being cracked up for being what they called 'a millionaire farmer with more acres under cultivation than any other land-owner in the south' never made him feel anything special: those things were factual. And as for physical bigness, except for Rin and Jake, he was used to being a head taller than most men around, used to having women look up to him physically. But she made him feel outstanding. She had given him a role. It was her way of recognizing the importance of his other experience, and his knowledge about the nature and power and waywardness of the land, that had given him the god-king feeling.

And it was true, the nature of things was important, he had known that for a long time, but unless you tried to discover the links in the chain that went back to the dawn of history and connected them to other links about things that still existed – such as the Queer Stone, or the structure of barrows, and intuition and sixth sense – then you wouldn't begin to see . . . But she did. She asked the right questions, asked him what he thought the significance was of Avebury and Silbury and the various henges and hilltop rings. She had sparked off thoughts and ideas in him that he would never have had alone.

She could look as brash as a tart or as beautiful as the Nefertiti head, yet she had a mind so sharp you could cut yourself. No wonder he had bloody wanted her so much.

He remembered how she had raised her eyebrows at him as she picked at the knot of the boot-lace shoulder-strap. 'You made a joke.'

It had occurred to him earlier in the day to wonder how the dress stayed up, what happened if the strap broke. 'I'm not known for my jokes.'

Whether it was intentional or not Nat didn't know then, nor could he guess now as he waited in Sid Postlethwaite's, but suddenly the knot unravelled and the question about the dress's engineering was answered. Without the strap it slithered to the ground, and left her standing in only bikini pants. Accident or intention, she just stepped out of the dress and walked towards the pool.

At the edge she stood for a moment; she was showing off, he understood that. She was proud of her body and wanted him to see every detail – and he saw. The perfect mounds of her behind pushing at the little triangle of white lace and cotton, the smooth sinuosity of her hips sweeping into the curve of her waist, the small swell of her belly with its perfectly central hole, and her low-nippled cupola-shaped breasts. He recalled his earlier comparison of her body to natural land forms, but whereas the land flows in a variety of curves, Kuan-Yin's had perfect symmetry, each side a mirror-image of the other. Sunbarrow pool was not one where women swam bare-breasted; maybe Jake would swim naked late at night, but as a family it wasn't done. Maybe Poppy did things like that in Greece – if she did then he certainly didn't want to know – and Daisy was sure to, because she half-lived on the Continent these days, but they didn't do it at home.

Stepping out of the pants she dived in. Words like nude or naked were too suggestive, there was nothing shameful in her body in its natural state. But she must know what she was doing to him. There wasn't a man alive who could look at a young woman poised with her arms stretched to dive and not halt his breathing and turn on the hydraulics of his blood vessels. As she moved to dive, a time-switch activated the underwater lights and lighted her as she surfaced and moved into a languid back-stroke, her torso rolling as her arms scooped up the water. He watched as she swam a couple of lengths and then as she relaxed hanging face-down and motionless in the water, her legs straight and her arms stretched sideways as she slowly and gracefully sank.

When she surfaced again she shimmered and sparkled in the beam of the submerged lights. 'You should come in, Tallentire, it feels wonderful.'

'All right, two minutes.'

She came to the side and leaned her elbows on the tiled edge of the pool, smiling up at him with her hair plastered to her head and water trickling from her face.

'Oh come on. Just get in, nobody swims in clothes these days.'

His dive into the water was less smooth than hers, but the feeling of freedom, even from the cotton shorts he usually wore in the water, was a revelation.

'Be with you next, Mr Tallentire.' Young Sid's voice brought him back from that voluptuous moment.

'No hurry, Sid. Give me a chance to read the paper.'

Sid had noticed that he hadn't turned a page in ten minutes.

He had thrown her a rubber ring which she caught on her arm and threw back to him. 'Oh, Tallentire . . . my earring!' They were at the shallower end and could see the jewel glistening in the light of the underwater lamps. As she dived to retrieve it, so he dived too and they reached the jewel together; and then Nat relived the moment when they surfaced in unison, their bodies lightly brushing as they came up.

The wonderfully alive and light-hearted feeling that had come upon him yesterday was still with him. He still felt no guilt about his desire. In the pool, he had suddenly felt no restraints, no guilt about wanting to make love with her, no embarrassment at being close to her and making the first tentative touch.

It came as an instantaneous revelation to him in the moment between the first touch of his hand upon her and her smiling response, that to love Kuan-Yin here in the water would not be unfaithfulness. Untroubled, he thought of Myrr. If she ever found herself in such a situation, he would understand. Married love was one thing and this was another.

Perhaps that was what Myrr was doing. It would explain the flash car, the blonde hair, and all the days and half-days when she was supposedly at the Centre or away on training courses. And if she was, it didn't trouble him.

With that one touch, Nat Tallentire, now sitting contentedly awaiting Young Sid's attention, liberated the passion from the self-disciplined, unfulfilled man. The man who had lived a hard life, sweated blood for his land and combated the elements to wrestle Sunbarrow for its crops. The man who suddenly realized, when he came round in the intensive care ward, that Death doesn't make any allowances for people who haven't found time for a bit of joy, and there's nothing else to come.

She said, 'Love me, Tallentire,' and his self-imposed taboos were undone.

She was slippery and cool and watery when, with her arms encircling his neck and his hands on her thighs, she lifted herself to him, sinking them both a little: was it possible?

Rising to the surface, he felt the warmth seeping through

her skin and into his. 'Love me, Tallentire.' It was possible. Water seemed to be the most natural element in which to make love. Wasn't that why the youth of the village used to gather at Goose Grass on summer nights and beside the stream's shallow pool?

In the expensively-tiled pool on the terrace at Sunbarrow, Nat Tallentire had felt a more powerful need, a greater virility than he had ever known. Her body, as though a part of his own, spiralled and floated with him and did not slide away at the last minute in panic, as Myrr's had once done, but with her arms encircling his neck and her mouth upon his, she drew him into her smoothly, strongly, endlessly. At the times when they sank beneath the surface, he could not recall the need to breathe. He saw, as though watching from above the water, the grace of the two-backed creature they had formed. Their mouths seemed never to part, yet he had seen the gleam of her teeth close to his face as she surfaced smiling, locking his gaze in hers as she breathed out in a gentle, ecstatic groan.

What Rin Tallentire wanted, now that his divorce was set in motion, was to tell somebody. He had rung home and Poppy had answered.

'Poppy, sweetheart, you're back. How was Greece?'

'Great, we plan to do France next year.'

'When do you get your A-level results?'

'Don't mention it. Not until the 16th. I'm sure I did badly.'

'Of course you haven't . . . everybody thinks that.'

'Talk about something else. When are you coming down? It's absolute ages since I saw you.'

'Didn't Mum tell you? Daze and me came down for the day not long ago.'

'Come again soon, Rin. I absolutely have to keep finding a new audience to tell about Greece.'

Rin laughed. He had always idolized his little sister. 'All right, what say I come down on the 16th?'

'And save me from leaping from a high place?'

'No, silly, to hear that you have three As and are being sought by every university in the land.'

'You're lovely, Rin.'

'I know.'

'Why did you ring? Mum and Dad have gone out in Mum's new car.'

'Good God, will wonders never cease?'

'Dad's terribly well now. He's gone all jolly and everything, quite different from when I went to Greece.'

'Take care of him down there, we can't do without the old bear.'

'Don't, Rin! I couldn't bear to go through last year again.'

'Has anybody heard from Daze? I haven't heard a peep since we went home together.'

'I don't know, I've hardly been home five minutes and since then I've had to practise for the doubles with Jake, and now Mum and Dad are out . . .'

'Poor ole soul,' he mocked, 'and did they leave you all on your own then?'

'Since you ask, no. My boyfriend will be here any minute and we're going into Winchester.'

'Boyfriend! How nice to be young and free.'

'You're not old.'

'But not sweet seventeen.'

'Then why don't you do something about being free?'

'Being what?'

'You know what. You and Mary should start afresh . . . but with other people. You probably think it's damned impertinent of your baby sister to say this, but I hate to see you wasting away. You'd be such a good husband with somebody else.' Poppy waited for her brother's response. 'Rin? You're not angry?'

'No, no . . . it's only the truth. It's just that I can't get used to the idea that you've grown up.'

Poppy wondered how he would react if he knew that she was on the verge of a full-blown relationship.

'I'll have to go, I can hear Mr Farenbach tooting his horn.'

'OK, sweetheart. Have a nice day, as they say.'

''Bye, Rin.'

'Poppy? Are you all right for cash? I'll put you a bit of pocket money in the post. And, Poppy, you can tell Myrr I've decided to start divorce proceedings. Tell her not to spread it around outside the family. I don't want a lot of gossip. OK?'

' Oh-absolutely-kay, Rin, I'm glad. Really, really glad.'

Her elder brother could have no idea that tears had welled up in her eyes. Although she was still only a young girl when it happened, she had been devastated by baby Nathan's death and had wanted, somehow, Mary and Rin to be happy again, as they used to be.

'So am I, now it's going to happen.'

Young Sid flicked out a cloth and tucked it round Nat's neck. 'You're looking miles better, Mr Tallentire.'

'I'm feeling better, Sid.'

He ran a speculative comb through Nat's crisp curling hair. 'Usual cut? Feels a bit wiry.'

'That's probably the chemicals in the blasted swimming-pool. You'd better give it a bit of a wash.'

'Righto, then.'

Young Sid had been cutting Mr Tallentire's hair every six weeks or so ever since he took over five years ago from his dad, Old Sid. Young Sid had modern ideas, had done away with his dad's barber-shop atmosphere and installed backwash basins and revolving chairs. Young Sid wore jeans and a T-shirt and sat on a stool to cut hair. He was London-trained and didn't mind charging his clients London prices, but he was proud of the fact that he had kept his dad's old customers. Customers knew what they wanted – a good short cut that would last – and Young Sid gave it to them and didn't charge nearly as much for this service as for the clients who booked appointments for their designer hair and beards. Condoms were on display in a wide range of sizes, flavours and strengths, and he provided newspapers, magazines, and a coffee-maker from which customers and clients alike could help themselves. His theory had been that eventually customers would get used to things. And they had.

And here was the evidence: Mr Tallentire seated at a backwash basin allowing Young Sid to shampoo and condition his hair.

'Look, Sid, Mrs Tallentire says she don't like the way I have it cut so short, what do you reckon?'

Sid lifted Nat's hair and let it fall back. 'I reckon she might be right, Mr Tallentire, you've got a really nice head of hair. I always think it's a shame when my Jenny has to sweep it up off the floor. How will it be if I just give it a tidy up, put a bit of shape in it?'

'Ah, all right. Just give it a try-out. Nothing fancy, mind. I can always come back another day for you to run the clippers up the back.'

'I'll have to charge you the new prices . . . I'll have to use scissors.'

'That's all right, I don't mind the cost, but don't go making me look like some of the newcomelately nancy boys you get in here these days.'

'Go on, Mr Tallentire, with shoulders like yours, there isn't much chance of that. You got Farmer wrote all over you. I shouldn't touch your beard, though. There aren't many that's got a fine beard like that. Beautiful colour – blond heads usually beard-up red and gingery. I told your Jakey he ought to grow one.'

'He won't do that, he does everything he can to stop people saying he's the spit and image of me. It's why he wears his hair like a blasted woman.'

'Well, I suppose you could say the same about me and my dad. You never would have seen him without his white overall and his collar and tie – heatwave or no heat-wave.'

And so Young Sid, with his inbred knowledge of what makes a countryman tick, chatted on with whatever entertained whoever was in the cutting chair until at last he rang up a Full Head Design, bottle No. 1 Conditioner, 6 pkts Mates. The latter item was surprising and Young Sid had no hand in promoting it.

But, there you go! Who said life in a village was dull?

Young Sid felt good as he watched Mr Tallentire striding out, his head nicely groomed but not too nancy and his blond beard shampooed and combed and six packets of Mates in his jacket pocket.

He's got himself a totty!

Young Sid had seen it happen before with men who wouldn't see forty again. But who'd have guessed the Old Man?

Not in a thousand years! But there you go – gave you hope for your own middle-age!

When Poppy reached the end of the front drive, Tom Farenbach and his father were leaning over the gate.

Rex Farenbach said, in his usual fruity voice, 'I heard you've got more rings showed up in some of your other fields. I'll bet your dad isn't best pleased: there was enough trouble with this one. But he's looking his old self lately. Fit as a fiddle: nobody'd ever guess he nearly gave up the ghost last year.'

Tom squeezed her hand, knowing how people often felt in the presence of his dad. You had to get to know him before you realized that under all the jolly landlord act he could be quite serious. All he wanted was for people to be cheerful, and he thought that by sounding cheerful and chatty himself it would brush off on them. Actually, it quite often did.

Poppy put her lips into a tiny kissing movement at Tom, who flicked a glance to see whether his father had noticed. One thing Tom dreaded was all the heavy-handed leg-pulling his father indulged in. Poppy joined them in looking at the crop-marks. 'I can't seem to get worked up about them any more,' she said. 'Two or three years ago, when I was into Gaea and stuff like that, it seemed like the earth might be sending messages.'

'Global 999 calls?' Tom's father squeezed her shoulders in his avuncular way and laughed.

'It's possible,' said Poppy defensively, wishing that he wouldn't do that.

'We'd better go, Dad,' Tom said.

'What about young Emma, haven't we got to pick her up?'

Tom and Poppy glanced sheepishly at one another, guilty at not having included her.

'She's not coming,' Tom said.

'Well that's a shame, seeing you have stuck together like the three musketeers.'

'Four,' Tom said. 'Matt Pridhoe was with us.'

'Ah, yes, I was forgetting young Pridhoe.' Young Pridhoe not really counting because he wasn't a true villager but came from a newcomelately family.

'Emma sometimes helps Mr Carter in the shop,' Poppy said, hoping that it would not get back to Emma that she had been left out.

They climbed into Rex Farenbach's brake and in not many minutes were coming into Winchester.

'You can drop us near the park, Dad, save you stopping in the traffic.'

He let them out of the car. They waved as he filtered back into the one-way system.

As soon as they had reached the tranquillity of the park, Tom stooped over Poppy in a very adult stance and kissed her in a very adult way. 'Oh, Poppety, I couldn't sleep for thinking of you last night.'

Hand in hand, Poppy wearing a long Indian cotton dress and a straw hat, Tom in black jeans and black vest, they were everyone's picture of love's young dream as they wandered beside the stream with its ducks and hired canoes.

Thirteen years ago they had started at the village school on the same day. Never very bothered about one other, they had gone on through every stage of their education at the same time, travelled on the same school bus, and sat in the same examination rooms without ever doing much more than register each other's presence.

Then the four young Childencombe students, Poppy, Tom, Matt and Emma, were drawn together as a clique within a group of twenty or so from other schools, and these two had suddenly noticed one another. 'Give it here, Poppy.' It had started like that, with Tom's unexpected gallantry when he had taken her hold-all and swung it up on to the rack and Poppy, shoving up close to Emma, had made room for him to sit beside her.

On the journey to London, Emma and Matt paired off and Tom and Poppy. During that time, Poppy discovered with great surprise that, although she realized that his voice had grown deep, Tom Farenbach now shaved and had very male whiskers. Her interest grew and, under cover of poring over a map with him, she took stock of the rest of him. By the time they reached London, she wondered how on earth this terribly attractive hunk had been living in the same village without her having noticed. Everyone knew that Matt Pridhoe could pull the girls, but Tom Farenbach! Suddenly Tom was fantastic.

Tom's discovery was a little less dramatic than Poppy's.

He had announced ages ago, to his equally coarse and callow cronies, that he thought that Poppy Tallentire would be nice nookie, but he hadn't realized that, beneath the college jumpers and blazers, she had been growing the most beautiful curves.

Of course, living in the close society of a country village, they were always seeing one another, and even if familiarity doesn't always breed contempt, it often breeds indifference. But unfettered hair, a pair of tight jeans and gauzy top on Poppy, and shorts, Reeboks and Young Sid's attention to the mop of black hair on Tom, had been enough for them to take off their blinkers.

Suddenly they were in love. Suddenly all those funny memories of being a mixed infant at the village school, of the ciggies on the school bus, and of the school plays, seemed to have tender romantic significance and to add to their sudden awareness that they had become adults.

In some societies they could have gone to the longhouse and spent a summer in consummate bliss and come out ready for life, but here in the park, they could only give one another the caresses acceptable in English society. The best they could do was to lie absorbed in one another on the brown grass and yearn for some way to gratify their unique desire for one another.

In the end they opted for an afternoon in the cinema, where, along with other couples who had no longhouse, in the air-conditioned back row they gave love to one another as best they could.

FOUR

Footfalls echo in the memory
Down the passage which we did not take
Towards the door we never opened
Into the rose-garden.

T. S. ELIOT, Four Quartets

We, who are no longer free to roam the earth – whose spirit lies captive in our cities, towns and villages, whose intuition is hampered by logic and science, who have been nurtured to be ashamed of feyness and mysticism – we still sense something.

What is it? What it is that lies in the subconscious of settled humankind? What relic of our dream time, what rusting knowledge? There is something there – but oh, the muddle.

Dragons, gods, shades, spirits? Instinct, intuition, foreknowledge? Having given them names, do these things then exist? We stifle our curiosity at birth with a pillow of ridicule and requirement of proof. Things that exist only in imagination and vocabulary do not exist. But they exist there? No. Yes. Oh, the muddle . . . the tug-of-war between proof and faith, science and spirit.

Kuan-Yin, her face shaded by a large straw hat, chinked the ice in her orange juice. 'My, my, I had no idea that li'l old England could have such weather.'

Mike Alexander and Kuan-Yin were breakfasting on the brick terrace at the back of his house. Jack had gone to stay with his Grandmother Alexander.

'Too hot for you?'

'I love it.'

'You needn't have gone to the Green Man, you know. Jack is quite a civil little boy.'

Kuan-Yin body-contacted him with her hand upon his

arm, a gesture of reassurance he often used himself. That was the trouble with two professionals in the same game. Mike couldn't decide at times whether she selected a particular body signal from her armoury of them, or whether it was a natural and feminine love of touching.

'Honey, I thought that he'd like to have you to himself.'

'Well, don't go abandoning me again. I love to have you here.'

'And I love to be here. But I must do some work. I've spent more than a week with only a notebook: I really must get some of it on disk.'

The garden was relaxing into full summer blowsiness. Large-headed roses dropped thick carpets of pink petals, yet still bloomed and bloomed. Hydrangeas with huge mop heads faded from their earlier sugary pink to paler more subtle shades. In the borders the lowest flowers of purple lavenders began to fade into grey, true geraniums revealed their crane's bill seed vessels and marigolds went over the top in trying to reproduce themselves by making green crowns of seeds. No damp humours arose from the borders and the moss between the stone slabs appeared dead. It was a time when it is best to follow the example of the garden and do no more than face the sun and catch any passing breeze. Yet, Mike sensed, Kuan-Yin was restless.

He knew what it was to enjoy research so much, and to become so involved, that you wanted to stay with it, but he also knew the right time to stop. And in any case, he had looked forward to taking what had promised to be an exciting relationship a step further. But so far it hadn't worked out. And then there was last night. He had thought in Washington that she was totally uninhibited and honest. He couldn't bear it if it turned out that she was not.

Mike turned her face so that he was looking directly at her. 'Kuan-Yin, you faked it last night. It isn't necessary to fake it with me.'

'Faking's no big deal. Women wouldn't do it if men

understood that it's not always necessary to go for a great Fourth of July display, all Roman candles and rockets.'

'Maybe, but with me it just reminds me of Ilse when she was sleeping around. If you don't want to make love, you've only got to say: Mike, I don't want to make love.'

'I did want to make love.'

He felt a prickle of jealousy and felt foolish. As yet they had nothing going except a casual relationship, nothing beyond their uninhibited enjoyment of one another. Since the day when she had landed up in Childencombe, he had begun to like the idea of something more. He knew that she had been at Sunbarrow all day and well into the evening. Jake Tallentire's reputation wasn't built on myths.

She came and stood behind him, crossing her delicate arms about his neck and speaking close to his ear. 'I guess you can have too much of a good thing.'

'Too much? Not any with me.'

'No . . .'

'With Jake, of course?' He felt annoyed with himself that he had allowed pettiness into his voice. Especially about Jake. Jake was such a stereotypical rival. Especially as Mike quite fancied Lizz Taylor, but wasn't likely to get much of a look in.

'Honey, that sounds . . . well, you know . . . a bit possessive.'

He remained unyielding, so she withdrew her arms. 'Mike, I'm sorry, but there's a whole lot of difference between faking and . . . Hell, no! What am I doing here, trying to explain myself?'

From those few moments of irritation that neither of them intended the other to take seriously, a schism developed. To have stopped it, all that was necessary was a scrap of sackcloth and smear of ashes, then they could have returned to the bedroom. But neither wanted to be the first penitent.

Mike didn't seem to be about when Kuan-Yin drove

back to her room at the pub. Still sore from her spat with him she asked herself why in all that's holy was she horsing around here when she could be anyplace else she pleased?

The truth of it was that, since she had become involved in work in a clinic on the Lower East Side, she had become very aware of the freedom that her plentiful dollars allowed her. Taking this sabbatical meant that not only had she cut her East Side work, but she was producing no income in the Park Avenue practice, and this trip was costing. If she had accepted a place on the official research project, she would have felt better about it, so for her self-respect she had to do the work she had set out to do.

And the phenomena on Sunbarrow were intriguing. She wanted to take a look at as many sites as possible, and then there was the possibility of there being further developments with the crop-marks in their increasing complexity. And then there was her proposed study of any effects on the Sunbarrow family . . . and where was that going? It had been interest in subconscious and tribal instincts during her second year in college that had led her to study psychology, and the longer she was in Childencombe, the more she found that she was experiencing that same excitement as when she was a sophomore.

And now there was this extraordinary thing with Tallen-tire. Her thighs automatically tightened at the memory of his urgent and uncomplicated love-making, something carefree that she hadn't experienced since AIDS put a stop to all spontaneity. She had had many other spur-of-the-moment lovers, but seldom one who had so unexpectedly fulfilled a fantasy as Tallentire had done. By making love in the pool, he had given her a sense of taking part in something ancient and mystical and of water as an element as natural for conception as for giving birth.

When she had invited him into the water she had known that it would happen, she had been allowing her imagination full rein as she floated face-down, sinking to the bottom of the pool. Their previous conversations had suggested to her that the Tallentires had a genealogy that was old and of equal importance to that of the Yins, so that the union between them was like the fulfilling of ancient custom. A union between equals that she had not experienced before. They had been discussing earlier the myths of the unions of god-kings and mythical goddesses. There came a moment when she and Tallentire had seemed to be the reincarnation.

There was also the matter of the closeness of the unexplained circles to the barrows and dragon veins. It seemed of such significance that she had telephoned Uncle Han.

She had been thinking how Tallentire had gradually revealed his inward self. An outwardly proper and conservative farmer enclosed a man full of unexpected knowledge and wisdom. In her professional life she spent her time helping clients to reveal what lay buried, but outside the consulting room she was frequently surprised at something her analyst self would have discovered at once. She had found him physically attractive right from the beginning, and had been intrigued by his detachment that morning at the church, but the revelation of so intelligent and sensitive a man captivated her as no lover before him had ever done.

She had been involved with a great many lovers since the time she was very young, but her affairs had not dulled her or made her cynical. An affair might last a week or a year, but to become an affair it must have some memorable element. She had supposed that her nice intrigue with Mike might have developed in that way, but the growing intensity of her feelings left no room for anyone except Tallentire.

When Rin Tallentire left his solicitor's office, he had a feeling as though his hands had been freed and he could now wipe cobwebs from his face. He had lived the years since the baby had died in a state of suppressed depression and its resultant state of inertia. His days filled with his work, his nights dulled by tranquillizers, his life was a familiar routine.

Mary had gone the other way, flinging herself into every new experience she encountered, anything to get away from life as it had been before. She grew her hair, streaked it with pale blonde, became thin and fragile, and more self-assured than anyone who knew the old Mary would have thought possible.

In the cot-death support group she had wept and wept and confessed her guilty feelings. Kindred hands had grasped hers and arms had hugged her. And again she had wept. When she came home from those meetings, Rin had often found her in a strange state of near-elation. She talked and talked and listened and listened and had her grief and anger drawn out and began to understand her guilt and depression. And she had managed it at a time when many inadequately informed experts, in looking for explanations, laid blame on parents. Parents, whatever they said, must be doing *something* to cause their healthy babies to die. Parents of longed-for and much-loved babies who perhaps subconsciously wished to return to the child-less state? Certainly Rin and Mary had not.

Rin was glad to see her dragging herself out of it, but nothing could persuade him to enter rooms filled with people who had had the same terrifying nightmare as himself, the experience of a chilly, still baby who did not stir hungrily in its fluffy nest. He had visualized rooms filled with anguish as crushing as his own.

Yet from such rooms of people, Mary had slid into

transcendental meditation where she found yet more sympathetic and loving people who took her with them to country houses for weekends of meditation and yoga. From these experiences she returned home friendly but distant. She wanted him to benefit from those same experiences, asking simply, 'Please come.'

But Rin's misery had been so severe that he did not trust himself to say anything about it out loud for fear he would lose control of his anger. He had dreams in which in a mirror he saw a single teardrop fall from his eye and shatter. Cracks appeared wherever the tear-shards fell, the cracks expanded into more cracks, so that eventually everything became crazed until finally the entire planet looked like a car windscreen hit by a missile ready to fall apart.

What he had wanted was to be with Mary somewhere where they could weep soft, healing tears; where they could meld their two bodies into one in their misery as they had once melded them in delight when she was pregnant, winding limbs, interlacing fingers, fusing torsos, exchanging tongues, coalescing breath. He could never in a million years have expiated his grief as Mary had done, in someone else's house, in the company of strangers.

'Time heals,' people said. Rin thought that that must surely be true, but what was it that healed? Walking through the park on his way from the solicitors, he wondered whether what they meant was 'Time forms a scab'. By the refreshment kiosk near a little playground where he often stopped for a coffee or an ice-cream, he sat and watched parents behaving as though that particular role was unassailable. It was here that he often allowed himself to finger his wound to see if the scab had become scar-tissue.

It had not.

When he saw a mother's attention wander from a toddler, or a father pushing a swinging child very high, he wanted to warn them. Between one second and the next every single thing in their lives could alter for ever. A toddler could wander until hit by a car; a child could lose its grip and fall on its head. But he sat as always, a layer of depression rising from his suppressed grief like mist over boggy land, a pleasant expression on his face as he leaned on his elbows over his coffee, a man with all the appearances of being at ease.

Anger, guilt, grief and depression. If he could somehow lose just one of these albatrosses weighing him down, then he could perhaps deal with the rest. By far the heaviest weight, and the one he would wish most to be rid of, was the depression. Like many depressives he kept it as shamefully hidden as Grace Poole's charge, or Maxim De Winter's dreadful secret in the sunken boat. His only release was the almost frenetic chopping-up of logs or the smashing of stored-up bottles and jars in a salvage skip.

Then, on that unbearably hot morning, he had awoken and some of the weight of the depression had shifted.

Daisy was surprised to open her door to find Rin standing there holding a container-grown plant, the pungent scent of its fluffy flowers filling her small porch.

'I hope that's not your after-shave. Come on in.'

'It's a myrtle.'

'Is it? I don't think I ever saw one.'

'It's for you. Evergreen. I know you like shrubs that earn their keep.'

She took the plant, smiling and inspecting the label.

'It is a myrtle. *Myrtus communis*.'

'The common myrtle. It went out of fashion and is about to make a comeback.'

'It's lovely. Thanks. I know just the place for it.'

'I thought I'd get Myrr one as well.'

'Oh, she'd love that, a plant named after her.'

'It's a wonder she hasn't got one already – she's got everything else.'

Daisy smiled as she plugged in the kettle and threw teabags into a pot. 'I don't think anybody enjoys money as much as Ma.'

Rin sat on one of the rush-seated stools and hooked his heels on its bar. 'Is that what she's doing? I thought she was compensating for something.'

'That's right, years of having nothing.'

'I think it's more than that,' Rin said.

'Children should never try to analyse their mothers. Have you phoned home lately?'

'Well . . . I don't know . . . about a week ago, I suppose.'

Daisy said, 'When I phoned that American doctor was there. I think that woman must have taken up residence.' She handed him a mug of tea and took the other stool alongside him at the breakfast bar. 'Apparently she is interviewing the Old Man about his old countryside lore and things like that.'

'That's nice for him. Nobody else was ever interested.'

Daisy lit a cigarette and ignored Rin's 'started smoking again then?' glance. 'Apparently she's interested in barrows.' She laughed. 'You know how you can practically see Myrr down the phone when she puts it all into her voice. I could tell what she was thinking . . . a bit of amusement and a bit of condescension . . . or patronage, I suppose.'

'Yeah, well . . . so long as the Old Man's got something to occupy him. Keep him out of Jake's hair.'

They fell silent as they each briefly examined their own images of life at Sunbarrow.

'You all right, Rin?'

'Funnily enough . . . yeah. I feel pretty good.'

'Why "funnily enough"?'

'We're getting a divorce.'

'Well, thank God for that. You should have done it ages ago.'

'I know . . . but, well . . . you know . . .'

Daisy smiled affectionately at her brother. 'Yes, I know, you always have needed a bit of Semtex behind you.'

Rin returned the smile. 'Maybe, but you can't deny that when I do get a kick in the bum, I move.'

She offered him the biscuit tin from which he took several, momentarily withdrawn as he laid them out in a row, compulsively aligning them with the tiles.

'Oh, Rin, spit it out. You've got something on your mind – you might as well out with it.'

'I used to believe you were a witch and could read my mind, Daze.'

'I could. When you were a kid, you were as transparent as the belly of a freshwater shrimp.'

He popped one of the biscuits whole into his mouth and realigned the rest. Daisy remembered this ploy from years back: when he was forced to announce something such as bad end-of-term results, he always did so through a mouthful of bread or potato. The result of his mumbled news was always having to repeat it clearly, but at least he had a few moments to listen to what it sounded like spoken aloud. Now, before he could open his mouth, Daisy said, 'And don't speak with your mouth full.'

As he broke another biscuit into small pieces and rejoined them like a jigsaw puzzle, he said, 'How do you think Jake would . . . well, if I decided that . . .' He dunked a biscuit into his tea until the soft end sank.

'For Christ's sake . . . Rin!'

'It's been passing through my mind that I wouldn't mind having a go back home.'

It took a few seconds before Daisy understood the meaning of this bit of news. 'You mean, go back? To live? To Childencombe? Live at home?'

'It has passed through my mind a time or two recently.'

'But you're a Londoner now. You couldn't go back. You'd ossify.'

He fished around in his mug with a spoon and ate the

mushy biscuit. 'I'm not that much of a Londoner, not like you.'

'Sure as hell you aren't a rustic, either.'

'You can't call Jake a rustic, not by any stretch of the imagination.'

'Oh come off it, Rin. Jake's as happy as Larry yomping over the Downs, setting the ram at the ewes and the bull at the cows and ambling down to the Green Man for a game of darts after supper, then getting his leg over to round off his day.'

'Put like that, I wonder why anybody'd want to leave.'

'Anybody'd want to leave because they couldn't stand twenty-four hours under the eye of the Old Man and seven days a week banged up in the heart of ye olde England. It was a disgusting life, suffocating.'

'Maybe . . . but the Old Man's changed since our day. Jake's boss of Sunbarrow now.'

'You reckon?'

'Yeah . . . I reckon, don't you? He's no fool is Jake. He's done a pretty nifty take-over there, so that the Old Man's hardly noticed how much power he's handed over. You might as well say that Sunbarrow's Jake's now.'

Daisy looked hard at her brother. 'You don't resent that.'

'No, no, no. I wouldn't want that kind of responsibility.'

'What do you want, then?'

'I've had an offer from that graphics place in Waltham. Apparently they were impressed by my Handy Dandy bath-cleaner animation.'

'You've been head-hunted?'

'Yeah, sort of.'

'Well, well. I'm impressed.'

'I wouldn't be an employee . . . it's an association.'

'You mean self-employed so that they don't have the same responsibilities they'd have if they employed you direct.'

'Don't be so cynical. It's a nice package. A new BMW, some index-linked PEPs for my old age, BUPA . . .'

'The kind of deal that would have qualified you for yuppie status in the eighties.'

'A slice of group contracts could bring me up to forty K annually, plus any accounts I can bring to the association.'

Daisy whistled. 'I'm in the wrong business. Publishing gets thinner and thinner.'

'Computer animation is still in its infancy.'

'With that kind of money, you could buy yourself a nice place on the Hamble River – you don't have to go back to Childencombe, just because it's close to Waltham.'

'Yeah, I could, but I just suddenly had a fancy to go back and live at home.'

'I suppose it can't be worse than mooning around in your Soho place on your own.' Briefly she squeezed his hand. God, why have I always felt so responsible for him? I can't bear it when he gets hurt. 'Just don't jump in with both feet – test the water.'

He smiled. You never noticed when I grew up, Daze. 'OK. I'll keep my place on for a bit.'

'For a year.'

'That will depend on my settlement with Mary.'

'Mary will do what you want.'

'Mary's changed.'

Daisy didn't quite know what to make of that, but she did know that it was the one area of his life where she could not intrude. Daisy would never forgive Mary for running away when the going got tough. When Rin had said that Mary was devastated with grief, Daisy had wanted to take Mary by the scruff of the neck and rub her nose in Rin's grief. Daisy was the one who had to stand by and see Rin's desolation. So, Mary's changed. Daisy could be excused for an inward curl of the lip.

On the Saturday Rin went to Childencombe. At lunchtime, he and Jake followed the old sheep-raike down to the Green Man. Rin was in smart, understated casuals and, Jake noticed, his hair was so well cut that, even when blown about by the wind, it returned to its style. Jake for once had put on a cotton shirt and some decent jeans: they felt coarse against his knees after the weeks of freedom in shorts. They walked easily together, with the same shoulders-back, hands-in-pockets, loping walk of their father.

Jake had been mulling over in his head what Rin had said about the urgent desire he had felt to come home for the weekend. 'Was it because of that Sunday when you and Daze came together?'

'Could be ... all of us being round the table on the Sunday.'

'It's not like that, not even on Sundays. Usually I go out somewhere for lunch, and by September there won't even be Poppy for Myrr to make a Sunday for. We're not the Archers and Sunbarrow's not Brookfield Farm ... the Tallentires haven't got the same scriptwriters.'

'Better scriptwriters than the "Rin and Mary" serial.'

'It seems a bit drastic to come back to Sunbarrow? You went to London in the first place because you couldn't stand village life.'

'I was young.'

'Christ, man, you still are.'

'I feel a hundred.'

'That's probably just deciding about your divorce.' Jake grinned at his elder brother. 'You never did much like having to make a decision. Give it a year and you'll feel different. They reckon divorce is about the most stressful experience you can have, don't they?'

'How would you feel about it if I did decide to come home?'

'Me? I'd feel OK about it, great in fact ... how should I feel?'

'You're the master here now.'

'Of Sunbarrow?'

'Yeah.'

Jake laughed. 'I'll never be master. I run the business, but I don't fit the Old Man's shoes. Managing Sunbarrow's a job. I'm quite good at it and I like being my own boss, but I don't have the same feel for the place as the Old Man.'

'I'm surprised. You've put your whole life into the place, the same as he did.'

'But he made the place, didn't he? Created the whole thing out of just Clump and Other Field, then added to them bit by bit. I run Sunbarrow all right, but he made it. I could never have the same commitment to it that he has . . . I don't expect to. You need to start small to love a conglomerate like this. I don't think that he's got any conception that we're a commercial operation like any manufacturer.'

'Yet he's not naïve. In fact the way he understands things like Europe and the Common Agricultural Policy amazes me.'

Jake laughed. 'I stopped being amazed when I came here to work. What fools everybody is that he still sees it as a place with the pig in the sty and Myrr throwing corn to chickens in the yard. He's an extraordinary bloak. He didn't get his understanding of commercial farming from education or books, yet it's been a textbook operation the way he built one bit on the back of the other bits. Whatever it is that he's got, he didn't hand on to me. I'm a decent enough farmer, but I haven't got the passion . . . the dedication or whatever. And I don't want it. It's too tough. Soul-destroying. I like life too much to want it dominated in the way his has been.'

'Couldn't you start small but in a different way? Like gradually changing to hydroponics or organics or something? Your equivalent to the pig in the sty and a wife selling eggs?'

'I have thought of that, but it would mean having a battle with the Old Man every morning . . . it'd drive me off my rocker. It took all my powers of argument to get him to give up fertilizer on those two north fields.'

'But he started with two fields.'

'He didn't have a bloody cantankerous father sitting on his back.'

They had reached the stile which separated Sunbarrow land from the main road. Rin climbed and sat on the top bar, Jake sat on the step, both brothers looking out across rolling countryside of fields bounded by ancient hedges and old trees. 'Looks good, doesn't it?' Rin said.

Head to one side, he looked down upon the unruly hair and clear profile of his younger brother. 'Why don't you just do it?'

Jake slapped his knees, rose and leaned upon the cross-bar facing the road. 'Because it's not my bloody farm, Rin, and it never will be.'

Rin jumped heavily on to the roadside verge and Jake athletically vaulted the stile and landed lightly beside him. 'I wish I was as fit as you,' Rin said.

Jake grinned. 'That's because you don't get any real ale, only that gnat's piss you call lager.'

'Then maybe I should come home for no other reason than for the beer.'

They headed downhill towards the village as cars sped by spattering them with last winter's road grit. Jake shouted back over his shoulder. 'You reckon you could stand the fast pace of country life?'

There were no customers yet in the pub, but there was that pleasurable feel in the wood beams and plaster walls of enjoyment remembered and anticipated: the smell of tobacco without the fug, of metal polish from the brass rail and pump handles, of the polished wood counter marinaded in beer fumes. For Jake, Rex Farenbach's front bar was a second home where, except for Lizz, he never brought any of the women he became involved with.

Jake leaned on the bar. Rin slid on to one of the polished wood stools. 'You like the Green Man, don't you, Jake?'

'I sometimes wonder if it's not this place that keeps me in Childencombe. Does it show?'

'Just something about the way you look at home here.'

Jake grinned. 'I'm practising to become a regular in my old age. I shall sit over there by the fire and tell the new-comelatelys about the olden days when the first crop circles came to Sunbarrow Farm.'

Rex Farenbach came in carrying dishes of crisps and peanuts. 'Wotcher, Jake. You're early today.'

'Dragged here by my big brother.'

Rex held out a hand. 'Nice to see you back again, Rin. Keeping OK? My Tom was asking me about you the other day – he wants to get into the advertising game. I told him: Get yourself a decent education first. You went to university, didn't you? Or was it art college? Well, you just tell him that when you see him. I'd appreciate it. Kids these days don't want to hear what their parents have got to say. Now then, what's it to be? No need to ask Jake . . . same for you, Rin? Right! Two pints of "Rex's Best" coming up.'

He carefully pulled two pints of ale and almost reverentially placed them on towelling mats upon the gleaming counter. 'Don't mind if I pop back down the cellar? Bit behind this morning, and now one of my waiters has fractured his arm so I'll have to fill in in the restaurant . . . never rains. Your dad's girlfriend's back.' He pulled up the corners of his eyelids. 'We've got quite a nice few guests in at the moment. This nice weather does it. That what brought you down, Rin? Can't say I blame you, bit of home cooking, a dive into that swish pool of your mum's. I don't know what she thinks about our Tom always hanging about the place. But there you are, love's young dream plus a swimming-pool. Moth to the flame. Give us a shout if anybody comes, will you, Jake?'

He disappeared into the less glamorous part of the Green Man.

'Cheers,' Rin said.

'Cheers. I hope everything works out for you.'

'Thanks, Jake. What do you reckon then ... about coming back home?'

'If it was me, I'd start off by putting my toe in the water. You don't need to sell your flat yet, do you?'

'No, as a matter of fact, I was wondering whether to offer to buy Mary's share and keep it on anyway. I don't think she wants it.'

'A pied-à-terre in London? Sounds OK to me. Why don't you do that, then? Even better, haven't you got some holiday due?'

'Yeah, still got five weeks.'

'Come home for two or three weeks then, give it a try.'

'I suppose I could, couldn't I?'

'What does Myrr think?'

'I haven't said anything.'

'Not about the new job?'

'No, so far I've only told you and Daisy. I thought that, if I told Myrr that the job was in Waltham, she would automatically assume that I would come home to live, and I wanted to hear how you felt about it first. I didn't want Myrr killing the fatted calf prematurely.'

There was the clip, clip, clip sound of high heels that automatically distracts men from their conversations. Both brothers turned towards the narrow stone-flagged passageway that led from the hotel and restaurant to the pub. Kuan-Yin entered, in loose crepe trousers and a short bodice, her hair in an immaculately shining plait swinging to the rhythm of her walk which hesitated for a second: it seemed that she had not expected to find the bar occupied.

She waved. 'Hey, look, it's you, Jake.' She flicked her gaze up and down him. 'Hi, Jake, how are things?'

They were two of a kind where the opposite sex was

concerned. He returned her look. 'Pretty good, Kuan-Yin. You haven't met . . .'

'Your brother. Rin. Am I right? No mistaking the Tallentire body.' She held out her hand which Rin took as he slid from the stool. 'I'm Kuan-Yin.'

'I know. We spoke on the telephone last week.' Jake was, to say the least, surprised at the sudden change that came over his brother as he took and held on to Kuan-Yin's hand. Throughout their developing years Jake never saw Rin as competition. Rin was good-looking, but staid; Jake was the one who pulled the girls at school, Jake was the one who knew the score at grammar school, and the one who surrendered his virginity early, ages before Rin.

Rin loved Mary. Jake loved women.

Until he saw that same absent-minded, prolonged hand-holding technique that he used himself, Jake had only half seriously thought about competing against Mike for Kuan-Yin. But here was his suddenly suave older brother breaking free of his marriage, with a single leap.

'Get you a drink, Kuan-Yin?' Jake asked.

'Well thanks, honey. Just spring-water and ice.'

Jake ducked under the counter and served her drink.

'Thanks, hon. I'm meeting Lizz, did she tell you? Have you come down for your ancient fair, Rin? I said I'd help, it sounds fun. And so interesting. Rex has made me an honorary villager for Ship Saturday. I guess it must be a first, a New York Childencombrian.'

'Oh Lord,' said Jake, 'I forgot. Aren't Lizz and Myrr putting on something?'

'Jake, you didn't forget? You were supposed to be our strong-arm man and help put up the bowling alley.'

He winked at her. 'No problem. I'll fix you your bowling alley.'

'Are you sure that it's bowling for a real pig?' She laughed, swinging her hair and showing her neat, unblemished teeth. 'Nobody will tell me what the winner is supposed to do with a *pig*? Rex says that it is tradition that the winner must keep the pig until it is full grown. Tallentire says that it comes as ham – I guess that sounds more reasonable. But I don't know ... it could be a live pig. This is a surprising place.'

Jake felt that he had begun to regain his position, but it was obvious from Rin's unawareness that he was devouring her, that she fascinated him – as she had appeared to have done to Mike, Rex, young Tom, all the regular drinkers in this bar and, for God's sake, the Old Man himself. Jake did not feel bewitched exactly ... but she was as sexy a lady as he'd ever had the good luck to meet.

Rex came back carrying a half-full gin and tonic, his crinkled hair slicked back and smelling of after-shave. Jake handed him some coins. 'One Malvern water.'

'Thanks, Jakey. Anyone want serving? No? Then I'll join you for a quick one before I have to go over to the restaurant.'

As he ducked under the hatch, Tom Farenbach came in. 'Dad ... ? Oh, hello, Jake. Have you got a partner for the tennis tournament? I was away so I'm looking for a partner.'

'I was partnering Mike Alexander, but he's had to call off. Are you any good these days?'

'Pretty good.'

'Right, you're on. But we're out to win. OK?'

Tom laughed. 'OK, Jake. That cup's as good as ours.'

'Is it an open competition?' Rin asked.

'Of course, don't you remember? It's the Ship Fair Cup.'

'Thinking of entering, Rin?' Rex Farenbach asked.

'Twist my arm and I might.' Rin smiled.

'You're here for a holiday then, Rin?' Rex asked.

Jake flashed an enquiring look at his brother and saw that the answer was aimed at himself.

'A couple of weeks,' Rin said. 'I've got time due to me,

and this weather looks set, so I thought I'd take a break.'

Tom said, 'It's a great tournament.'

'More of a drinking contest, if you ask me,' Rex said.

'I haven't played for years,' Rin protested, but it was obvious that he wanted to be drawn.

'It's the Ship Fair Cup, everybody knows it's not cut-throat,' Rex said.

'Not much!' Jake said.

'It's not, Rin. All you have to do in the men's doubles is to keep sober until the others are pissed.'

'Oh, come on, Dad,' Tom said. 'You make it sound like a drunken orgy.'

'Just my joke.' Then, flashing a look at Kuan-Yin, Rex asked, 'What about me? I'll tell you what, be blowed to Mike Alexander, let's you and me show 'em, Rin.'

But Rin didn't hear.

Jake had watched how deftly Rin had moved so that Kuan-Yin, who was seated upon a bar stool, had become corralled by Rin and the stool he had vacated. Several regulars now came in and Rex went behind the bar. The room began to get hazy from tobacco smoke and pungent from the pints of Real. Jake could not hear Rin's conversation with Kuan-Yin but he could tell from the way she held her head, the way her eyes zigzagged over him, the openness of her gestures, that they were tentatively coming on to one another.

He called along the bar to them. 'Hey, you two, we'd better cut along and see about this pig.'

Rin acknowledged Jake but continued to nod at what the Dragon Lady was telling him. Jake had to wait for five minutes for them to emerge, laughing together as though they had known one another for ages.

Watching them, Jake smiled to himself and thought: She's a right bugger, she can't talk to a bloak without giving him the come-on.

Which, coming from Jake Tallentire, was a bit rich.

When Jake and Rin went to Lizz's to find Myrr, Lizz had had a phone call to say that Myrr might be late but to carry on regardless.

Roz's train was due. When Myrr had finished her stint at the Community Centre, she went along to Winchester station in plenty of time only to find that it was running twenty minutes late. Myrr bought a beaker of coffee and sat to wait. Roz had phoned her at the Centre.

'Myrr? I have to come to Winchester, could we meet?'

'Of course, you don't need to ask. When?'

'Actually . . . today. I'm sorry, but . . .'

'It's all right, Roz. Just come.'

'I can't talk over the phone. There's too much . . . it's too complicated . . .'

'I've said, Roz. Why not come for the weekend? We've always got a bed made up.'

Myrr had for the moment forgotten that Rin had landed home at a minute's notice.

'Oh, I didn't mean . . . I thought we might meet in our old cafe.'

'It's Ship Fair week, I'm doing the bowling for the pig. You can help.'

'I have to see Duncan. I may not be much of a weekend guest.'

'I'm not expecting you to be entertainment. Just come. I'll meet you off the train.'

Roz breathed a heavy sigh down the phone. 'Thanks, Myrr, but I'll have to see Duncan anyhow. Thanks.'

In the station cafe, Myrr put down her coffee and almost furtively slipped a large envelope from her document case. A faint smile of satisfaction softened her mouth and she smoothed the envelope like a pet before she slid out a sheaf of papers, forms and large, glossy booklets. She had already had a brief look at them earlier and had dipped a toe into the new jargon. Open University modules. Credits and half-credits. Tutor groups. Summer schools.

This time she allowed herself to look properly at the prospects within the covers of the booklets. In this envelope was the door to everything she had ever dreamed of doing during those years of making some sort of a life out of next to nothing. Making butter, making cream, making children into sensible adults and making do. In the envelope was the kind of education she had seen her kids get and longed for herself. Looking at paintings and finding out what made one thing art and another kitsch. Comparing classic and modern sculpture. Finding out what Corn Laws actually were, and why they were repealed. Reading literature and discussing with other people why Jane Austen could be as exciting in her way as P. D. James and why P. D. James was 'genre' and Jane Austen 'classic'. For as long as she could remember, Myrr's mind had been full of Whys? Imagine getting up in the morning and spending a whole day reading history and writing your opinions about it.

The contents of the envelope were not new. They had arrived two years ago when she had filled in the application form and been turned down because the list was full. Last year she had re-applied and then had to withdraw because Nat was ill. She had put the papers away in a drawer at the Centre and put the prospect of Open University at the back of her mind until earlier this year when a duplicated letter looking very much like a bit of junk mail had offered Myrtle Tallentire a place on the Arts Foundation Course.

This was the year. Not a single obstacle lay in Myrr's way – not lack of money, or time, or transport. Norah Pack would do whatever housework Myrr couldn't manage, Nat was well again and Poppy would be off. They had all had their fair share of her life, what remained was fairly her own. Nobody could begrudge her that.

When, in good broad Hampshire, the Bournemouth to

Waterloo train was announced, Myrr carefully slipped her wonderful future back into its envelope and put that into her document case.

Roz, carrying only a bulging canvas shoulder-bag, stepped down from the train at the far end of the platform from where Myrr waited. Myrr watched her as she strode out, her exotic-looking hair shining and bouncing as she went. She had grown younger since she had got away from Duncan.

'It's great to see you, Myrr.'

'And you. You look wonderful. Where shall we go?'

'You said you had to help at the Fair.'

'Ship Fair will go on whether I'm there or not. Anyway, it doesn't need half a dozen pairs of hands to knock up a bowling alley and make a few notices. Let the next generation find out how it's done. If you and I never run another fund-raising stall, we've done our share. I've rung them to say I might not get there yet.'

They bought some sandwich packs and cans of drink and walked through the precinct filled with shoppers, and on past tourists being Leicaed in stone archways and Nikoned at the old Butter Cross. When they reached the grassy environs of the cathedral they sat under a tree which looked old enough to have been a sapling when the foundations were laid.

Roz snapped open a can of Pepsi. 'It's Patrick – Duncan's brother.'

'The one Malcolm and Ian are with? In America?'

'Patrick's got AIDS! AIDS! For Christ's sake, I didn't even know he was gay.'

'Oh, how awful.'

'It's Ian and Malcolm I'm worried about.'

'But they don't live with him, do they?'

'No, but they visit. I mean . . . can you catch it by using the same swimming-pool?'

'No, of course you can't.'

'It doesn't say so on these.' She took a bunch of crumpled leaflets from her bag. 'Screwing around, fucking and buggering is about all they tell you about. How do we know that our kids don't?' Her voice broke and her large eyes became awash with tears which welled into the lines beneath her bottom lids. Myrr gave her a tissue and tentatively grasped her fingers. It was an awkward gesture, for until now their friendship had not had to deal with many overt displays of emotion. Roz briefly returned the grip.

Myrr waited as she would have for a client at the Centre.

The temperature had risen to the high eighties and, in the middle of the day, the cathedral threw very little shadow. Some visitors wandered about, the massive walls of the cathedral drawing their eyes upwards, tourists rested on seats or grass, a few people lay flat on their backs with handkerchiefs spread over their faces, locals went by laden with Sainsbury's and green M & S bags. Organ music trickled out from the cathedral. Black-skirted clerics hurried, from somewhere to somewhere. Where? Elderly men in black medieval tunics and hats came out through side doors and went back through others. So many men in black. What happened to make them stick with that fashion? Why had it never changed?

Myrr thought: The cathedral's like a great hive and it's as though they are all coming and going tending their queen bee god. What do they do? Why are there so many? Where are the worker bees who keep them all going? Waiting for Roz to regain composure, Myrr knew that here was another image that would become permanently fixed in her memory. She had many, in which she had total recall of the quality of light, the temperature, the scents and smells and texture of everything connected with a particular scene. She could step outside and look at herself within it, to see herself and Roz as a passer-by might see them. Myrr guessed that the AIDS thing was only the trigger that had released Roz's pent-up feelings. Roz had, as Roz would put it, fucked up her life and was finding it difficult to un-fuck it.

Roz balled the damp Kleenex, thrust it into her pocket and breathed out heavily. 'Oh well, better out than in. Sorry, Myrr.'

'There's nothing to be ashamed of.'

'I always feel such a bloody wimp. If I'm supposed to be able to help people sort themselves out, then I surely ought to be able to sort myself out.'

'Well you probably can't, and neither can I, or anybody. We're too involved.'

Roz ripped open a packet of crisps. 'Was there ever a time when you wondered whether Jake or Rin were . . . homosexual?'

'Jake and Rin . . . ?' Myrr considered. 'No, I don't think so.' She smiled wryly. 'Certainly not Jake, he preferred girls from when he was four.'

'It was the first thing that flashed into my mind when Malcolm phoned. I know really nothing about Patrick except that he's rich. I didn't even question whether he'd be a suitable person.'

'Roz, this is crazy talk. Your kids went to live in the same town as your brother-in-law, that's all. And all this talk about being gay. Stop trying to punish yourself because you're worried about Ian and Malcolm. Jake sleeps around, and Poppy went off to Greece, don't you think it hasn't crossed my mind – the thought that they might get carried away and make a mistake? God knows, it's easy enough. Remember how it used to be when we were teenagers? We had heard about the pill, but nobody knew how to get it.'

'I remember. Getting banged up was a fate worse than death. Except that it wasn't worse than the fate kids face now.'

Myrr thought: Didn't stop us getting the terrors if we were late, though.

Her own memory of finding herself pregnant before she

was eighteen was still not far from the surface. The feeling of dread after the twenty-eighth day of the month. Thirty-two, thirty-three, thirty-four ... seven days overdue ... two weeks ... a month. She had supposed, from seeing other women with their babies, that nature would put it right and that her twins would compensate for those dreadful days, of cycling steep hills, and of lying in scalding baths drinking gin.

'I always felt that I had something to make up to Daisy and Rin for that.'

Roz looked puzzled: Myrr's last statement appeared to be apropos of nothing in their conversation.

Myrr said. 'They were my fate worse than death.'

'I never knew. You weren't very old.'

'Seventeen when I found out that standing up wasn't very good contraceptive advice.'

'Poppy's age.'

Myrr nodded. 'It's a different world now.'

Roz drew out the ball of Kleenex and blotted her eyes and nose. 'Christ! I always look such a bloody sight when I weep.' She breathed out heavily again and leaned back against the tree. 'Do you know something ... I've asked myself this every day since I've been on my own, why did I ever marry him? Why? I wasn't even pregnant ... Lord knows, I deserved to be.'

Myrr said, 'It's funny really, looking back from here, the problems of the sixties and seventies were handleable ... just fear of getting pregnant and the bomb.'

Roz made a wry face. 'Products of the swinging sixties. Ours was the last generation to be able to swing. Isn't that a terrible thought?'

'I expect they'll survive. I managed without a single love-in, and very little grass.'

'I had a lot of lovers and a lot of joints.'

The redness began to ebb from Roz's face as she returned to her more usual self-possession. She handed Myrr one of the packets of sandwiches and unsealed one for herself. 'I think I'd like to come for the weekend.'

'I'll drive you up to see Duncan. You'll feel better when you've done that.'

On the way out to Ridge House, they dropped into silence. Eventually Roz asked, 'What would you have done if attitudes had been different in your day, would you have married?'

Myrr's answer came immediately. 'No. I would have had it terminated and tried to get some sort of education.' Then she paused. 'Nat and I are OK and I love my kids, but . . . well, to be honest, I've always had the feeling that it was just filling in . . . like girls who go au pair or do VSO until they decide what they want to do . . . a kind of practice run for when my real life starts.'

Roz looked shocked and did not notice that they had reached the St Cross area that she had run away from. 'I have always thought that you had the most enduring marriage I know of.'

'We probably have.' Myrr swung in at the wide gateway of Ridge House, the gates of which were newly painted, and up the freshly gravelled driveway where abundant, well-tended roses dripped from posts.

Roz looked around her as though trying to place where she was. 'I still feel as though somebody tugged at the rug under my feet.'

Whilst Myrr had been sitting with Roz on the Cathedral Green, Chrissie Pack, who had just finished off at Sunbarrow, did a quick change in Myrr's bathroom, exchanging her jeans and sweater for something that would make their eyes water in the bar of the Green Man.

'I done, Poppy,' she called through the house. 'You there?'

Poppy came downstairs two at a time to where Chrissie

was putting the finishing touches to herself in the hall mirror. 'OK, Chrissie. Mum left your money on the dresser.'

'It's all right, I found it. Tell her we run out of Sanilav, and tell her I don't like that new cleaning stuff that smells of vinegar.'

'It's ecologically sound, doesn't pollute the water.'

Chrissie, only about five feet tall, had to stretch to see herself in the Tallentires' hall mirror. 'I know that, but if you ask me, it stands to reason that stuff that won't kill a fish won't kill a germ. Anyway, I put bleach as well down all the lavs and plug-holes just to be on the safe side.' She teased her hair and renewed her lipstick. 'I suppose Tom Farenbach is taking you to the fair.'

That was the way of things in the village. First, everybody knew your business before you knew it yourself, and second, when a couple went out together then it was the boy who took the girl. Poppy smiled. 'No he's not, Chrissie.' Chrissie looked disappointed. 'I'm taking Tom.'

Chrissie flicked her hand at Poppy and smiled. 'Oh, go on with you.' She had twisted a scarf, turban style, round her head. 'Do that look right to you?'

Poppy centred the knob of the scarf. 'Looks good.'

Chrissie was only a little older than Poppy and in their junior school years they had sat together in class and played together over Goose Grass. Chrissie, though, had left school at sixteen and gone into the Sunbarrow dairy making yogurt. It was Mrs Pack, Chrissie's mother, who was officially Myrr's domestic help, but nobody at Sunbarrow was ever surprised to find Chrissie or her sister Susie or even Granny Cole energetically pulling furniture out and vacuuming into corners.

There were a good many newcomelatelys who would have paid way over the rate to get the Pack treasures into their houses. But that was precisely why the newcomelatelys would never get the chance, nor understand why. The Pack women had no intention of ever demeaning themselves by becoming anyone's treasure. They were bright, honest and hard-working women who knew that they did what they did well. They expected to be treated with the respect their experience deserved and paid well, but they were not up for grabs to the highest bidder.

Mrs Pack had no reservations about working for Myrr Tallentire. She well knew that Myrr was capable of getting dirt under her own nails – mucking out animals, scrubbing kitchen floors and bringing up four kids – and that even now, when Sunbarrow owned half Childencombe, Myrr wasn't really any different, she didn't have a bit of side to her:

Good luck to her that's what I say. There's always somebody who's going to get the crock of gold, so I say let it be one of our own kind. I'd rather have twenty pound for cleaning the Tallentires' kitchen than twenty-five for being treated like I was a servant by some toffee-nosed solicitor's wife.

Chrissie bit on her lips to secure the lipstick. 'I said I'd help out in the pub whilst the fair's on, our Susie's helping out at the Tea House. Mr Farenbach is opening all day till Wednesday, always a lot of visitors as you know. One of his waiters is off sick so he's having to do the restaurant himself. I expect there'll be more than ever this year since your field was in the paper.'

'Don't mention it. It's a sore point in our house.'

'Mimm Carter said he offered to charge to let people into your field and share it with your dad.' She laughed.

'I know, I thought it was a good idea.'

'D'you know what, Mimm can't get enough strawberries from their own field to satisfy demand: they had to go and do a pick-your-own down at Titchfield to keep up with it. I don't know if it's true, but their Emma said that Mimm made over a hundred pound in a single day. I shouldn't mind that, should you?'

'Mimm always did have the knack of how to make a bit of money. You remember how he used to get packets of biscuits from his dad's shop and sell them singly at the school gate at break time?'

'Yeah. I was only in the infants, but I remember he bought himself some mirror sunglasses. That kind of thing's all right, but I prefer nice steady money.'

'Want a cup of coffee before you go?' Poppy asked, walking through the house with Chrissie.

'Better not. I said I'd be at the pub as soon after midday as I could. Mind you, I'm not so much bothered about pub work these days – not since your Jake worked out this bonus for us.'

'I didn't know about that.'

'It's a production bonus.'

'Oh, good,' said Poppy. 'Perhaps I've got some to come. I did a lot of casual work at Christmas and Easter.'

'Oh it's really, really good. It's not like a bonus you get every week in your pay-packet. Your Jake calls it profit-sharing and we get it twice a year. It mounts up to quite a bit, you'd never believe.' She yanked the family bike up on to its wheels. 'I'm putting mine into a building society account.'

Poppy held the bike for Chrissie to thrust her jeans into the saddlebag. 'You're never saving up to get married, are you, Chrissie?'

'Me? Married? Not bloody likely. I've got the offer of a nice little TR2.'

'A sports car?'

'Oh, it's lovely. Vintage. Pale blue and a lot of chrome, only partly restored, but our Rich could do the rest.' Rich Pack was the eldest of the Pack children, who, if he wasn't roaring around the countryside on a Harley-Davidson, was attending to the guts of cars with the delicacy and assurance of an experienced surgeon dealing with the human gut.

'It sounds as though you've already got it,' Poppy said.

'Oh well, I have really . . . I would have if our mum wasn't such a stick in the mud.'

'Doesn't she want you to have a car?'

'It's not the car . . . it's me taking out a loan for it. I told her, everybody buys things on HP these days: Never a borrower or lender be, she says. Oh, she's that smug, she says: Everything we got is bought with money. I never owed nobody a brass farthing, she says, what I can't afford, I don't have. I bet your mum isn't like that.

'Well that was all right in your day, I told her. But she won't hear of it. Anyway, I've been putting in a lot of overtime, and your Jake's summer bonus is due this month, so with what I get from Mr Farenbach I shan't be far off, and our Rich says he knows the chap selling the TR2 and could probably do a deal with him.' She mounted the bike and hooked her heel on to the pedal.

Poppy said, 'Well, good luck with it then, Chrissie.'

'Thanks, Poppy. Nobody knows how much I want that car.'

'Where will you go in it?'

Chrissie gave Poppy an old-fashioned look.

'That isn't nothing to do with it, Popp. It's about being independent. It's a symbol.' She held her fist in a power salute. ' "Up the Women!" I'll bet your mum would understand.' She waved and called back. 'You can keep your fellas – I'll have my TR2.'

Poppy went slowly back into the house wondering about Chrissie always flying off to some job or other, which led to her thinking, as she did more and more these days, about how it had come about that things were shared out so unfairly. In Greece she had noticed it particularly – luxurious yachts anchored off islands whose inhabitants were living off a few goats and a small olive grove. When she had mentioned it to Tom, he had said that maybe she should have applied for the LSE. The truth was, Poppy had to admit, it had never occurred to her to apply for anything except what her college had suggested, never to wonder whether she really wanted university at all.

Noticing her father cleaning out the pool, she made him a drink and carried it out to him.

'Good-oh, Poppy love.' Taking the drink he perched on one of the pool-side stools. 'I'll only stop for a minute. I promised your mother I'd go down and see Jez Carter and pay for the side of bacon or whatever it is. Though why they can't just take the money instead of going through all the rigmarole of bowling for it, beats me.'

'You know why. You're just being an old grouch. People like to do things. It's fun. Anyway, they'll probably double what you give, and even if they don't, a lot of people will have had a lot of fun. It's keeping the village traditions going. I always thought you were all for that.'

Poppy, who had been picking seedling weeds from Myrr's flower tubs, looked up and caught him watching her over his mug. He looked tanned and well, and happier and more relaxed than she could remember seeing him for ages. So well. Not young in years, but young in the way some old actors seemed, people like Joan Collins and Sean Connery. People you could still imagine dancing and making love. You could never imagine somebody like Emma Carter's mother in bed with anyone, and she had never let herself think of her own mother . . . She did allow that her father might . . . But not the two of them together . . . She flushed at her own thoughts and went to pick and pull at the other tubs.

'What are we doing for lunch? Did your mother leave any instructions?'

'No, I expect she thinks that two adults are capable of arranging food for themselves.'

'OK, Mrs Pankhurst, let's have less of the feminism and more suggestions. Would you like to go down to Farenbach's?'

'Ah . . . which: bar-food or restaurant?'

'If you'll put these cleaning things back in the pump-house, I'll stretch to the restaurant.'

Wonders will never cease! But she didn't say it aloud, just in case he should take fright at the prospect of being seen entering Farenbach's restaurant.

Rex Farenbach, who was friendly but formal in his role of temporary waiter in his own establishment, attended to them himself and led them to a table in a bay where they could look out over the stream which he had recently paid a lot of money to have landscaped.

Poppy, feeling pleased at being in the Green Man Restaurant with her father, said, 'Isn't this place smashing now?'

'I remember when it was the old stables and that stream was no better than a quagmire.'

'Well, even I can remember that, Dad.'

'He's got some money invested here. Must be up to his neck with the bank.'

Poppy opened her menu and looked over it to see what her father's reaction to Green Man prices would be, but he appeared either not to notice or to accept that double figures for a few slivers of Parma ham or a pot of smoked salmon pâté were normal in 1990.

'Soup. Steak. And bread-and-butter pudding,' he said, when Rex came to take their order.

'For two?'

'Yes.'

She didn't want to put him in a bad light, but neither did she wish to be treated like a child and told what she must eat. She smiled at him, then at Rex. 'My Pa has forgotten that I went vegetarian.'

'Ah . . . so I did. Better tell Rex yourself, then.'

Rex, very different now from his role as Tom's dad or

landlord behind the bar, said, 'I can recommend the goat cheese en croûte. Greek recipe, local cheese.' He raised his eyebrows a fraction, no longer treating her as a schoolgirl.

'Oh well then, that will be perfect,' Poppy agreed.

'And I'd like a beer,' Nat said. This time he remembered. 'And what about you, Poppy, I expect you'd like a glass of wine?'

The steak, which Nat Tallentire's heart man had removed from his diet-sheet, was fillet and perfectly cooked to his taste. He closed his eyes as he took a forkful into his mouth. 'Mmm. My God, that tastes good. Don't tell your mother I've been eating bloody meat.'

'Oh go on, Pa, don't exaggerate, she'll be pleased that you've come out to enjoy a meal. You should do it more often.'

'Ah . . . I suppose we might come down here occasionally. It's not bad.' He leaned across the table. 'But did you see the prices? Is that what you've got to pay for a meal out these days?'

Poppy smiled, loving him for his unworldliness and wishing to protect him from any sense of feeling at a disadvantage. 'No, you can get a decent meal in plenty of places for the cost of a starter here. This place is in the Michelin book, people come a long way to eat at the Green Man.'

'Is that so? Ah well, that would account for it.'

'For what?'

Again he leaned towards her, not wanting to be heard talking prices. 'What Dr Yin said she was paying for a room here. I said she was being robbed and could get a decent enough room at the Dickey for a quarter Rex's prices. But she said it was peanuts compared to what you'd have to pay in London. She reckons London is dearer than New York.'

'She's probably right. She'd know, she's always jetting around the world somewhere, isn't she?'

'Makes you wonder how people afford to live.'

Poppy had no idea how well off her father was: he must be worth quite a bit, yet he never seemed to believe it. It was a joke in the family that Myrr could always find something new to spend money on, but really, when you looked at some of the outsiders, professional people who had come down from London to live in the village, Myrr wasn't anything exceptional. They just weren't used to having money.

Most of the spending was on the farmhouse. Her father still went to the same shop in Winchester to buy his clothes as he had always done. Jake went about in old jeans and his yomping boots, and certainly Poppy herself didn't get as much pocket money as Emma Carter. She withdrew from her thoughts and turned her attention to the juicy, runny cheese in its crisply-baked filo wrapping, and was about to say something to her father when she saw that his attention was totally focused outside the window. A smile softened his face. She followed his gaze and saw the Dragon Lady leaning over the small arched bridge which spanned the stream with its graceful young willows and ferns.

'Your Dragon Lady makes quite a picture,' Poppy said, feeling ridiculously embarrassed – Tom's father was always looking like that at women.

'She isn't *my* Dragon Lady.'

Poppy endeavoured to be grown-up about it. 'She obviously thinks you're the cat's whiskers. What is she doing over here?'

'I don't know. She's got this theory that there might be some connection between barrows or the contours of the land and those things in the corn.' He picked at some cheese and was lost in thought. Poppy was not upset, her dad was like that. Always had been. She got quietly on enjoying her food whilst he was preoccupied with his own thoughts.

Nat hadn't spoken to her since she had phoned him when he came back from Bere Forest with Myrr. He had been half-expecting that she would call. According to Jake, she had gone up to the farm quite soon after he and Myrr had left. She said she wanted to look at the plan of the dragon veins. Jake had searched out the ley-line map for her.

'You went and got it from my desk? You've got a bloody nerve, Jake.'

Jake had been unusually shirty. 'I didn't know what to do, did I? She seemed to know a damned sight more about it than I do. She knew where you keep it, and she knew what it was all about and that you had told her she could have the map any time.'

'I meant when I was there.'

'Then you'd best tell her that. I didn't know. Don't start on at me. I'm not supposed to know what's going on with you and her.'

For a moment, Nat had thought that there was something behind that, but obviously not. He calmed down. Jake had only done what he thought right. 'I didn't mean to bark at you like that.'

Jake had nodded. 'Do you know what an omphalos is?'

'A what?'

'That's what I said to her. Well, she reckons that the Queer Stone in the dip could be one.'

He knew it! In latter years he had come to believe that it was a stone of some significance, though exactly what he had never fathomed. It didn't look anything much, but it hadn't come there by accident: a pit had been dug and the stone dropped into it. It was weathered so that you couldn't tell how much it had eroded. Perhaps it had been six foot tall at one time, but you couldn't tell. He had wondered whether at one time there had been some kind of dais there, or perhaps some pagan altar. Although it was smaller, it had always reminded him of one of the Avebury stones. His father had called it the Queer Stone. He had said that it must never be moved or the Tallentires would fall. When Nat was young he had thought his father pretty stupid to believe that kind of a tale. But if the stone had been there for thousands of years, as was reckoned, it wasn't doing any harm leaving it be.

Jake had wanted to take the tractor and tackle to it, but Nat had forbidden anybody to do anything to it and so tractors, harrows and harvesters had always had to interrupt their straight lines to avoid the stone. It was only later, when Nat had tried his hand at divining, that he had discovered that all the ley-lines that traversed the old Sunbarrow land at some point touched the dip with the stone. When Kuan-Yin had talked to him about the dragon veins, he had not said anything about the Queer Stone. He couldn't have said why; perhaps he had wanted her confirmation that it was a thing of significance.

Jake said, 'An omphalos.'

'Oh.' Nat feigned uninterest, but had soon gone and looked up 'umphalas' and had been disappointed at not finding it. Then, under 'O' he found:

a sacred stone of a rounded conical shape, in the temple of Apollo at Delphi, fabled to mark the central point of the earth: a central point . . . centre, hub.

And he knew that Kuan-Yin had confirmed his own instinct that the Queer Stone wasn't there by accident.

Poppy broke into his thoughts. 'What does she think about the crop circles then, Dad?'

'I don't know.' Sharply.

Poppy caught the cageyness of his retort and wondered what had been going on in his mind to change his mood.

'She don't think anything as far as I know.' He recovered his good mood. 'Seems that back in the sixties there was something going on in Australia. Something to do with Aborigines. She reckons they thought it was the old flying saucer thing again.'

Poppy was surprised. He was about as likely to mention sex as the 'old flying saucer thing'. He looked up from his plate and then away. The subject was embarrassing. A lot of people in Childencombe found it so. And ridiculous. They preferred to forget the time when a number of people driving on the Childencombe to Winchester road reported that they had had their car stopped by some light and saw men in silver suits.

'Flying saucers didn't make that big pattern on Clump Hill.'

'Give it a rest, Poppy.'

'I don't know why everybody gets so het up about it all. I'm like Jake, I think it's nice having a sort of mystery on your own doorstep. Like having the Loch Ness Monster.'

'Ah, and the people living round Loch Ness are probably as fed up to the back teeth as I am having people rubbernecking around their private property.'

'Oh, Dad. Nobody's done any harm at Sunbarrow.'

'Give them time, give them time. You mark my words, some newspaper won't be able to resist setting somebody up to make them look fools and themselves superior. It's what they did before. You were too young to remember. It didn't matter whether Jobe Culpepper's car was or wasn't stopped by a light, it was just evil crucifying him like they did. He answered their questions and they made him a laughing stock. I still say it was the press that killed him.'

'All right, Dad, you don't have to get worked up. But this is different. The corn circles are lovely.'

'That won't stop the newspapers making something of it, and I don't want them doing it on my land. I've told Jake, but he goes his own sweet way.'

Poppy said nothing further to make his blood pressure rise, and gradually his gaze softened again as they both watched Kuan-Yin at ease in the garden.

Rex Farenbach came back to see if they were ready for their coffee, and again stood looking out. 'You'd think I had her in mind when I had that Japanese garden made, wouldn't you?'

'Except that she's Chinese,' Nat said.

'Well, yes, but you know what I mean.'

They continued to watch as Kuan-Yin stopped wandering and seated herself on a cedarwood garden seat set beneath the trailing fronds of a willow. Tom came into the scene, and Poppy's heart dropped.

Oh, Tom.

His romantic sixties curls had gone and his hair was cut short, making him look like some American preppie; he was wearing his old, unfashionable grey flannel trousers and white shirt, and was carrying a drink on a tray. The Dragon Lady said something to him and he laughed politely.

Like a waiter.

As Poppy watched, the bronzed Tom Farenbach of the Greek islands – that Tom whose shoulder-length hair had curled behind his ears, and who, dressed in old denims and sleeveless T-shirt, had shaped himself around her closely that night – that romantic and carefree Tom had faded and the old conformist Tom was reinstated.

Poppy noticed that diners at the other two window tables were looking out. All that was happening was that a woman was being served a drink, yet somehow every attention was riveted upon the scene – upon her. The only other person Poppy could think of who had that effect upon people was Mrs Petherbridge. She too never seemed to have to do anything to make people look at her. But Roz Petherbridge didn't have half the class and style of the Dragon Lady. Mrs Petherbridge was just plain sexy.

'That cost me fifteen hundred pounds,' Rex was saying.

'The whole job?' Nat asked, still not turning away from the window.

'What job?'

'Making a garden out of that tatty old bit of land.'

'No . . .' Rex laughed, 'the seat, man. It cost one and a half K.'

Now Nat slowly withdrew his gaze from the garden. 'You mean you paid fifteen hundred quid for a garden bench?'

'It's a one-off, hand-made by a craftsman. Beautiful job, isn't it? It wasn't the dearest.'

Nat frowned and returned his gaze to the window. 'It's no wonder you have to charge eight quid for a bit of bread-and-butter pudding.' It was the kind of forthright thing Poppy was used to hearing from her father, but usually belligerently and not with the faint but genial smile and a touch of irony in his voice.

'Would you like to take your coffee out there?' Rex asked.

'Have we got to buy tickets to have a go on your bench?'

'Compliments of the house, Nat.'

'All right then, why not.' And he left the table eagerly, without reference to Poppy.

Tom didn't move until he saw Poppy and her father coming from the restaurant. 'I'd better dash,' he said. 'We're short-handed.'

'Bring us a couple of brandies with our coffee, lad,' Nat said.

'Tallentire! How triffic, I never expected to see you here.' Kuan-Yin clutched his fingers and drew him to sit beside her. 'And Poppy. Oh you do look great, honey. I just love your hair.' She moved her skirt so that Poppy could sit too. Poppy did not take up the suggestion but lowered herself on to the lushly-growing grass beside the water.

'Look,' she said: 'green, green grass. I thought there wasn't any left.'

Chrissie Pack came out with the coffee and Nat's brandy order and stood looking questioningly at him as to who should have them.

'One for me and one for the lady. Just the coffee for Poppy.'

Poppy rolled her eyes at Chrissie, who grinned as she served the coffee.

'Tom said to tell you he would be getting off at three-thirty.'

'And . . . ?'

Chrissie shrugged. 'He didn't say anything else.' She winked. 'Men's wish is our command, isn't it? You and me could always push off on our own and have a walk round and look at the fairground like we used to, if you like. I'm finished in ten minutes.'

Poppy turned to her father who was listening avidly to something the Dragon Lady was telling him. 'Is it all right if I don't come back with you, Dad? . . . Dad, is it?'

The second or two's pause before he responded indicated that he had probably forgotten that she was there. 'Of course . . . do whatever you want. Dr Yin here is going up to look at the Clump Barrows . . . you'll give me a ride up there?'

Poppy was disconcerted by the look that passed between her father and the Dragon Lady, it was like meaningful arrows in a Victorian illustration. This wasn't her dad. Her dad wasn't like that.

'Of course, honey.' The Dragon Lady took his fingers, familiarly as she had taken Tom's.

'I could come and hold the end of the tape for you.'

'Would you, Tallentire? That's real sweet of you. But I don't want to crowd your lunch date with your daughter.' Now she reached out and touched Poppy, and Poppy saw that was how she was – how Americans were. They were much more into touching people than the English, you saw that on the TV, men slapping one another, a lot of hugging.

FIVE

Leaping through the flames, or joined in circles,
Rustically solemn or in rustic laughter
Lifting heavy feet in clumsy shoes,
Earth feet, loam feet, lifted in country mirth . . .

T. S. ELIOT, Four Quartets

Western people are again beginning to wander the earth giving their atrophied spirits little outings. Visits to Delphi, Easter Island or Iona. Walks to kiss the Stone of Galway, vigils at the Rollright Stones, tours of henges and stone circles. Using vacations to study meditation, yoga, self-awareness. We, the weekday sceptics and searchers after proof, take the human spirit to walk in forests, and undertake gruelling motorway journeys to seashores where we leap with it into the waves. We immerse the spirit in lakeland waters and stand with it on high mountains, ancient tors. Half-believing, we watch the parading of Kali and Mary, and our mouths go dry with anxiety as we wait to see whether the sun will actually rise through the sarsen stones on Salisbury Plain. And when we hear speaking in tongues and watch fertility rites and ancient fire rituals, the human spirit gnaws like Nidhoggr.

Having sent Tom a message that she was going to the fairground, Poppy went off there with Chrissie.

'Let's call for Emma, shall we?' Poppy said. 'It will be like old times.'

Emma Carter was sitting at the check-out in her father's shop. 'Oh, I can't go now, I have to see to the till, the Saturday girl has gone to dinner.'

'Can't your dad do it himself?'

'He doesn't like doing the check-out.' Mocking, she sucked her cheeks in. 'Women's work.'

Chrissie raised her eyebrows and rolled her eyes. 'Oh come on, Emma, ask him.'

'I have to earn my allowance.'

'I wouldn't have wanted to work for my dad,' Chrissie said.

'You go and ask him, Poppy,' Emma said. 'He's more likely to say yes if you ask him.'

'Oh, all right. Where is he?'

Poppy knocked on the stock-room door and called, 'Mr Carter? Can I come in?'

'Is that Poppy? I thought it was. Come on in, I'm just trimming up the flitch your dad ordered for the bowling.'

The room smelled of the side of smoked bacon laid out on a heavy wooden chopping-block. Poppy remembered the room from when she and Emma were little. She had loved being allowed to help Mrs Carter scoop out beans and lentils from drums to fill brown paper bags for the 'Wholefood and Deli' department Mrs Carter had started up at one end of the shop. Mrs Carter's deli, like the off-licence the Carters had taken on, had expanded and prospered.

'Nice side of bacon, think your dad will be pleased? Dare say it won't be long before he sets up his own curing parlour.'

'Oh, I should think he'll be pleased. But I don't eat dead flesh these days.'

'Dear oh dear. You young women these days. You got that many ideas ... opinions about everything.' He covered the bacon with muslin and came to the stainless steel sink to scrub his hands. Myrr had always said: One thing you can rely on in Carter's, is that things are clean.

'What do I owe this visit to then? Haven't seen you hanging round my store since you and our Emma gave up pinching the Mars bars.'

'Did you know we took them?'

'I run a tight ship. One gross in, one gross out, one gross

accounted for. Missing Mars bars was always you and our Emma and missing packets of Rolos is always our Mimm – he still does it.'

He dried his hands on paper towels and straightened the sleeves of his white shoulder-fastened jacket that suggested dentist or doctor rather than grocer. 'And now you want to persuade me that Emma can leave the check-out and go randying off with you.'

Poppy smiled at him. 'I knew you wouldn't mind, Mr Carter.'

'Jez. Makes me feel old a lovely young thing like you calling me Mister. Everybody calls me Jez.'

Poppy couldn't imagine herself calling him Jez. Mr Carter. Emma and Mimm's dad. A touch of anxiety in her midriff.

'I'll bet our Emma put you up to it, though. She was always the one to make the bullets and you was always the one to fire them.'

'Emma's nice. I'm going to miss her if I go to university.'

'What do you mean "if"? I thought it was a foregone conclusion. Your mum's set her heart on it.'

'I know, but I hate counting chickens. I might not get my A-levels. I'd rather think the worst and then it's a nice surprise if it comes all right.'

He gave her shoulders a friendly squeeze. 'Poor little Poppy. I've said to Phil many a time that you had an old head on young shoulders.'

'Emma can come with Chrissie and me to watch them put up the fair, then?' Poppy, knowing that he was going to say yes, put her hand on the door-handle.

He took out a bunch of keys. He didn't appear to have heard her question. She waited as he inserted one in the store-room padlock. He sighed deeply as he reached across to the light-switch. 'Beautiful young shoulders though, young Poppy.'

Walking with Emma and Chrissie towards the field

where the fair was being erected, Poppy functioned on two levels – chatting to her friends whilst deep in thought. Suddenly she couldn't bear it any longer. She had to be on her own. Chrissie and Emma and the fairground were just too much.

'Listen,' she said, breaking into the chat. 'I think I'll have to go and get some Tampax. You go on.'

'No,' Emma said. 'We'll come with you.'

But Poppy ran off before they could protest, calling, 'I won't be long. I'll see you there.' And cutting off down a narrow alleyway she found herself in Goose Grass Lane before she realized it.

Whereas in the years of her early childhood she had spent hours, days and weeks playing here, it was now ages since she had come down Goose Grass Lane. If it were not for the fact of the fairground being erected, then the place would have been echoing the voices of Childencombe's children on holiday from school.

She stepped off the path and on to the children's track that led to the stream. Hazels grew on either side. Many years ago the trees had been coppiced so that now the branches sprang out at an angle from the base of the old trunks.

The cobs were early this year. The hot, dry weeks had started the green nuts ripening weeks before usual. When she had come here nutting three years ago it was to be her last time. Since then that season had become the time of new subjects, new classes and teachers. Three years ago, at fifteen, she had thought that she was already a woman. But, as she now realized, she was still an innocent girl. Being a woman was as of now.

Goose Grass was deserted. Leaves rustled and wood-pigeons made curdled sounds behind their crops. She sat on a railway sleeper the children had dragged from some-where to make a solid dam. Cyril Parker would be after them for that. It was against the rules. If they dammed the stream at all seriously, so that the head of water could not burst through at the end of the day, then Cyril Parker would have to come in and break it up. Cyril – water bailiff and the children's pet ogre – was endlessly patient and left Goose Grass undisturbed from April to October unless they made a solid dam, but then he would put up a notice and keep them away until they had learned to respect the chalk-stream.

Dangling her feet in the same clear water that flowed through Rex Farenbach's garden and beneath Lizz Taylor's millhouse studio, Poppy began to feel in control of her emotions again.

Being a woman was now. Being a woman was having to deal with something you never expected could happen, and dealing with it on your own.

She could hardly believe that he had actually done it. Mr Carter. Emma's dad.

The shocking scene played itself to her in slow motion. She put her hand on the door-handle: Emma can come with Chrissie and me . . . ? As she depressed it, he had reached for the light-switch. In passing, he had deftly slipped his hand up under her loose blouse and briefly cupped his palm under her breast. He had lifted it a little, running the ball of his thumb over her nipple – now the thought struck her – as he did when selling a grapefruit. She had jumped and opened the door. Even then he had not let go but had squeezed gently as he snapped off the light.

The whole thing had not taken more than a few seconds. Then she was back in the normality of the shop where, as though nothing had happened, he went to attend to a man waiting at the off-licence counter. As though nothing had happened. 'Off you go then, Emma. You girls always could twist me round your little fingers.' He had shaken his head at the customer. 'Girls today. They aren't children five minutes.'

The automatic doors had opened for them and suddenly Poppy found herself in the bright sunshine once more and was scarcely conscious of Emma and Chrissie as they had all made their way through the village. The tacky scene vivid. Her indignation and anger repressed.

Why didn't I say something? Why didn't I shout, 'Don't!'? I bloody trusted him . . . I bloody trusted him because he's Emma's dad. How could he! The dirty old man, the bloody dirty old man. Heavy tears ran down her face. Their feel was irritating; she smeared them away.

She had looked down at the breast expecting some visible sign of his touch. And then, as she had walked with Emma and Chrissie, she had become sensitive to its every movement beneath her black muslin top, aware that she was repeating with every step the bounce that he had given it.

Sitting on the end of the railway sleeper with her feet dangling, Poppy had a sense of things falling apart.

Tom Farenbach who had appeared so romantic and sophisticated on the Greek island had reverted to the old Tom serving his father's customers.

Rin, who had always been there, reliable in his brotherly pigeon-hole, was about to become a divorced man. It was so unlike the old, safe Rin, to suddenly turn up at home unexpectedly.

Her father, for whose attention she had never had to compete, had this morning forgotten her presence whilst he had flirted about with that American shrink.

And . . . Emma Carter's dad had groped her as casually as though she was one of the slags who hung about the bus shelter near the college.

Before the holiday in Greece her future had seemed to be happy and uncomplicated; now, suddenly, it was spoiled – not least her friendship with Emma. Even now she felt embarrassed at the thought of what it would be like being with her. She folded her arms across her chest. She shouldn't wear a top like this.

She withdrew her feet from the cool stream, dried them on her skirt, put on her espadrilles again and sat hugging her knees. Why shouldn't I wear whatever top I want? If I wear no top at all, he's got no right to think he can touch me.

Emma and Chrissie would wonder where she had got to.

And Myrr . . . What was wrong with her parents all of a sudden? What was it that had got into her mother? She had sensed it when Myrr had come to the station to meet them off the train. Poppy had seen her mother waving and had sensed that there was something changed. It wasn't just the blonde hair – Myrr had often had it darkened or reddened – nor was it Myrr's pleasure at having got the car she had wanted – Poppy was familiar with her mother in one of those moods. A couple of times over the last day or two, Poppy had thought that Myrr was about to tell her something, but had changed her mind when it came to it. Perhaps she was pregnant . . . perhaps she was having an affair . . . being pregnant wasn't likely to account for Myrr's light-heartedness. Myrr had pulled Dad's leg about the Dragon Lady, but didn't seem bothered about it.

They were just too normal to be doing things like having affairs. Yet the way her dad had looked at the Dragon Lady was disturbing.

But . . . who seemed more ordinary and normal than Emma Carter's dad? He was old and going bald, he wasn't even good-looking like her dad was and yet he had . . . She flinched. A fifty-year-old tubby grocer had bloody groped her. It was revolting.

A dry twig snapped and she leaped to her feet. Further upstream she saw Cyril Parker making his way along the river bank. More than once, over the years, she, along with a gang of other guilty village children up to tricks with the flow of the stream, had fled from Cyril. Again she fled, springing lightly along the familiar track that led through the woods to Goose Grass Lane.

This time she did not know why she fled from him, he was a really-really nice man. But until today Poppy would have said that Emma's father was a really-really nice man.

At Sunbarrow Farm, Roz Petherbridge opened her eyes to a sloping, beamed ceiling and for a moment thought that she was back in the attic room at Ridge House, until the sunshine coming in at the leaded lights reminded her that she was at Myrr Tallentire's. She had intended to put her feet up for only a few minutes but had fallen asleep. Somebody had thrown a light cover over her, so she guessed that Myrr had been in.

Sitting on the edge of the bed and looking out across the acres and acres of ripening corn, she felt wonderfully at peace. Myrr had taken things in hand and gone with her to see Duncan. At Ridge House, the garden had been sorted out and bits and pieces of repainting and repair had been done: it really looked quite splendid.

He had kissed her in a friendly way on the cheek and said that it was nice to see her, then taken her in through the porch which had been cleared of its collection of Roz's geraniums and bits of cuttings in yogurt pots. In the hallway the floor had been cleared of its usual accumulation of family detritus and polished so that the oak stripwood showed its grain beautifully. It looked very much like the house which, when they had first moved in, she had always expected it to become – and might have, had it not been for the ennui of their marriage and awful lack of money.

'Everything looks beautiful, Duncan.'

He had made a deprecating gesture. 'I got some garden people out of the Yellow Pages, and the estate agents found some women called Cooks and Bottlewashers or something.'

'Estate agents?'

'Just a valuation. We're not committed. They reckon about 350K.'

'Three hundred and fifty thousand pounds? That's ten times what we paid for it.'

'We'll have to talk about it.'

Myrr had declined Duncan's invitation to go into the house and was waiting in the garden where Roz could see her sitting by the lily-pond, its stonework revealed and restored. Roz had expected to feel overflowing with emotion and to find Duncan uptight, but going back had been quite easy. She had smiled: 'I feel like a prospective buyer.'

'You said that you had something important . . .'

'I'm sorry, they shouldn't have phoned me, they should have phoned you direct.'

'Who should?'

'It's your brother.'

He had only one brother, but he asked, 'Patrick phoned?'

'No. It's Patrick who is ill. I'm afraid it's bad news. He's in hospital. He's really terribly ill.'

'Who phoned?'

'Malcolm.'

'What is it, his heart?'

Roz had shaken her head. 'Worse . . . it's AIDS.'

From Duncan's expression one would have thought that he had never heard of the condition. 'Patrick has AIDS?'

'Malcolm says he's very ill, Duncan.'

He had not gone to pieces as she had done, but was the perfect clergyman faced with human tragedy. 'Poor Roz. I wish that they had phoned me.'

'I expect Malcolm didn't want to be the one to give you such terrible news. He always chickened out when it came to . . .' She had been going to say: Things like this. But there had never been anything like this until now.

He had gone to the well-stocked drinks table, poured

them both large scotches and, indicating the bottle, said, 'What about Myrr?'

'No, she never does when she's driving. Will you go out there?'

'He's my only brother.'

Sitting on the arm of the sofa, he raised his glass in a half-hearted gesture – 'Cheers' – and downed a mouthful, gripping his teeth and tightening his lips at the sting. Roz walked to the window and thought: I could live here. If Duncan just ceased to exist I could be happy here. And she glimpsed herself some time in the next century, an old lady in a cliché of a battered straw hat tending the kind of garden that featured in magazines and TV programmes.

'Can I do anything?'

'I don't think so. I was preparing to fly out there anyway. There's some advertising man on the West Coast who Rupert has persuaded to do something for the charity.'

'Didn't you know that Patrick was gay, Duncan?' She had been surprised how calmly she was able to ask because of her swallowed anger.

'Gay? Patrick's not gay.'

'What do you mean, he's not?' She had felt her face flush. He was still telling himself lies. Just as he always had done, telling himself what he wanted to believe. 'Don't be stupid, Duncan. For God's sake, at least once in your life face up to something. Your brother is dying of AIDS.' She drank off her whisky. 'And our sons are out there with him.'

He had then come to where she was standing and, cupping the side of her head in his hand had turned her face to him. 'That's better, you haven't looked directly at me since you came in. I know you well enough to tell that you are in one of those states where it won't take much to make you explode . . . and I don't want that.'

Now, leaning on the bedroom windowsill at Sunbarrow, Roz recalled that, for a brief moment, she had felt herself aroused by him and she had seen the same in his own look.

She wondered what might have happened had she responded differently. What if she had rested her head in his hand? His fingers would have wound around her hair, she would have closed her eyes and he would have kissed her. That was how it had once been. A long time ago, it would have happened like that. They would have gratified one another quickly and then gone to bed and been languorously generous to one another. That was how it had once been . . . a long time ago.

Instead, she had pulled away before he had scarcely touched her. 'Of course I feel like exploding. I'm afraid. I've been nearly sick with worry. I imagined what it would be like getting another call, this time to say that . . .'

'That what? Go on . . . that what?'

She remembered that same expression in his voice many times over the years: Stop being so damned hooked on crises. Make yourself say it, Rosamund. Say it. Listen to yourself, you're just making a crisis out of a piddling little problem.

Suddenly, she had felt ridiculous. Outside herself, she saw the mother that she'd always been – he was right – the mother who was always sure that an earache was meningitis; that a tin of corned beef they had just eaten was one of a batch being recalled because of some deadly contamination; that any small swelling was malign.

'I had the idea that Patrick might have wanted a couple of young . . .'

'Young what . . . lovers? That Patrick asked them to go out to Los Angeles for the purpose of buggering them?'

That had always been his technique to turn away her point of view. The rough side of his tongue and coarseness. 'Don't, Duncan.'

'Don't what?'

She didn't reply.

'I thought when you phoned to say that you had to come

to see me that you might have been going to say that you wanted to come back. I was pleased, really pleased. I thought about what a pleasant sort of a life we could live here. But it's not on, is it?'

Roz had shaken her head.

Thinking about it now, until the moment when she had felt his hand on her head, she had supposed that they had parted company on the Sunday afternoon when she had walked out into the downpour and jumped on the train to Southampton. They hadn't really parted until that moment when she felt as though she was being offered a choice – turn and kiss him, or turn away? The restored Ridge House, money, security, travel and the position of administrator's wife was the one option – insecurity, tatty accommodation and freedom to be Ms Redhead the other.

The air out in the cornfields was still and hot. The only movement was that of the fast-ripening corn and the only sound was that of shrilling larks and the rustle of bristles in acre upon acre of barley – or perhaps it was the distant rush of motorway traffic. The crust of the red earth and lumpy chalk was crisp underfoot and the sky was an amazing clear blue against which the dark green boughs of the barrow yews looked black.

Nat had helped Kuan-Yin to measure and photograph the barrows and taken her on to where the Queer Stone sat in its pit out of which green blades of grass grew in what must be the only moist patch anywhere about. The stone was a quite beautiful object, appearing more sculpted than natural, weathered, and pitted with holes of differing size. If there had once been corners and sharp edges they had been eroded into undulating curves.

'Come this side and half-close your eyes.'

Kuan-Yin did as he bid her and stood with her back to him. 'What am I supposed to see?'

'I always thought it looked like a kind of Buddha, or perhaps a fat cat with no ears.'

She held her head this way and that. 'Maybe. Ah . . . I see, I see. Those indentations could be eyes.' She turned to him, exaggerating the slant of her own eyes with her middle fingers. 'What sort of stone is it? It looks kinda strange with all those holes.'

'I haven't a clue, we don't have yellow stone in Hampshire. Here, put your finger into one of the holes.'

She did so.

'There,' he said. 'What do you feel?'

She felt around and then tried another and another. 'Hell,' she said, looking at the faint marks on her forefinger; 'they're spirals.'

Nat shrugged his shoulders. 'I had a cowman once who said he'd seen another piece down in Devon somewhere and it was reckoned to be a thunderbolt.'

'With spirals?' She held out a hand and grasped one of his. 'It is so warm, let's sit in the cool, Tallentire honey.'

'Your air-conditioning puts sweat-glands out of gear I shouldn't wonder.' Nat allowed himself to be led into the shade of the yews where it was cool and from where, settled with their backs against the rough terracotta bark, they could see down over the acres of restless barley.

'It's lovely here. I'm glad you came with me. I wondered whether I would be welcome at Sunbarrow again.'

Thoughtfully, he ran his fingers through his spiky hair. 'I should have thought it was more that the boot was on the other foot and you wouldn't have come back again.'

'Not come again? More than anything, I wanted to come.' She took his hand and stroked her cheek with his knuckles.

Turning slightly to look at her, he studied her from head to foot. 'Dammit, woman, I'm a worn-out farmer. Why would a beautiful creature like you want . . .'

She stopped his words with the palm of her hand and then fingered his beard. 'I like unique and enigmatic men. Rare men, like you. When I first saw you in church, I knew that I would not go back to the States until I had got to know you. I think . . . I assumed . . . hoped that something would happen between us. You looked so . . . ? So unknowable that I guess I made up my mind that I would know you.'

He grasped her hand. 'You aren't going back? No.'

'Not yet, but it's my home, it's where I work. I have to go back.'

Taking her at first gently, and then more urgently he kissed her. 'Don't go away. Please. I couldn't bear it.'

She pulled back a little way and studied his face. 'You're serious. Oh, don't, Tallentire. You've got a good marriage, your family, your farm, everything. You're terrific, I have enormous respect for you, but I'd never bust up any marriage. I don't hold with the idea of sin, or any of that crap . . . I mean I don't think that it exists, it's something thought up by men who saw an easy way of keeping control, so I don't have hang-ups about sleeping with whoever I like so long as nobody gets hurt. But I do hold with stable relationships and it's stupid to destabilize wantonly. You have a good marriage. You wouldn't last five minutes outside it . . .'

'I'd chance it. We've only one hand to play, and it wasn't until last year that I suddenly saw that I had thrown away most of my best cards. You're my ace of trumps, and I won't waste you.' He thought he read the signs of panic on her face. He did, but he mistook the reason for it. He could hardly know that he sounded so sure of himself and of her, that she was thinking that she would not be able to put a stop to the affair.

'Tallentire, I don't go in for long-term relationships.' She held his shoulders, talking to him as though he might not understand her language. 'I'm a loose woman, honey. I sleep around. I've had three different men since I've been in Childencombe.'

He was surprised that he didn't feel any jealousy. Perhaps he knew, perhaps her assuredness that she was her own woman was part of what attracted him. 'Rex?'

'It doesn't matter who. It's the way I am. If I need food, I get myself a meal; if I need sex, I get myself a man.'

He frowned. 'I don't believe you.'

'Tallentire, I sleep around. Less these days – at least not so thoughtlessly as I did once – I take more care, but I'm a psychologist, I know my problem and I don't want it sorted out.'

'If you had wanted a quick bit of sex, there are plenty of young bloaks who'd have given you that – our Jake wouldn't have needed asking twice. I don't believe you. I know a she-animal on heat when I see one, and you weren't that.'

She turned away from him, letting her gaze roam free across the wide, golden acres of his farmland. He said nothing and they sat close, but not touching, quiet and cool in the shade of the ancient trees. She took out a cigarette and handed him her lighter. As he touched the flame to the tip, she looked up at him, lowered her eyes, drew deeply on the tobacco, then let the smoke out in a stream.

He watched her, his emotions quite under control, his agitation showing only in the way he pulled at individual hairs in his beard.

At last she said, 'You're right, it wasn't like that.'

He waited, but she said no more. 'Then what was it like?'

She shook her head.

'Tell me. You will go back to America and I shall go on growing old.'

'Oh balls, Tallentire. Don't try the hearts and flowers, I see through that kind of thing every day.'

'It's not balls, I must know what it meant to you. Do

you want me landing up on your doorstep? I shall need a brain doctor if you don't talk to me about why you seduced me. You did, I wouldn't have dared. But by God I wanted to.'

'So did I.'

'Then just tell me – what was it like? I'm not asking for comparisons with your Mike Alexanders, I don't mean performances – I'm a bloody farmer, I know when a bull or a ram is doing his stuff – I mean what did it actually mean to you?'

Fiercely she ground out the cigarette and putting her arms about his neck, kissed him aggressively. 'OK, I'll tell you! I guess I thought I'd found the thing I have been searching for since I was twelve years old. Maybe I thought that I had found that half of me that was always missing and that I need to make me function. Who knows? All that I know is that it was sublime, an out-of-body experience.' She laughed and tugged his beard. 'What crap I talk at times! It was a total in-body experience. It was ecstatic. It was fulfilling. Did you ever see the movie *The Man Who Fell to Earth*?'

Under normal circumstances, Nat would never admit to having wasted time on such a film. 'That skinny singer?'

'When he remembers what it was like to make love to his wife on their home planet . . . they coalesced.'

'I know the bit.'

'It was like that.'

He nodded, wryly. 'Without the spacesuits.'

'And, for Christ's sake – it was so crazy that I can hardly believe that it happened – underlit by floodlights . . . I mean! Oh, Tallentire!'

He was still as still except for his eyes which moved up and down and back and forth, taking in every detail as she laughed. She threw herself back and lay with her head on his knees.

'Somebody saw us, you know.'

Now, it hardly seemed to matter. He ran one hand over her features and the other over the profile of her torso. 'That don't surprise me. Myrr's pool isn't exactly a dewpond, is it? It's a wonder it didn't attract half the village. Only person I saw was you. Was it our Jake?'

She looked up at him. 'You really don't care, do you?'

'I'd care if it was Myrr or Poppy, but I know it couldn't have been. Nobody fetched the police . . .' He gave her a wry smile.

'Lizz Taylor came across the garden. I caught a glimpse.'

He raised his eyebrows in interest now. Nat Tallentire's smiles were more an expression in his eyes than any movement of his lips. He smiled. 'Did she now?'

'She hot-footed it away. I guess the secret's safe with her.'

'It wasn't wrong.'

'Why are you so blasé about it? Do you lay other women?'

A flare of anger that died down at once. 'I've never been with another woman! I haven't ever wanted to. And it wasn't like that . . . you just said so yourself.'

'Then what was it like, Tallentire? I'd sure like to know.'

He fell silent. On the still afternoon air, the motorway traffic and barleyfield sound was joined by fairground organ music coming from the direction of the village. The western face of the earth was beginning to turn towards the sun. 'There was a time in the old days when they picked a couple to perform publicly. In mythology they were chosen to become god and goddess for the time it took to make the fields fertile.' He smiled. 'I often wondered whether it wasn't that humans didn't quite trust the gods to know how to do it, so they laid on a sort of demonstration – country people are like that, you know, we think nobody knows anything except us.'

Her eyes crinkled in amusement.

He continued. 'I felt that it was that kind of thing . . . a pagan rite. I felt joyful. Christ, yes! That's what . . . bloody joyful. I can't say I felt that many times in my life.'

'It was innocent?'

'I don't know about that. What's innocence? But I had no bad feeling then, and I haven't now. There never was when the village watched its green man and its corn queen. I reckon you're right about sin . . . that only came on the scene when they stopped people having decent sorts of gods with human flaws, and went in for having just the one with a capital G.'

'I noticed that you didn't join in when I saw you in church. If you're a pagan why do you go?'

'I never said that . . . though you might be right. I like the place. There's been some kind of worshipping place there since Saxon times, probably a lot longer ago than that. When I'm there, I get a real sense of all the other Tallentires there must have been before me. Maybe it's Tallentire bones that fed these yews.'

'These trees aren't old enough.'

'No, but you get the general idea. You understand . . . being part of a whole something? There's times when I stand up on the ridge and imagine myself rooting there like a willow sapling. You know about willow? Break a piece off, jam it into a place where it belongs and it will root. You can't spend your whole life looking after the land and not feel part of it.' He ran his hands tenderly over her face and neck. 'The Tallentire spirit is in these fields close to the house.'

'And after you?'

He pursed his lips and gazed inwardly. 'I don't know.' Shaking his head.

'What about Jake?'

'He's a Jeavons. Only Tallentire by name. This place needs somebody who feels something for it. Jake's all full of queer ideas. I think if he had his way he'd go back to the old strip-fields and let everybody grow for themselves.

If it was left to him he'd put the clock back two hundred years, he'd go back to relying on muck and luck like my father. Land has got to be farmed intensively these days. All this talk about agrochemicals being harmful. Look at that,' indicating the acre upon endless acre of ripening barley, 'nobody ever saw a crop like that when I was a lad. New strains of seed. Feed and keep feeding the land, stuff it to its eyeballs with the minerals and trace elements that growing takes out; feed the land and the land will feed you, that's all you've got to remember.'

'What about pâté de foie gras, Tallentire?'

He frowned at her.

'The goose dies, honey. It gets so sick from being stuffed full of nourishment that its liver packs up.'

'Jake been getting at you?'

'No.'

'Won't you talk about . . . us? What are we going to do?'

'Nothing, Tallentire. There is nothing left to say that hasn't been said. You do know that.'

'I shan't give up.' This time he grinned, crinkling his eyes, almost laughing as though having recently learned the art he was hooked on it. He leaned across and kissed her gently. 'I put Rin's little dragon in the glove compartment of your car. I want you to have it.'

'Won't Rin mind?'

'He made it for me, and gave it to me. He knows it's probably as important a token as I've ever had . . . he knows how I feel about it. That's why I want to give it to you. If Rin needs to know why I gave it to you, then I won't mind telling him.'

Now it was she who bent over him, but she neither kissed nor touched him, but for long moments looked at him with a serious expression which still did not entirely obsure the turmoil she was feeling.

After a few minutes he said, 'It'll be all right. Just don't do anything until we have talked about it. Please.' An unusual word in Nat Tallentire's mouth when spoken in that tone of voice.

'All right, but that doesn't mean anything. You understand, Tallentire? It doesn't mean anything except that we'll meet again and we'll talk.'

'That's all right.' His eyes crinkled happily. 'I reckon I ought to get down to the fairground. I promised I'd help a bit.' He handed her to her feet and gave her a brief, warm kiss upon her mouth. 'It's the one night and the one place where you can still get a whiff of the old green man and the corn queen.'

'Before they got the God with a capital G?'

'Ah, and before they invented things like sin and guilt.'

'The very things that keep Manhattan shrinks in business.' She laughed. 'Just think, Tallentire, if hadn't been for sin and guilt I might never have been able to afford this trip.'

Roz Redhead was the name she intended to use from here on.

At Sunbarrow, now refreshed and wide awake, she went downstairs. On the landing floor was a note: *Roz, I didn't like to wake you. I've gone down to see how things are going for the fair. Everybody seems to have gone somewhere. Food in fridge, make yourself a drink. Come down to the field if you like, or have a swim – spare things are in the changing hut. I'll be back during the evening.*

The idea of a swim wooed her out into the golden afternoon sun.

An entire swimming-pool to oneself was the height of luxury. The surface of the water was glassy in the warm, still air. The faint sound of the fairground music came up from the village. As she poised on the edge looking down, a small glittering object caught her eye. She dived in and came up with a long, beautiful earring. Certainly gold and very expensive-looking. Not Myrr's style and too classy for Poppy.

After about half an hour, Roz climbed out on to the warm surround, dried herself, and tied on her cotton skirt and top. She was about to pull on her pants and sandals when she heard quiet laughing voices, and saw through a small gap in the border an astonishing tableau. Beside a Jaguar car that was hidden from the house was a slim woman kissing some sort of a toy animal, then drawing Nat Tallentire into a long, kissing clinch.

From the height and stature, she had thought for a second that the man was Jake, which would not have been surprising, but clearly it was Nat. She could not draw her gaze from the riveting scene. The woman wrapped her arms about his neck, and Roz could not control a prickle of arousal from the sensuous way the woman drew Nat towards her and the way he responded, pressing her petite body to his large frame, wrapping his long arms well about her.

Nat had always been a very handsome man, tall, with a hard and muscular body from years of physical labour, but Roz had never known him to have either a wandering eye or a wandering hand. Even on that jamboree of misrule Ship Fair, she had never known Nat to have any sort of a fling with another woman. She had taken him to be a high-minded and moralistic type: certainly when she and Duncan had lived in Childencombe, Roz would never have dared to joke or flirt with him when she was about her parish work as she often did with more responsive men. Nat was introverted and Roz liked extroverts. But . . . look at that! Roz watched, fascinated, as he ran his hands down the young woman's back. When her conscience got the better of her and it dawned upon her that she was being a voyeur she slipped out through the border, clutching her pants and sandals, and went quickly and quietly away.

When she felt safe from discovery, she finished dressing. Her hair was wet and her bag was in the house where she didn't want to go in case they came in, so she decided to walk down to the village. God only knew how she would face Myrr. Why had they been so careless? She could only suppose that they believed they were out of sight. But anyone could have been sitting where she had been, Myrr, Poppy, anyone.

Nat Tallentire . . . of all people. For the second time that day, Roz felt the ground shift beneath her feet.

The day of Ship Fair was for villagers only. Outsiders could not be stopped from coming to Childencombe, but they could be kept from entering the enclosed area on the edge of the village close to Goose Grass.

This was the day that Nat had said had its roots in the mists of history, the day when they let down their hair. The safety-valve. This was the day when all the traditional contests were held. Although modern-day inhabitants of the village did not go in for bare-fist fights, bull-baiting, ring-dances by flower-bedecked virgins and youths, nor fertility rites and blood sacrifices, there were still events that derived from a more pagan community. On Ship Fair Day village bobbies and local vicars usually found it politic to be away from home. In spite of their corn dollies and intellectual knowledge of *The Golden Bough*, none of the newcomelatelys had come to be accepted except in supporting roles.

When Duncan had first been vicar here, he and Roz had made history by remaining in the village and turning up in kaftans. So she did not feel like an intruder as she walked down to the field.

Myrr, Lizz Taylor and Jake were setting up the traditional Sunbarrow contribution of a simple bowling alley, next to which was a small pen in which a young pig rooted around. The pig was the prize for a winner who wanted to rear or butcher it, but most were better pleased with the flitch that Sunbarrow paid for.

'Oh look, here's Roz. Is your hair wet?'

'I . . . ah . . . had a swim and thought I'd let it dry out on my walk here.'

The partial collapse of the pig pen ended any more discussion on that score.

Jake asked, 'You didn't happen to see the Old Man, did you? He was supposed to be looking out the bowling balls.'

'He wasn't in the house,' Roz said.

'I thought he'd be back by now. Didn't Poppy say that he'd just gone with the Dragon Lady to do something up at the barrows?' Jake said.

'I wouldn't be surprised,' Myrr answered laconically.

'Now, Mum,' Jake said. 'You should be pleased he's got somebody at last who's interested.'

'I know,' Myrr said. 'I am. She's really very nice.'

'But just a bit much?' Lizz was trying to think what she would have said had she not had the swimming-pool scene at the front of her mind.

Myrr smiled enigmatically.

Roz, also conscious of the more recent scene and feeling that at any moment her cheeks would burst out in an embarrassed flush, said, 'I seem to be spare here: for goodness' sake somebody, give me something to do.'

'You could have a walk round and find Poppy. Tell her we're going over to the tea tent if she wants us.' The tea tent being less to do with tea than with a powerful barley wine and a strong ale brewed especially for Ship Saturday.

By now, Poppy had regained some of her composure and was wandering around with Emma and Chrissie amongst the travelling people who were erecting the rides and roundabouts.

When they had been in Greece, like Poppy and Tom, Emma Carter and Matt Pridhoe had paired up and, like

Tom, Emma had thrown off her rather sullen but dutiful air, born of generations of poor rural workers. Now though, Poppy thought, like Tom Emma was slipping back into her old role of grocer's daughter.

'Why didn't you wear that super skirt and top you bought, Emma?' Poppy asked.

'Mum said it wasn't decent.'

'Why not? You couldn't see anything through it.'

'You could if you stood with the light behind you.'

'Only your legs.'

'Well that's what she means.'

Chrissie said, 'You've got a nice pair of legs, Em, what's wrong with showing them off? Anyway, that dress you've got on makes you look old-fashioned.'

'Thank you very much!'

'Oh, Em,' Chrissie placated her. 'You know what I mean, you're ever so pretty . . . my mum reckons you're the prettiest girl in the village. You ought to make the most of yourself.'

'You should have seen her when we were abroad,' Poppy said. 'She wore her hair up all the time, didn't you, Emma? And she's got smashing boobs when she lets them out.'

Emma flushed. 'This isn't abroad though, is it?'

Poppy thought that Emma sounded almost bitter and fell silent. There had been so much talk everywhere lately about abuse and incest, but it was like AIDS and smoking, you sort of knew that it must be true but it was hard to take it personally if it didn't affect you. But the smoking thing had come home to her when she had seen her dad in hospital. Emma's father wouldn't . . . ? But he had done it to herself which was as bad. Perhaps Mrs Carter knew what he was like. Perhaps it was why she had been so keen for Emma to go off with the youth group – Mrs Carter wasn't usually like that. Yesterday Poppy could not have believed such ideas possible.

Today she could.

Even probable.

It had seemed such a familiar gesture to him, that it could hardly have been the first time he had fondled a girl in passing. Then Poppy remembered Daisy saying something, when they had been mulling over the possibility of Poppy going to university: 'Don't let the male tutors persuade you to go for any private tutorials.'

Myrr had said: 'For goodness' sake, Daisy! Not all men are like that.'

And Daisy had said: 'Ha!'

Poppy snapped out of it. 'Who's coming to see if they've got the ferris wheel ready?'

'I'll soon have to go to work,' Chrissie said. 'I'm on the tea tent.'

On Ship Saturday afternoon, as soon as each of the rides was erected and tested, the children and young people of the village were allowed to ride free. It was always impossible to get on the bumper cars for little boys who, having once secured a car, would not give it up until they were turned off physically. The ferris wheel was already turning slowly when the girls reached it, and an oily-fingered young man, having fed his own image of devil-may-care with a bit of back-chat and suggestive eyebrow raising, stopped the wheel for them.

With Chrissie in the middle, they rose slowly up into the hot July air. At the apogee of the wheel's cycle it stopped again and they were left hanging with a view over their home village.

'Look,' Chrissie pointed. 'It looks like that model village we saw when we went with the school to the Isle of Wight. There's the Green Man, it do look little. It isn't often you think about it as being like that . . . you know, everything fitting in with everything else.'

Poppy found the corner of the field where the little group of people must be where they were fixing up the bowling.

'I can't see my dad down there, perhaps I ought to go and see if Myrr wants any help.'

'Oh, let's just have a couple of goes round first,' Emma said. 'I love the big wheel. I think that's what I should like to be – the owner of a ferris wheel.'

'You'd always have to be away from home,' Chrissie said. 'I couldn't abear that. I wouldn't want to go off to some university miles away like Poppy. I don't like it when I don't sleep in my own bed.'

'I do,' said Emma emphatically. 'I loved it in Greece. Once, we had to sleep rough, didn't we, Poppy? It was super. I wished it wouldn't ever end.'

'I didn't know you liked it that much,' Poppy said.

The wheel moved on one to allow somebody else on.

Chrissie said, 'That's because our Poppy was all took up with Tom, wasn't it?'

Emma said, 'I thought you would have been with Tom today. I was surprised when you came in to call for me.'

'We always come, the three of us. Ship Saturday wouldn't be the same if we didn't do this, would it?' Poppy said.

The wheel was now full and beginning to circle faster. Chrissie rocked the gondola, and Poppy and Emma laughed and protested. The youth with the oily fingers waved and whistled as they passed. Poppy caught a glimpse of Mrs Petherbridge, who waved. Chrissie shouted, 'There's your dad, Em, he must have shut up the shop.' Mr Carter was craning his neck, looking upwards at the passing gondolas full of laughing girls and whistling youths. Emma did not look in his direction. 'I expect my mum's looking after it.' As they passed him a second time, Chrissie said, 'There he is again: hold down your skirts, girls.'

Fortunately, when they stopped Poppy was able to turn her back on Mr Carter and go to Mrs Petherbridge. She heard him saying, 'Emma, I want you to nip home and fetch me that red scarf for the tug-of-war.' And Emma's reply: 'Oh no, Dad, that's not fair, you go, it's your game. You said I could come with the girls.'

To Poppy's amazement Emma did not submit to doing exactly as she was told as she usually did, but went off with Poppy and Chrissie to where Roz was standing.

'You was brave, Em,' Chrissie said. 'You don't usually stand up to your dad like that.'

Poppy didn't know what to make of Emma's look. 'No, I don't, do I?'

Whenever Roz saw Poppy, she wished that she had a daughter like her. Most of the young girls Roz spoke to these days had come to the Centre, traumatized from some encounter with some violent man, so it was gratifying to see these three girls high on the ferris wheel, laughing as light-heartedly as she herself at eighteen.

'Are you stopping over, Mrs Petherbridge?'

'Your mother has twisted my arm.'

'Good, it's nice having visitors.'

'Oh well, I don't feel so much of an intruder, then.'

'Myrr will be pleased, she likes you better than anybody.'

Such a spontaneous comment made Roz feel quite flushed with pleasure. Myrr would never have said so herself. She had got over her own overreaction to the news about Patrick and, having seen Duncan and made a decision, she was in a better mood than she had been in for ages.

'And I like Myrr. It's not difficult, she's such a nice person.'

They had reached the tea tent, where Chrissie went on duty serving ale and Emma volunteered to help wash glasses. Myrr and the others had not arrived and Poppy bought drinks for them both.

'I feel such a fool,' Roz said. 'I just walked out, didn't even bring my bag, not even a comb.'

'It's nice to change places for once. You've bought me plenty of Cokes in the past.' They sat at one of the tables already littered with empty glasses and plates.

Roz said, 'You don't have to sit with me if you want to go with your friends.'

'It's all right, I'd rather. Chrissie's got to work. Unless you'd like to have a walk up home. You could get your bag and I could fetch the bowling balls and I could change into something else.'

'That's lovely.'

Poppy pulled at her cropped top. 'It's hardly decent.'

'With a tilt like yours have got, nobody would complain if you went topless.'

They took the bridleway from the fair field to Sunbarrow. The sun was sliding down towards evening, and the air was golden and heavy with pollen from the Sunbarrow crops. The ground was dust dry and where in winter the water running from the downland had made runnels, the bared chalk was knobbly and fissured. As they walked, white dust puffed up at every step and settled on their sandals.

'It's going to be hot for dancing this evening.'

'Not as hot as dancing in Greece.'

'Of course, you're not long back. And you went with Emma Carter and some others, didn't you? It's nice to see that you're still friendly with Emma.'

Poppy nodded, Roz thought, half-heartedly.

'You always seemed an unlikely pair, even when you were little. Emma's such a . . .'

'Mouse?'

'Well, perhaps I should say that she always seems so timid and you always seem to have that much extra life in you.'

Pausing, Poppy looked into the distance for a few

seconds. 'If I'm honest, Emma and me haven't ever been very close, it's Chrissie and me who are proper friends. Everybody says we are, even we say we are, but I think it's more like loyalty or something – for me anyway. Emma would be hurt if she didn't think I was her friend, but really it's only because we started school together and then went on to the same sixth form . . . Gosh, what a relief to have said that out loud. Do you understand what I mean?'

'I do.' Roz didn't reply at once, pausing as they neared Sunbarrow and the image of Nat and the American woman returned. She would have liked to be able to tell someone about that. 'It can be just the same when you start having boyfriends. You go out with one a couple of times, and maybe you meet his friends, and then you go to his house, and his parents think: Thank goodness he hasn't got himself a bimbo, and your friends think he's a swinger – what's street-language for "swinger" these days? – anyway, it isn't long before everybody thinks of you as a couple . . . you even begin to think it yourself. And if you aren't careful that's what you become, whether you ought to be or not.'

'Is that what happened to you and Mr Petherbridge? I'm sorry . . . is it all right me asking you?'

Roz shrugged. 'I don't mind. Ours was that other kind of mistake – being caught on the rebound by somebody who is physically attractive.'

'Mr Petherbridge?'

Roz laughed, 'Yes, Poppy, Duncan Petherbridge. You might not think so, but he was an extremely attractive young man twenty years ago.'

'Oh, I didn't mean . . . You know . . . it's just that I only knew him as the vicar when I was in Sunday school. It's awful, I know, but to me then he was an old man who wore a long black dress on Sundays . . . I mean . . . he was quite good fun and all that.'

Roz laughed again. 'You're right, he went from being my young man in a long coloured dress – he used to wear a kaftan and ponytail when I first met him – to your old man in a long black dress.'

'Do you mind talking about it? I mean, Mum has said that you and he . . . had split up . . . well, that you've gone to live in Southampton.'

'No, I don't mind. In fact it's nice to talk to somebody like you. Young people usually cut right through all the nonsense older people use to dress up problems. Either that, or we hide our eyes so that we don't really see a problem until it's too late: there are usually enough mean little problems to sort out, without tackling the big ones. Sufficient unto the day and all that. You just hope that if you ignore it long enough then it will go away. Of course it never does.'

Poppy, idly pulling the seedheads from ripe grass, said thoughtfully, 'Do you think it would be better if people always said what they think straight away . . . I mean . . . if something happens to make a friendship fail, or a relationship . . . is it better to do something about it at once, even if it is hurtful . . . ?'

Roz made a moue, inwardly wondering what would happen if she were to do something about what she knew about Nat. 'Lord above, Poppy, Claire Rayner makes a fortune answering that kind of question. Actually, I tried to live with it . . . mostly for the boys, only partly because of inertia. I think though, on the whole it's probably best to do something as soon as you discover you've made a mistake. Not so much time wasted. Soonest ended – soonest mended.'

'I've decided to tell Tom Farenbach that it's over.'

'Tom? I didn't know it had begun.'

'It hardly has. Oh, he was so different when we were away.'

'You don't sound particularly heartbroken.'

'No. Disillusioned . . . maybe a bit sorry that the Greek island Tom wasn't true.'

'Classic ship board romance, Poppy. When we touch land our feet turn to clay. Perhaps it's as well. Now you can go off to university footloose and fancy free.'

Poppy opened a five-bar gate between the bridleway and the pathway running beside Clump Field, and as they emerged from the hedgerow Roz saw with relief that the American woman's car had gone. Concentrating on fastening the gate, Poppy said with obvious casualness, 'Would you have been disappointed if Ian and Malcolm had turned down the chance of university?'

'I don't know. Well, yes, I suppose I would have. I expect that we should have been more disappointed than they would have. I wish now though that I had tried to persuade them to choose an English university. But then, we never know how these things are going to turn out.'

'Aren't they happy in America?'

'Oh, I think so . . . it's a long, long story. Anyway, surely you haven't got any doubts? You've always wanted university.'

When they were within a few hundred yards of the house, Poppy said, 'How do you think my mum would take it if I didn't go?'

'I think she'd say the same as I would. I know she set her mind on all you children getting the education she never had.'

'That's not fair, though, is it?'

'Probably not. We all do it.'

'Why? It's just imposing your ambitions on your children.'

'For love of our kids, I suppose.'

'And kids go along with it for love of their parents.'

'Good Lord, Poppy, we are getting in deep.'

'It isn't really any different from what we were saying just now about drifting into a relationship because people expect it of you.'

'Are you saying that you don't want to go to university?'

Poppy nodded. 'Yes ... that's what I am saying – at least not just now ... maybe later. I don't want to be like Jake when I'm his age.'

'Jake? He did well, didn't he? And he has found his niche.'

'Everybody thinks that. But I don't think that Jake wants to be a farmer. He does it because of Dad. I think that's terrible, to have to live somebody else's life because it's expected of you. I expect Jake and Lizz are one of those couples we were talking about – people always invite Jake if they're inviting Lizz and vice versa. Jake's being made into a married farmer because of other people.'

'Jake's a big grown-up man: he can make up his own mind.'

'I could make up my mind and dump Emma, but I probably won't. She needs me and she'd be hurt.'

Roz suddenly felt the burden of what Poppy was telling her. Within the span of a few hours she had learned secrets that were at the heart of the Tallentire family. She had enough of her own problems. Marriage, what was going on in LA, money, whether she was a good enough play-wright to get something accepted, how to deal with her longing for sex, yet not wanting Teddy to go so far as to leave his wife on account of a few friendly lays: I've come to Myrr's to have a break from it all.

She decided that Ship Fair was just the time to get pleas-antly drunk.

Rin seemed in high spirits when he returned to Myrr's bowling alley. 'Daisy's coming.'

'Daisy?'

'I rang her and twisted her arm, she'll be here by seven. Not that she needed much persuading. I think she wants an escape route from one of her boyfriends who's getting too serious.'

'You'll have to share with Jake, then,' Myrr said. 'Roz has got your old room.'

'I'd rather share with Roz.' He winked at Roz, who made a mock seductive face.

Myrr thought how lovely it was to see Rin behaving more like his old self. She only hoped that he wouldn't go mad.

By early evening, the fairground rides were going flat out, each one sending out pop music to compete with the disco that Young Sid was putting on in a large marquee. All the village shops had closed early and Childencombrians were already bending the elbow for Rex's special ale, having a good excuse because the evening was so warm.

There was a lot of laughing and joking going on around the various contests and competitions put on by the village; Myrr's effort was not the only one where people were throwing their money about with abandon and making daft wagers with one another, then giving the winnings to the stall-holder. Occasionally a cheer would go up when some youth got to the bag at the end of the greasy pole, or a heat was won in some contest. Myrr had already collected a tidy wad of notes when another small cheer of bystanders greeted Nat.

'I thought you were never coming,' Myrr said.

'I took Dr Yin over Avebury way to let her see some stuff she wanted to take pictures of.'

Jake, who had spent quite a lot of time at Rex's bar, gave his father a friendly punch in the arm. 'You're doing all right there then, Dad?'

'You got a one-track mind, lad. She's doing some serious research. She knows more about ley-lines and hidden watercourses than you'll ever know about farming if you live to be a hundred.'

As when she had seen Rin flirting with Roz, so now Myrr felt a similar prickle of misgiving – he *was* doing all right there.

Roz could only admire Nat's aplomb. 'Hello, Nat,' she said.

'Well, if it isn't the Vicar's Wife. What are you doing back in Childencombe? Come to kick over the traces?'

'That and to eat you out of house and home for a couple of days.'

'Well we shall have a houseful, then. Myrr? Did you know Rin has told Daisy to come down?'

Myrr nodded. 'It's all taken care of, Nat. Here, come on and have a go for the pig.'

'I don't want any pig – I gave the damn thing. Here.' He gave Myrr a high-denomination note.

'You could always present it to your Dragon Lady like a proper champion,' Poppy said. 'She fancies Dad. Did you know that, Roz?'

'Well,' said Roz, her two barley wines brightening her eyes, 'I'm not surprised. Your dad is a good-looking man.'

Rin protested: 'She's too young for him. She's more my age.'

Myrr said, 'Perhaps we should tie her to the end of the greasy pole and all the men in the village could climb out after her.'

Nat frowned. 'You wouldn't like it if you went to America and people said things like that,' and stopped any more ribbing by saying he was going to the beer tent and if anybody wanted a drink, he was going to buy a round.

Roz, who had watched with concern and interest, detected the tartness in Myrr's voice, but for the rest it was the good-natured banter that goes on inside a family.

Daisy didn't arrive until nine o'clock and she felt like a guest arriving late for a particularly successful party. Under the influence of barley wine, dancing and fooling around on the fairground rides, hair had been let down in both senses. She was surprised to see Jake flinging Roz Petherbridge about the wooden dance floor and Rin being taught some arm-waving dance by a Chinese woman she supposed was the American doctor. They were too preoccupied to notice her arrival, so she pushed her way through the beertent crowd to where she saw her father's head above the rest.

'Dad.'

'Daisy.' He opened his free arm to her. He wasn't drunk, but it was getting close. 'Come here and let your dad buy you one of Rex's special barleys. Look, Rex, it's our Daisy come home for Ship Saturday. I tell you, they go off to London where it's all theatres and they have to come back to the sticks for a bit of real entertainment. Nobody there knows how to entertain themselves any more. You have to come to a true English village with history to find proper entertainment.'

Daisy kissed her father and, whilst Chrissie poured the drink, he remained with his arm about her shoulders. The only times she had ever seen him as mellow, were on one or two Ship Saturdays way back.

'D'you recognize this young woman, Daze?'

Chrissie made a half-wink at Daisy.

'. . . this pretty young woman is Chrissie Pack. D'you remember little Chrissie, Daze? Well this is what she grew up to. You got a good little barmaid there, Rex.'

Chrissie smiled benignly at the mellow Mr Tallentire as she had never imagined he could be and said to Daisy, 'When I was growing up, I used to love seeing what fashions you would come home wearing.'

Daisy was glad then that she had taken the trouble to change into some new stylish full-legged trousers and a stone-washed matt-silk shirt. She was aware that in the village she had a reputation as the high-flyer who had her own house in London and worked in the West End.

'You seem to be doing all right then, Dad.'

'I'm fine, Daisy. Never felt better in years.' He thumped his chest. 'Quacks! They don't know a thing. Not too much drinking, Mr Tallentire . . . well, I've been drinking. No red meat, Mr Tallentire ... well, when they got that pig roasted, I'm going to have a nice slab of pork as fat as I can get it and plenty of butter on the bread ... no animal fats, Mr Tallentire.' He had to shout over the noise of the ale-drinkers crushed around the bar.

'Where's Myrr?'

'I don't know. I think she's just sorting out who won the pig.'

'I'm too late to have a go, then.'

'You can give her the money. Your mother ...' he weaved slightly but, as always, kept his dignity. 'Your mother ... can spend money like it was going out of fashion. But when she sets her mind to making it, she's got the knack. It's the patter, you see. I've said to her she ought to have set up on the market years ago, and she'd a made herself a fortune.'

Rex, who was wiping down the bar, caught the end of Nat's lecture. 'What would Sunbarrow want with another fortune then, Nat?'

Nat pointed. 'Now that's where you're wrong, Rex. Sunbarrow hasn't got a fortune. It's all land and buildings and machinery. Capital and investment in plant and machinery. You should know all about capital investment.'

'Oh I do, Nat. It's what keeps me poor.'

'Hark at him, Daisy. Poor poverty-stricken poor old four-star restaurateur and Egon Ronay publican. Right, Rex?'

'Haven't got a swimming-pool or a white MG-C. And I sleep above the shop.'

Daisy said, 'Poor old Rex, my heart bleeds for you.'

Rex – who had probably sampled more of his own barley wine than most and although more used to it was nevertheless slightly running his words together – leaned close to Daisy. 'And you been making mine bleed for years, Daisy Tallentire. You should come back to the village – there isn't many 'vailable women around here and none of 'm as good-looking as you.'

'You must have been going about in blinkers, Rex. Look, the place is full of pretty women.' She indicated where Chrissie and Susie Pack were serving one of the tug-of-war teams.

'Too young, Daisy, they're more my Tom's age than mine, the village is full of tasty little fillies. Two women I always fancied – Daisy Tallentire and Jenny Mumford, and Jenny went and married Young Sid.'

'Doomed to remain a widower then, Rex,' Daisy said gaily. 'I'm off to find my mother or she'll still be working at midnight. I'm quite sure the village fund has raked in enough money by this time. You coming, Dad?'

Nat, consulting the amount he had left in his glass, nodded. 'Ah, better see what's what or I shall get my ear bit off.'

She took his arm as they made their way across the trampled grass. 'There seems to be a lot of people here this year. A few new faces every year. I suppose some of the incomers are getting accepted. What is it now, down to twenty-five years' residence to qualify as a Childencombrian?'

'The place is growing. They converted the old malt-house . . . call it The Maltings now. Some of that lot Rin's thinking of going in with live there. Then there's about a dozen council retirement bungalows, that let a lot of old cottages on to the market to be tarted up. And I dare say Rex has told anybody staying at his place it'd be all right to come to the fair.'

'Looks as though they all have.'

'Makes a difference, the weather being good.'

In the fresh air, he seemed to have regained his composure.

'Rin seems to be enjoying himself,' Daisy said. 'I saw him dancing. He hasn't looked like that for years. He was with the Chinese woman.' Daisy sensed that she had said something wrong, but being Daisy that didn't stop her. She knew very well who the woman was; she had picked up bits and pieces over the phone and knew about the doctor who was claiming a lot of her father's time. 'Who is she then, from The Maltings? She looked the type.'

'She's a scientist from America. A Dr Yin. Likes people to call her Kuan-Yin, but not me.'

'I can imagine.'

'Your mother calls her the Dragon Lady, but I reckon she's more Madam Butterfly.'

'Oh, Dad, I do believe you actually like her . . . an American . . . I never thought I'd live to see the day.'

'She isn't really American, her family comes from a very ancient and important Chinese line.'

'Not as old and important as the Tallentires, of course.'

'Our ancestors were engineering when the Chinese were still learning to count. Not a lot of people know that fact. Oldest culture in the world, we are.'

As Myrr had earlier, so too did Daisy now feel faintly apprehensive. It was the way he obviously liked talking about the woman, and she had rarely known him so approachable and talkative.

'Is that the woman who's come to see the corn circles?'

'And she's interested in ley-lines . . . dragon veins, the Chinese call them. That's how your mother first came to call her the Dragon Lady.'

'You've been going out and about a bit with her, then.'

He didn't seem to have heard, but stood looking at the crowd dancing under the flashing lights outside the disco tent. Following the direction of his gaze, Daisy saw that he was staring at Rin, now without jacket and tie, who was still dancing and laughing with the Chinese woman: They're going to start rowing all over again. What on earth possesses Rin to believe that anything has changed? They'll drive Myrr round the bend. Fancy thinking of coming back here to live.

She decided that she would lay down the law to Rin. There were times when he could be the absolute pits: We're a bloody self-centred family one way and another.

Myrr came upon Nat and Daisy standing at the edge of the crowd, watching the dancing. 'I wondered where you'd got to.' She was glad to see Daisy.

Daisy brushed a kiss on her ear and Myrr smelled barley wine on her breath.

Daisy knew what she was thinking. 'I haven't been here long. I just had a drink with Dad.' Why must I explain myself? Why am I still ten years old when I come home?

'I meant Nat. I wondered where he'd got to. I haven't seen him for five minutes all day.'

'I've been about.' Myrr could tell almost to a glass how much he had had to drink. His doctor would say it was far too much, but Myrr felt sorry that these days he was denied most of his few small pleasures.

'No, he hasn't, Daisy, he's been gallivanting off with his fancy Chinese lady. If it hadn't been for Lizz and Poppy, I should have been left to run the pig by myself.'

Myrr wondered what that look was that Daisy flicked from Nat to herself as she said, 'Dad couldn't gallivant if he tried.'

'You don't know the half of it,' Myrr said. 'You wait, he'll be over there dancing before the night is out.'

It was as though he had suddenly made up his mind to something. 'You never said a truer word, Myrr. And I shall have some of that beast that Mr Singh's got on the spit, and some barbecued sausages, and I shall say – Sod all dieticians and cardiac specialists. And if you want to come back with me, I'll buy you a glass of Rex's special barley in return for me not helping out on the pig.'

'I will after I've checked this money in to Norman

Anstey. We made three hundred and fifty. Most we've ever taken.'

'There was a time when thirty quid was,' Nat said.

Daisy said, 'Childencombe's full of fat cats these days.'

'Plenty of poor people still about,' Myrr said.

'In Childencombe?'

'Yes, in Childencombe.'

'I know about the poor,' Daisy said. 'I pass them every day. The poor live in their cardboard boxes.'

'They are the destitute.'

'You can't deny that Childencombe's full of fat cats who've been given the cream.'

Myrr felt ill at ease. Partly from knowing that Daisy was right, and that the most cream which had floated to the top had been poured over Sunbarrow – and partly from wanting everything to be nice this evening. Here were all her family and her best friend, and it was Ship Fair. 'Perhaps it's just our turn. When you were born, we were lucky if we even got the skim, let alone the cream.'

'I know. I meant all the dentists and barristers and accountants . . . and that lot Rin's thinking of going in with. Publicity and advertising! God's gift to Britain in the nineties. Oh, Myrr. Don't feel so bloody guilty. You do your bit, nobody expects you to give it all away. You can't do anything if you live in a country that likes a government that gives hand-outs to millionaires and lets its kids sleep in boxes.'

Myrr had heard it all before. There was a lot of truth in what Daisy had to say . . . perhaps that was the trouble: nobody liked to hear uncomfortable truths. But Daisy herself had always been trouble where politics was concerned. It was never easy to have a conversation when she was around because it always turned to politics in the end.

Myrr, like all the Jeavonses, was old-fashioned Labour, if Nat was anything it was probably some sort of wet

Liberal, Rin and Jake didn't seem to be anything very much. But Daisy. She must have joined her party on the first day she went to Sussex University. It was the main reason why she had settled in London, and probably why she didn't come home more often. There were none of her kind in Childencombe. Myrr knew that she didn't really mean that the Tallentires shouldn't feel guilty.

Myrr found herself deep in her thoughts standing beside Daisy who was still watching the disco. Nat had slid off whilst she and Daisy had been talking. 'I didn't see the going of Nat.'

'I think he's gone back to Rex's tent.'

'I'm going to get rid of this money, and I've got to find Lizz, then I'll be in Rex's tent. If you see Roz Petherbridge, tell her where I am.'

'The last I saw of Roz Petherbridge she was giving Jake a run for his money. Jake's a bit of a bugger, he just can't help himself.'

'With Roz? She's my age.'

'What's age got to do with it? I'll bet he thinks that she's fair game if she's here on her own. But then . . . isn't that what Ship Saturday is all about?'

As Myrr walked to the treasurer's tent she thought how right Daisy always seemed to be about that kind of thing. Intuition. She had said ages ago, even before Mary got pregnant, that Rin's marriage was in trouble. Daisy had a lot of intuition. But Jake and Roz? Jake was her favourite, but Myrr had often had to admit that he didn't have much of a conscience where sex was concerned. He picked up and dropped Lizz just when it suited him. She didn't seem to mind, though. Myrr saw it happening all the time when she was in her counselling role at the Centre, but it wasn't possible to be dispassionate with your own. Now that Roz was free she would develop her full potential as a man-eater. Why do I always expect trouble?

Because that's what you're most likely to get. Expect the worst and if you're wrong, it's a nice surprise.

Daisy must have known them both pretty well for, at the time when Myrr was counting out her takings with the village fund treasurer, Roz and Jake were enclosed in a mutually devouring and uninhibited embrace in an area of darkness away from the disco lights.

'I suppose I should feel guilty,' Roz said, her mouth close to Jake's ear. 'But I don't.'

'I should hope not. Night of misrule. I've got the Range Rover parked behind Rex's.'

Nobody saw them go.

'I should say it's misrule all right, when a woman's being felt up by a man young enough to be her son.'

'Sod age. You're just a fantastic vintage, Roz. We've both got what it takes, who cares when we got it?'

He guided her through the trees away from the fairground. She needed no persuasion.

In the car park he held her close. 'I'm supposed to be taking part in the village pull tonight. Where shall I get the strength if you get me up there on the golf course?'

Roz, the flames of pent-up desire fanned by the joy of liberation and the heat of Jake's hard body, responded to his lips and tongue. 'Is that where I must take you to get my way?'

'Do you know anywhere else where the grass is still green and soft?'

She laughed. 'I don't know that I can get you back from there in time for you to be in your team for the pull.'

He gave a low laugh. 'I hope you won't try. God, I fancy you something rotten.'

They got into the Range Rover and he drove off very fast, one hand steering. 'And you fancy me, Roz.' He laughed. 'Tell me you fancy me something rotten, too.'

'Fancy you? Like I might fancy a *petit four*? Or a titbit for my jaded palate?'

He turned down a bit of overgrown disused road with such assurance that she knew he must have been here a hundred times. He knew exactly where there was a gap in the hedge that led on to soft grass.

'If you don't fancy me, then what?'

She let her hands run over his body, as he also let them. 'Delicious hunger . . . relish . . . finger-licking gusto . . . self-indulgence . . . zest . . . shall I go on?'

'Have you got a talent for anything else besides words?'

He discovered that she had.

It was like that on Ship Saturday night.

They were away for an hour.

When they reappeared, the trials of strength were about to take place and at the calling of his name over the tannoy system for the village rope-pull, Jake looked sideways at Roz and grinned, making an exaggerated display of fatigue. 'Don't put your money on the Green Man team.'

'You'll manage. I'm sure you always do.' Giving the rear of his jeans a discreet squeeze.

But not quite discreet enough.

When Lizz Taylor saw Jake return Roz Petherbridge's squeeze, her mind leaped to the underlit scene she had stumbled upon at the Tallentires' swimming-pool. When she hadn't seen him for the last hour or so, she had guessed that it had been his Range Rover that she had heard roaring off out of the village.

Like father, like son. Jake would always be the same. Another face, another body, another bed, another lay. She had thought when she had seen him dancing with his mother's friend in that way, that they would be in bed together before the night was through.

Do I want a lifetime of that?

Do I want to come home and find red hairs on the pillow? Or brown, or blonde, or . . .

With Jake, wouldn't there always be the chance of finding some woman's pants stuffed down the back seat of the car?

Maybe an older woman was exactly what Jake needed. Although Lizz did not know her well, she had read the signs of the bony, hungry face, the full, moist mouth, and how and where her dry eyes rested on a man. She would indulge him. She would pick up his clothes as his mother always had, cook him his favourite foods, go to bed at the drop of a hat. His casual expectation that some woman would always look after him had always irritated Lizz – even though he was the only man she had ever felt really close to.

The price a woman must pay for taking Jake long-term was higher than Lizz Taylor was willing to pay.

All that she wanted to do now was to rush back to her new canvas and paint. By the weekend she would have her big work finished. At the sight of those long, red-nailed fingers clutching at Jake's behind, Lizz Taylor set herself free of her on-off, casual, uncommitted, everlasting affair with Jake Tallentire.

It was simple now. She walked through the deserted village to her flat. She felt energized, eager to finish the canvas that was going to make her name.

SIX

Who then devised the torment? Love.
Love is the unfamiliar Name
Behind the hands that wove
The intolerable shirt of flame
Which human power cannot remove.
We only live, only suspire
Consumed by either fire or fire.

t. s. eliot, Four Quartets

We, inheritors of the pinned-down Spirits – dragon, python, intuition, instinct – have kept their powers shut away for so long that they have become alien to us – mechanisms whose workings we no longer understand, forces whose use is lost, nostrums about which we know nothing and so assume to be toxic.

Alchemists who once sought to recover the lost knowledge were overtaken by scientists. Scientists look for existence only where proof lies. Nowhere else may a thing exist. Yet we cannot throw off the remnants of things spiritual and intuitive. What muddled half-alive creatures we became once King Ludd had encased the spirit of the screaming hearth-dragons in stone.

From where Kuan-Yin was standing, talking to Rin, she saw Lizz watching Jake and Roz. She saw Lizz leave, saw the lights snap on in her studio. Kuan-Yin was not surprised. The end of the affair had been there when she had first visited Lizz. Her advice to Lizz would have been the same as for Mrs Shamalla: if she wants to keep that sort of man to herself, she must buy a pearl-handled pistol and remove the opposition.

Jake Tallentire was not a one-woman man, he was, as she knew herself to be, too easily aroused by the prospect of a new experience.

But Tallentire? The thought of leaving him was painful. He would leave a scar.

She had allowed herself to become too involved. Before

it went any further, she must send out signals saying that there was nothing serious between them. She would signal with his son: Look, Tallentire, Mike Alexander, Rex Farenbach, Nat Tallentire and now Rin, and maybe Jake will be next. You don't want a woman like this. He must get the message.

She would soon be leaving for the States. He'd soon forget and then begin to enjoy life because of it. He would soon see it as a romantic interlude. A summer affair.

Emotional entanglements between shrinks and clients were an inevitable part of the process of delving into another person's life, which was what she had done with Tallentire. When clients came to her with their lives crabbed and distorted, her job was to become involved and hold their hands until they were more at ease with themselves. He was not her client, but she had responded to the pleasureless life he had imposed upon himself. All that she was doing at first was to say: Come on, honey, loosen up.

'Kuan-Yin?' During her musing, she had been absorbed in watching a large Asian man slicing through the charred skin of the spitted pig to reveal the succulent pink flesh within it. She had been curious about him and wanted to ask how he came to be pig-roaster at this English fair.

'Mike!' She was glad to see him. 'Isn't this super? It is so wonderfully ancient. I had no idea that such traditions still existed.' She kissed him lightly on the cheek. 'Look, a whole animal turned for hours and hours on a spit. How primitive, yet how natural. Do you know whether there is any connection between this and eating the long pig?'

He took her hand and lacing his fingers in hers held it tightly. 'I've missed you.'

'I came to the house, but it was all shut up. It had the look of a house that was unoccupied.'

'I took Jack on holiday for a few days.'

'That's good . . . good for you both.'

'Come and dance with me.'

Rin, returning with two cardboard plates of fat sausages and thick bread, chose not to hear. 'Hi, Mike. Long time no see. I didn't know you were here or I'd have brought you a plate of grub. Still, the queue's not too long, or you can share ours.' He held out a plate to Kuan-Yin. 'I'll bet you don't often get hand-made bangers in Park Avenue.'

'Go grab yourself some, Mike honey, and come back and sit with us, we'll be with Rin's family. Rin is going on the tug-of-war rope.'

'Mike will be too . . . won't you, Mike?'

Mike hesitated, not wanting to leave Kuan-Yin to Rin Tallentire, who looked as though he was in possession of her.

It was the early hours of the morning when the fairground rides shut down and around a huge fire everyone from white-haired elders to toddlers gathered to watch the village rope-pull, which was a test of both strength and technique. In modern times this had no serious intent; but it was a platform for the young men of the village to strip off their shirts and show how they had not been wasting their time and money pumping iron in a Winchester gym and for the older men to hang on to tall tales of prowess and of the days when they had more muscle than fat.

'Don't, Nat, please. That's about the worst thing you could do in your condition.'

'What bloody condition? Look at me, woman, have you ever seen me in finer fettle?' He had stripped to his broad chest.

'You look great, Nat, but that's because you've been taking care of yourself.'

'Listen. Today I climbed to the top of Silbury Hill, I've drunk God knows how many barley wines, I've just eaten about a pound of sausages and I'm just waiting for some pork.'

'Well, good for you. I'm glad to see you enjoying yourself.'

'And that's what I intend to do in the future.'

Myrr felt her hackles rise, but their argument was taking place in hissed tones surrounded by people. One thing the Tallentires didn't like to do was make a show of themselves in public.

Jake, against whom Roz was leaning back to back, stood up and said, 'I'll have to go and see to the drawing out of names for the two teams. Save my pork till later. I can't pull on a full stomach.' His hand lingered on the dip of her waist.

Rin, joining them now with Kuan-Yin, said, 'Barley wine, Jake, that's the best ballast,' and finished off his glass.

Kuan-Yin, as she had been doing all day, quickly fired off her camera at the Tallentire group, catching Nat in a dominant stance, then sat at one of the trestle tables on a bench stool. Rin sat close, asking her what she thought of the goings-on of simple English country folk.

She smiled enigmatically. 'Aw, come on, honey, simplicity has nothing to do with what is going on in this community tonight.'

He winked at her. 'You should a been here when we used to do our roistering in the baronial hall.'

'I see great similarities between a gathering of your family and a full gathering of Yins at my grandmother's Number One Blossom Park restaurant. It is always interesting. I could write a book on family gatherings.'

Myrr said, 'You'll have a whole shelf-full of books, what with families and the circles and the barrows and Silbury Hill.'

She sounded bitchy, Nat thought. He didn't think that he could explain to her what this was all about. He didn't know that he would even try. If she wanted to take it hard, then that's what she would have to do. He hadn't asked for it to happen and even if he could put an end to it, he didn't want to. He would have to tell Myrr soon. How did you do a thing like that? Short and to the point? Sorry,

Myrr, but I fell in love with her. She's brought all this joy into my life, just when I thought there was no point in anything any more. I can't afford to waste any more of my life, I'm not getting any younger.

He could scarcely keep his eyes off Kuan-Yin, his mind going back again and again to her painted eyes looking down and the feel of her light body as they made love on the ridge.

Kuan-Yin tried not to look back at Tallentire, but she was aware of his eyes following her. The sensible thing would be to pack her bags and go back to New York at once. Every day she spent in this village, the more strongly she became attached to it. There were times when she longed to be part of it, yet she couldn't stay.

Poppy, who had been dancing with Matt Pridhoe, came back. 'Oh Mum, you're never going to let Dad do the rope-ring?'

'Whoever let your father do anything?' Myrr bridled. 'He's his own boss.'

Nat said, 'There's older men than me going on the rope tonight.'

'Nobody's saying anything about old, Dad,' Poppy said. 'We're talking beta-blockers here.'

'Well, Dr Yin,' Nat demanded, chest out, fists on hips. 'How much would you charge for a consultation on this? Is this the body of a man who's likely to drop dead from heaving on a bit of rope?'

Kuan-Yin glanced at him, then away, shaking her head, saying, 'I'm just your average, overpaid shrink, I'm not an authority on the male body, Tallentire.'

Roz concentrated on her food.

Myrr said, 'You should ask her to examine your head.'

Rin, speaking quietly in Kuan-Yin's ear, said, 'Better if you examined his ego.'

'Honey!'

'You're right. Poor Dad. He's been Tongue-man for

twenty years. Nobody wants to step out of the limelight.'

Myrr said, 'Has anybody seen Daisy? I've got her ticket for the food.'

'She's gone home with Mimm Carter on his motor-bike,' Poppy said.

'Why do they need to ride a motor-bike up the road to Carter's?' Nat said.

'Not to Carter's, Dad. Mimm said he fancied a swim and was all for going down to the Bliss. Daisy said they could go up to our place.'

'Didn't they used to knock about together at one time, Myrr?' Roz asked.

'Not for long. I'm surprised at our Daisy, I thought she'd be too sophisticated these days for a chap like Mimm.'

'Ha!' Poppy said. 'You haven't seen Mimm Carter on demos. I should say he's just right for Daisy. When he's not selling strawberries he's out selling some anarchist newspaper.'

'Lord above,' said Myrr. 'You can live in a village all your life, and still not know the half of what goes on.'

'D'you want to bet?' said Jake, coming back to the last bit of the conversation. 'By the way, I forgot to tell you that Daisy went off on the back of Mimm Carter's motor-bike.'

'We know,' Myrr said. 'She's taken him up to the house to give him a swim.'

Rin and Jake made punching motions towards each other. 'There you are, Rin, I told you our Daisy wouldn't get up to no mischief. She's gone to give Mimm Carter a swim.'

'Pack it up,' Nat said.

'Come on, Dad,' Jake said, holding up some tickets. 'You and me are both pulling on the pub side. Rin and Mike are on the side of the angels.'

The two teams were known as the Sacreds and the Profanes. If the Sacreds won the winnings would go to the church repair fund, and if the Profanes pulled the rag tied to the rope across the no man's land, then the money went on barley wine for all comers.

By the time the teams were organized, had another drink, a pee, a change to heavy boots, and generally larked about looking for team members who were said to be last seen heading for Goose Grass with Mary Acker, it was getting on towards three o'clock and dawn. As usual, around about one and two o'clock when the meat was sliced, the roaring fire had subsided to a heap of red, and the dancing stopped to draw breath; a pleasant quietness had descended; people ate, drank, sang and snoozed. Now, refreshed, the festivities began to wind up to the climax of Ship Saturday.

Roz came and stood by Myrr as she watched the circle of rope being ragged and knotted. By now Roz had had time to recover composure enough to be able to act nonchalantly, telling herself that if one couldn't throw one's cap over the windmill on Ship Saturday then when could one? Most societies would be better for such a safety-valve. It was not unknown for incest to be committed unwittingly twenty years later, when a youth conceived on Ship Saturday might easily bed a girl who was his Ship Fair sister. One year, when Duncan had been vicar here, he had baptized three babies from different families, each child with its inheritance of Don Anstey's unmistakable red frizzy hair.

So, Roz's hour of exuberant passion with Jake was in the spirit of the celebration. Anyway, unless she had upset Myrr, she didn't really care. It had been great. She had been great, she knew it. He had said that he would come to the houseboat. They had made a tentative plan to take the Range Rover and do a week together roaming around Tuscany.

He had said: 'You're a knock-out, Mrs Petherbridge.'

Perhaps he said, 'You're a knock-out' to all his women, but who cared? She was on her way out of a disastrous marriage, and a young, desirable man had said, 'You're a knock-out.'

Myrr said to Roz, 'I wish Nat wouldn't do it.'

'There are times when we can't do anything but stand back and watch people do stupid things.'

Myrr nodded, and Roz realized that Myrr would be well aware of the irony of that. She had probably been watching her family do just that all day.

Chrissie Pack came and hooked her arm through Poppy's. 'They don't never grow up, do they?' she said. 'Look at my grandpa, I know he isn't pulling, but he'd curl up and die if anybody took away his job of judging who wins.'

The criterion for a place on the team was a growth of beard sufficient for a youth to prove that he had reached manhood. The origin of the circular tug-of-war was lost in time, but it was said to come from a fertility rite when a virgin would have been the prize at the centre of the ring and would have been impregnated by the winning team. In time, any male child resulting from that rite could lay claim to the title of 'Tongue-man'.

Now, the late twentieth-century Childencombrian teams took their turn in the history of Ship Fair, appearing to be very little different from the muscular field labourers of the past.

Because of the fire that they were to brave, their faces and chests were smeared with a lotion containing soda and wood ash which dried eerily white. Traditionally, the Sacreds wore a sacking loincloth, whilst the Profanes had a kind of posing pouch of leather with a tail of long, knotted thongs. Having bared their masculine thighs and breasts for the other team to anoint with the lotion, they now strapped on to their opponents' waists wide leather belts with iron rings through which the rope was then passed. The two 'Tongue-men' leaders then ceremonially each attached a long red rag to his opponent's pouch. A wide ring of dry wood chips and shavings had been laid, with a heap of sawdust dead centre. Now, to the playing of an old skin drum, red-hot ashes from the bonfire were placed on the ring. And now, as soon as the shavings were burning, the teams must pull.

Watching for the exact moment, Grandpa Cole held up his large white straw field-hat and the men dug in their heels and leaned back against the taut rope. The ring of fire was complete. He brought his hat sharply down and there was a cheer from the audience and a shout from the participants as they strove to keep themselves from the fire by pulling their opponents into it.

'It's not exactly a demonstration of your sexual equality here tonight,' Chrissie said with mock severity.

Poppy burst out laughing. 'I know, did you see Matt and Tom, they couldn't wait, could they? Men are like children.'

'I know,' Chrissie said. 'That's why I don't really fancy marrying one of them.'

'Marry me, then,' Poppy said.

Chrissie linked arms and tightened hers on Poppy's as they watched the two teams inch one another close to the fire and then be pulled towards it themselves. 'Nice of you to offer. Thanks, but no thanks. I'll tell you one thing though, Popp, our boobs stand up better than Tom's dad's.'

Their uproarious laughter caused Myrr to look across at them and say to Roz, 'Thick heads in the morning. This is the first time Nat would let Poppy have any of Rex's special.'

'Oh, Myrr, come on, since when did girls not drink barley wine when their fathers told them not to? I'll bet she had her first taste of Special when she was six.'

A cheer went up as the Profanes were dragged towards the barrier of flames, then another cheer as they pulled back from it.

Kuan-Yin was stooping down at the front of the supporters firing her camera flash after flash. Before it started the floodlights had been switched off and a dry resinous fir bough had been dragged on to the red base of the fire. Now it crackled, sparked and flared, lighting up the bare and sweating torsos of the white-smeared men. Men who in the morning light would revert to their normal soft pastiness appeared, in the red Tartarean light, to be powerful and muscular. The ring of shoulders and biceps around the circle of rope looked like some snake-like creature. Grandpa Cole on the sawdust island at the centre of the fiery circle, straddled and bent-kneed, scuttled back and forth sideways like a crab, his straw hat held ready to cut down at the first tongue of red rag to singe in the hot ashes.

Roz said, nodding at Kuan-Yin's flashes, 'It's all pretty primitive when you think of it. I wonder what she makes of it all.'

Myrr said tartly, 'I don't know. But you can take it from me, she's sure to write a book about it.'

Roz, perturbed by Myrr's tone, said, 'Thanks for setting me back on my feet.'

Myrr nodded. 'It wasn't about Patrick or AIDS or your boys really, was it?'

'No. I guess I felt alone and palely loitering . . . or was it not waving, but drowning? Anyway I don't feel that any more. I'm glad Duncan and I didn't fall out. You're great, Myrr.'

'I wish I was great enough to stop my stupid, bloody husband from doing that to himself. He knows what the score is, but just look at him.'

Nat was thumping the heels of his boots heavily into the grass, making a hollow and a ridge against which he could lever his body. Rivulets of sweat washing away the white lotion left shiny cracks. Nat and Jake heaved and leaned together, their blond heads close, matching height for height. They were magnificent, and Roz, like Poppy and

Chrissie and other women who usually scorned men's macho antics, felt her breath shorten at the transformation of the men of the village. In their ragged sackcloth in the red darkness, Rin looked fitter, Mike Alexander younger, Tom mature, and Rex's good-life portliness looked better naked. But none of them looked as awesome and unassailable as Nat and Jake.

Myrr thought: Except for his beard, he hardly looks any different from the first time he went on the rope.

She remembered how she had stood and watched him then. He hadn't so much hair on his chest in those days, but he was glorious. That night, she had stood in this same field and was so proud that she longed to tell somebody: I'm carrying his baby.

It had been back to normal next day. Their enforced marriage hanging over her. She suffered dreadful morning sickness. They would be as poor as church mice. Sunbarrow land had been neglected and the harvest was going to be sparse. But on the rope that night he had been a Sacred, and he had looked magnificent. She had never forgotten that for a moment she understood how the stories about old gods having their way with country maids had come about.

Now, as she watched him, a fine but foolish man of fifty, she smiled to herself. What a thought, to be proud of being knocked up by some marauding old god. And now what she wanted most was a piece of vellum – did they still use vellum? – anyhow, a piece of paper which said on it: Myrtle Anne Tallentire BA – preferably Hons. And in the getting of it she would fill the holes in her education, and belong to the same club as people like Roz who could throw in the odd significant quotation – 'Alone and palely loitering' or 'Not waving, but drowning'.

Roz, mistaking Myrr's smile and where her gaze was held, wondered what was going to happen next in the Tallentire family.

A shout went up. The Sacred's rag was on fire, and Grandpa Cole stood ramrod-straight holding his hat high above his head saluting the Profane team.

What did happen next in the Tallentire family was that when Kuan-Yin went close, flashing her camera at the winners, Nat looped his red rag about her, drew her to him, and kissed her long and hard on the mouth. There was a cacophony of whistling and whooping as both teams thumped the air at the Old Man's triumphant claim of the woman.

Only Jake heard what the Old Man said to her. Coarse, farmhand's language that Jake had never heard his father use till then, the language Jake had used to tell Roz Petherbridge on the way back from the golf course. There can't be a lot wrong with the Old Man's heart.

Nat poured himself his usual strong morning cup of tea, but not from the Teasmade as usual, for he had awoken on the sitting-room couch, his stomach a bit queasy – pork had always done that to him – but his head perfectly clear. Rex Farenbach must have made a really good brew for anybody to wake with a clear head after a night on barley wine. He couldn't remember how he got home. The last thing he could remember about the fair so far, was Madam Butterfly and her camera.

He took his tea outside where he could sit and look out over his land and think about her. Facing him was the huge circle with the rings, which Jake had agreed with the university to leave uncut when the combines had come in last week. Not that he needed reminding, but the circle with its boss brought back vividly the feel of her pressed against his bare chest last night. The rest was a bit hazy, though he did remember wondering whether Jake overheard what he said to her. If he did, then he knew what they'd been doing in the afternoon. He'd got home somehow. The burn lotion had gone – he thought he must have gone for a swim. He remembered passing out on the couch.

He guessed that he might have burnt his boats. Whatever happened now, there wasn't any going back. Her coming to the village had changed him, changed everything. Until now, he'd been only half-alive. He had been only half-alive because he was just a kid when his father had died, yet on that day he had had to take on the responsibility for Sunbarrow and everything and everybody on it. When he looked back now he saw how fanatical he had been. It was no good condemning a youth because he hadn't wanted to give anybody the chance of saying that the boy wasn't half the man his father was. He had hardly had a bit of pleasure, Sunbarrow had sucked everything out of him.

Myrr had come along when he had ached with bloody loneliness. She wouldn't have married him if he hadn't got her into trouble. And she wouldn't have been in trouble if he hadn't practically forced her. Trouble. Nobody seemed to think of it as trouble now, but back then it was about the worst sort of trouble a working girl could find herself in. He had tried to make it up to her. As soon as there had been money to spare he had let her have anything she wanted. She had earned it. She wasn't happy . . . never had been, but who was?

He was . . . Christ, yes! Nat Tallentire was. Half-way through his life and he had had a month of happiness.

He suddenly felt extremely peaceful. It was as though he could at last look at a crop circle in his fields with a quiet mind. He had recorded and paced them out, but until now had not allowed himself to wonder what was going on. And something was going on and had been for quite a few years now.

Before universities and television crews had started taking an interest – when the first small circles had appeared suddenly on his land – he had realized that there was something queer happening. He was familiar enough with crops to know what wind-damage looked like and knew his own land well enough to know about its micro-climates and whirlwinds. To a man who has tilled the same plots all his life, something like that happening was inexplicable in the same way that his ability to divine how subterranean watercourses and ley-lines ran was inexplicable. In his youth he had taken that ability for granted: his father could find underground streams and wells, as could his grandmother. Nat had grown up not thinking it anything special, no different from being able to hear something you couldn't see. Later on, when the press was making laughing stocks of people about flying saucers, he'd been glad that he had not told anyone about the circles. He couldn't have borne being associated with that kind of notoriety. But once the circles had started appearing in a big way, there was nothing he could do, they had become public property as Jake said they should be. Jake was wrong; they appeared in Sunbarrow fields, which was one of the reasons he had started keeping records of where and when they appeared.

It was as though he had been waiting all his life to find somebody who would understand his obsession with his enigmatic land. He smiled to himself. She could detect some of the ley-lines ... dragon veins, but not underground water. This Uncle Han she was always talking about, he sounded like a man who would understand this land, would be in tune with it, her Uncle Han would be able to read in the same way as himself. Tallentire. That made him smile. What American nonsense, yet he liked the way she had adopted that name for him. A thing that had attracted him right from the first was how totally different she was from anything in his previous experience. She had made a beeline for him outside the church that day, she said because she had picked him out as different from the rest. She had seemed so unreal, she had reminded him of a little willow-pattern statue his mother used to have.

She was the only other person who had set eyes on those corn circles records which showed their alignment with the Sunbarrow ley-lines.

Tallentire! These are terrific! Oh, if only my Uncle Han could talk with you.

She had taken his hands as they had sat in the conservatory with his papers spread out before them. The relief he felt that morning. At the time, he had thought of the irony of it: A rich Chinese lady all the way from New York . . . a little bit of a thing . . . a headshrinker, for God's sake. Yet she's turned out to be the only one who has ever got to know who the real Nat Tallentire is.

She had come to stand behind him as he pointed out the features of his maps, casually, as though she had known him for ever, instead of being a stranger. She had linked her arms about his neck, her cheek had brushed his ear. He recalled the perfume of her hair and the bony feel of her arms. He couldn't remember that he had felt anything really sexual then. Intimate. That was the word.

In some ways she was a bit like Roz Petherbridge. She made entrances, held people's attention, said things for effect, flirted with anything in trousers . . . but the difference was that in Roz Petherbridge it was irritating, he always wanted to say: For goodness' sake, woman, stop showing off, act your age.

Yesterday she had talked about her Uncle Han popping over from Hong Kong to see Sunbarrow.

'Popping over from Hong Kong! As though it was a trip up from Brighton. You're like a butterfly on a buddleia bush.'

'Why so, Tallentire?'

'You've got everything you need on one branch, yet you have to flit from place to place, like a butterfly, drinking a drop of nectar here and a drop there.'

Yet . . . if she wasn't like that, then she would never have landed up in Sunbarrow, and the lump of ice that

Nat Tallentire had become would never have thawed. That thought had come to him on the day when he had gone to see his solicitor.

He had not had a chance yet to talk to Myrr about the changes he had made to his will. He would do it today. There was a lot to settle today. Now, he listened to the early bees working their hearts out on the clump of borage in the border. Things about last night were coming back gradually.

He went into the kitchen and made himself some more tea and some toast which he brought back out. They had come home to find Daisy and Mimm Carter having a swimming contest, with Mimm Carter wearing Nat's new shorts and Daisy as topless as if it had been a French beach.

The smell of the toast reminded him that Poppy had been making some in the early hours. She had brought the two Pack girls home to stop the night, and they had all had a swim. Now, he remembered coming home in Myrr's car. They had started making sandwiches and toast. He remembered hearing the Range Rover come up the back road. Jake was a bloody fool, he must have been well over the limit.

What about Rin? The last he remembered of him was taking a photo of Madam Butterfly. If it came out it would be damned good, a great shower of sparks going up into the night sky, sparks the same colour as that tarty dress. The tarty dress he had bought for her and she had worn for him.

That dress. It had been made for her. Letting him pay for it had put them on a different footing. They had both understood that. It was the first time he had ever entered a boutique in his life . . . almost the first time he had gone into a woman's shop of any sort. Once, years ago, he had gone to one in Winchester and bought Myrr a fluffy jumper for Christmas – the Christmas she was expecting Poppy.

On the way back from Long Kennet Barrow where she

had gone to do some videoing, they had stopped at a teashop and she had persuaded him to come in to see how she looked in the dress she had seen in a boutique window. Just like the sparks of that bonfire.

In it she had looked oriental and desirable. The soft stuff had shown the swell of her belly, even the little dip of her belly-button, it had moulded to her backside and caressed and clung to every dip and curve as she walked out of the changing room. The dress had a little sparkling silver top with strings on one shoulder like that other one she had dropped when she dived into the pool. He had never seen a woman wear a dress yet look so naked.

'How do I look, honey?'

'Like a top-price Chinese tart.'

'Noo Yoik tarrt, sweetheart.' She had smiled and shown him the tip of her tongue. 'OK, honey, then we'll take it, shall we?'

The girl in the shop didn't know what to make of it. Well, perhaps she did. A middle-aged man and a Chinese princess buying sexy, tarty clothes like that. He had felt extraordinary.

That same day she had gone with him to Cockrill, his solicitor, to add a codicil to his will. Later she had promised with great understanding that, even if it was another thirty or forty years before he died, she would come from wherever she was to see that his arrangements were carried out.

'What about Mrs Tallentire? Your children?' Cockrill had asked.

'They wouldn't want to do it. Dr Yin will save them the hassle. She knows exactly my wishes.'

'Very well, it's your funeral, Mr Tallentire.'

Nat had liked that.

Lee Han had arrived in England on the Saturday afternoon, but although he rang the number she had given him several times he got no reply. So he stopped overnight in a hotel close to the airport and ordered a car and driver to collect him very early the next morning.

This car was no limousine and the driver was no personal chauffeur, but Lee Han enjoyed being driven through the English countryside. The impression he had of Britain was that, although not as packed as Hong Kong, it was a small, crowded island. But once away from the airport, he saw that his impression was a mistaken one, that there were stretches of quite beautiful countryside in which there were very few dwellings. Villages were small and at this time there were few people about. It seemed hard to understand how this country had once been the hub of a great empire.

It was when he reached the environs of the village where he was heading that he saw the nature of the disturbance Kuan-Yin had told him about. A deep man-made gorge sliced into what appeared to be a tiger configuration. In places where the existing road ran alongside the cutting, everything – trees, hedges, vehicles, machines, huts – was whitened by the slicing away of the calcareous haunch of the tiger hill. Lee Han instructed the driver to go up and down the road several times whilst he took stock of the landform features which were most interesting.

When they turned off at the Childencombe signpost Lee Han saw the row of tumuli on the skyline. This must be the configuration that Alison had found so greatly exciting.

'I don't really know how to do the geomancy, Uncle Han. I am not practised enough to set up the *lo p'an* . . .'

'Alison,' he had admonished, '*lo p'an* was gift only, not for practise of *feng-shui*.'

'And I'm keeping my promise: the *lo p'an* you gave me is on the wall of my apartment. I bought one for myself in London.'

'It is not possible for a woman to practise *feng-shui*.'

'So what will you do, Uncle Han? There is this great man here, he has made charts that would make your eyes stand out from your head. He has never ridden the dragon in his life, yet he knows every underground watercourse and every vein of *ch'i*. And he is a dragon year man — surely that's some kind of omen?'

'I am working on a correct burial site for an important banker.'

'He can wait in a temporary grave. I'm sure there is a dragon's lair here but if you can't come, then I'll have to try to ride the dragon myself.'

Lee Han had capitulated. 'It is fortunate that the man with the charts was born in year of dragon. I will come.'

'You won't be sorry, honey.'

The hire car turned into the long drive towards Sunbarrow and Lee Han had the driver stop well away from the house as he did not intend intruding at this time, but would come later and more formally with Kuan-Yin. He looked around at the configurations she had described and nodded to himself. She had interpreted it very well. He thought that he would like to take a quick look along that ridge and saw that there was a pathway. Having taken the wrong fork he found himself coming out close to the house.

As he rounded the bend, Lee Han saw two heart-stopping sights. On the slope facing the house was the huge wheel and boss shape in a harvested cornfield, precisely as Kuan-Yin had described, though in reality it was very much larger and more impressive than he had visualized it.

The second sight was on the terrace of the house facing the wheel. There, sprawled, was the inert form of a man who had obviously fallen from the terrace bench. Food was scattered about, and a plate and mug smashed to a score of pieces.

Lee Han ran to him and bent down. He did not attempt to move him: not only was he too heavy for Lee Han's frail arms, there was no point, the man was dead. For a minute Lee Han squatted beside him. There were few men who were as tall as himself, but this one was as tall and much more broad and muscular, with narrow hips and long thighs. He had the large hands of a labourer, but their skin was fine and uncalloused. Because of his well-proportioned features, he would be considered to be a handsome man by any race. In much the same way as he read land form, Lee Han read the human form. He knew intuitively that this was the owner of the land that had excited his niece so much, the man who had been born with all the luck a dragon can bestow. This was not luck, for the man was still in his middle years. He felt a great sadness sweep over him.

He straightened the legs, collected the undignified debris, placed his own linen jacket over the head and went into the house where all was silent.

Something had disturbed Myrr. She lay staring at the ceiling, trying to place what it was. It had sounded a little like the wind-chimes in the garden, but there was not enough wind to even disturb the curtains. She lay on her back and let her mind wander over yesterday.

The worst of days, the best of days. She was glad that it was over, out of the way so that she could give her attention to organizing her new life. Today was reckoning day. She had already made up her mind to say to Rin that it would be best if he looked for a place of his own. He would understand, and if he didn't then Myrr was determined to stand her ground. If she didn't think of her own future, then nobody would think of it for her. Nothing . . . nothing at all was going to prevent her from doing the OU Arts Foundation Course. And she would give Jake an ultimatum. She would employ Mrs Pack permanently – it was already arranged – but Jake would have to mend his ways. Mrs Pack would not clear up behind Jake. He had to grow up. Myrr had let him go on too long behaving as though it was his right to have a servant. Nat wasn't really any different except that he never expected Myrr to be a personal servant: just head cook and bottle-washer. Well, no more. She had given them half of her life, they couldn't begrudge her having a bit of the rest of it for herself. And in any case, she didn't care.

What he had told her last night on the way home . . . He'd been pretty drunk, but she knew that it was the truth. It was obvious once it had been said. She wasn't ready to think about Nat yet.

There was a crunch of gravel as a car came down the front drive. Who was that, this time of the morning? She hadn't heard Rin come in although she hadn't fallen asleep until it was getting light, but Rin didn't have a car. She thought it was Rin she had seen with his arm round that sparkling dress going into Rex's, but she hoped she hadn't seen that in view of Nat's maudlin admission. She could deal with that kind of thing at the Centre, but not in her own family.

She couldn't help herself. The scene at the end of the evening developed like a photographic plate until it became clear and vivid. The red glow of the fire upon the bare bodies of the team, the Dragon Lady's flashgun lighting them up, the flame-colour of her skirt, the red rag around her waist, then Nat yanking her to him, bending over her. She had fallen willingly into his arms, laughing up at him. They could have been posing for the cover of a romantic paperback. She had not shown the slightest surprise. Anyone seeing the way they moved into the kiss must surely see that they'd done it before. It hadn't been a playful kiss like winning racing drivers gave to bimbos . . . she had seen as clearly as though she had been standing beside them that they had opened their mouths.

She leaped out of bed. Ship Saturday affairs were supposed never to have happened. But this was no Ship affair, it must have been going on for weeks. If only he hadn't told her about the swimming . . . I couldn't help myself, Myrr.

You understand? I never intended. She had felt sick. Perhaps their salvation today was that they had a house full of people. She tied a housecoat round her and went downstairs.

He hadn't come upstairs, nor was he still asleep on the couch. She heard a movement in the kitchen. She had no idea what she would say to him. At the moment she felt like hurling something. She had never believed that she could feel so violent.

As she came through the saloon swing-doors, it was a moment before it registered what she was seeing. In her kitchen was a tall man wearing immaculately creased trousers, white silk shirt and blue tie. A tall, thin Chinese man. He jumped as the doors swung. She too started back. He held up his hands as though to placate her. He had a sad, sombre face, made more sombre by a thin, drooping moustache.

'Madam. I beg forgiveness. I could not find doorbell.'

'It's . . .'

'I am sorry, there has been accident.'

'Oh! Where? Is it bad?'

'Madam. Please, if you will sit. Please be calm.' He pulled out a kitchen chair and gently forced her into it.

She shied away involuntarily. 'My husband . . . my son, let me call my son, he will telephone.'

'Please. Breathe very deeply. I am not intruder. My niece is Miss Yin. I believe you know.'

Myrr drew in her breath. Dr Yin? 'Yes, I do know Miss Yin.'

'There is no way to tell bad news. I regret that you must hear grievous happening from this stranger.'

'Nat!' She started from her chair. 'It's my husband, isn't it?'

'I believe it must be. I have seen same thing before. I think his heart . . .'

'Oh, God. Where is he?'

'In garden. Please wait, you have son at home? I regret he is dead before I discover. Too late. Please. Allow Lee Han to get man member of your family.'

Although she felt herself trembling, she was cool and calm. 'No. It's all right. Just come with me, please.'

Except that it was such a strange place to be lying on a Sunday morning, and except that a man's linen coat had been placed neatly over his head, Nat did not look dead. He might have been sunbathing.

But he was dead.

When the man bent down and almost reverentially removed his coat, she saw that Nat was dead. Dead and faintly smiling. He must have died in an instant.

'Please. Perhaps you would like me to cover him. I am afraid that he is too heavy for me to lift.' Lee Han's hand hovered about her shoulder, not quite touching.

'Yes. He's six foot six. That's big, isn't it?' Anything one might say in such circumstances sounds trivial in the telling, but to Myrr it was only Nat's size that seemed to have any relevance. The dead man was six foot six, like Nat.

'I am myself over two metres, but I have not fine physique of this man. He is giant.'

'There is a big shawl on that cane settee in the conservatory. Perhaps you would fetch it to cover him.'

As he did so, Myrr said, 'I don't know why we cover dead people, do you?'

'Privacy, I think.'

'And dignity?'

'Yes.'

He helped Myrr to her feet. 'My name is Lee Han. I am sorry that I was chosen to be messenger with such tragic news for you.'

For the first time since that first scary glimpse of him, she looked at him: he had such a nice kind face and his eyes were wet. 'I'm sorry for you. It must have been awful finding somebody like that. But you have been kind.'

Why am I not crying? Why am I not rushing through the house calling for Rin and Jake?

'I think I must fetch my sons.'

'Perhaps I should make coffee. I am very efficient in kitchen. Would you like coffee?'

'I would, if you don't mind.' She held out her hand, 'I'm Mrs Tallentire – Myrr.' She imagined herself telling Roz. It was so weird. This long, thin Chinese man in my own kitchen asking, would you like coffee? She found it difficult not to laugh. It was the funniest thing in a long time. And as she left the kitchen she heard Myrr Tallentire of the Centre saying: It is a perfectly usual thing to happen with sudden bereavement, any of us can do really strange things. We can all behave in a way that would shock us in normal circumstances.

She found herself standing staring down at the couch upon which the indentation of Nat still showed in the goose-feather cushions and remembering a talk on grief in which a group of trainee counsellors had heard anecdotes of respectable women finding themselves in bed with some sympathetic neighbour before they had been widowed for a day. The group had felt embarrassed at their desire to snigger, until the tutor had said that it was all right, it actually was pretty funny when you came to think about it.

There was not a sound inside the house. They were all obviously sleeping off their various orgies. She tapped on Jake's door. Opening it she saw first that Rin's bed had not been slept in, and second that the body about which Jake was wrapped was Roz's. And it didn't seem to matter.

'Jake?' She shook his shoulder and he turned towards her, snapping awake as he had always been able to do. Roz, hardly disturbed, turned away and sighed heavily. 'Jake. Get up. It's your father.'

In a second he was out of bed and pulling his jeans over his naked body. 'What's wrong?'

Myrr shook her head and stepped out on to the landing.

He followed her, barefoot, zipping his jeans. 'Is he . . . ?' He knew. 'He's dead.'

She nodded. 'On the terrace. Heart attack, I think.'

'Are you sure he's gone?'

She nodded. 'The Dragon Lady's uncle found him. He's downstairs making coffee.'

'Her uncle?' Jake ran his hands over his face and through his hair, stretching his eyes apart as he did so. Then he pulled Myrr to his chest and rocked her gently. 'Poor Mum.'

Why don't I cry? People cry.

'Poppy's the only one ever calls me Mum.'

He released her. 'What shall we do first?' They were whispering. 'Rin's not here.'

'I know, I think he might be down at the Green Man. Come down and see if we can at least get your father on to the garden bench.'

In the kitchen, Lee Han was stirring a jug of steaming coffee. He clasped his hands and bowed when Jake came in.

Myrr said, 'This is my son, Jake. I'm sorry . . . you did tell me your name?'

'Lee Han.'

'That right,' Myrr said.

'Yes, Kuan-Yin is niece.'

Jake nodded. 'I am sorry that you had to arrive like this. I'd better go and see . . .'

'Death seldom comes at convenient time.'

Jake thought that there was a surrealistic quality here. Who gets up on a Sunday morning and finds an old Chinese man, a complete stranger, quoting Chinese sayings and making coffee – and their father dead?

Jake and Myrr went outside.

Myrr said, 'I thought I should cover him.'

Jake pulled back the paisley shawl.

337

Oh, he was dead all right.

This was the first dead person Jake had ever seen, but he knew that the Old Man had gone. Gone. He couldn't seem to get his brain in gear.

'Go and have some coffee, Myrr. I'll see to him.'

Alone he lifted his father's sixteen stone on to the garden bench, then squatted beside him. He looked all right. Why had they always called him the Old Man? He wasn't at all old. He was bloody good-looking. Now, with his bare, brown chest, his fine profile and the bright shawl draped across him, Jake remembered that image of him when the Profanes had won.

The Old Man had looped her in his Tongue rag and bent over her as though he would have laid her there and then. For a moment, every man there must have wanted to change places.

Jake had been standing closest and had heard the groan his father had given when he had kissed her . . .

He pushed back the lock of hair that always fell over his father's brow and thought: Jesus, Dad, how can any-body put a man like you in a grave or bring you home in an urn?

What a bloody waste. Between one second and the next, all his knowledge – of farming, of all his hard-won experi-ence of what was best for Sunbarrow land, of his store of country lore, of legends and all the other obscure things that had absorbed him and bored the pants off his family – all gone. Never again would there be another mind that would contain just such a collection. Jake suddenly wanted to know it all, wished passionately that he had listened. Too late! The Old Man was gone.

He felt Myrr's hand on his head. 'He looks OK, Myrr. He didn't know a thing.'

'Can we get him indoors? I don't want Poppy or the Pack girls . . . Where's Rin?'

Jake shrugged his shoulders.

'If Rin was here we could probably . . . ?'

'You have that coffee. I'll go and tell Daisy and Poppy and get Roz to keep Poppy and the girls out of the way until we've seen to everything.'

'I think Rin might be at the Green Man.'

Jake nodded. 'So do I.'

In the kitchen the respectful stranger had found cups, heated milk and strained coffee into a jug, and made a pile of toast which stood neatly in the toast rack. It was the gentle man's offering the only bit of comfort he knew how that at last brought Myrr's tears flooding. He quietly stepped forward, nodding, and seemed to tentatively offer the crook of his arm. She took the tea-towel that he had been using and sobbed quietly into it. She felt his hand tighten on her arm and then hold her head. She sensed his awkwardness. Small movements indicated that he was still nodding. He was permitting her to cry. She felt that she had known him for ever. People are kind, she kept thinking. People really are kind.

She heaved a sigh and the man let her go, turning away to attend to something on the dresser whilst she composed herself.

'Madam, if you permit, I have a young strong driver . . . with your son we shall carry your man to more suitable place.'

From that moment, the day formed a pattern that would remain in the minds of all of them for the rest of their lives.

Rin awakened to a familiar sound and, of late, a less familiar feeling. The sound was the tuck-tuck, tuck-tuck of a computer keyboard being operated, the feeling was of acute desire. Propping himself up on one elbow and looking into a stream of sunlight, he saw Kuan-Yin absorbed in watching the screen of a lap model as her fingers flew over the keys. Without looking away from the screen she waved her fingers over her shoulder at him. Flopping back on the pillow he smiled and groaned.

'Just look at you, fresh as a daisy . . . how on earth do you do it? We didn't have much sleep.'

Still typing very fast, she said, 'The need for sleep is all in the mind. Geniuses and successful entrepreneurs often don't take more than three or four hours' sleep.'

'Ah . . . but how long do they stay in bed?'

Kuan-Yin stood up, depressed two keys with her forefingers and went across to the bed where she dropped down facing him with her fists under her chin. 'I don't think anyone has done a paper on that.'

Rin reached out and rubbed his knuckles against her cheek. 'OK then, genius, if you've had your five hours' sleep . . .'

'Four.'

'OK, you had your four hours' sleep, now come and have four hours' bed.'

He followed every movement as she walked to the bathroom. Even though he lived close to a Chinese community and saw lovely oriental women every day, he had never seen any to touch her. There was something delicate and perfect about oriental women – it had been the features Mary had inherited from her Filipino grandmother that had first attracted him to her. The telephone rang.

'Leave it,' Rin said.

'I have to . . . it's probably my Uncle Han . . . he's due in today.'

Rin was towelling his hair in the shower when she came back and stood in the doorway.

He held out his hand for her. 'Come here, let me dry you. Was it your uncle?'

She stood there, looking pale and wide-eyed. 'Yes.'

'What's wrong?' He wrapped a bathrobe round her.

She put her hands over her face and rubbed it as though

340

awakening from sleep. 'Uncle Han was phoning from Sunbarrow.'

'Sunbarrow?'

Her chin began to tremble and she clasped a hand over her mouth.

'What's wrong? What's happened?'

'It's . . . Oh, Tallentire!' She stared into space, seemingly unaware that streams of tears were running down her face.

It was the bloody awful morning all over again.

He grasped her shoulders and raised his voice, 'For Christ's sake . . . what has happened?'

'Oh Rin, your father is dead . . . it's Tallentire . . . he's dead.'

He rushed into his shirt and jeans and rammed his bare feet into shoes.

Unhelpfully she picked things up and put them down again. 'Rin, I am so sorry . . . I don't . . . I can't . . .'

Her mind was in turmoil. She had taken Rin home with her as a message to Tallentire that he must not think of taking anything seriously. Rex or Mike wouldn't have done, Tallentire wouldn't have taken notice of any message that did not hurt. Taking Rin or Jake was needed.

She put her arms about him and for a minute they clung together. 'Do you want me to drive you home?'

Rin shook his head. 'No. I'll go across the fields.'

At the door of her suite he kissed her gently. 'I thought I would get round to asking you to marry me.'

Her face creased and she bowed her head against his chest. He caressed her shoulder. She shut her eyes to try to stop the flow of tears but they would not stop, then she looked up at him, her mascara from yesterday running down her cheeks.

'As soon as I met you, I had no doubts.' He smoothed away the mascara. 'I was too late, wasn't I?'

Broken, she nodded. 'I was going away from him. I

341

didn't know . . . He didn't . . . It was an accident. You should go home now.'

'There's no hurry now, is there?'

They held one another, each glad of the understanding caress of the other in their remorse at not having done things better.

She insisted that he go.

'Will you be all right?' he asked.

'I will be my normal self the next time we meet.'

'You won't go away yet.'

'I can't now. I made a promise to Tallentire. I have to keep it now.'

Later, after he had gone, she put up her hair and made up her face and observed herself closely in the mirror. The face reflected was no different from the one she had studied yesterday morning, and yet it must be so altered as to be someone else. Everything was changed.

She studied her mouth as she painted the outline. How many men? Scores? Hundreds? It wasn't something to play the numbers game with – Hell, that was too damn scary. Some women too, not many.

But Tallentire . . . She saw the grief in her own eyes. How many times had she seen depression from the suppressed anger of a lover who had no right to grieve. She'd be all right. She was tough as carbon fibre.

Just a couple of days ago, when he was so solidly and joyfully alive, she had gone with him to his lawyer and promised to arrange his last rites. She wasn't sorry that she had had last night with Rin: except perhaps for Lizz Taylor, there was no one else to whom she could acknowledge her involvement and show her grief. Now that she had got the weeping over, she was ready. Her reflection showed her well-groomed usual self.

She went downstairs and found Rex Farenbach.

'Enjoy yourself yesterday, Dr Yin? Bet they don't do it like that in New York.'

He had obviously not seen Rin.

'You didn't see Rin Tallentire.'

He grinned. 'No, but I would have turned my blind eye.'

'His father has died.' Her mouth wanted to tremble.

'Jesus! Nat? Dead? He shouldn't have done the pull yesterday.' He rubbed his hand back and forth across his chin, then took her elbow and led her to a window seat. 'What happened?'

'Coronary, I believe.'

Rex shook his head. 'Bloody idiot.' It was said with understanding. 'Fancy going on the rope last night. But there, we were the same age, and I still think of myself as a young man. What a waste . . . he was a really decent bloak. He worked like a black all his life and then . . . can you imagine, out like a light. What a waste.' He shook his head. 'Old Nat was nobody's fool, he brought that place on from a few scratty little acres to one of the biggest family farms in the south. Poor Myrr, just as they were going to sit back and enjoy some of it. I'm damned if I'm going to let that happen to me. As soon as this place is finished, I shall sell out . . . go to live on Tenerife or somewhere . . . Normandy perhaps.'

If Kuan-Yin's face held any expression of her inner feelings, Rex wouldn't have noticed.

'I can't get over it. Old Nat, dead.'

Sundays were always quiet, but particularly so today when Lizz Taylor looked out over Childencombe's square. She had painted all night and only now did she notice how much her body ached from the prolonged work on the large canvas. She stripped off the clothes she had worn to the fair yesterday and stood under the shower, allowing the pulsating needle jets to revitalize her circulation. Then she went back into her work-place and stood in front of an enormous mirror, not to look at herself, but to get a reflected view of the canvas.

It was stunning. She had known that it would be the best thing she had ever done. It was trouble, but there wasn't much she could do about that. As often happened when she was involved in an intense and long session of work, her subconscious had been active. Jake had been sorted. Even had she not seen Jake and the woman coming on to each other, she would have come to the same conclusion. It was over. Finished. There was nothing left for either of them. It was great fun, but it was just one . . .

Mike Alexander, probably in a fit of pique about Kuan-Yin, had asked Lizz up to his house for lunch and a game of tennis today. And for the first time in ages, Lizz felt interested at the thought of a date. Mike was OK. It didn't matter if it had been because of pique, they could bitch together about the crassness of Ship Fair.

The painting was large and done in acrylics. She had used a restricted white, blue, ochre and green palette and as she studies it she can see that she has got the nature of the disturbed water right as the dominating figure of Poseidon erupts through the glassy surface.

There was a ring at her door. When she answered the intercom Kuan-Yin's voice asked if she could come up.

Lizz was about to cover her canvas as it stood directly in the line of sight of anyone coming in, but she thought better of it. It would be her most important work in her new show in September. Sooner or later she had to see it . . . they all had to.

Lizz sat in the window where she could see Kuan-Yin's reaction.

She had probably imagined most reactions to the canvas except that Kuan-Yin would cover her eyes and begin to cry silently as she did. 'He is dead.' She turned away and left Lizz shocked and listening to the echoing click of high heels.

Clutching her bath-towel round her, Lizz rushed downstairs after Kuan-Yin but she was too slow to catch her before she was in her car and away. She went back and stood where Kuan-Yin had stood.

He is dead? Mr Tallentire? Everybody said that he was better. This summer he had returned to being the man that she had always known.

She picked up the phone, but before dialling she stood and concentrated on her life-size representation of Poseidon and Gaea – Jake's father and Kuan-Yin. It was virtually the scene that night when she had stumbled upon them in the Sunbarrow pool. Poseidon, jubilantly bursting through the surface of a domestic swimming-pool, is holding the goddess Gaea, his large hands are in her delicate armpits, water cascading over his pectoral muscles, streaming from his hair and pouring from a crown of seaweed and shells, his lips are parted in a triumphant climactic shout.

If Lizz Taylor's reputation had so far rested on her portraits and her erotic paintings that in the main appealed to women, then – however much she might deny it was her intention – this was aimed at a wider public; for, although the Poseidon figure showed only the torso above an incipient maelstrom – the rest of him being tantalizingly hidden in the turbulence of the water – no one could be in any doubt as to the source of his moment of ecstasy. Poseidon was the god in love with love and life.

And the Gaea? Elation. In Lizz's version it is the goddess who has seduced the god. She has dived to the sea-bottom and come up with her prize. Although she is shown only quarter profile, she is unmistakably Kuan-Yin. The ivory skin, the high cheekbones, the upward slant of the eye. An oriental Nereid with strands of her long jet-black, wet hair caught in a distinctive earring.

With a lump in her throat she touched the fast-drying paint with a nail. Poor Mr Tallentire. Let's hope he's gone where he can be himself.

It was the kind of picture that could easily draw flak, but she had no regrets: it was a truthful portrait, she would tough it out with the family if she had to.

She dialled the Sunbarrow number and when she heard Roz Petherbridge's voice she asked for Jake.

'Ah ... he's ...'

'I know. Tell him it's Lizz.'

Jake answered in seconds. 'Lizz.'

'Jake, I heard something about your father ... ?'

'I was about to come and see you and tell you myself. Who ... ?'

'Kuan-Yin.'

'Ah. I'll be down in ten minutes.'

'It's not ...'

But he had put the phone down.

By the time she heard him let himself in, she had put up her hair and slipped on a cotton skirt and top and hung a length of butter-muslin over the canvas. She looked at herself. Presentable. That was all she wanted to be.

When he went to kiss her, she turned her face so that the kiss landed on her cheek.

'I'm so sorry, Jake. Really, very sorry. I was very fond of your father.'

'I don't know ... I'm still waiting for it to hit me. We're all like that up there. Everybody being polite and concerned for each other. Poppy's in a state.'

'She adored him, didn't she? How about your mother?'

'Brilliant, just as you'd expect. I expect she's still in shock, but she's doing it her way. She's organizing things, telling people what to do. She's got me sorting out his things. She's even putting the clothes he wore yesterday through the washing machine.' He dropped into a rocking chair and sat rocking. 'It's weird, really.'

'Are you all right, Jake? Have you eaten? I could get you something.'

'It's pretty rotten having to go through somebody's pockets.'

'It has to be done, best get that sort of thing over.'

'It's as well I did. Look.' He delved into the side pocket of his jeans and came out with the packets of condoms Nat had bought from Young Sid in a moment of bravado. 'These were in the pocket of his new jacket.'

Lizz watched him as he inspected them as though he had not seen a condom packet in his life. She felt terribly sorry for him. He'd always had everything, looks, personality, money; he'd been the golden boy with a charmed life and no problems. This would hit him harder than most; he had no experience of grief. Poor Jake.

'I've never known him very well, not as you'd expect to know your father.' He scrunched up the packets. 'Bugger all, Lizz, I didn't know him.' He rose and threw the packets into the stove. 'I didn't bloody know him at all.'

As he passed the canvas his arm caught the muslin, which fell off.

'I'm sorry, Jake. I didn't mean you to see it – at least, not yet.'

He stopped her from covering the picture. 'No. Let me see.' She had never seen Jake with tears in his eyes. 'You knew him, all right, Lizzy.'

'It's my job, I paint portraits.'

'I don't think he was ever unfaithful before, do you?'

'That's only a story, Jake. Poseidon seduced by Gaea, it's turning the myth on its head. The picture's not about your father being unfaithful, he was just the model for Poseidon.'

'Come on, Lizz, that's not the truth.'

She had nothing to say. Long ago she had learned not to underestimate beauty, obesity or disablement. And it never did to underestimate Jake: he was perceptive and intelligent inside his easy-going, charming exterior.

'Anyway, I heard him last night . . . he told her what a fantastic lay she was. He was cock-a-hoop, and he didn't care who heard. I'd never have thought my Old Man knew what joyfulness was, not in a thousand years. I don't know how you did it, but you've got that same expression.'

'I could do it because I know you. Your father was never intended to be dour and angry. If he'd had the same start in life that he gave you, then I think he would have been as laid-back as you are, but he got nipped in the bud, clobbered. I know everybody says that you are like your mother, but I've never seen that – I think your mother is a tough cookie. I think you take after him, the only difference is that you've grown up in a nice sunny world.'

'I'm glad I saw him like that last night. She gave him something none of the rest of us has ever given him. Do you think there was anything in it?'

'On her side? Yes. I think she was as banjaxed by it as he was.'

He sat with his head bowed and his hands hanging loosely between his legs looking dejected. 'That's a tough one.'

'She'll cope. She's the Pagliacci type. She'll paint her eyes and you'll never know she wept.'

He turned again to the painting. 'It's the best thing you've done.'

She nodded. 'Yes. It will be in the exhibition.'

'It will fetch a good price.'

'It won't be easy to let it go.'

He made a move towards her as though he would put his arms round her and as casually as she could she went to pick up some brushes. She felt mean; he probably wanted all the comfort he could get at the moment. He followed her and, standing behind her, put his arms beneath hers, wrapping them around her, a hand over each of her breasts.

'Let's leave it, Jake.'

'I can't. When I was looking at the Old Man stretched out . . . I should stop all this fucking around.'

They had stood like this scores of times, looking out of the studio window or standing on the Downs, or criticizing a new painting. This was Lizz and Jake together. Lizz and Jake. Jake and Lizz. A couple, an item.

'That was when I first realized that I didn't really know him. There was this bloody awful sadness came over me. He and I had wasted twenty years. We were together nearly every day. I don't know whether he wanted to ask me things about me . . . but sure as hell, I know now that I wanted to ask him things about him.'

Lizz felt acute heartache for him. No matter what was happening to their relationship now, they couldn't ignore all the years up to this moment.

'Let's get married, Lizz. I can't absolutely vow that I won't ever be attracted by another woman . . . and I don't expect you to be any different. But if we married I might feel different about sleeping around, you know what with a family. I really do want kids, Lizzy. I want stability, I want to be married, Lizz, and there's really nobody except you.'

It was now or never. This was the end of Jake and Lizz as an item. Whatever happened now, they would either marry or put an end to it. They couldn't go back to the old casualness now that marriage had come into it.

Last night when she was painting the lovers, she wondered what had happened when Poseidon returned from his affair with Gaea. Jake's father had had thirty years of commitment to their marriage, but when push came to shove she guessed that he might well choose Kuan-Yin. Commitment isn't love. He'd found love at the eleventh hour – but he'd found it. The one thing that a film-maker or writer can do that a painter cannot is to tell everything. In *Poseidon and Gaea* she had only been able to reveal one moment of their love, but she was sure that she knew the rest of the story.

She felt Jake's familiar shape and warmth and smelled his unique odour. And if I never have this experience again? She had already glimpsed her future with Jake if she married him. She had glimpsed it last night when he and Roz Petherbridge couldn't keep their hands off one another, and she had a full view of it now on the canvas. Lizz knew that she was not the woman to make Jake cock-a-hoop with joy.

'No, Jake. One day you'll find a Gaea, but you know that it's not me.'

As he went back up to Sunbarrow, Jake no longer felt as fresh and young as he always did when walking carefree between Lizz's place and home. His breezy youth had been blighted. Now all the decisions about Sunbarrow would be his own, not merely reacting or putting an opposing view to his father's. If Sunbarrow was to continue in the old way, then he was responsible for it. He felt too young to have the weight of all his father's hard years of sacrifice hanging around his neck.

Ages ago he had toyed with the idea of going to Zimbabwe or Australia. If he had done it then Sunbarrow would now be somebody else's problem. It was no use anybody pretending that Sunbarrow was now the responsibility of the whole family: they all knew that the responsibility for Sunbarrow was Jake's.

He was angry at the Old Man. He hadn't died, he'd thrown his cap over the windmill and bloody killed himself.

* * *

The telephone interrupted as Rin and Daisy were trying to write down a list of things that needed to be done. They had been out of their depth with Poppy, she had cried and cried until Roz Petherbridge had said, 'Wouldn't you like to get away from this place for a few hours? I'm sure nobody's going to mind.'

'Are you sure? I don't want to leave Mum if she wants me.'

'Where do you want to go?' Rin asked.

'Down to the Packs. I'll be all right with Chrissie. Do you mind, Daisy?'

'For two pins I'd come with you.'

Poppy said, 'It's the thought of him being in there.' She nodded in the direction of the small room filled with books in which they all used to do their homework. It was apart from the rest of the house and the only place where Rin and Jake could erect a simple bier on which the Old Man was now laid out. It was difficult, being Sunday, but the doctor had called and issued a certificate of death and had promised to get Ray Lavender the undertaker to call and arranged with old Mrs Lavender who would: See to Mr Tallentire and make him look nice.

It was strange, but the absence of the Old Man's spirit or ego or whatever it might be, was as affecting as its presence had always been.

Roz had felt herself an intruder. She had been ill at ease knowing that she had not gone back to her own room last night and being discovered in Jake's bed by Myrr. 'If I can't be of any help, Myrr, then I think I will go.'

Roz knew that her friendship with Myrr was damaged. No woman can lay her friend's son and remain his mother's confidante.

Myrr had nodded. 'Thanks, Roz. You helped with the most important thing, sorting Poppy out. I was just out of my depth with her.'

'I'm sure it was the right thing to do.'

'Of course. It's just that my brain went overload and I couldn't see the wood for the trees.'

'Myrr, I'm sorry . . . about last night. It's not that I'm ashamed, but I wished you hadn't found out.'

'Put it down to Ship Saturday.'

Roz wanted to say: Try to think like that about Nat. 'A moment of madness.'

Myrr nodded. 'We all have them.'

'I'm sorry, Myrr . . . about everything.'

So, whilst Jake was at Lizz's, Roz discreetly withdrew by taxi to Winchester station. All the way back to Southampton she wrote furiously in a notebook; once back on her houseboat she went to her typewriter and wrote the first ten minutes of a radio play.

Rin answered the phone and, as Daisy noted, lowered his voice and turned away. Even so, she heard him say: 'OK . . . Well, look, Jake's out at the moment and we're waiting for the undertaker . . . Yeah, well all right, if you can wait there, I'll be down as soon as I can.'

Daisy thought: He needn't be so coy, it's bound to be her. Where the hell does he think we think he slept last night. She said, 'If you want to go out, Rin, it's all right.'

'It's like living in a bloody goldfish bowl here.'

'So, why are you thinking of coming back here to live?'

'I don't know that I am. Will you be all right if I go down to the village for an hour?'

'Go, brother dear. Give me and Myrr a chance to try to get things sorted.' Suddenly she felt stifled by the place and the thought of what it would be like for the next few days. 'I ought to go back tonight.'

Rin raised his eyebrows. 'Ought?'

'OK then, want to go back. Unless Myrr and Poppy need me, then there's not much point in sleeping here. It only makes more work. I'm only at the other end of a telephone. I can be here in just over an hour.'

'It's OK, Daze. There's nothing Jake and I can't cope with. Myrr said that the funeral could probably be next Friday.'

'I suppose it's a cremation?'

'I don't know. I'd assumed so.'

'Shall I ask Myrr?'

'Where is she?'

'In the book room,' Daisy said. 'Sitting with him.'

'Oh Lord, she's not being . . .'

'She'll be all right. Myrr's strong.'

'I can't imagine this place without him.'

'I know,' Daisy said. 'And Poppy will be away.'

'So she will. Are you going in to see the Old Man?'

'Jesus, no! I've been sitting here thinking about it, I couldn't do it. It would be like the time when I was about ten and I went dashing into their bedroom. He was just sitting gazing into space daydreaming. Except for you and Jake, that was the first time I had seen anybody completely naked. It wasn't shocking in that sense . . . not of seeing his body . . . it was seeing him with his guard down. Even though I was only ten I felt embarrassed, not about catching him without his clothes on, it was because he didn't have his face on.'

Rin nodded.

Daisy said, 'It's why I dread ever having to have an operation, and why I don't want anybody to see me after I'm dead. That's why I don't want to see him.'

Daisy couldn't remember either of her brothers ever having made any comforting moves towards her. Daze had always been the strong one. Daze would defend Rin against bullying. Daze would look after Jake. She had once fallen in the playground and caused a ten-stitches cut and she had been the one who had done the comforting when Rin had cried at the sight of her blood.

'Nobody's going to make you, Daze.' He put his arm round her neck, pulled her into his shoulder and ruffled her hair. 'Remember him with his face on. Remember his frown, and his scowl. Remember how it used to get bright red from frost and dripping wet from hay-making. Oh, poor Daze. I thought I was the only one of us who ever cried.'

She took his handkerchief. 'I bloody well loved him, Rin. Sod him . . . it was just like him to go and die before I found the courage to tell him.'

'He wouldn't have known what to do if you had.'

'That's the trouble with us Tallentires. Anyway, it wouldn't have mattered if it had embarrassed him, at least he would have heard me say it.' She blew her nose and straightened her hair. 'Listen, you, I'll say this once only.' She brushed his cheek with her knuckles. 'I'm glad that we came out twins, but it's been bloody unbearable looking on these last few years. For God's sake, kiddo, try to grab yourself a bit of happiness before it's too late.'

The Packs' home was totally different from the Tallentires'. It was an end-of-terrace labourer's cottage built a hundred years ago with modern facilities only just beginning to appear there. Mrs Pack had rocked Poppy like a child saying: There, there. You have a good cry, love, let it all come out. If you can't cry when your dad dies, then when can you cry? I'll get Susie to make us all a nice sweet cup of tea, and then Chrissie can take you down to see Lassie's new puppies. Lord alive, I don't know where she gets them from and that's a fact. This lot look like their fathers must of been a reg'lar united nations, they're all colours under the sun.' And Poppy had wallowed briefly in the soft arms and the soft meaningless words. Susie had made strong sugary tea and given Poppy a cigarette.

'There, that's better, isn't it?' said Mrs Pack when Poppy took a second cup. And it was.

But Poppy couldn't bear the thought of her dad being dead. 'It's thinking of him being at everybody's mercy, Chrissie.'

They sat on a pile of old wood watching Lassie lying in a box suckling her puppies.

'He was awful when he had that other attack. He wouldn't do what anybody told him. He didn't like anybody to see him weak. But when you're dead, you're at everybody's mercy.'

'They won't do anything to your dad, Popp.'

'He has to be put in a coffin, though. It's awful, the thought of him being put in a box. Sometimes, when I was little, he used to let me ride with him on the tractor. You could hardly hear him over the engine, but he would be humming away. He hardly ever said anything. Only sometimes he'd say something like: "We're living under a great big blue bowl, Poppy." And it is, if you look at it like that – see, it starts on the horizon, goes over your head and down the other side.'

'I can never imagine Mr Tallentire saying things like that, not poetic sort of things. Though he used to talk to me a bit when he was laid up ill last year. Not really talking to me, but getting me to talk, asking me things about what I was going to do, was I going to be serving in bars all my life and didn't I mind cleaning up your house. I told him I was just doing it until I got myself my car. I remember he said, "What you going to do then, drive against Fangio." I said to him, that dates you a bit, Mr Tallentire. I thought it was so sad because he said, "When your sell-by date comes, Chrissie, you've got to get off the shelf." And I said to him, he was just being morbid and I'd send my mum up to sort him out if he didn't watch out. He was nice, your dad.'

Poppy found it difficult to imagine her dad and Chrissie

chatting like that. There was a lot you didn't know about people, even your own father. 'Chrissie? Do men try to touch you up when you're serving in the Green Man?'

Chrissie picked up one of the puppies and made a fuss of it. 'There's always the odd one. Why? Somebody been putting his hand up your skirt then? Never Matt Pridhoe last night.'

'Oh, that's different. He's my same age.'

'Well, you know who Childencombe's most famous feeler upper is. Is it him?'

'I didn't know there was one.'

Chrissie patted Poppy's arm. 'You shouldn't be let out on your own, Poppy Tallentire. You get that preoccupied with your head in books . . . Emma's dad.'

Poppy blushed and folded her arms across her breasts.

'It was him, was it? I thought you were being a bit of a divvi yesterday, going down to his store-room to find him.'

'I didn't know.'

'But I thought you must know and could look after yourself. My mum told me ages ago: Don't get anywhere where Jez Carter can reach: he's part gypsy so he's got Romany hands. He didn't try anything, did he?'

'Lifted my boob. I suppose it's my own fault for not wearing a bra.'

'Dirty old sod. Of course it's not your fault, that's what's the matter with us, we always let them get off. No reason why you should have to wear a bra just because that old sod can't keep his hands to himself. You should have told your mum.'

'I'm nearly eighteen.'

'I would tell my mum if he did it to me. Your dad would half-kill him. Sorry, Popp.'

'It's all right. I hope people aren't going to start shutting up when my dad's name is mentioned.'

'I expect they will. They say don't speak ill of the dead,

but when my dad died people didn't hardly speak of him at all.'

'Chris. Don't tell anybody about Emma's dad. It would be awful if Emma got to hear about it,' Poppy said. 'Fancy knowing that people knew your dad was like that.'

Chrissie wondered where Poppy had been when her dad had kissed the Chinese lady like that. It hadn't been like an older man kissing, it had been like seeing Sean Connery, you knew he was old, yet he was really sexy so you didn't think of him as old. 'You can stop the night if you like. My mum says the first night's the worst.'

'I expect my mum will like me to go home. She's going to miss my dad. They hardly ever slept a night apart except when she took us on holiday.'

'Are they keeping your dad at home?'

'Yes. Otherwise it means Mr Lavender's Chapel of Rest and he wouldn't want to go there.'

'Ugh. All those dusty velvet curtains and that plastic wreath in the window.'

When Daisy asked Myrr what she thought, Myrr said: 'If you wouldn't mind, Daisy, I'd quite like it if you stopped tonight. Just to get used to the first night. Just us, his family. He set a lot of store by doing things like that properly. You remember how he was at Rin's wedding and some of Mary's people got all mixed up with ours in the church. He didn't reckon much to that.'

When, at last on that disastrous Sunday, Myrr and three of her children were left with no more phone calls, or visitors bringing flowers and letters of sympathy, Jake poured them drinks and they sat in the conservatory which had now taken over from the old kitchen as the natural gathering place in the house.

The brave faces were abandoned and it was now that it was possible to see that it was only Daisy who had inherited the Tallentire carapace. It was she who sat with a notebook, prepared to deal with the practicalities of her father's funeral.

'I wish there were still black horses with plumes,' Poppy said. 'It seems so undignified for dad to have to be carried in Mr Lavender's hearse.'

'It seems undignified for him to have to be carried anywhere at all,' Myrr said. 'He made such a fuss when the ambulance men brought in a stretcher-chair to carry him to the ambulance, that they eventually had to give in and let him walk out. He hated all of that being in hospital.'

'Well,' Jake said, 'he can't get out of it this time. He's going to have to let us deal with it.'

'Jake!' Rin said. 'Don't be so callous.'

'Jake's right,' Daisy said, 'like it or not, we've got to decide – how many cars and what time . . .'

'He wouldn't want a religious service,' Myrr said. 'He often said he was going to find out about Humanist services and make his own arrangements.'

'But that's like making a will,' Rin said. 'It's always something we intend doing and keep putting it off.'

'Oh he's made a will, ages ago,' Myrr said. 'You know what it says, don't you?'

'I don't,' Daisy said.

Myrr said, 'He's tied it up so that the farm is left intact – he was very insistent on that.'

Jake said, 'I think there's some sort of covenant which says that if the place is ever sold on outside the family, it must be sold as a going concern and kept as it is now. He didn't want there to be any prairie farming. The old farms that we've added to Sunbarrow over the years are to be kept as separate farms and run much as they were before.'

'I think that's nice,' Rin said. 'It would be dreadful if it was owned by some big company – that would destroy Childencombe.'

Daisy said, 'It's already owned by a big company. Has it ever occurred to you, the size of Sunbarrow Farms?'

'Not a public company,' Rin said. 'It's a family business.'

Daisy said, 'Let's get back to deciding something.'

The phone rang and Daisy answered. 'It's her.' They all knew who. 'She says when would it be all right to talk to you, Myrr?'

'What does she want?'

'I don't know. She says if it hadn't been important she wouldn't have intruded.'

'Shall I speak to her?' Rin said, and took the phone from Daisy. The others watched and listened.

'Hi . . . Will I do? . . .

'That's all right. No . . . not at all. It's just that the phone hasn't stopped ringing all day . . .

'No, no. I realize that . . .

'I see . . .

'I see . . .

'Hmm, hold on . . .'

Turning to Myrr he said, 'Do you feel up to seeing her for half an hour? Privately . . . she says it's important.'

Myrr shrugged non-committally.

'OK, Dr Yin, come up.'

'Christ!' Daisy said. 'What on earth can she have to see Myrr about on a day like this?'

Rin shrugged.

Myrr said, 'I'd best go and run a comb through my hair. She always makes me feel hot and sweaty and pulled through a hedge backwards.'

When Kuan-Yin arrived she was dressed in the plain grey silk she had worn on the Sunday when she had gone to Childencombe church. Rin jumped up to answer the door, ushered her in and offered her a seat. She looked her usual elegant self, but for the first time they saw her looking entirely unflamboyant.

'I am sorry,' she said. 'Please believe me, I would never have intruded if it hadn't been necessary.'

Myrr came in.

'Mrs Tallentire . . .'

Myrr said, 'You don't have to call me Mrs Tallentire because Nat's dead. You've always called me Myrr before, haven't you?'

'Of course. I am so sorry for your loss.' The muscles of her mouth tightened as she worked to control herself. She gave Rin a quick look that he could not interpret. Although Rin had not said where he had spent the night, they all guessed that it was with her.

None of them guessed what it was that Nat had told Myrr.

'I'll get you a drink,' Jake said.

'No, thanks, Jake, I have my Uncle Han in the car.'

'You've left him outside? Of all people, Mr Han is welcome here,' Myrr said. 'Jake, go and invite him in.'

Lee Han came in apologetically. Myrr took his hand and insisted that he be comfortably seated. 'I shall always be in your debt, Mr Han.'

He gave a gracious little bow. 'I am culprit making my niece come here. Sorry for intrusion. Alison, tell family of predicament.'

She spoke to Myrr. 'Do you remember that a few days ago your husband came with me to Long Kennet?'

'Wasn't he always somewhere or other lately?' Myrr said.

Rin thought: She knows what was going on.

Daisy watched Rin watching Kuan-Yin. She hoped he wasn't going to get hurt again just as he was climbing back. She was certainly beautiful, like Mary. Rin had always been a sucker for looks. She was the sort that men couldn't help making fools of themselves over.

Jake said, 'It was great for the Old Man, having somebody who was interested in the old barrows and knew what a ley-line was. None of us ever was.' He had to admire the way she had control of herself: it couldn't be easy. Even if she didn't know about Lizzy's little bombshell, she must know that she and his Old Man hadn't been invisible in the glow of the bonfire.

'On the way, he asked me if we could stop off at his lawyer. He said that he had never given Mr Cockrill instructions about . . .' Few people had ever seen her floundering. She looked at Lee Han.

'My niece is naturally embarrass. Sometimes we say yes to things and do not see consequences. To say yes to friend who make simple request is understandable. Mr Tarrentire ask for special way of . . . I am sorry, Madam . . . of disposal of remains.'

Kuan-Yin spoke directly to Myrr. 'I would not have agreed if I had thought for a minute that he wouldn't have time to tell you what he had in mind. I suppose he didn't? He said he'd wait until you were all together.'

'Like we are now?' said Daisy.

'I think he was going to arrange for you to be together and . . . well, to try to show you why he wanted you to carry out his wishes. I don't find this easy, you know.'

Lee Han said, 'Alison has show me photocopy of your husband's records.'

'What records?' Poppy asked.

Kuan-Yin answered, 'Geomantic records.'

'Geo-mantic?'

'Maps of various courses . . . water.'

'He could always dowse for water, everybody knew that,' Myrr said.

'And why would he want to give you records?' Daisy asked.

'Because I was interested, am interested. I have records of Faery paths in Ireland, Spirit paths in South America.' She clasped the fingers of her uncle as though to draw support from him. 'My uncle has given me records of dragon veins in parts of China, your father had records of ley-lines on Sunbarrow. I shall use them in a book. Tallentire had a theory about a connection between the dragon veins here, and the barrows and the corn circles, he was going to contribute a chapter to my book.' She looked at Lee Han, who nodded encouragingly. 'But it is too late.'

Daisy was the only member of the family whose mind wasn't being disturbed by the thought that they had lived their lives with a man who had a side to him they didn't know existed.

Kuan-Yin said, 'His records go back to 1956.'

Daisy said, 'He wasn't hardly in his teens then, was he?'

Kuan-Yin cut across them. 'If you will please ask Mr Cockrill tomorrow, he knows the difficulties Tallentire has created. I know it wasn't very wise of me to agree but I ... but ... Well, I've agreed and I shall do my best to see that it is done.' She faced Myrr again. 'If you've got problems with me ... maybe you won't mind Uncle Han making the preparations.'

'For Christ's sake!' Daisy said. 'Does he want burying at sea or something?'

Lee Han said, 'If you allow, Lee Han will conduct proceeding with great dignity. Many times in China Lee Han is call by important family at time of death of most important father. You will see, Madam, arrangements will be suitable for head of great household.'

Jake, who had been the most likely candidate for involvement with Kuan-Yin, had remained unentangled. They had met frequently over the weeks, and they had been easy-going with one another, whether it was on the tennis courts or looking at circles. With the exception of his father, he was the member of the Tallentire family who knew her best. He had liked her from the first. He had seen Lizzy's picture and seen the élan with which his father had captured her in the red rag. Seeing her sitting there looking composed but defeated, he felt a lot of compassion for her, and wanted to let her know that at least somebody in the room understood what she was going through.

He said, 'All this must be pretty bloody for you. The Old Man put you in an impossible situation. We're sorry you had to be drawn into our family affairs like this. It's not your fault, you didn't ask to become involved.'

She gave him a faint smile and nodded, then turned her gaze to Myrr. 'Jake's right, I hope you won't blame me, the last thing I wanted was to become involved at all, but what we want and what we get are two different things.'

Only Lee Han did not know the sub-text of these last exchanges.

Myrr looked away and then back at her. 'You'd better tell us what you promised Nat. We've arranged next Friday with Dick Lavender.'

Kuan-Yin didn't ask what had been arranged with Dick Lavender, she felt outsider enough as it was. Neither did she know that the man with whom she had so unexpectedly fallen in love was laid on a hurdle just a few rooms away. She had assumed that he was resting in some chapel or funeral parlour.

Jake went out at first light to meet Lee Han and Kuan-Yin. He stopped himself thinking any more about her – he had spent last night organizing his thoughts, sorting out Myrr and Kuan-Yin and the Old Man; having sensed, or observed, that Myrr knew that something quite serious had happened – whether the Old Man had been unfaithful or not. Jake had eventually concluded that the situation had resolved itself by the Old Man dying; the only productive action on his own part was giving non-partisan support to Kuan-Yin as well as his mother.

There is always a morning, when the summer is at its fullest, that a smell, a breath, a shade or ghost of winter past or future rises up before and after the sun as a reminder. In full summer it never seems possible that leaves will ever become red with sugars and then fall, that grasses will no longer be able to photosynthesize or plants make seed. In the middle of the weeks of hot, dry weather, Jake, as he walked up towards the ridge at the top of Clump Field, felt that brief foretaste of a November morning.

He shivered. It was barely light, but he was glad to be out of the house. He didn't think he could stand the tense atmosphere of the family under one roof, living with the Old Man back at the centre of it; there and not there. No matter what sort of conversation was going on, nobody could get away from the presence in the book room. It wasn't the fact of living close to a corpse or anything like that, but because he was still at the centre and dominating everything, and until they had let Lee Han and Kuan-Yin get on with their thing, nobody seemed able to breathe properly.

On the ridge at the top of the field, he saw Kuan-Yin and her uncle setting up various pieces of equipment. The sober presence of Lee Han and Kuan-Yin's face, wan and pale in the weak, grey light, seemed to make even the most normal exchanges of greeting too light-hearted. Jake himself felt sombre and withdrawn.

He was surprised at her changed appearance. Few people had seen Kuan-Yin wearing jeans and sweater and with her hair under a band; even when she had come to the tennis club, she had not abandoned her exotic make-up and complicated hairstyle. Jake thought how amazingly small she was; had she been unmade-up and dressed like this that evening when Mike had first brought her to the Green Man, Jake would have described her as a pretty little woman.

In the presence of Lee Han at work, Kuan-Yin felt quite inadequate and of a lower order. Being used to having half a dozen young men around him for the task, he instructed without a please or thank you. She was glad that Jake had offered to come, she had sensed his empathy in her situation over the carrying out of Tallentire's wishes. The whole family had listened to what she had to say in an unemotional silence, and had accepted it almost without question. She wondered whether they really understood what it was that he had instructed them to do. She knew very well that they could simply say no: they had every right to do so, Tallentire's instructions had no law to back them. Perhaps it was all so extreme that they simply could not cope with objecting to it.

Lee Han said, 'First I shall walk entire ridge. No need of assistance at present. Erect stool and place *lo p'an* securely. Compass must be flat. Check needle.'

He left, walking eastwards, away from the barrows with their clump of yews, striding sure-footedly like a man half his age, stopping to scrutinize the Queer Stone. Jake helped Kuan-Yin dig out little dips in the ground for the legs of the *lo p'an* stool.

'Don't mind him if he treats you like a bellhop, Jake, it won't mean anything.'

'I expect he's used to better help than two unskilled labourers.'

'He won't mind. The Chinese like to be with a *hsein-sheng* at work, he's used to amateur helpers . . .'

'I wonder what he actually feels when he hits one of these . . . forces he's trying to locate.'

She didn't look at him. 'You should have asked your father, Jake: he knew.'

Jake wondered what kind of conversations the Old Man must have had with her. How had he ever got round to talking about his own last rites? The sun appeared over the horizon and caught the opposite slope. 'Jesus! Will you look at that?'

Lower down the slope from where they had set up the *lo p'an* and close to the Queer Stone was a new set of symbols stretched out for two or three hundred feet or more.

She turned slowly and raised her head to look. 'I know.'

'You knew it was there?'

She nodded. 'We saw it on Saturday.'

'You . . . and the Old Man?'

'Yes. When you were down in the village.'

Everyone had gone to the fair. She and Tallentire, walking back towards the farmhouse, had sat and rested on the ridge, seeming to be quite alone in the landscape. The heat of the day had been intense, but nothing like the furnace of New York in a heatwave; out on the Downs although the air had been hot it had seemed clean and refreshing. It was idyllic, she had never remembered ever feeling as contented and peaceful as on that day.

Tallentire had held out his palms to the clear sky. 'I can stand any amount of this, I love it when it's really hot.' He had laughed in his short, expletive way. 'I've always thought that we shouldn't be surprised that there's spirits running about graveyards: I'd run myself if anybody put me in the cold ground.' He had shuddered. 'Myrr knows not to let them put me in cold storage.' He had smiled. 'We've got our Old Mrs Lavender down in the village, you know, she "sees to" all us authentic Childencombrians when we pop off. She likes to know in plenty of time what we want to be dressed in.'

'She would make her fortune back in the States. What happens when there's no more Old Mrs Lavender?'

'Oh, there always is one. There has to be, none of us villagers would know how to get over to the Other Side if there wasn't. The Young Mrs Lavender eventually becomes Old Mrs Lavender. She likes you to let your preferences for dress to be known by the time you're forty-five. Then she doesn't have to bother the family when the time comes.'

'That's great. So practical and nice.'

'I always reckoned I'd like my best check working shirt

and corduroys, but I've rather taken to these ones and the dark blue shirt.' He had laughed again. 'You've got a lot to answer for, Doctor. Nat Tallentire in pale blue trousers – God above, the village must think I've gone soft.'

With every hour they were together, her interest in him grew; she had noticed how he began opening up, softening, allowing himself to enjoy, letting her through. She remembered the half-wink he gave her when she had said, 'Well, haven't you gone soft?'

So light-hearted, no serious thoughts of dying; how was death possible out there on the Downs, with sun and sky so warm and bright, with Tallentire so full of joyful life?

He had named the flowers around them in the long grass. 'Cocksfoot, carline thistle, birdsfoot, wild basil . . . ?'

His accent broad. His voice soft and deep. She found it exotic. Memories of her high school English Literature studies suddenly came into her mind. Mid-term a good-looking teacher from Cambridge, England, had taken over the dreary course and had breathed life into nineteenth-century British farmers. Richard Reingaud. He had been passionate for the Thomas Hardy novels. Reingaud's classes became notorious amongst the students for an explicitness that was unusual for the times, and he had tried to hide his Englishness: Hey people, take a look, it's all there on the page . . . Lucetta is one sexy lady and Thomas Henchard is quite a stud. He hadn't known that it was his Englishness that they loved.

Sex in all its adult possibilities had burst forth all around them.

Gabriel Oak, Thomas Henchard, Jude Fawley, Clym Yeobright.

Is that what this is all about? Her heart thudded as always when she made some self-discovery. Tallentire was in their mould. Outwardly dour, obsessive men, all burning with terrific sexual passion. She remembered how much more stimulating than her teenage boyfriends she had found those men. In many of her fantasies at that time, it was an amalgam of Reingaud and the tragic heroes who had yielded to her . . .

'. . . Wa'frin' tree, germander and saxifrage.' The long, open vowels of an English southerner.

With all the ease of a practised lover he had gathered her to him and kissed her long and tenderly and said, 'You looked as though you needed that.'

'A bit more than that, Tallentire.'

It had not been only a sexual hunger for him that she had needed him to satisfy there and then, it was that she wanted to assure herself that he was not tainted with the tragedy of her fantasy lovers. She wanted to do for him what Eustacia, Lucetta and Sue had been unable to do. She wanted to make him happy, very happy.

She would never forget. Time had passed as though the pause-button of a video player was being depressed and released, producing a series of blurry still shots. Her own deep intake of breath as he released her. His suntanned arm with golden hairs the same colour as the corn. The feel of his dry hand on the back of her own. The rivulets of perspiration that trickled from her temples. The afternoon heat shimmering the landscape. A wonderful stillness and silence. Silence broken by a shrilling, soaring lark.

She had felt that her mind had slowed down until it came almost to a halt as it dwelt on the one sensation of their skin coming into contact. The experience of making love to him was so intense that she could hardly think.

'It's all right, I brought all my mates with me.'

She opened her eyes to see him grinning boyishly at her.

'Joke, Doctor. Make a note of the date, it's the one when Old Man Tallentire made a joke.' She had not understood until he had playfully stuck a condom packet to his forehead.

'Don't,' she said, taking it and throwing it into the grass. When they released one another from his smooth, overwhelming glide into her receptive, eager body, he said, 'All I want . . . is to do that every day for the next fifty years.'

With a mock pout she had said, 'Not enough by half.'

He had pulled her to him and kissed her. 'In a hundred years I'll be a hundred and fifty . . . and I doubt if I'll make it much past a hundred, the rate I'm going lately.'

'And I'll be a hundred and thirty. So it will have to be done at twice the rate and in half the time. Twice a day?'

'I'll settle for that.' He had raised himself on one elbow and was tenderly caressing her.

'Not necessarily in quick succession, honey, or you won't make it past ninety.'

Hell, she was falling for this guy. Really falling. Momentarily unaware that she was doing so, she found that in looking into his blue eyes, through which he had lately revealed so much of his previously pent-up desire and unspoken thoughts, she had allowed him to penetrate her beyond her gaze as easily as he had her body. She might have been prepared when it came to his physical outpouring, but against his strong, silent declaration of love he gave her no protection. Before she could snap her own guard in place, she knew that it had gone too far and she had let him go further than was safe in a light-hearted affair.

Now, brushing her hair and putting on lipstick she reflected upon it, since the first day when she had arrived here, she had felt that she was living in some kind of enchanted circle. Childencombe standing isolated in the heart of miles of downlands, and Sunbarrow encircled by the prairies of ripening corn. Apart from her real world. Away from the sidewalks of New York. Separated from the Blossom Parks, from Addie, and Huband and the partners, and from clients with guilt problems who wanted to dump on her – wives who cheated on their husbands and husbands who beat up their wives.

Here there were only beautiful stimulating women like

Lizz and desirable men like Jake and Mike, and a lover who could take on the form of a god. In this enchanted place she had twice thrown caution to the wind, both times because of Tallentire. First physically when they had played gods in the swimming-pool, and now emotionally when she had let him glimpse how she felt about him.

Recovering, she said laughingly, 'Ninety's good.'

He had pointed to the complex pattern of triangle, circles, rings, spirals, arcs and ladders inscribed in the cornfield. 'Can you read the Circlemaker language?'

'Not too well.'

'It reads: "Kuan-Yin, don't go away".'

She had taken the opportunity to break the spell and jumped up. 'That's the first time you called me by my name.'

He too got up and stood beside her looking at the pictogram. 'OK, Doctor, so it reads: "Dragon Lady, don't go away" – the important part is the "don't go away" bit.'

Now the early morning sunlight appeared through trees and caught the pictogram obliquely. Lee Han, who had been making stamping and turning, stamping and turning actions close to the Queer Stone, was now climbing up to the ridge.

'My God, it's beautiful,' Jake said. 'It's really, really, so beautiful.'

Lee Han too must have seen it for he stopped his intense activity and stood looking.

Kuan-Yin nodded. 'Tallentire thought so.' She looked subdued, quite desolate.

Jake's instinct was to put his arms around her and say something, but he felt that whatever he might say could only come out sounding trite and conventional. He said, 'I never like taking the harvesters into those fields.'

'Neither did he.'

'You're wrong there. He liked to get the harvesters in, he couldn't stand having circles appear on Sunbarrow. I always had to battle with him if somebody wanted to film them. He didn't have much time for corn circles I'm afraid.'

'He did, Jake, of course he did. When he saw that, his response was the same as mine and yours – wonder. Isn't that what you feel?'

'And respect. That's what I feel . . . and awe. If there were no modern media and tin-brain reporters, or if there weren't heat-sensitive cameras and Japanese technology, I think we'd see it all in a much different light.'

'You mean that we've all gotten used to seeing the fantastic?'

'Have you ever wondered what the general reaction would be if the Archangel Gabriel appeared?'

'Somebody would announce it as a hoax.'

'Perhaps it is. Does it matter? The effect is much the same. If it all turns out that the SAS has been creeping about Sunbarrow at night, somebody, somewhere had the marvellous idea of doing it.'

She showed a flicker of interest. 'That's quite a profound thought, Jake.'

He now did what he should have done when he first thought of it and put a friendly arm about her shoulders.

'First one I ever had then.'

Their attempt at some sort of normal conversation soon foundered. They kept withdrawing into their own thoughts. Not knowing what to do until Lee Han came to instruct them, they stood gazing towards the latest crop symbol.

Kuan-Yin was subdued but, psychologist or not, Jake thought, that wasn't surprising; it was a bloody peculiar occasion.

Jake watched as she worked at levelling the *lo p'an* with little folds of paper tucked between it and the stool. She looked so small and vulnerable, her breasts soft and flattened beneath her skinny shirt, her tennis shoes, her

371

schoolgirlish, waterfalling hair. That day when he had come across the frog orchid, she had looked so powerful that he had felt almost intimidated by her. Yet the Old Man hadn't been. They had understood one another. He thought of the little packets he'd discovered in his father's jacket pocket, the assured way he had captured her with the "Tongue", his groan of sheer delight when their mouths had met.

Half to herself, she said, 'I don't think he could decide whether Sunbarrow was being blessed or cursed.'

She sat down beside the *lo p'an* stool. Jake did likewise and pulled out a crushed packet of cigarettes from his shorts pocket. 'Daisy's,' he explained, and offered her one which she took.

Lee Han had disappeared over the crest of the ridge, and it was now quite light. They fell silent until she said, 'Can I ask you . . . ? Maybe I've got it all wrong . . . Well, y'know you don't seem too . . . Hell, this isn't going to come out right . . . no signs of grief, Jake, where are the tears?'

'I might ask you the same.'

She looked away sharply.

'You mean because I can stand around speculating about strange happenings when my father's hardly cold?'

'It's the way some of us cope with our feelings?' She raised her eyebrows questioningly. 'Isn't it?'

'You should know, you're the shrink.'

'Shrinks don't always have the answers.'

He drew the cigarette smoke deep into his lungs and released it, it was the action of a smoker whose body won't ever give up. 'What is the question?'

'Did you love him?'

Jake couldn't look directly at her. Jake, a thirty-year-old, sociable, tolerant man, was not easy in a situation where he could not flirt or joke. He sounded abrupt: 'Yes, I s'ppose I did.'

He sensed her forming a follow-up question and wanted to ask: And did you?

She pressed. 'And did you feel that he loved you? I mean as you expected to be loved by him? Were you satisfied with what he gave you?'

Looking back, even over the one day that he had been dead, it was difficult to remember the Old Man as father. Until now, Jake's mind had only been able to cope with the immediate images – the inert body on the terrace, the still body on the garden bench, the stiff, formal corpse in everyday clothes stretched out on sheep hurdles resting on trestles, like a poor farmer of a century ago. Did he love you?

Love? Was a father with an obsession, such as the Old Man's obsession of having control of huge tracts of fertile land, able to love his children? Jake was sure that it had never been wealth for its own ends that had driven the Old Man. Unlike many farmers Jake knew well, his father had not been interested in being a rich man, yet he seemed to have the feel for growing money in the way that he had the knack of growing many another cash-crop better than his neighbours. The profits from Sunbarrow Farms were simply the means with which to acquire more land and to buy his way out of the hands of the banks, and after that the means of securing the future of Sunbarrow. Nor had it been the status ... certainly not the status. It was a standing joke in the village that Nat Tallentire had made a million and never even bought himself a decent car or worn anything better than off-the-peg clothes from the same shop he had used for years. Nor had it been the power a big operation like theirs wielded. Love? The Old Man had loved his land – no, he had a passion for it. Passion.

Suddenly he saw his father more clearly. His Old Man was not a man for such a manageable emotion as love, at least, not for falling in love as Jake understood it, but was a man who would become involved in uncompromising passion – perverse, undocile, destructive passion. Jake realized that his father's forceful, exuberant declaration to Kuan-Yin made by the light of the Ship Fair bonfire was in keeping; as was the Old Man's need to always get what he set out to get, in any way he could get it. Single-mindedness. Even though he was dead, he was still getting them to take part in a bizarre procedure because he had set his mind to seeing that it was done. If it wasn't for the heart attack, the Old Man would have got Kuan-Yin.

Kuan-Yin seldom got a quick response when she asked this question professionally. She saw the signs of a man who was, for the first time, trying to answer a very basic question about himself.

The signs that the Old Man had been incapable of moderation had always been there, but Jake had always been too close, or too familiar with them, to see. It was the way the Old Man was, the way he'd always been. It wouldn't have been difficult to see that nor to understand what he was capable of, had Jake given two thoughts to what made his father tick. Lizz had seen, so presumably had Kuan-Yin. Was it the father and son rivalry that was supposed to exist? Jake didn't know about that kind of thing. It was only when Kuan-Yin came upon the scene and then when he had found the condoms that he'd even given much thought to the sexual nature of the Old Man. Nobody ever liked to give much thought to that side of their parents.

Now that he thought about it, there was plenty of evidence that his father was more capable of passion than his dourness seemed to point to, but it had been channelled into obsession. As well as the single-minded gathering in of the land surrounding Sunbarrow, there was the continual expansion of their operations; no aspect of the chain from soil to consumer was overlooked; Sunbarrow Farms was all-providing; then recently there had been that map of ley-lines and tumuli. Finally there had been the going overboard with Kuan-Yin. When overtaken by an aspiration or when an ideal had been embedded in his mind, he had been incapable of moderation. So that once he had been captivated by this idea of leaving life like a dynast and he had invested it with his single-mindedness, the idea would have no option but to gather momentum and go like a snowball downhill.

He visualized the small idea, started rolling by Kuan-Yin, then with the Old Man's enthusiasm it had gathered to it Mr Cockrill's willingness to buck the system, Myrr's willingness to acquiesce with whatever he wanted just to get it over, and the rest of them willing to, at least, see to it that the Old Man got something to show for nearly forty years of holding himself in check. Nothing as trivial and vulgar as the personalized number-plates with which other wealthy farmers indulged themselves.

'No, he didn't love me,' he said at last; 'but I think that I've been satisfied with whatever it was that he did feel for me. It wouldn't have been much use being otherwise. I think he gave as much as he was capable of giving. Even when I was quite little, I think I understood that he wasn't an ordinary kind of man. I could never imagine myself equalling him in size, you know.' He smiled reflectively. 'I'm a bit taller, actually, but I always do this,' he held his hand about six inches above his head, 'if I ever describe him – "My dad? He's a really big guy." I dare say I'll always wish that I'd known him better. How was it that he could talk to you?'

'I make my living at it.' Her eyes followed Lee Han as he moved about in the pictogram. She shivered. Jake took off his sleeveless jerkin and put it round her shoulders.

He shook his head. 'No. Your conduct with my dad wasn't at all professional, was it?' She tried to smile. He chafed the bare shoulder that poked bonily through the armhole of the jerkin. He felt terribly protective towards her. It was confusing. It was quite probable that his family would have broken up over her, yet somehow it seemed to be more the fault of the family than of her. He felt peculiarly guilty that he had been the one to bring her to Sunbarrow. The lovely exhibitionist who wanted to see their corn circles had gone.

He said, 'You say that he found the circles awesome, yet he'd put up notices stopping other people who might find them awesome and only wanted to come and have a look. I argued with him, but he never mentioned awe or momentousness. For God's sake, I knew it couldn't be that we couldn't afford to lose the twopence ha'penny-worth of corn that sightseers might have damaged.'

'Don't you think that he just might have been trying to protect the circles and not the crop?'

Jake went silent; he tried to see her expression, but she had turned away. 'You haven't answered my question. Why couldn't he have talked to me?'

'Y'know, Jake, you're a real social guy, you're carefree, laid-back . . . you've got all those things that he thought were too extravagant and luxurious for a man with responsibilities.'

'He resented my nature?'

'No, I don't think he did, but he wouldn't have found you the easiest person to open up to.'

'Who was?'

'Perhaps an outsider who was on his wavelength.'

The word 'outsider' brought a lump to Jake's throat, and, as Lee Han appeared once more on the ridge, Jake put his arm round her narrow back and hugged her gently. 'It's all right, I've no problems with seeing a shrink crying. If anybody's got reason to grieve for him, it's you. You loved him?'

But she didn't cry, she looked across at the symbol dry-eyed and in obvious distress, clutching his other hand tightly.

'Loved him? I fell for him, Jake . . . I sure as hell fell for him. It was like walking on a firm floor and suddenly falling through a hole. I had no idea ... I thought I knew all about love ... perhaps I do ... but I don't know about that kind of passion. Oh, that theory about male and female being two separated halves, each half always searching for the other ... that's how it was. I felt that I had found that piece of me I've been looking for. I'm sure that he felt the same. I had no intention ... can you understand? I mean, if we were going to go in for a grand passion, we'd both have been pretty dim to choose each other, wouldn't we?'

Lee Han was now striding back in their direction and when he reached them he pointed to the symbol. 'Most extraordinary!' He was brisk, and the thought flashed through Jake's mind that perhaps Lee Han had disappeared purposely so that his niece could talk. 'Ah. You can be useful.' He went to the *lo p'an* and adjusted the needle, looking back and forth between it and the ridge along which he had walked. Pointing to a place along the ridge, he said, 'That is place on back of dragon where I must start.'

'Uncle Han, it must be me. I am going to do it.'

'What must you do?'

'I have to be the one who rides the dragon.'

'This is not possible. Female cannot ride dragon.'

'You can guide me, I will do precisely what you say.'

'Not point of argument. Is wrong, female is against tradition.'

'Probably not. It is more than likely that originally the rite was carried out by a woman ... most mystical rites were. We used to be the ones who performed rituals. We've got to begin doing it again.'

'There is danger for woman.'

'No, Uncle Han, honey, the danger for women is in not doing the things we ought.'

'It is necessary to run with abandon . . . go where dragon runs. The omphalos . . .'

'I know, I know the omphalos, Uncle Han, I have been here with Jake's father.'

Jake could see assertiveness surge through her, filling her out, making her grow. Her breasts no longer seemed childlike as she stood up to him. She took off the ribbon band and with it tied back her hair and, as she spoke, she thrust her body and chin slightly forward. 'I have to do it for Tallentire, Uncle Han. You can be with me or against me, but I shall do it.'

For what seemed ages to Jake, they contested with only their eyes. Age and youth, male and female, old ways and new, Eastern and Western cultures faced it out. She was the stronger, or perhaps it was that she was more passionately involved, had more to lose. Lee Han nodded gracefully and conceded the contest.

He pointed to a place and said to Jake, 'You and I shall position ourselves downward of flow from first point. Usually I have several assistant but we shall manage. When my niece is riding, please do not stand in way or be tempted to stop her, even if it appears she is unable to halt. She will stop.' He took some thin, extending rods of cane, some of which he handed to Jake. 'Please mark exact spot at which Kuan-Yin dismounts.'

Jake positioned himself just below the Queer Stone, where the steep slope of the field levelled out; not knowing what to do or what to expect he took up a similar stance to Lee Han, who stood sideways-on to the slope. Kuan-Yin went to the point on the ridge which Lee Han had marked earlier with one of the cane rods.

At a signal from her uncle, Kuan-Yin launched herself in a flying leap from the steepest angled point along the ridge. Then she came at full tilt. Downhill leaping towards them. Running headlong, almost flying, her feet seemingly hardly touching the ground. Down the slope, across the corn circle and up the slight rise in the ground, with her head held back and panting lightly she slowed down, then stopped. Lee Han ran to her and stuck one of his canes upright at her feet.

He pointed to the ridge. 'Now to the second hump. Do not direct yourself, but ride dragon, let him go own way.'

This second starting-point was a good many yards away from the first and again she launched herself almost wildly as though leaping from a cliff. At first running and leaping diagonally. Then downwards, her momentum carrying her fast downhill. Over the circle again she crossed the path of her first descent and came to rest at a point well beyond it, which Jake marked.

She made a third, fourth, fifth and sixth headlong flight from separate points along the ridge, by which time the sun was well up in the sky and lighting the hillside. It took quite a long time for the three of them to attach lengths of red plastic tape between the start and finish markers of each of Kuan-Yin's flights. Where they crossed, Lee Han erected a red-painted marker.

'Here!' he declared unnecessarily.

The three of them stood silently. The point at which the red marker stood, at the centre of the web of tapes, was at the outer edge of the dip in which the Queer Stone rested, close to the new pattern.

Lee Han nodded. 'Your father must have been *hsein-sheng*, that is place he has chosen as most appropriate. I have felt flow of *ch'i*, Alison has confirmed.' He bowed formally to her. 'Perhaps old men have been mistaken. You wish to become master of *feng-shui*, I will instruct. This has been good ride.'

It was as though the name 'honey' had never entered her vocabulary. Appearing totally oriental in spite of her jeans and skinny shirt, she returned his bow. 'I should prefer to become mistress of *feng-shui*. What is the feminine of *hsein-sheng*?'

Jake looked at the web of red plastic and canes. At first sight it might appear to have been marked out, not by geomancers with *lo p'ans* and running leaps, but by surveyors with tapes and theodolites. What with that and the Gaea symbol on the facing slope, Jake felt weary. Daisy had always said: Don't ask Jake to think about it, he's afraid to bend his brain. Just now his brain did feel bended, it was all becoming too weird.

'I ought to get across to the office quite soon. There's a lot to be done, I'll have to see to some pretty prosaic things like telling the newspapers . . . the radio . . .'

'Jake, can you get the field harvested quickly?'

'Don't worry, I'll get it done.'

'But not the symbol.'

He nodded thoughtfully. 'OK, if you say so.'

When Jake got to his quiet, empty office he was glad to be drawn into a normal working day organizing the roping off of the circles and mustering all the combines he could. He supposed that now that the Old Man wasn't here he could take over the other office and the king-size chair. He went into his own corner of the main office and sat as usual on the draughtsman's stool. It was OK in here.

SEVEN

When the tongues of flame are in-folded
Into the crowned knot of fire
And the fire and the rose are one.

T. S. ELIOT, Four Quartets

Midday on that same Monday morning brought Mr Cockrill to Sunbarrow. Daisy and Poppy had gone to Winchester for no other reason than to get away from the house where their father lay in state giving Poppy the creeps, so Cockrill was greeted by Myrr and Rin.

'This is such a strange request, Mrs Tallentire, that I should like to have discussed it with the entire family. You understand, of course, Mr Tallentire, that a deceased person has no say in the disposal of his or her remains. They may request – as Mr Tallentire has done – but the actual deed, as one might say, is done by the surviving family and should there be any dispute, then it is for the next of kin – yourself, Mrs Tallentire – to make the final decision . . . it is hoped, of course, without pressure from anyone. Do you understand?'

'Yes, of course. You mean that Nat's body is mine and whether he's cremated or buried is up to me.'

'Something like that . . . yes. But you already have an inkling, have you not, that his request is, to say the least, somewhat unusual?'

'Unusual?' Rin said. 'I should have thought it was unique in England.'

'Not totally unique, there was an occasion . . . ah, special circumstances . . .' His discomfort made Myrr and Rin feel ill at ease.

Myrr said, 'This can't be easy for you. But I – we – the whole family, we have decided that if my husband went to such lengths to make his wishes known, then the least we can do is to try to carry them out.'

'All we really need,' said Rin, 'is to know what the legal situation is.'

'Of course, I have had little time to ascertain very much information, but the Cremation Society have furnished me with . . . ah . . . certain particulars. Since the Act of 1902 there has been only this one occasion . . . as I have said . . . at Woking . . . July 1934.'

'Nearly sixty years ago,' Rin said.

'Of course,' Cockrill said, 'things were very different . . . ah . . . There is no question of its being permitted in the easy-going way that it was then.'

'And we would need permits, a licence or something?' Myrr asked.

'I believe that you must consider something less . . . ah . . . I explained to Mr Tallentire at the time.'

'He asked very little for himself, Mr Cockrill; the least we can do now is to try. It's nothing very difficult.'

'But against the law, Mrs Tallentire.'

Mr Cockrill had seen this kind of thing before . . . well, of course, not this kind of thing, but certainly cases where the family of the deceased had bent over backwards to try to acquiesce to some whim of the deceased. Families could behave very strangely over the remains and the ashes. He was really quite against cremation himself. It was so final, no chance for a pathologist in a case that turned suspect. Clean fire, people said. Didn't they think of the billions of motes of humans that must rise from crematorium chimneys only to descend again? And with burial you had no doubts about what happened to the coffin, you saw where the brass furniture ended up. No such assurance with cremation: as far as anyone knew, there could be some sort of black market in used items.

Rin knew that Myrr's silence did not mean acceptance. She would battle it out now that she had set her mind to carrying out his father's instructions.

'What would the penalty be?' she eventually asked.

'My dear Mrs Tallentire, I think you must put it out of your mind. It would be most distressing ... can you imagine ... ?'

'Would it mean imprisonment?'

'No, no. A fine. I have a copy here.' He handed one to Rin. '"Contravention of the Act of 1902 or of any Regulation made thereunder, Section 8(1)" ... ah, here it is ... "would be liable to a fine of £50". Fifty pounds in 1981 (this is a 1981 copy) – it would be higher now.'

Rin read on. '"Provided that any person aggrieved by any conviction may appeal therefrom to the Crown Court." Which means, I suppose, that it would be a summons in a Magistrate's Court and a fine?'

'Something like that.'

Myrr said, 'Then it's not worth arguing about, Mr Cockrill. I'd stand up in court any day and argue the case. It's not as though we live in the middle of London.'

Cockrill foresaw trouble. But then such determined country families as these had been the backbone of his own family's practice for generations and had always been trouble. Cockrills throve on the bloody-mindedness and stands against the law of the smallholder and farmer. Cockrills had defended inarticulate farm labourers against the iniquities of the old system where lowly men and women were tried by their lords and masters. Cockrills been the mouthpiece for men who had stood up for the right to come together in combinations and unions and defended them when they stood in jeopardy of transportation. If the Cockrills were anything, they were old-fashioned and liberal-minded; it had long been their philosophy that people have a say in their own destinies.

This wouldn't be the first time that a Cockrill had had to stand up and be counted. 'So be it, Mrs Tallentire,' and he shook hands firmly with her and with Rin. 'You can rely on me.'

He brought forth another sheaf of photocopies. 'These

make rather stark reading, but in the circumstances it is essential that we know what we are doing.'

'What are these?' Rin asked.

'To be frank, I came prepared, as I had a notion that you might come to the conclusion that you have, Mrs Tallentire. This is an excerpt from "Cremation of the Dead"; it is how to prepare a bier.'

'What made you think I would go ahead with his crazy scheme?'

'I have known you all for a long time. You and Mr Tallentire didn't make Sunbarrow Farms what it is today by submitting to pen-pushers and red-tape merchants.'

Myrr nodded, 'I appreciate that, Mr Cockrill. The Jeavons family have been in hot water before today for arguing with authority.'

Daisy and Poppy sat in the buttery of a hotel in the centre of Winchester. Poppy said, 'It's been totally ace having a sister to go shopping with. I wish you'd come down more often.'

Daisy wasn't often seen with such a gentle smile. 'It hadn't occurred to me that I had a sister old enough to go shopping with. When you're at university you must come up to town, we'll do Regent Street, Bond Street. I've enjoyed myself – I doubt that I'd have bought such an itsy-bitsy, teeny-weeny, yellow polka-dot bikini if I had gone shopping with one of my London friends.'

'That's probably because they could see you'd put them in the shade. You've got a super body . . . but super.'

'Poppy, my sweet, you must package me some of that mood lifter. There are times when I need telling that I'm not over the hills and far away.'

'Do you think we're alike? Do we look like sisters? I can never tell. Chrissie Pack says that we do.'

'Maybe a bit, but you aren't like me. Inside I'm like the Old Man and you are like Myrr.'

'Don't you think it's weird, us sitting here as though nothing had happened? I remember when Chrissie's dad died, looking at her and wondering how she managed to look just the same as always. I mean . . . she cried and all that, and she was sad and she said she missed him . . . yet she could still talk about ordinary things. Just the same as we've been doing this morning. You know . . . that girl who served us with the swim-wear, she couldn't have guessed that our dad was back home lying in state.'

'The saying "Life goes on" had to come from somewhere. Poppy, I have to ask you . . . are you all right with this . . . God above, I have to call a spade a spade . . . are you all right about this funeral pyre?'

'Of course I am. I said so last night. I would never have thought of it, but now that it's in my mind, I couldn't bear letting Dad go any other way. It seems so, so . . . right. It's right in the way that some women are insisting on having their babies at home with their family in the room. I don't think that I would want any if I had to have them in a hospital . . . hospitals are for sick and dying people.'

'That's going a bit far; there are maternity hospitals.'

'Hospitals! That's what I mean. Anyway, I feel the same way about dying. People should die at home, and we should all return to the days when people you knew did it all. When Mrs Gilks our Guide captain died I went to the crematorium. It was dreadful. Dead bodies were practically queuing up to get in. There was canned music, some hymns, and the vicar said something. Then, when the coffin disappeared you could almost imagine that any minute the vicar was going to say *Voilà!* like a conjurer, and he'd open the velvet curtains and Mrs Gilks would jump out again well and alive.' She bit her lips. 'Stop me, Daisy, I think I'm going to giggle.'

'Don't worry, it's only the result of living on your nerves for twenty-four hours.'

'I won't be like that on the day. Honestly. I do think it's a wonderful way to say goodbye to Dad. Don't you?'

'Yah, I do rather. When that woman first said what he wanted her to do, I was mad as hell. Then, when I'd had a chance to simmer down, I saw that what I was mad at was her. I was indignant that the Old Man had gone off with a woman like that to nominate her as executor or whatever it is that she's supposed to be.'

'I think she's sincere. I really do think she's sincere in carrying out Dad's last request.'

'You're probably right. I gather she's rich as Croesus, so she wasn't after his money.'

Poppy looked shocked. 'Of course she wasn't.'

'Take no notice of me, I spend too much time in hard-nosed company.'

'Mimm Carter's not hard-nosed.'

Daisy gazed inwardly for a moment, smiling. 'He's got a hard nose for business ... but you're right, he's not smart and cynical like some of my workmates.'

'Is that why you like Mimm?'

'I guess it might be. Also he's not half bad-looking, and he's great in bed. Or are you too young to know how important that is?'

Poppy tried to appear urbane. 'I'm beginning to understand that a relationship can't work without it.'

'Also It isn't the only ingredient in a relationship.'

'I certainly know that. A relationship needs a bit of magic, doesn't it?'

Daisy smiled softly at her young sister who was suddenly a woman. 'Yah. That's the hardest one.'

'Daisy? Can I tell you something? Swear you won't make a fuss, it's just that I want to tell you. Mimm's father ...'

'Jez has had his hands up your skirt.'

Poppy looked at Daisy in astonishment. 'Does everybody know that and do nothing about it?'

Daisy heaved a sigh. 'I suppose yes, people do know what Jez Carter is like with his hands. And no, we do nothing about him. I dare say he gets a knee in the balls, but he's harmless.'

'He's not! He touched me and he had no right to. He took something from me that he had no right to.'

'You can't stop them, Poppy. There are hands everywhere you go in town. The best you can do is say in a loud voice: Get your filthy hands off my tits. It's your best shot. They always get off next stop.'

'I went walking all over Greece without once being touched.'

'Don't kid yourself that Greek men are any different. Listen, Poppy, I'm not much of a one for handing out advice to the young and that, and I don't want to come the older sister now, but as I told you once before this, when you go up to university, don't have any naïve ideas that academics are gentlemen with special morals and codes of conduct: given half a chance they'll do you a Jez Carter – or worse. But for God's sake don't let that blight your life. You'll love university, enjoy yourself, have the time of your life. If you want men, have them, but *only* if you want them. It's your body, you only share it if and when you want. Make sure it's you who makes the rules and knee all the others in the balls.'

Daisy paid the bill and they went out and walked to the car park through the cathedral close where Roz and Myrr had sat a couple of days ago. The heatwave still lasted, the afternoon was dry and the air was filled with particles of dust and brown grass, and in the shade of the ancient flint archways over the pavements, the shadows were as purple as on a Mediterranean afternoon.

'I'm not going, Daisy.'

'Where?'

'To university. I tried talking to Roz Petherbridge, but she's loyal to Mum. I believe she thinks like Mum, that I'll regret it for the rest of my life.'

'Maybe you will – probably you will. But it's your life, not theirs.'

Daisy was so unexpected. Poppy wondered whether it was that she had never really understood her sister until today, or whether it was Daisy who had changed or Poppy herself. Perhaps it was that they had seldom been alone together. Usually when Daisy came to stay, Poppy was involved in her own world of school then college, and Daisy would go off with Jake to walk over the Downs or play tennis down at the club. Jake had always said: Our Daisy's all right, you've just got to understand her a bit. But Poppy had always been in awe of her sharp, sophisticated sister, who was making it alone in London.

'You won't try to persuade me, then?'

'Not I. People said much the same thing when I decided not to come home to live after I graduated.'

'And you don't regret it, do you?'

'Nope! Only that I've sometimes felt a bit out of things to do with Sunbarrow. Nothing serious, just day-to-day things. Like Myrr's changes to the house. I expect you pored over leaflets and things together, and talked about wouldn't it be nice to have a swimming-pool, and then which was the best place to put it. You'll probably miss that kind of thing. And you'll probably have a moment of resentment that they've been and gone and changed things since you were last home. But nothing's free in this world.' She lit a cigarette, then looked at it. 'Sorry, pet, I really have stopped. This is just temporary till things simmer down. I say, you aren't thinking of giving up university because of Myrr being on her own, are you?'

'No.' Poppy paused as a thought struck her. 'I wasn't intending to live at home, you know – you don't think I should, do you?'

'I do not!'

'I would, you know, if she wanted me to.'

'I know you would. You've got Myrr's nice kind streak in you. I'm as egocentric as the Old Man.'

'Daisy? It won't be gruesome, will it . . . a funeral pyre?'

'If what the lady shrink says is true, it won't be much different from an ordinary bonfire.'

'She seemed to know all about it, didn't she?'

Daisy said, 'She told Rin that she went to India when she was studying suttee and saw the entire process. Though heaven only knows where one gets sandalwood and the proper oils.'

'I'll bet she does,' Poppy said, and Daisy smiled at her perception.

Before he left, Cockrill asked if he could pay his respects to Mr Tallentire. Myrr took him into the oldest part of the house, to the little library with its low, beamed ceiling where Nat had frequently banged his head, as had Jake and Rin when they too had grown past six feet tall. The walls of the room were immensely thick so that there was a very positive quality about the quiet. The two windows were small and diamond-paned, letting in filtered light and little outside sound. In here there was always a stillness able to calm and soothe. It was the place where Myrr had always made up beds and lit fires when the children were sick.

She had sweet memories of this room. Nat had given her Poppy on the floor here, later Myrr had suckled the pretty, sweet-natured baby here, and nursed her through childhood ailments as she had all her children. And now the man who had both blighted her youthful ambitions and given her a very different career from what she had dreamed of having, was gone.

'You must be relieved that he died not knowing it. Would that we could all go like that.'

'But not so early in life, Mr Cockrill.'

'True. There seems to be no sense in a world where a child like my Enid can survive for twenty-five years not knowing that she is a human being, whilst a man like that is taken in his prime.'

As Cockrill looked down on the man he had known ever since he, newly appointed to the Cockrill partnership, had been given the Sunbarrow folder on the death of Nathaniel the elder, as he had become when the boy Nat had assumed the role of Master of Sunbarrow, he felt more than a pang of regret, he felt really sorry. He had liked young Nat Tallentire for his determination as he had liked the mature man for his single-mindedness. Over the years the thin folder of papers had grown thick until it had become necessary to give an entire filing cabinet drawer to the Sunbarrow affairs. There was no doubt about it, being legal adviser to such a successful business had given Cockrills a leg up in the world.

'Your sons will be hard put to it to fill his shoes, Mrs Tallentire.'

'I don't believe they want to try.'

'No?'

'I have the feeling that Jake only took on Sunbarrow to please his father. It would be terrible if he felt that he had an obligation to continue.'

'And what about your elder son?'

'Rin's no farmer: never has been, never will be.'

'But Sunbarrow is made now. It could run for ever with good farming and estate managers.'

'It wouldn't be Sunbarrow. Nat was Sunbarrow. If Jake wants to go his own way, I shan't try to stop him.'

'You know that the farm is not to be split up and sold in units?'

'I know, nor is it to be sold to a consortium or whatever

you call it. Nat was always specific about that.' She looked down at his handsome face and could have made believe that he was asleep, had she been given to fancifulness. But he did look fine. She would miss him dreadfully. He had been a dominating and dour man, but they had had their moments, mostly in bed, and they had grown used to being husband and wife. The boys had erected the traditional farmer's bier out of sheep hurdles, and he lay in his red plaid shirt open at the neck and his dark brown cords. At his open neck sprang fair curly hair that had not been there when Myrr had first made love with him. It had grown and thickened as he matured until recently it was beginning to show grey, as was the hair at his temples and in his beard.

'He thought that he could make provisions so that Sunbarrow could be set in aspic. I have done everything I can to secure that into the foreseeable future at least, but things change . . . who would have thought that we should ever see a motorway sited out there? However . . . I sincerely hope that you will see your grandchildren running around Sunbarrow.'

The short drive back to his Winchester office was slow because of the log-jam of vehicles caused by the upheaval of the great engineering operation cutting the highway into the Downs.

Travelling a few feet a minute Cockrill allowed himself to ponder on his mental picture of Nat Tallentire lying on the hurdle bier looking – as Cockrill imagined – like some ancient noble tribal chief with his broad chest and calm face.

Compare that with the – again as Cockrill imagined – rather randy-looking man whom he had watched from his office window. He had been laughing with the American woman, and he had put his arm casually around her waist and let his hand rest upon her hip as they had walked to her car.

And there was the third image, now nearly thirty years old, of the tall boy who had looked scared but fierce when he had come to hear the reading of his father's will which had bequeathed to him the then tiny Sunbarrow Farm – and all the troubles of producing sufficient to provide for the family of ailing women Old Nathaniel had left him.

He turned his mind to his immediate problems. He had left a message at the hotel for Dr Yin. She had already telephoned his office and left certain names and addresses on his answering machine. Cockrill felt out of his depth with a woman like her. She had telephoned her office in New York and had them do the searching from there. He thought some of the excesses of wealthy Americans to be exaggerated – nobody spent money like that. But she had. She had needed to discover sources of sandalwood, camphor oils and frankincense in Britain, and it was done for her. Money talked. All that Cockrill had to do was to check that a supply was delivered before tomorrow evening.

He wondered what he would say if the supplier enquired as to the use of the sandalwood. Did they sell off-cuts like a timber merchant? And there was no way that he could ask vital questions such as its dryness and combustibility. Except . . . yes, he must prevent himself from thinking like a country town solicitor. This was no big deal, pop stars must have lawyers who must deal with stranger requests than providing sandalwood for their clients.

The traffic still crawled but it gave him time to plan his calls. He must at least make enquiries about cremation on private land. It was against health regulations, illegal but not criminal. That was important; he might be reprimanded by his professional body, but he would not want to risk disbarment.

On the Tuesday, when Cockrill again went to Sunbarrow, he looked at the aromatic wood stacked in an empty barn and asked himself what he had got into. He had never in his life until today misled his wife: I have to attend to the reading of the Tallentire will this evening. She had looked doubtful: In the evening, Maurice? Yes, Kathleen, in the evening.

Not surprisingly he found the atmosphere in the Sunbarrow household strained. He guessed that the presence of the body was not easy to cope with. It was a thing that was common at one time, but in his experience it was only those landed people with private chapels who continued this tradition these days – and the Irish, but they were sensible enough to get their funerals over and done with.

Mrs Tallentire and all four of her children were there, though young Jake came and went in a pair of torn shorts and T-shirt covered in harvest dust. The elder son, who Cockrill had always thought stood in the shadow of his twin sister, seemed to feel comfortable in his role and took him into a quiet room to confer.

'I'll be glad when this is over, Mr Cockrill.'

'No changes of plan, Mr Tallentire?'

Rin said, 'No changes, Mr Cockrill. The site has been selected by Dr Yin, it is on our land and not overlooked. Are there any problems?'

Cockrill raised his eyebrows at Rin. 'There are many problems, some of which may be insoluble – I'm not even thinking of them. Outdoor cremation was banned in the early 1950s and the only licence was revoked. So I have to advise you as your solicitor that what you propose *is* against the law.'

'I understand.'

'And as your solicitor, I should not be looking after your interests if I did not advise you not to go ahead with it.'

'I understand that, too. By the way, we've – that's Jake and Daisy and I – read the information you left about the . . . ah . . .'

'Funeral pyre?'

'Yes. It isn't easy to actually talk about. Daisy's always had a very prosaic nature, doesn't mince words, and Dr Yin is very knowledgeable on the subject, she seems very confident that it will be all right. I wish that we could leave it to them.'

'Perhaps you should.'

Rin frowned. 'It's not the kind of thing one would want to leave to women.'

'Mr Tallentire, in normal circumstances I might agree – and if my wife could hear me say this, she would wonder whether she has ever known the man she married – but in my experience women are frequently found to be very much the better sex at coping with practicalities and I would not hesitate to let those who know how – do.'

'Now that you know about what's going to take place, are you supposed to inform the police or anything?'

'I . . . ah . . . Put it this way, if there are any enquiries after the event, then I shall be hard put to explain my prior knowledge of how Dr Yin obtained on behalf of your family a large quantity of sandalwood, faggots and volatile oils, to say nothing of posts and planks. But that is not a consideration likely to prevent me from doing my best to see that an old and valued friend leaves this world in the way he wished to do. I see no more harm than the same process taking place in an automated incinerator.'

'Would you come?'

'I shall be honoured, Mr Tallentire.'

Once more stuck in the coned-off contra-flowing traffic, Maurice Cockrill compared the new head of the Tallentire family – suave, well-educated, stylish and at ease – with the inarticulate, village-school boy in hobnail boots shoving his cap in his pocket with large red hands that stuck out four inches below the cuffs of his camphor-reeking jacket, who, even in his poverty, had stood in the alien territory of Cockrill Partners' offices looking as imperious and digni-fied at nineteen as he looked in death thirty years on.

This one would never be Master of Sunbarrow if he lived to be a hundred.

When the vicar called to ask what the family wanted in the way of a service, Daisy was alone and told him the first thing that came into her head, which was that her father was to be cremated and there was to be no service until later. 'We thought later in the season ... perhaps somewhere about Harvest Festival time. We are arranging a kind of wake for the village.'

Except for the cremation, because he favoured graves with headstones, the vicar thought that an excellent plan. 'Quite in the old country tradition. The squire was always good for at least two suppers in his lifetime – one for his birth, one for his death.'

'My father is hardly squirearchy,' Daisy responded sparkily.

'He was the nearest Childencombe had.'

Daisy hoped that she had made it plain that the 'wake' was only for the village and Sunbarrow employees.

Myrr, not wanting to risk the chance of any outsider being at Sunbarrow on that day, arranged everything with Mrs Pack, who said to leave it all to her. Granny Cole and Mrs Pack baked in their own old-fashioned iron ranges, preferring them to Myrr Tallentire's peculiar arrangement that cooked by light bulbs. 'Funeral meats!' Granny Cole was back sixty years. 'I haven't seen no real funeral meats since I was in service. If it wasn't for the fact that a good man has gone from our midst, I should feel fair lighthearted.' She hummed as she weighed ham and skinned tongue, and hummed hymns as she instructed her daughter and granddaughters as to the correct lay-out of a table.

By eight o'clock the sun had gone from the side of the house where Nat lay. Candles were lit and a steady flow of Childencombrians came to pay their last respects. Rin and Jake stood grey-suited and pale. Myrr, Daisy and Poppy in new, subdued dresses. Everything traditional and proper. Only Nat, in his cords and red plaid shirt, looked familiar.

The hum of conversation in and around the tractor shed was low and respectful, even though there was plenty of ale. Old men who had worked at Sunbarrow came to shake Myrr's hand and weep for her. Girls who worked in the creamery stood together in groups, in awe of the occasion. Skilled workers and labourers, sheep men and agricultural students wondered what changes would be made.

Old men stated that: Young Jake's all right, but he's too easy-going.

Young men argued that: The Old Man had been all right, but he never learned how to deal properly with the unions.

Creamery girls who were all a bit sweet on Jake wondered if he'd get married now: There wasn't nothing to stop him before. Yes, but he's the boss now, properly the boss. He'll get married now he's the boss. They felt a bit lost knowing that there wasn't a Mr and Mrs up at the house.

Poppy looked strained and hollow-eyed. 'Come on, Popp,' Chrissie said. 'You look terrible.'

'It's the dark dress.'

Poppy longed to tell Chrissie what they were going to do, but Daisy had said that some big-mouth in the village was sure to blow it. And if Jez Carter got to know he'd be on to the *Sun* in a minute. So Poppy wandered about, longing for it all to end so that they could do the terrible thing that her dad had wanted.

She didn't want to know how it would be done. All that she did know was that Rin and Jake had gone up into Clump Field and driven a kind of barrier of poles over the Queer Stone. And that Jake had brought a tractor and trailer into the yard and they had loaded it with the wood that had been delivered yesterday.

Myrr came and tucked Poppy's arm through hers. 'You don't have to come, love. Your dad wouldn't think any the worse of you.'

'It's not that I don't want to do it, I want to, because it's what he wanted. It's just standing around thinking. I keep imagining that it won't work.' Which wasn't true: the dreadful vision that Poppy had was of Mr Singh at Ship Fair.

'It will work. I'm sure the Dragon Woman knows what she is doing. She saw it quite a few times when she was working in India, and Mr Cockrill has found out quite a lot.'

Daisy joined them. Myrr said, 'Poppy's afraid it won't work.'

'You don't need to worry. Dad wouldn't have asked for it to be done if he thought it would be upsetting . . . Whatever else he was, he wasn't unkind in that way.'

Poppy was reassured. But Daisy was not. The worst part was not knowing how long it would take. Was there enough wood? Would the brushwood catch? Well, it was too late now. They'd made the decision.

Rin wondered how Jake could be so relaxed. He wished that he had persuaded Kuan-Yin to come to the villagers' wake, but she had said that it would be intrusive: Honey, can you imagine? No, I'll come later with Lee Han.

Gradually people drifted away until those who remained were seventy or eighty men and women who Jake and Rin had, throughout the evening, quietly asked if they would stay behind. Hand-picked villagers that the family knew they could rely on. People like Rex Farenbach, whose family had been in the village as long as the Tallentires, and a fair number of the men and their sons who had taken part in the tug-of-war on Saturday. The Pack women and women Myrr had known since they were girls. Country people who kept their own counsel and themselves to themselves.

When at last Kuan-Yin arrived with Lee Han, Jake asked Rin, 'Shall you speak to people, or shall I?'

'You. I don't belong here any more.'

To gather them in a close bunch, Jake and Rin brought out bottles of spirits.

'I'm sorry,' he began, 'but in a way you've been asked to stop behind on false pretences, and what I've got to tell you is bloody difficult.'

He did not notice Lizz arrive. Except for Kuan-Yin, her uncle and Mr Cockrill, she was the only person outside the family who knew of the Old Man's directions for his funeral. Jake had been to see her.

Lizz had never seen this Jake. She had seen him wearing a formal suit once or twice, but never with his hair cut short and wearing such a serious expression. A flash of an image of Mr Tallentire, not as Poseidon but as he was as master in his own home: Don't stand there on ceremony, come on in, my girl. But Jake was too much his own self to take on the role his father had left.

'We've asked you because you are all people we've known all our lives. Some of us have got the same ancestors, and we've been inter-marrying going back generations. Well . . . you know my Old Man, he never made life easy for anybody – perhaps least of all his family. He drove himself hard and thought the rest of us were made the same as he was. Even though he's gone, he's still ruling the roost.' Jake smiled to show that he wasn't running his father down. People smiled and nodded.

'He was a close man, as you all know; even we didn't know much about what went on inside his head. Well, to cut a long story short . . . not long before he died, he got it fixed in his head that he didn't want to be buried nor did he want to have to go over to Winchester crematorium. He once told Myrr . . .' he dropped into the native broad

Hampshire '. . . "My father got me on my mother in that ole barn, I was born on Sunbarrow and don't never plan on living nowhere else, and with a bit of luck I 'a die here."' People who knew the Old Man when he was Young Nat and before Myrr Jeavons polished him up a bit, smiled and recognized the old country brogue.

'Well, he did die here. Not much over fifty. Most of his life spent working night and day to drag Sunbarrow out of the eighteenth century and into the twentieth . . . and people who have seen the new creamery will agree into the twenty-first. I'm not standing up here to tell you about Nat Tallentire. I'm here to ask those of you who will to fulfil his last wish. We are doing it against the law, and if there's anybody who doesn't want any truck with it, then nobody's going to think any the worse of them. We don't even rightly know the way to do it. If it goes wrong then we shall be in deep shit.'

Rex Farenbach said, 'It won't be the first time we've been in that, Jake. Go on, spit it out.'

'He wants to go like some old Viking, or as they do in India on the banks of the Ganges. A funeral pyre on his own land.'

Into a short, shuffling silence, somebody said, 'Jesus Christ, Nat!'

Nobody went home.

The funeral procession, if that is what it could be called, was casual and unorganized, except for Grandpa Cole who, as well as being Hatman, was one of the Tallentire clan: as the natural leader he walked before the bier. It wasn't possible to find four other men tall enough to match Rin and Jake to act as pall-bearers, but as Daisy pointed out, because they had to walk up the slope of Clump Field, some shorter bearers in front would make for better balance.

They started out with Jake and Rin plus Young Sid, Rex, Mimm Carter, and Vic Tatum, Sunbarrow's senior cattleman – but it was hot and very humid and the weight of Nat soon took its toll so that the bearers were relieved when others joined in; two more Tallentire cousins of the Pack/Cole family, Tom Farenbach, even Maurice Cockrill for a short distance, none of them perhaps wanting to be left out of what was after all a historic event that would be talked about for many a long year. With mostly women leading, but behind Grandpa Cole, they wended their way from the house up the same pathway that Jake took most mornings, and along which he had taken Kuan-Yin on her first visit to Sunbarrow, that day when he had shown her the great pictogram which she had said was the Vajra symbol, and on their way back had found the unexpected frog orchid. The same path down which Kuan-Yin and Nat had walked on Ship Fair Day after making love on the Downs and Roz Petherbridge had not been mistaken when she had thought they were kissing as passionately as lovers.

'Is that it?' Poppy asked when they rounded a bend from where Clump Field was visible from the pathway, not referring to the field but to the wooden structure on the Queer Stone spot.

'That's it. Yes. You OK?'

'Stop treating me like a kid, Jake.'

'I didn't mean to, I just want it to be right for the Old Man.' He glanced up at their father's profile which was all that could be seen of him, the rest being covered by a heavy sheepskin that had been taken years ago from the enormous snail-horned ram that had been the sire of the first of Sunbarrow's pedigree flock. That had been Rin's idea, and in a way it did seem more appropriate than the tartan blanket and belts that strapped Nat to the hurdles.

'Sorry, Jake.' Poppy squeezed his elbow from which

sweat was running. 'I didn't expect it to be in that kind of shape, I thought it would look like those you see in films about the Ganges.'

'Mr Han says that . . . Christ, Poppy, do you really want to know?'

'No, not really, Jake. I'm just talking for the sake of it.'

He smiled sideways at her and shrugged his shoulders as best he could under the weight he was bearing.

With Kuan-Yin and Lee Han's guidance, and with Vic Tatum's help, the brothers had built a kind of stockade of tinder-dry pine poles within which the more familiar wooden platform was constructed of cedar and sandalwood. Beneath the platform were piles of dry faggots. What Jake had baulked at explaining to Poppy was that by concentrating the fire within the 'stockade' it would become a kind of furnace in which Lee Han believed that the heat would become fierce and more quickly consuming. Lee Han had not voiced his other thought, that when the pyre eventually collapsed, he hoped that the structure would also act to shield the final stages of the cremation from what Western eyes would probably consider gruesome.

Myrr and Poppy and most of the villagers went to sit on the barrows, but Daisy went with her brothers to watch as they put their father into the enclosure. Kuan-Yin offered her a large wide-necked jar holding probably a litre of reddish oil. 'I thought you might like to have this.' Daisy held it to the last of the evening light. Kuan-Yin said, 'It is just some sweet kind of oil, not really volatile . . . I guess I thought . . . y'know, instead of flowers.'

Daisy was suddenly cut to the quick by the poignancy of the other woman's situation. 'The Other Woman' were absolutely the words that formed in Daisy's mind. Sudden death and a family gathering, every mistress and lover's put-down. Only secret grief was allowed for those involved in extramarital love. Daisy still had the scars from being excluded from a lover's grief when his wife had had a stillbirth. Being Other was the pits.

From what Rin had told Daisy, the Old Man had fallen head over heels in love with this Dragon Lady: she reckoned he was ready to give up everything to get her. Jake was cagey, but she had prised out of him what had happened on Saturday after she and Mimm had left Ship Fair. 'All right, Daze! If you must know, it's quite probable that the Old Man was fucking her, I found a pocket full of "Mates" in his jacket. Did you really want to know that?'

As always, when she had got what she wanted by needling him, his capitulation had upset them both.

'Oh Christ, Jakey, I'm sorry. I can be such a bitch.'

And Jake, as always, was understanding. 'It's all right, Daze, it's no big deal. But just keep it to yourself.'

'Aw, come on, what do you take me for?'

By now the three of them knew it had become impossible and a mess. On Saturday night, it had been Rin and not the Old Man who had slept with her; which complication, according to Rin, she hoped would put the Old Man off her, even though, according to both Jake and Rin, she was just as deeply involved with the Old Man as he was with her. It may have seemed improbable that he could be even thinking about a woman as young as that, but Daisy knew better. Bill Sloane at the age of fifty-five had given Daisy more happy days and nights than any of her other lovers, and if she ever settled with any man, it would probably be Bill.

For years Daisy had suspected that there wasn't too much left in their marriage for either Myrr or the Old Man, but she had expected that they would go on rubbing along, probably for ever. Since the Old Man had died, Myrr had erected a barrier which Daisy could not and did not wish to try to breach. If he had been fucking around with the Dragon Lady, then Daisy would rather not be drawn in to having to take sides. It was pretty impossible to be neutral when your parents split up. Daisy guessed that Myrr would continue to behave as though nothing had been going on. And she was right: what was the use in making waves now? The Old Man was dead, so there wouldn't be any scandal. It could all stay hidden. The Childencombrian gossips could nod and wink to as many blind donkeys as they chose, but the real scandal would lie hidden, like Jez and his groping hands, like the incestuous affairs that were all right during Ship Fair, like the blackened eyes and bruised arms on women who walked into doors, like all the hundred and one bits of corruption and humbug which Childencombrians hid under a sham of decent, honest countryfolk and which Daisy could not do with.

The two people here who loved him best are probably Poppy and the Dragon Lady — and nobody cares a shit about her.

But Daisy was wrong. Rin cared. Although as he now knew she had slept with him only to make the break with the Old Man, she had been good for him. Jake cared. He said, 'Kuan-Yin should pour the oils on the Old Man, Daze?'

'That's nice, Jake.' Daisy handed the bottle back to Kuan-Yin. 'Yes, I think you should, it will probably mean more to you than to the rest of us.' Daisy turned away when she saw that tears had welled up in the Dragon Lady's eyes, and said, 'Perhaps I could light it, Jake?'

'Why not?'

Kuan-Yin went into the stockade and soaked the ram's skin with the oils. Jake saw her slip Rin's little dragon beneath the skin. Then Mimm and Vic helped Jake and Rin drop the last of the pine poles into the post-holes, so filling the gap and completing the circle.

By the time Daisy touched the first of the bundles of dry furze with a lighted tarred stick, the last of the daylight had gone. Except for Lee Han and the Tallentire brothers, the rest retreated to join the others on the barrows. At first the fire caught like a garden bonfire, a few sparks and red flames licking out through the spaces between the poles. The tinder-dry bracken, furze and wood-shavings crackled and fizzed as they fired a pile of thin timber offcuts. A night-wind, the first for a month, swept down across Clump Field and was sucked through the spaces between the poles. The fire roared as a great long tongue of flames was funnelled upwards, frightening in its threat to go out of control. Suddenly the pyre burst into a great conflagration, the heat from which singed the hair and skin of those close and drove them back up to join the others on the barrows.

There, the watchers were mesmerized by the great pillar of heat and fire. Except for Rex, who said, 'Christ Almighty! What a way to go,' they watched silently. Again the wind swept across the fields and was sucked in by the fire. Soon the circle of pine poles began burning, at first licked by flame and then blazing more fiercely until they became long firebrands between which the white incandescence at the heart could be glimpsed as through the door of a furnace.

A sharp and sudden crack made the watchers jump. Some clutched their necks, others held their cheeks, some almost turned briefly towards their neighbours but could not take their eyes from the flaming beacon. What was that?

Kuan-Yin's voice from somewhere at the back said, 'Don't worry, it's OK – the heat has probably split a rock.' She had expected it. The Queer Stone was porous from the hundreds of little spirals that Tallentire had shown her, guiding her finger into some. It was at the Queer Stone that Tallentire had plotted the conjunction of ley-lines and subterranean watercourses, and there too that Kuan-Yin, in her role as *hsein-sheng*, had traced the crossing of many dragon veins. Lee Han had agreed, the Queer Stone was at the point where the most favourable *ch'i* gathered into a pool. He too had concluded it to be a place in which the spirit of a person of extreme importance might rest for all eternity.

With the explosion the pine poles collapsed inwards, sending a huge column of sparks high into the air. Then, except for the crackle of the wood and the roar of the wind-fanned flames, there was total silence. No moon or stars were visible, no lights in Childencombe houses, no streetlights nor those of cars passing along the main road. All that existed for the watchers was the circle of fire that appeared to be hanging in a black void.

A hilltop fire in one of the most ancient centres of human habitation.

A ceremonial fire. Little different, except for what was at its heart, from many fires that had lit the faces of people down the ages.

Only Kuan-Yin knew how truly satisfied Nat Tallentire would have been: I sometimes fancy to myself that I'm a direct descendant of some of the Neolithic Tallentires who came up here to build the barrows. I reckon I've got genes that are pure over four thousand years. Tallentires then, Tallentires now, Tallentires yet to come.

He had laughed, a bit embarrassed at his own fancifulness: Tenacious buggers, aren't we?

As with that other fire at Ship Fair less than a week ago, when he had been 'Fire Tongue', so now his final show died down at about three in the morning. And as it had been then, so now, no one present had any real sense of the passage of time.

They straggled away almost silently, finding their way down the chalk path by what skylight there was and an inborn sensitivity to what was beneath their feet when they walked.

Rin wanted Kuan-Yin and Lee Han to go back to the house, but they would not. They shook hands formally where the path divided leading to the road where Kuan-Yin had left her car parked.

It was daylight when Daisy and Jake eventually got back to the house. Neither of them had wanted to leave until they were convinced that there was nothing awful to be discovered in the light of day. Lee Han had offered to stay, but he had looked tired and frail. Jake had said that he would fetch a tractor and plough as soon as it was light. He and Daisy had sat on, drinking from a flask of whisky Jake had put in the tractor box, not saying much to each other, watching the smouldering circle and the occasional flurry of firefly sparks which the wind fanned up. There was a short, slashing shower from which they sheltered in the clump of yews. The ashes hissed and steam arose.

Jake, planning ahead a bit, had left a tractor and small plough close by. The ground was still hot, and now steamy from the storm. Daisy wanted Jake not to risk taking in the tractor yet because of the danger of the fuel igniting. There was no risk of that, but for a reason he could not have defined he did not want to let go of this last act of the Old Man's life, so they sat on the crest of Clump Field drinking and smoking cigarettes and watched the sun come up.

'I'm going down now to take a look,' Jake said.

'Will you be all right? I'll come if you like.'

'No. It's my job, Daze. And it's OK. Honestly. You've been great. We ought to . . .'

'Yah . . . get together more often. We always say it.'

'We will.'

Daisy thought: He's the best of all of us. He just lives and lets live. He does what he's got to do and never makes much fuss.

As he got up she caught his hand. 'What you see is what you get with you, Jake Tallentire. Right?'

'Pretty much I suppose, Daze.' He squeezed her hand.

'You're OK, Jake. Don't waste yourself.'

He ruffled her hair in the way that used to infuriate her when he was about twelve and within the space of a few months had suddenly leaped ahead of her in the growing race.

'The Old Man was a bit of a bugger, wasn't he?' she said.

'He was a lot of a bugger. But he didn't really have a chance. He was clobbered from the day he was born. He went from Young Nat to the Old Man and nothing between. He'd got good reason to be a bit of a bugger.'

'Like I said, Jake. You're OK.'

When eventually Jake went down to the circle of white ash and blackened earth, he found nothing gruesome, which had been the secret worry of all of those involved – only the Queer Stone which was broken into several pieces. Daisy watched as he ran the tractor back and forth across the steaming land, and then walked back with him down the chalk path to Sunbarrow where, immersed in their own thoughts, they undressed and dived into the clear blue pool.

It was the first morning on Sunbarrow without the Old Man.

A letter from Declan O'Phee to his girlfriend Maria Mallory in Castle Rey.

Dear Maria,

I thought I would send you these bits out of the English papers because it took place here just above where we are working. Such a thing to happen in a place like this. Fair English countryside and no mistake. You'd never believe farming people could get up to such tricks, would you? And rich, they own half the county by all accounts. Many's the time I've been in the village pub for a quick pint or in the shop for some smokes. Haven't I told you that the place looks like it was invented for the television, and I reckon I've not seen a ragged ass or a flapping boot sole all the months I've worked here. Everybody's got work and a place to live. Anyone would think it was paradise.

You'll see it says that a pall of smoke hung over the village, but that's the newspapers for you. Our mess van isn't but half a mile from where they burnt up the old fella, and we never noticed a whiff of anything. The first we knew was when a posse of police cars parked in our compound and went charging up over the cutting and the rumour went round that there'd been a murder. Well of course they were too late, weren't they, it had all happened the night before. It's all rumour of course because they're a tight-*** lot in the village, you'd never get as much as a word out of them, but they say he was a giant of a fella well above six foot tall and it took hours to do the job.

There's a young fella sells strawberries just off where we're working and he's doing a roaring trade with the reporters, but he's not saying. They say it was this one's old fella who sold the story to the *Sun*. If he hadn't done that, I reckon nobody would have ever been the wiser. It's a five-minute wonder and the papers are sure to have another go at it when they take the sons to court. One of our lads has made a book on what he will get. The fine's only £50 which is not a lot when you think you can get more than that for just breaking a window. I've got long odds that he's going to get off with a caution or something, and quite apart from what I shall win, I hope that he does. It does your heart good to know that there's still a few who won't knuckle under.

They say there is to be another public enquiry about the route of this motorway, but don't worry, either way we win. If the locals lose we shall go on with this route, if they win we shall have to detour. So there's a good many more months good pay and bonus to come, then we'll buy the ring and tie the knot.

Your ever loving, Declan.

Extract from *The Daily Independent News*:

FARMER'S DEATH RITES
RITUAL BURNING IN CORN CIRCLE VILLAGE

Funeral Pyre of Aromatic Woods
Childencombe, Wednesday

The burning ghats of the Ganges were brought to the Hampshire countryside yesterday when the villagers of Childencombe, Hants, were present at the secret burning of the body of wealthy landowner/farmer Nathaniel Tallentire.

Today, in this rural village, hidden away in a corner of the rolling Downs south of Winchester, it was difficult to find anyone who was prepared to admit that they were present or that there was any mystical significance in a ceremony that appears reminiscent of Saxon or Viking burial rites.

This is not the first time that this secretive village has hit the headlines. In the mid-seventies there was a flush of reportings of strange moving lights and UFO sightings. Later, it was again the centre of attention when the first of the mysterious circles began appearing in its cornfields. Again, in June of this year,

---

hundreds of sightseers came flocking to try to get a glimpse of the 'Great Pictogram', as it has become known.

Childencombe is situated very close to Operation Blackbird. 'Blackbird' is the continuous field-watch for circles by a group of international scientists whose 'discovery' turned out to be a hoax.

Although police were called to the scene of the secret funeral pyre, it was stated that there are no suspicious circumstances surrounding the death. Family solicitor, Maurice Cockrill of Stockbridge Road, Winchester, stated: 'Mr Tallentire suffered from a heart condition and died from a massive coronary on Sunday morning.' When asked about the midnight ceremony, Mr Cockrill said: 'All that I have to say on behalf of the family is that they obeyed Mr Tallentire's instructions and see it as a very private matter.'

Statutory regulations covering cremations state: 'All cremations shall be carried out . . . under the appropriate statutory provisions and regulations . . . no cremation shall take place except on the written authority of the Medical Referee.'

The penalty for contravention of the Cremation Act, 1902, is a fine of up to £50.

Extract from *Sportsnews 'n Fun Weekly*:

CHARLIE CHAN, MADAM BUTTERFLY and MICHAEL CAINE IN STRANGE DAWN CEREMONY

World Exclusive

When continental lorry-driver Phillipe Mouet (30) of Tour, France, was caught short at dawn, he went into a field and came upon 'something very strange'.

The story he told *Sport 'n Fun* reporter was how he saw two 'Japanese' and a white man marking out patterns in a cornfield. 'I was curious. The girl I call Madam Butterfly, went many times to the top of the hill and ran in all directions.' Phillipe went on to describe the wild dance performed by the girl before the two men. 'When she came to a stop one of the men stabbed a stick into the ground at her feet.'

The two men he describes as one looking 'like Michael Caine' and an old man. 'He was like Charlie Chan I have seen in late-night movies.'

Sport 'n Fun reporter, Guy Chapstick, who uncovered the infamous Satan Ring, pressed Phillipe for details of the dawn ritual.

Speaking in his native French, Phillipe told Guy Chapstick: 'When the poles were placed they were linked by a network of ribbons. At the point where all the ribbons crossed "Charlie Chan" stuck a red upright pole.'

When Guy asked what he thought they were doing, Phillipe said, 'I thought that there might be some secret rite, or they were making one of the patterns.' By patterns, Phillipe meant one of the corn circles that had already hoaxed the Japanese scientists who have set up a 24-hour watch on the fields where the mysterious corn circles have been appearing.

Two days after seeing the strange dawn rituals, Phillipe was waiting to go on board at Portsmouth's continental ferry port, when he happened to tune in to a local radio station.

The news item which caught his attention was a report of the 'Viking Funeral' arranged by the heirs of wealthy farmer Nathaniel Tallentire, whose wheatsheaf and 'Sunbarrow Farms' logo can be seen on any supermarket shelf.

'I know this village, it is on my regular route and I know it is where I had stopped on Sunday morning.' Putting two and two together, French Phillipe rang *Sport 'n Fun* with his story.

Childencombe is a picture postcard village nestling in the rolling Downlands of Hampshire. It is Mister Kipling and Hovis country rolled into one. A place where local hotelier Rex Farenbach (54) makes his own 'exceedingly fine' ale. But although Mr Farenbach (as do all Childencombrians as they call themselves) admits to being a lifelong friend of the millionaire Tallentires, he insists that he knows nothing of any Viking funeral.

'There have been no peculiar goings-on of any kind in Childencombe – and you can quote me.'

Funny goings-on there may not be, but it is a fact that until recently two Chinese people – a beautiful young lady and an old man – have been guests in Mr Farenbach's four-star Green Man Hotel.

This is a close community where inhabitants

who have lived here for twenty years are still known as newcomelatelys. It is wise monkey country where nobody sees, nobody hears and certainly nobody tells.

Something happened here, that much we know. Phillipe Mouet saw the preparations and, even though the site of the pyre has been ploughed, a dark patch marks the soil. Why it happened may not be so easy to discover.

Sport 'n Fun won't let that deter it.

Extract from *Winchester Times*, November 1990:

LOCAL BROTHERS BOUND OVER

Winchester Magistrates Court

It was standing room only today in the public gallery when Aneurin Tallentire (32) of Vigo Street, London, and Jacob Tallentire (30) of Sunbarrow Farm, Childencombe, nr. Winchester, appeared before Winchester Magistrates charged with having contravened the Cremation Act, 1902.

Readers will recall that the brothers had been jointly charged after they admitted wilfully and knowingly procuring the disposal of human remains not in accordance with the regulations of the act.

The brothers told magistrates that their father had left detailed and specific instructions regarding his funeral and that they tried to see his wishes carried out.

When questioned about the involvement of others in the ceremony, the brothers said that no one else took part in the preparation of the 'funeral pyre' and that close friends who attended thought that they had come to attend their father's 'wake' and could therefore not be held responsible.

The very tall and impressive brothers stood quietly together, heads raised when the Chairman of the Bench told them that even though they had done what they did to carry out their father's last request, it was nevertheless not a thing to be tolerated by society.

'Regulations are regulations and they have been brought into being to protect society. No one is outside the law. However, we feel that you are men of excellent character and are not likely to re-offend.'

The brothers agreed to be bound over.

Extract from *The Daily Independent News*, November 1990

Today saw the final chapter in the extraordinary 'Viking Funeral' story, when two of the heirs to the wealthy Sunbarrow Farms estate were bound over to keep the peace by Winchester Magistrates.

It will be remembered how on a hot night in the midst of this summer's heatwave, about fifty inhabitants of Childencombe in Hampshire attended the cremation of millionaire farmer

Nathaniel Tallentire on a funeral pyre on his own land. When questioned by the police, the deceased's two sons admitted that it was they who organized and carried out the ceremony.

When the news of the macabre affair broke, questions were asked regarding the constant appearance of symbols and 'pictograms' in the cornfields of Sunbarrow Farm.

Local vicar, Rev. David Hawthorne, questioned at the time about any significance that might be attached to the huge symbol of 'Mother Earth' discovered in the 'cremation field', said: 'It looks more like a baby's rattle to me. We shall probably find out that these "happenings" are hoaxes – they appeared everywhere this last summer.'

Rev. Hawthorne, when asked yesterday whether he thought that the symbols had anything to do with the army, said, 'This country has two million idle hands,' but would not be drawn when asked if he meant that the Devil was finding work for the unemployed. Again questioned on the strangeness of the cremation of Mr Tallentire, he said, 'Many country people are still attached to the old ways.' When asked if he meant the 'night of misrule', in which Mr Tallentire had taken part on the night before his death, Rev. Hawthorne would not comment.

Writer Jenny McLusky who, during the long, hot summer of 1990, spent a great deal of time in this area of Hampshire investigating the 'Circle' phenomena, came to the conclusion in an exclusive article for *The Daily Independent News*, that 'it would need a small army of highly trained people, working quickly, in organized teams in the dark and with no lights,

> often close to busy main roads, to create these gigantic symbols.' In another article at the end of the '1990 Circle Season' Ms McLusky has written, 'I can think of only one body capable of such covert operations, but cannot think of a single reason why the SAS should wish to do so, unless there is something more phenomenal than the pictograms to cover up.'

NEW YORK

The head waiter at Yin's Number One House made a smiling obeisance to Miss Alison and led her over to the family alcove. 'You are first to arrive, Miss Alison. Mister George and Lady Yin are usually first.'

'And I am usually last.'

'We saw you on tee-vee, Miss Alison, you looked great.'

'Why thanks, Jimmy, but did you enjoy the show?'

'I sure did. Those shots of that . . . whaddya call'm . . . pictograms? I've never seen anything like it. Impressive, Miss Alison. How's the book coming along?'

'OK, Jimmy. Mostly pictures, not too much writing.'

'We shall look forward to it, Miss Alison.' He bowed briefly and pulled out her chair.

George and June and Lady Yin arrived. June Yin said, 'Why look, George, she is already here,' and kissed her daughter. 'We began to wonder whether you were ever going to return home. Let me look at you. Nice dress, but you've put on a little weight. Heavenly saw you on tee-vee, said she supposed it's all that roast beef they eat in the UK.'

Kuan-Yin knew she had arrived home when her dress and her figure came under scrutiny. 'Great to be back, Mom.' Kissing her grandmother's knuckles in her usual greeting, she said to her, 'Uncle Han was very much liked by the English, Lady Yin.'

Lady Yin nodded, indicating: Of course.

George, organizing everyone, said, 'Henry will not be eating, he has staff problem in Number Six, but Louis and Heavenly should be here.'

Burt grinned. 'Heavenly is taking Louis to baby classes.'

Lenny said, 'I never would believe that those two would suddenly become like nesting swans, fuss, fuss, fuss. You would believe no one had a baby before Heavenly.'

Kuan-Yin said, 'From Heavenly's point of view, no one ever did.'

George said, 'Enough of babies, let's eat, I'm hungry.' He put up a finger and at once a flutter of slim little smiling waiters alighted at the table.

Kuan-Yin watched as her family pored over the menu. Most evenings it was the same procedure, anything up to eight Yins each choosing anything up to ten separate dishes apiece. The family meal had become a ritual; she wondered whether it had come to represent something they had left behind when Lady Yin and her three sons fled mainland China. Everything done just so. Her father, being the senior son, ruled the proceedings, but only with the tacit agreement of uncles Lenny and Burt.

She had news, family news, but no matter how important – and hers was important – the first courses were not the place to impart it. She had never liked to be the cause of her father's frown and: Alison, let us at least have sufficient food inside us so that we can give news full attention. Even more important than her own news was the fact that she wanted to request a Kitchen Meeting. Kitchen Meetings were few and far between. They were the more or less formal business meetings in which the whole board of directors met to discuss anything that it was not possible to do under the eyes and ears of the staff. Seeing that the board consisted of only the Yin family, it was usually arranged after dinner but before coffee, with Martin How, their lawyer-cum-company secretary, present. One didn't ask for a formal meeting to be arranged, one simply suggested that they invite Martin How to join them.

Only gossip was permitted with first courses, so with half her attention given to smiling and nodding, she let the other half drift back to England.

To Mike who, before she returned home, had formally and sweetly proposed marriage to her. He had it all worked out. He was always being made offers to work in America, but he liked his house and his work in London. They could live half in New York and half in London. She could keep her practice. They were good together in bed, weren't they? That was important, a good foundation for marriage. He really was good at marriage, Ilse had been a youthful misjudgement. And she loved Loxwood, didn't she?

'Alison.' June Yin's voice penetrated. 'I don't think you heard a word.'

'Sorry, Mom, I just remembered something.'

Louis and Heavenly arrived, Heavenly wearing something loose and gathered below her bump which revealed to its utmost her advanced pregnancy. She became the focus of the family's attention. Now that she and Louis were married and Heavenly was a Yin and was going to produce the first child of the second-generation American Yins, her status was enormously elevated. Heavenly drew any possible fire from Kuan-Yin's tardy attention to the family since her return. Perhaps she would not tell them of her own plans just now.

Perhaps she had still not absolutely decided what they were. The Kitchen Meeting could wait.

EIGHT

Houses rise and fall . . .
Old stone to new building, old timber to new fires . . .

T. S. ELIOT, Four Quartets

The first rain in weeks fell on Sunbarrow as Jake drove back there from London. He and Rin had driven up together, Jake to go to a preview of Lizz's exhibition, and Rin to sort out things with Mary. They were to have met up again at Daisy's, but when Jake arrived there, Rin had left a message to say: Change of plans, stopping over in London.

Daisy had said, 'If you want my opinion, she wants him back.'

'Mary? I thought she had set up house with some woman.'

'Mary was never a full-time lesbian, she had men as well . . . quite young ones . . . sometimes more than one at the same time. I met her recently: she was very willing to talk. I think she believed that if she could create some sort of a different Mary, then she could forget what happened. She wants Rin back.'

'I can hardly believe it, after the hell of a time she gave him.'

'That seems to be pretty much the case in marriage generally, doesn't it?'

'You're not half the cynic you make out. Do you reckon that's a good thing? I mean, Rin has seemed to be his old self lately.'

'Because he had a one-night stand with Dragon Lady? That's your style, not his. Rin's old self would be settled and conventional.'

'And with Mary? You don't really believe that they'll get back together?'

'I shouldn't be surprised.'

'It couldn't be the money, could it? Rin's going to be well off from his share in Sunbarrow.'

'If we sell. You know Mary, she's not like that. She certainly wasn't after his money the first time round, Rin hardly had two pence of his own to rub together.'

Rin and Mary had met at the solicitor's office and signed papers and then gone back to the house to sort out some of their tapes and books. Rin had offered to make coffee which Mary seemed delighted for him to do. They had been friendly but a little awkward with one another, politely doing little deals over jointly-owned books and tapes, until the photograph of baby Nathan had fallen from between the books where Rin had thrust it when he had smashed the picture-frame glass. Rin had tried to snatch it up before she saw what it was, but she saw and held out her hand for it.

She had sat and looked at it for a long time. Rin had felt apprehensive: the visit with the baby to the photographer had been such an event. They had photographed him at a day old, and had said that they would start an album and have him photographed every six months all the time he was growing up. They had joked about who he would look like once he started to get features. Now, he half-expected her to break down sobbing, or leap up and run from the room, or fling the nearest object at him, as she used to. Instead, she had run her finger over the baby's pudgy face, put the photo in one of the boxes and said, 'He was so sweet, Rin, so wonderful . . . wasn't he?'

Her question wasn't rhetorical, she wanted an answer. 'Wasn't he just. He was a great kid . . . great.'

'Wouldn't you like to try to make another one? Not a replacement, not a substitute, but make a different one?'

Unnecessarily, he said, 'Together?'

'Nobody else could do it for us.'

Of course. Who else was there who could live with Rin

when a particular model of a Mothercare baby buggy squeaked by and his blood stopped flowing for a moment, and who else in the world could possibly understand why Mary had been so unforgiving of the old Mary that she had tried everything to obliterate her?

Relief made him feel light-headed. He had known, even as he thought of setting up with Kuan-Yin, that there was no way that they could make out in any relationship longer than a night or two. But that night he had felt himself come back to a quite wonderful state of normality in which the notion of marriage was prominent.

Later, when he had time to think about it, it had crossed his mind that his night at the Green Man had been an attempt to prevent what he feared was going on between her and the Old Man. Much in the way that children will carry out some destructive act to try to stop their parents arguing.

Mary's smile was not gentle as it had once been; to those who know, the scars which the death of a child leave are permanently there in and around the eyes and in the set of the mouth. Hers was a brave smile because she knew that he had plenty of cause to reject it. But a smile, something that Rin himself wasn't brave enough to offer, was the bridge they both needed to cross over to one another.

Whilst Jake and Daisy were discussing Mary's motives, Rin was back in his familiar home, in his familiar bed, with his arms about Mary's familiar body, holding one of her soft familiar breasts, not giving a damn for her motives.

Mary, having been once flung into the darkest oubliette of despair, knew that whatever might happen from now on, nothing could ever be as bad again. Life is a real mad dog, and once it has savaged you, you never again make the mistake of approaching it as a friendly puppy.

A few miles north of Winchester, where the road climbs and dips steeply, water had run off the baked surface of the Downs and flooded the road. Had Jake been in his Range Rover he could have driven through, but he had borrowed Myrr's MG. The chassis was too low to clear the water, so he pulled into a gateway to wait to see whether there was a chance of the water draining away. He still had some of the bread-rolls they had taken with them that morning, Myrr always kept cans of soft drinks in the glove compartment, and the radio was a good stereo. Jake decided that he didn't mind if he had to wait a couple of hours. He was glad to have time on his own. The weeks since his father had died had caused him the sort of hassle he found a bit hard to handle.

He ate a couple of the bacon rolls and drank half a can of drink. The drum of raindrops on the canvas hood was soporific; he closed his eyes and listened to some music as stranded traffic piled up on the road. He thought about Lizz: although they had parted company, they had left one another without spoiling the good times they once had together. She had ribbed him about the beard he had grown.

'It never had strength enough to grow before I took up celibacy.'

They had exchanged fond, friendly looks. She had said, 'I hope you soon find a woman to shrivel it for you. At least you look the part now, Jake . . . Master of Tallentire.'

Jake had scorned the suggestion, but Lizz often seemed to know him as well as he knew himself. And when her agent had joined them before the picture, and had said: To the life, Lizzy, Jake knew that it wasn't much good trying to deny it himself. Whilst the Old Man was about, Jake with a full beard would have made him appear a poor copy of the original.

Did he now feel that he was an original? He couldn't answer himself that question.

Reflecting on the gallery where Lizz's exhibition was housed, he had to admit that he had been surprised to discover that it was such a prestigious place. Lizz had said that her show was in a London gallery, but until he saw its space and style, Jake hadn't really understood the implications of being shown in the West End ... Lizz had arrived.

Certainly the *Poseidon and Gaea* caused a stir, and was exhibited with a red spot which Lizz had said would keep her for a year. Taken with the rest of the exhibition, it was easy to see the direction in which her strong, forceful work was now taking her. And watching Lizz, assertive and confident in press interviews, Jake saw that she would go in the same direction as her work. Whilst her previous pictures of the male nudes were calm and studied, one could see an analogy of the warm and vibrant figures erupting from the still, blue water, with the hot thick, tactile acrylic paint bursting out in the midst of the cool, beautiful erotic young men.

Because of Myrr, Jake was glad that it had been sold to an overseas buyer. Even if she did know that they had been having an affair, a thing like that was best out of the way.

The rain stopped and the sun came out, gleaming on leaves that already appeared more turgid and green from their soaking. Jake wound down the window and smelled the earthy steam rising. Often when he was out in a parched field and a sudden storm quenched it, Jake fancied that he could hear the earth sucking and gasping with relief. Listening now, he was reminded of something Kuan-Yin had said when he had taken her to see the Great Pictogram.

Her smile had been enigmatic: Message from the planet, Jake. Gaea to humans. Person to person call.

She was an enigma herself. She had been through medical school yet could talk of Gaea the Earth Mother. Westernized to her very teeth, but, he guessed, subconsciously with oriental grass-roots. A beautiful, womanly woman who lives her life like a man. And, Jake thought, she's better at it than I am. Her success is self-made but I was made by the Old Man. She seems to have her lovers, and no regrets, and she comes and goes as she pleases.

When she had mentioned Gaea, she had not joked as he would have himself, but mentioned the goddess as unfazed as a clergyman can mention the Trinity – as a fact of life. In the days following the Old Man's funeral, it seemed that he hadn't been able to turn round without finding her there. And during that time he had seen quite another side of her nature. Perhaps one she had let the Old Man see and he himself had glimpsed the morning when they were preparing the funeral site.

Understandably he might easily have fallen for her. Certainly he had fancied her. She had spent quite a lot of time perched on a stool in the farm office after Lee Han had gone back to Hong Kong, when there seemed to be no reason why she should not return to New York; she had logged the local tumuli, and collected the maps which the Old Man had said in a letter to Maurice Cockrill that she must have. There would be no more circles this year because all the fields had been harvested, yet for days she had hung on, apologizing until he had got through to her that he was pleased to have her there.

It was during those days that she had planted seeds of ambition in his heart. Not the five-bean seeds like those that the Old Man had planted and watched grow from family farm to food factory.

'If your family sells, will you stay on at Sunbarrow?'

'Not if it means staying tied into the agri-chemical deal.'

'Is there some law that says that Sunbarrow must always produce edible crops, Jake?'

She had gone home leaving that seed of an idea germinating. Inedible crops. A spinney? A wood? Eventually perhaps a small forest. No returns for forty years. A bit of Sunbarrow given back.

And what if next year, as she had speculated, the circle

business got more complicated and involved? She already knew of several universities who were preparing to research. She had told him about her Golden Flower prediction. She had speculated on a chrysanthemum symbol and the Old Man had plotted it on his chart.

What would he do if he was still managing Sunbarrow? Let the crops take second place to the sightseers and researchers. It wouldn't break Sunbarrow.

She was an enigma and he had not been able to stop thinking of her since the day she left; and she was what had drawn him to the exhibition. He quite longed to see her in that ecstatic pose before it disappeared. It crossed his mind that he might even take a trip to New York. He was due a holiday now that the harvest was over.

Daisy, back in the place she liked best, her own conservatory in her own house, amidst her own jungle of plants, was doing what she liked best, being delighted by the manuscript of a teenage girls' book with totally new ideas and a lot of humour.

Rin and Mary were gently feeling their way back into one another's lives.

Jake, still waiting for the storm to go over, was thinking about the viability of planting a large tract of Sunbarrow with broad-leaved trees. He would need to talk it over with Kuan-Yin before he committed the land. He had no idea why.

Whilst her elder children were thus occupied, Myrr sat in her conservatory with a large gin and tonic watching the clouds burst over Clump Field. The sky was so dark that it was impossible to see through the slashing rain which was ridge and which sky. The times she had sat and looked at that same scene over the years. When she had first arrived there had been no conservatory, of course, just the scullery with a stable-type door, now part of the extended kitchen.

She recalled watching another such storm break thirty years ago, whilst trying to swallow her deep and resentful misery at finding herself pregnant and suffering the nausea caused by it. Old lady Tallentire had still been here, bedridden downstairs; and Nat's two sisters, whose health was too delicate to contribute much to the upkeep of the place. Those first years were almost too awful to recall. First she had given birth to twins instead of the expected one, then soon after that old lady Tallentire had grown more and more sick until she died, quickly followed by simpleminded Kit.

Within too short a time she had somehow become pregnant again. God only knew how, she had tried as well as she knew how to prevent it. Now, of course, it was impossible to think of a world without Jake, but at the time she had taken enough stuff and jumped down from enough heights and humped about enough heavy bales, for a less determined embryo than Jake to have lost its grip. She smiled to herself. Jake . . . he had probably lain there not noticing anything untoward was going on.

Then things had got slightly better. Nat's sister had undergone a series of injections for her asthma and she had so improved that she got married. Then they had had a great windfall. It was the year when practically the entire potato crop south of the Scottish border failed, yet the Sunbarrow potato harvest produced a crop that Nat had said had a resistance to blight. It had been like finding oil on their land, dealers were fighting hand over fist for their crop. That year Nat had had a modern stove and washboiler installed and with a bank loan had bought up the Glasspool's piggeries when the family had emigrated to Australia.

The first of the circles had appeared in that field. A small, single circle. Then two together. Nat had said that it must be whirlwinds, but she had seen him go up there with hazel wands in his pocket and had watched as he had walked across and around the circle. Next, three circles, then four evenly spaced. When Myrr had said jokingly: It's God playing poker, Nat, he had got ridiculously angry. When the five in a pattern had appeared, she had kept her mouth shut. Jake, home from agricultural college, put his foot in it by saying that they should tell somebody, but Nat had been furious. He had always hated to see people who had no business on Sunbarrow land. If he'd had his way he would have ploughed up or barricaded the bridle paths and rights of way that were close to Sunbarrow and he would have fenced off the barrows so that they were included within the Sunbarrow boundary.

She felt the comfort of the gin relaxing her neck muscles and watched the sheets of rain drive across the black mark where, she presumed, small atoms of Nat still remained. She had thought, on that night when they had all agreed to go along with what Nat wanted, that she would find it all too macabre. But it hadn't been. In its way it had been the perfect and fitting end for a man like Nat. When she had seen the fierce flames leap from the loose hay and ignite the tinder-dry wood surrounding his body, she had been unbearably moved.

And now they had all got to apply themselves to the future and what they must do with the place.

The place, the place. What should they do with it? Nat was so possessive of it, yet it appeared that none of their children really wanted it. Why? Why, when Nat had felt so passionately about it, are the rest of us so indifferent to what happens to it now?

Certainly it had not taken Myrr long to know that, without Nat, Sunbarrow meant very little to her. She had no sentimental attachments to it and not that many fond memories. It had been her home – at least, it had been their home, her and Nat's home, but now that there was to be no more 'them', Myrr didn't want to stay. It would have been nice if one or other of their children had caught a bit of Nat's feeling for the place. In the same way Myrr would have preferred one of them to have wanted to live in the house she had done so much to create. The Sunbarrow agent had said in passing that on the open market the Sunbarrow house alone would fetch close on a million.

Close on a million ... Myrr could have laughed and cried at the irony of it when she heard. All those rotten years when she had had to hands-and-knees wash quarry tiles that had been put down in Nat's father's day. The heating up of water in the old copper boiler to get enough water for six of them to bath. The collecting by hand of hundreds of eggs, and the wringing by hand of hundreds of necks, to buy some decent chairs and curtains. Until the Common Agricultural Policy had thought of making butter mountains, and Nat had thought of going in with an ice-cream manufacturer, and building a slaughter-house and opening a farm shop, and converting barns to chicken percheries, and God only knew what else, until then, it had all been so bloody. Cold and mean, pinch-penny and hard.

And now her home alone was worth close on a million.

In the village there had been talk and some resentment. Jez Carter was never slow to tell her – jokingly of course – what was being said: They say if you leave an old harrow in a ditch, Nat Tallentire will buy it cheap and find a market for it.

Myrr never let him know how that had hurt: More fool they then, Jez, to let somebody make money whilst they're all going broke. But then there are always more big mouths about than big brains. Jez Carter always laughed, knowing that he couldn't afford to upset the Tallentires these days.

Poppy came running in through the rain.

'What are you sitting in the dark for, Mum?'

'It doesn't seem dark, I expect my eyes have grown used to it. I was watching the rain. When the wind is in that direction, it always sweeps over Clump Field in sheets like that.' Poppy had been for her driving test and until her mind had started going back to the past, Myrr had been on tenterhooks for her. 'Well . . . how did you get on?'

Poppy plumped down on the sofa beside Myrr. 'How do you think I got on? Look at it! I could hardly see through the windscreen, and people kept rushing out into the road with umbrellas, and on the hill start the engine acted up . . . it was a disaster.'

'Well, never mind. Stay there and I'll make some tea.'

Poppy flung her arms about Myrr's neck and hugged her. 'I love you, Ma.' She laughed. 'I said it was a disaster . . . I didn't say I hadn't passed.'

'Poppy, you did it!'

'The examiner complimented me on driving with such skill in such bad road conditions. I passed, I passed, I passed!'

Poppy's acquisition of a driving licence had meant a great deal to her. In one way Myrr had half-hoped that she would fail, thinking that if the one option was removed, then she might reconsider and apply for a university place. With her three good A-level passes she could still get a place. But a children's nurse . . . a nanny. Surprising everybody with a fait accompli, Poppy had got herself the job and then arranged for Myrr to meet Mr and Mrs Stylianopoulous with whom she would live for two years. Two years is enough time to know whether I am going to be any good at it and whether I want to continue. Myrr hadn't been able to fault the Greek family, and the only proviso Mrs Stylianopoulous made was that Poppy should have a clean driving licence so that she could collect the elder Stylianopoulous child from school and take both children on expeditions.

'Only a fortnight then,' Myrr said.

'I can hardly wait. I adore Greece. You'll come and see me, like the Stylianopoulouses said?'

'Of course I'll come. I expect it will help me with my OU studies.'

'You are the one who should be applying for university,' Poppy said. 'They'll always find a place for mature students who can pay their way. Why do it the hard way? You have no reason to.'

Myrr halted on her way to the kitchen, finishing her gin and tonic. 'I couldn't do that . . . I haven't a single A-level.'

'They might take the O-levels you did before Dad was taken ill into account, and all the different courses you've done at the Centre. If you don't ask, you don't get.'

'But I've paid my Open University fees, they'd be wasted.'

Poppy laughed. 'Oh Mum, you are sweet. There you are, part-owner in an enterprise worth a bomb and you're thinking about a couple of hundred pounds.'

'Oh, not really that much. I'll make that tea. You get your wet shoes off.'

It took Myrr ages to make the tea. Before each operation she stood gazing, her face suffused and warmed by the excitement of the thoughts that raced around in her head. She returned to the conservatory with the tray, where Poppy had switched on some lamps and was pressing back the aerial into the phone. 'How do you fancy linguistics at a Poly?'

'What's linguistics?'

'To do with language. You remember that book by Crystal you read when you were doing English Lit?'

'Oh yes, I thought it seemed a bit like learning algebra – not that I know much about algebra.'

'But if you were offered a full-time three-year course of study?'

'They wouldn't offer.'

'Mum, they've just instituted a new course. Tom told me about it, it's true, they've got places to fill. I just rang, they are open to applications from anybody at the moment.

Mature students can be considered on personal interview.' She handed Myrr the handset. 'Ring them. You've got nothing to lose.'

Myrr took the handset and sat with it in her lap, her eyes fixed on a line of yellow outlining the ridge where the barrows lay. 'It's clearing. I hope Jake's all right, I was going to get that hood checked, I wondered whether it was properly rainproof.'

Poppy took her mother's hand. 'It's frightening, isn't it, when you actually think you might get what you want? I know that I want to go to Greece and I know that I want to work with children, but when the examiner handed me my certificate I trembled with fright that I no longer had any excuse not to do it.'

Myrr gave a little nod of acknowledgement that perhaps Poppy was right.

'You could have your BA by 1993.' Poppy watched as her mother's eyes grew moist and she bit her lips together. She pressed on relentlessly. 'And maybe your MA by 1995 or 6.'

Myrr pulled down her face with both hands. 'Heavens above, child, I haven't even asked if there's a chance of a place.'

'Here's the number,' Poppy said, 'or do you want me to dial it for you?'

Myrr suppressed a slightly hysterical desire to giggle. 'There's not much hope of me getting any sort of degree if you think I can't make a phone call under my own steam.' And she dialled the Polytechnic's number.

Lizz Taylor sat in Delgado's swish trattoria and, for once, allowed her ego to be massaged. She scarcely knew whether she was host or guest at the table, where, with her agent Charlotte fielding some of the questions and prompting some of the answers, she was agreeing to consider any number of proposals from a half-hour television her-life-and-work type of feature to a show in Paris and another in Sydney. Lizz was a shrewd enough woman to know that — although she was probably the flavour of the month in the art world — it wouldn't last, and that she must grab every chance with both hands whilst they were hot for her.

She had been so glad that Jake had come to the preview. Jake was Jake, the eternal bachelor. Today she had been able to let him go. She knew that this was the world she wanted, a world of £40,000 tags on her pictures, showings in distant cities, television and London life. She had enjoyed being described as Extraordinary! Fantastic! and Truly-truly exciting.

NEW YORK

Louis and Heavenly's baby, Carole, was brought on its first visit to Yin's Number One House where the family fussed and chattered volubly at this first new Yin for twenty-five years, and for the first time in her life, Kuan-Yin experienced a maternal instinct. 'Oh, she's so cute, let me hold her.' The baby curled its mouth into a smile, locked its tiny fist on to her finger and Kuan-Yin was smitten. 'Oh, how I should like one of these little things,' she said jokingly.

June, not joking, said, 'Then you have no time to waste, Alison. Babies need parents, not only mother' — sending a well-concealed pang through her daughter.

This was to be the evening of Kuan-Yin's requested Kitchen Meeting and Martin How, the company secretary, was to join them to oversee the meeting.

June and George Yin, their heads held in sentimental poses, drank in the sight of their daughter as a beautiful Madonna. Lady Yin's shrewd old eyes watched as Kuan-Yin jiggled the baby Carole's hand.

Lenny Yin said, 'It is high time you made George also grandfather, Alison.'

Kuan-Yin felt herself unable to control a blush when she looked up and saw that the whole family was watching her make a fool of herself with the baby. 'Henry's turn first,' she said, 'he's older than I am.'

Louis said, 'But that would only make Pop a grandfather twice over. Now come on, Ally, time you did something about it.' He held out his hands to take his new prize and show them all what a really good Pop he was. He was the greatest authority in New York on everything homo-generative from pre-conceptual diet to breast shells.

With the arrival of Martin How, they all retired to the Kitchen Meeting. Years ago the board meetings had taken place literally in the kitchen, but now a pleasant and comfortable room was always kept ready at the Yin Number One. Before they started, Louis demonstrated his skill at diaper changing, then baby Carole was put down to sleep in a basket crib so that, as a member of the board, she was both present and absent. She would not get a vote until she was seventeen, so she slept, a presence in the room who, from time to time, drew surreptitious looks from all the rest.

Martin How said, 'We'll make a start then?' He addressed his question to Lady Yin, the titular Chairman, seated next to him. 'This Kitchen Meeting was requested by Alison. She has given me an outline of her proposals . . .' He passed papers round to each of them. 'If you'll just read it through, you'll see that it is a straight-forward investment proposal. Do you want to speak, Alison?'

'OK. It's all down here, but briefly . . . I'm suggesting that we diversify. The Blossom Parks are all making nice profits but we have all our eggs in one basket.'

'There's nothing wrong with that,' Henry said.

'Not whilst Americans like to eat Chinese,' Kuan-Yin

said. 'But already the Mex and sushi places are becoming popular.'

Burt said, 'Chinese food is part of the American way of life.'

'Ally isn't suggesting that we close down the Blossom Parks,' Louis said, 'but that we have another line, and I'm inclined to agree.'

'OK,' Henry said, 'but this investment is in England. Who has ever been to England?'

'I have,' Kuan-Yin said.

'So have I,' said Louis.

'It's a great place,' said Henry.

Heavenly said, 'Will somebody tell me what is an arable-cum-thing complex?'

'It's just a darned great big dirt farm with sheep and pigs and processing plant,' Kuan-Yin said.

Heavenly pointed to the page with the sets of figures. 'There must be one hell of a lot of sheep and pigs. I mean, this is very big potatoes. What rate of return could we expect?'

Oh, Heavenly. How the Yins loved her. Not only was she pretty, and a producer of grandchildren, Heavenly could read and discuss a balance sheet.

Martin How said, 'I've had the chief accountant go over the figures. On paper it's a pretty sound investment.'

'But why England?' Lenny said. 'If we want to diversify we don't have to go to England to do it.'

'Uncle Lenny,' Kuan-Yin said, 'it's nearly the twenty-first century.'

'Ally's right, Pop,' Louis said. 'It's high time we began to think more expansively. Do you know how many American companies have been bought up by the English in the last ten years? I say: Sonofabitch! Let's go buy up some of theirs.' He crashed a fist into his palm.

Kuan-Yin shuddered inwardly to think what Tallentire would have thought if he could have heard his precious

Sunbarrow being haggled over. But it was necessary. If, as seemed likely, the Tallentires were going to put Sunbarrow on the market, then she would move heaven and earth to take possession of it.

They argued back and forth for an hour. Lady Yin, silent but listening and shrewdly weighing them all up, sat patiently waiting for them to run down. When she made a move, the discussion came to a stop.

'June,' George said, 'go to bathroom with Lady Yin.' But Lady Yin refused June in her own tongue and held out her hand for Kuan-Yin who walked along the passageway with her grandmother.

The little decorated anteroom had a few stools and a couple of chairs and a lot of pink mirrors. Lady Yin said in her strange, halting American. 'Sit, Arison. I don't need pee, I wish ask important.'

'OK.'

'Pre'nant, Arison?'

Kuan-Yin looked wide-eyed at her grandmother, who pointed accusingly at her. 'Dumb girl, no.' She rubbed the palm of her hand around Kuan-Yin's belly. 'Baby? Pre'nant?'

Of all questions, this was the last she had expected. She didn't reply immediately, but viewed a multi-reflected glimpse of herself in the mirrors: Do I look pregnant?

'Yes, Grandmother.'

'Not long?'

'I have just one moon, but I have a positive test.'

'Englishman?'

Kuan-Yin nodded.

Lady Yin smiled and took her granddaughter's hands affectionately. 'You want marry pig-sheep farmer.'

Kuan-Yin shook her head. 'Not possible, Lady Yin.'

Lady Yin wagged her head. 'Arison allow marry man put baby in?'

Kuan-Yin nodded. 'I'm afraid so.'

'Arison, all make mistake.' She smiled and squeezed Kuan-Yin's fingers. 'All make mistake.'

'I guess it might not have been too much of a mistake, Gran.'

'Understand.'

'I didn't plan it, or go about trying to seduce him for that purpose, but it wasn't exactly an accident.'

'Understand. I tell. Young woman,' she patted her own chest, 'almost marry. Freedom army come Mao Tse Tung so'iers.' Her eyes lit up. 'So'iers hungry. Rag shirt.' She held her fisted hand against her flat chest. 'Fighting spirit men. Young woman love at once . . . one only man. One only night. Baby made quick.' She tapped her own chest. 'Young woman . . . not plan.'

Kuan-Yin had never heard her grandmother string together so many words of English and was impressed. All these years playing dumb. That she halted and stumbled did not matter because the telling of the love-story was in her face. Kuan-Yin nodded.

'He is happy marry?'

She held on to her grandmother's fingers as she said, 'He is dead, Grandmother. He had no idea that I got pregnant. Nobody knows except you and my gynaecologist.'

Lady Yin put her hand over her mouth and looked sad. 'All same story. Mao Tse Tung fighter is kill next day.'

'That's a sad story, Lady Yin.'

The old lady shrugged her shoulders and her eyes wrinkled to her smile. 'Not so sad. Quick love make Lee Han . . . gift of heaven. Young girl marry.' She nodded in the direction of the passageway. 'George, Lenny, Burt . . . gift of husband.'

'I'm glad, it's a half-happy ending.'

'Is happy now Arison make Lee Han come visit Lady Yin. Lee Han soon come many time. Happy end. We make two bit happy end? Baby belong to pig-sheep man?'

'Yes. He was in love with his land, it's called Sunbarrow

440

and it's very beautiful. His wife has never liked farming and his sons and daughters would prefer to sell. I want . . .' she clasped her belly, 'this child of his to learn how to fall in love with Sunbarrow. The child belongs there. The only way for it to happen is for the Yins to buy the place. It would need our sort of money, and apart from my baby growing up in its own place it would be a really terrific investment for Blossom Park. And . . .' she kissed her grandmother, 'it needs our sort of understanding of the place, it has to be owned by a family.'

'We go back now.' Kuan-Yin crooked her arm for her grandmother. 'Lady Yin belong nowhere. Husband bring young woman and sons, America – he die! Young woman not pass lan'uage test. Not belong in US not belong China . . . not belong. This child marry man put in belong Engrand.'

George, June, Alison, Henry, Heavenly and Louis voted for the proposed investment, Lenny and Burt against. Lady Yin's votes were not needed, but she voted anyhow. The next day, on behalf of Park House Investments, a preliminary offer was made to the agent for Sunbarrow Farms.

CHILDENCOMBE

Considering Poppy's voice was coming from Athens, it sounded to Myrr remarkably undistorted. 'I really don't mind, Mum. I think Jake should have the say.'

'But you mustn't just push it aside like that, Poppy. There is a great deal of money involved and once the offer has been accepted there will be no going back. Don't you mind if the place is sold off?'

'I've told you, Mum. If I come back to England, I wouldn't want to settle in a place like Childencombe. I don't suppose that I'll want to settle anywhere at all for a long time, and it certainly wouldn't be Childencombe.'

'It's a big step. You might think differently if you were here.'

'I wouldn't. I promise you, I wouldn't. You don't want to stay on there now, do you?'

'No. I've already got this place I've found close to the college: I'm longing to show it to you.'

'Well then, if shove comes to push and Mr Cockrill wants you to vote on it, then I give you my proxy. What about the others?'

'Rin's absorbed in mending things with Mary. You'd think this was just a little cottage we are contemplating selling to these Americans. But I think he'd rather like enough money to start his own agency.'

'I don't think Daisy's ever been very attached to Sunbarrow, has she, Mum?'

'You know Daisy, you can never tell what she's thinking. She comes out with her Marxist things – I think she'll have to face up to a lot of questions if she suddenly gets a load of money.'

'Well look, Mum, I'll have to go. I'm supposed to be packing. Mr Stylianopoulous has to go to Rome for a month, and he's taking all of us. Give them my love at home.'

Myrr pushed down the aerial thoughtfully and looked round the kitchen, rather expecting that some poignant memory would jump upon her, and that all this talk of selling Sunbarrow was nonsense and her course at the college was just pie in the sky. But it was just a kitchen. Beautifully designed, expensively fitted, cleaned and polished by the Pack women, true, but even so, it might easily have been just an advertisement, or a set in a glitzy soap opera.

Since she arrived an hour ago she had been right through the house, and it all felt like that. She had the impression of being shown around some desirable residence that was on the market – which of course it was: The Master

Bedroom, with pine-clad sauna off and bathroom with double handbasin, bidet and genuine jacuzzi bath, plus separate wc, handbasin and bidet. Five further bedrooms and two shower rooms. Two wcs, with handbasins and bidets. Attic conversions with plank floors. Conservatory – purpose-built and sympathetically designed to be in keeping with a house of such age and charm. Exterior, shrubberies and flower beds, many mature trees. Large swimming-pool with bottom lighting, changing rooms, patio with barbecue . . .

A lovely house, Mrs Tallentire.

Very nice, but not really what I'm looking for. I had in mind something smaller, perhaps a small house in the centre . . . perhaps close to the cathedral and the college.

Myrr wished that Roz was here; she would have understood what was going on in her head better than anybody. But Roz was in Bristol this week, sitting in the studios as her first play was recorded for radio: My producer thinks it might well go forward for the Sony awards, Myrr. Isn't that great?

Great, Roz. Her new play was a one-hander . . . about a woman who has a one-night stand with a young man half her age . . . it's all going on in her head . . . a kind of soliloquy. It's cathartic for her . . .

Myrr guessed that Roz had hyped her play to so many people that she had forgotten that her research for it had gone on under Myrr's roof. Myrr was glad that they had got back together again. The old Centre days had gone and their friendship had moved on, but there was something in what they had now that Myrr preferred. Two ambitious career women. Starting later than the new young women who wore short tight skirts and men's shoulders, but she felt – excepting that they had not so much time – she and Roz were none the worse for starting late: it was just the fact that they had less time which made them seem greedy for success.

Rin had suggested that she might like to meet up with him and Mary in London and they could have made a night of it and taken in a show. But Myrr had said that they should be at Sunbarrow to make the decision, looking at what they were being asked to part with.

'Good Lord, Myrr, we know only too well what it is. It's the same place I parted with years ago.'

'I still think it should be here, Rin.'

He had agreed and so had Daisy. They were driving down together. Not Mary. Rin said that she wanted to reunite with the family, but on another occasion.

Myrr heard Jake's footsteps and went to the back door to meet him. Oh, why had he grown that beard? With the light behind him . . .

'Jake . . . Oh, you do look like your father.'

They hugged and kissed and he ruffled her hair demonstratively – in an un-Tallentire manner. 'Hmm, it's great to see you. This place feels a barn without you. I've stopped down at Rex's a time or two.'

'Oh, Jake.' Now that she didn't have to curse him for spattering the stove with fat or for leaving his clothes where they dropped, it pained her to think of Jake fending for himself. 'I'm sorry I haven't been back as much as I thought, it's just that, with it being the beginning of term, there is so much going on.'

'Hey . . . it's all right. I'm a big boy, you know. And Mrs Pack just loves cleaning the place.'

'Don't you treat her like a servant, Jake.'

'Mrs Pack just loves having a man to look after, she told me. If she can't find any polishing to do, she has the oven going and does baking. The freezer is full of stuff.'

Myrr would have loved to have been able to pick him up, as she could when he was six, and sit with her arms about him for five minutes. Jake was the one who liked being cuddled more than the other three. Daisy and Rin never wanted all that unless competing for it: then each would try to squirm into the other's territory. Poppy never wanted to sit still for five minutes. 'I'll make us some tea.'

He sat and watched her as she opened and closed cupboards, looking for things in unfamiliar places that were now Jake's and Mrs Pack's. 'Well, come on then, what's it like being a student?'

She looked at him for a long moment, then let out a bubbling laugh. 'Oh, Jake, it's absolutely wonderful. I sit in lectures, I sit in libraries, I sit in groups – nobody seems to think anything about a woman my age being there. Of course, I'm not the only one. There is a black woman my age, she's on another course doing women's studies, we've become friendly and there's another widow, younger than me, she's doing some diploma in social work, I think. We all keep coming across one another. I shouldn't mind doing women's studies. I think it's possible to change over. I'm going to enquire about it.' She laughed again. 'And I belong to the Student's Union.'

As she poured the water on to the teabags he came and put his arms about her. She felt the beard by her ear. Dear, nice Jake. He put on his happy face so as not to show what was behind it. In his way, he was as close as Nat.

'You sound happy. I'm glad it's turning out so well.'

'Thanks, Jake. I don't think it's happiness, it's fulfilment. I haven't been anybody for over thirty years, and now at last I'm back to being me. I . . . ah . . . I decided to call myself Myrr Jeavons . . . saves questions about whether I'm anything to do with those Tallentires, you know what I mean? People might think I wasn't serious about my studies.' Jake nodded. 'I'm a mature student reading linguistics. I don't suppose you've got any idea what it means to me to be able to say that.' She laughed. 'I sometimes go into bookshops and order a book just so that I can hear myself say: It's a book on linguistics I need for my course at college.'

'Are you getting over Dad?'

She nodded. 'You can't be married for nearly thirty years and suddenly switch off.' Then she fell silent, her gaze withdrawn for a few moments. 'It's funny, you know, but I don't find him here. I thought that everywhere I went I would have memories of him . . . but I haven't, except in the book room. The day he died – after Mrs Lavender had laid him out and you and Rin had put up the hurdles – I sat with him for ages . . . you remember? You might think it's a funny thing to say, but that was the first time I was ever with Nat and felt on any sort of terms with him.'

Not knowing what to say, Jake drank his tea.

'I don't suppose you understand what I mean . . . I hardly do myself, but it was as though all the years of our marriage there were things going on in his head that I couldn't understand, it was as though we were from different cultures . . . well we were in a way, you know what the Jeavonses are like.' Jake smiled at brief images of some of his stocky, rumbustious, demonstrative, horse-dealing, gaming kin. 'The only thing we had in common was you four. It wasn't much of a life for either of us at first. I used to say to myself: Poor old Myrr. Not pitying myself, but sort of saying: Never mind, it will be all right one day. When I sat with him that Sunday, it suddenly came to me: Poor old Nat. He really didn't have anything.'

'He had Sunbarrow. Maybe it was all he wanted.'

'I think it was until he found that he had actually got it and there was nothing much left to do to it except play about with what he'd got. I think he loved it . . . but it never loved him back. So . . . poor old Nat.'

Jake too had been surprised that, although every inch of the house seemed to have some ghost of Myrr with the four of them doing something, saying something, being there, he sometimes had the feeling that the Old Man never had been there. Jake had missed having Lizzy to tell such things to. He couldn't make out where the Old Man had been all those years, or where he was now. It was almost as though he had never been in the house. The only trace of him was in his four children.

'Well, what do you want to do about this offer, Jake?'

Jake spread his hands. 'I think I'd go along with selling. I don't feel that there's any reason for me to be here.'

'Of course there is. You run the place.'

'So could any competent general manager with the kind of staff we've got here.'

'Listen, Jake, if you don't want to sell, then we won't. I'm only asking you all as a kind of courtesy, Sunbarrow belongs to me, but I want you all to be put on the spot and actually say what it is you would like. I think I know what I shall do, but it's not settled. If I say "No deal" to these Americans, then you'll all have to be content to have just your share of the profits and wait until I'm gone for your inheritance. Now whether you stayed on under those circumstances is something you'd have to decide, but let's get it quite clear – nobody expects you to.'

Jake nodded.

'Don't just nod. No way will I have you feel that it's your duty to stay on here. That's what happened to Nat, and I don't want to see you doing the same. He became obsessed with the blessed place.'

'I don't think it's in me to be like that. In any case, he hasn't left anything for anyone else to do.' He could have told her about the idea of creating woodlands and the distant plan for a small, broad-leaf forest, but he wanted them to decide without taking him into account. He wanted them to accept the offer if they wished without feeling obligated.

She looked at him. If Poppy had been Nat's joy child, then Jake had been hers. It wasn't that she had not loved Daisy and Rin, she had . . . did, but they were an accident, the result of Nat not being careful when he had promised he would; she would have given anything if they would have dissolved inside her in those first months of her

447

pregnancy, but they had stayed there and grown into two healthy babies and been born into a penniless household.

Poppy had been a kind of accident too – more like serendipity. But she had got Jake in a rare and beautiful moment of being close to Nat. The twins were still babies and Myrr saw nothing but work and scrimping for years ahead. And one night she had gone into the room that had become the book room, and come upon Nat with his head in his hands and tears streaming down his face. All he had said was, 'I'm sorry, Myrr, I didn't ever mean it to be like this for you. You are too bright and nice for this bloody place. I would give my right arm to turn the clock back to that day over Goose Grass.'

To see his handsome young face – dead tired from the hours he put in pulling the farm up by its bootstraps, so full of misery – had been just too much for Myrr; the only way that she could think of to assure him that she had no regrets was for her to be the seducer this time. Jake, easy-going, nice-natured, beautiful . . .

The beginning of October and, although the days were shorter, the afternoons in Childencombe were like spring. Jake, still undecided about his future, started a long walk over the Downs, not purposely to look at their flock of sheep, although they were certainly worth a look, but simply to enjoy being out in the crisp air and the warm sun. As he walked amongst the watchful sheep they scattered, still grinding away at mouthfuls of grass. Jake had always liked sheep. They were nowhere near as stupid as their reputation had them be, but as with the reputation pigs had for being filthy, it was lack of human understanding that was at fault.

Sheep-rearing was something that he knew about, and one of the options he had considered for his future. He didn't know where, but abroad probably. He had taken Lizzy out a couple of times, and told her of some of the options that were open to him. Perhaps he had been hoping that she might show a spark of enthusiasm that would have rekindled their old affair, but any interest she showed was for the idea, not for any part she might play in it. He still fancied her, but she had slid away quite expertly when he had made a tentative move. He guessed that she still fancied him, but whatever glue it had been that had held them together during their affair, had dissolved.

When he reached the place known as the Other Field, he hitched himself upon the stile at a place where one could see a great part of the later annexations to Sunbarrow, the ice-cream manufacturing unit, the yogurt plant and the creamery. If the Old Man hadn't been so adamant about the place not being split up, those businesses could easily be sold off separately. So could the slaughter-house, which wasn't even attached to the rest of Sunbarrow land.

For a while he reflected on his part in the recent development. Even before he went to college, he had understood how the various parts fitted beautifully together, but it wasn't until he had been through agricultural college that he had begun to see the perfection of a place like Sunbarrow. The Old Man had been a bloody intelligent entrepreneur. No one had ever told him how a successful business is built, but he had known, and he had done it. On reflection Jake had to admit that the Old Man had been right to prevent its division. Sunbarrow was a great deal more than the sum of its parts. To split it would be like dividing up some valuable collection made piece by hard-won piece over a lifetime.

His mind went to Kuan-Yin. She had certainly put the cat among the pigeons. When Maurice Cockrill had said he had a proposal he needed to discuss with the family, Jake had expected nothing like that. Cockrill had read the formal offer from Park Investment NY straight. Jake recalled the expression on Cockrill's face when he came to the end of the document.

'You probably will not have heard of Park Investment.' He had handed Jake the accompanying letter. 'Read the small print at the bottom.'

Jake had read: Chairman – D. F. Yin. Directors – George Yin. Lenny Yin. Burt Yin. Louis Yin. Henry Yin. Dr Alison Yin. Mrs Heavenly Yin. Carole Yin.

Mr Cockrill's eyebrows were at full mast. 'You understand who these people are?'

'Of course I do.'

'She has telephoned me from New York.'

'Do you know who all these other Yins are?'

'Her family. They are very big in restaurants, apparently.'

'I knew about that, but I never suspected they had the kind of money that could buy Sunbarrow.'

'Oh yes, I've made some enquiries. They are doing very nicely indeed. They not only have this unique chain of very up-market restaurants serving only Chinese food, but they are importers of anything Chinese. It's still a family business. Like Sainsbury's, they've never gone public.'

'I think you should tell the family about the offer without calling their attention to the small print.'

Myrr had said: 'An American investment company? What do they want with an English farm?'

Cockrill had said: 'It might easily have been an oil sheikh. Of course it is an outline offer,' he explained. 'Normally, the sale of a business such as this would take months . . . viewings, brochures. But, of course, you realize that the covenants created by Mr Tallentire will effectively rule out a large number of would-be buyers. I am inclined to the idea that this offer from a family concern is very much in the spirit of your late husband's will.'

Daisy, having taken the original letter from Cockrill, said, 'A *Chinese* family concern?'

Jake had seen Maurice Cockrill open his mouth to comment, but think better of it. He supposed that they all must have had some comment on the tips of their tongues. Myrr had said, 'Your father had an idea that nobody should have Sunbarrow except Tallentires. But let's face it, which of us wants it? Not Mary and Rin, not me, not Poppy. Do you, Daisy?'

'Not if you paid me.'

'So what then? I certainly won't have Jake left with it hanging round his neck in the way it was left hanging around Nat's. Jake needs to be free to make up his mind without feeling he's got any duty to either us or the farm. So if you haven't anything else to say about it, Mr Cockrill might as well get his head together with Phil French – that's the new agent – and the Yins' representative.'

Jake, now sitting on the stile in the Other Field, wished that he hadn't given up smoking. Several times he had felt like this over the last three months, but knew that if he had the first one, he'd have to go through all that business again as he had after the *feng-shui* morning and the night he and Daisy had sat on watching the ashes cool. So he reached for a twig to chew. Poor substitute for what he needed. The hedge between the Other Field and the Downs was festooned with large red hips, red honeysuckle berries, and a few nightshade, and there were blackberries galore. It was a wonder the Childencombe children hadn't been up and had the lot: they would have done in Jake's day.

No, probably not, not this late in October, when the Devil sits on the bramble bush – or spits – or shits, according to which version you were brought up on. It amounted to the same thing. There it was, luscious fruit glistening in the October sunshine, as black and juicy as it was ripe and tempting. He remembered Daisy, scoffing at him for believing old wives' tales, making him and Rin go with her to collect the October fruit. They went all along the hedgerows, but most of the berries dropped off or disintegrated in their hands; they had managed to pick some but when they arrived home the basin was crawling with tiny maggots.

He wished Lizzy was with him now. She was easy to talk to. She'd have it in one, what he felt about things being blighted:

On the day when the Great Pictogram appeared, everything had been totally great: after that things had started to go rotten.

Rotten, Jake?

You know what I mean. You've gone, the Old Man, Myrr, Poppy and now Sunbarrow. Yeah, Lizzy, rotten.

Not the pictogram's fault.

No . . . that was terrific. He chewed the stick, sliding slivers of wood satisfyingly between his teeth. OK, so the Devil shat on my fruit and so I'll . . . ?

He wanted sudden inspiration.

. . . and so I'll go sheep-farming in Australia . . .

. . . and so I'll put up some cash into an expedition to . . .

. . . and so . . .

He leaped down and as always poked about in the long grasses to see whether anything interesting was growing, and noticed that on these bramble bushes the fruit looked good and wholesome. He picked half a dozen berries and inspected them: Good as gold, not a maggot or web or mould. He poured them into his mouth and squashed out the juice between the roof of his mouth and his tongue, letting it trickle down his throat. It had all the magic of his boyhood.

There was nothing, but nothing that brought it all back like the tastes and smells of things that you grew or picked yourself. He thought of picking the cob nuts at Goose Grass, remembering the bitter taste of the green calix of unripe nuts, collecting horse mushrooms . . . the land the other side of the barrows grew enormous ones.

And cereals. That indescribable grassy taste of grass in unripe milky corn, and the nutty flavour when it was ripe and ready to harvest. He looked at his watch: three o'clock. He had promised that he would phone Maurice Cockrill at three-thirty. He didn't much relish the idea of going back into the house, where it would be shining and tidy and smelling of Mrs Pack's Brasso and Mansion Polish, but he didn't want to phone from the office, there was already too much speculation and uncertainty going on. Understandably, people were edgy when changes were in the offing and their jobs might be under threat. He felt a bit more cheered when he remembered that Mrs Pack had said that she'd make some malt bread and a few apple pies.

As Jake approached the steps to the terrace, he thought he heard someone dive into the pool. His spirits rose. Lizz. Except for himself, she was the only one who had used it recently. He was glad that he'd not turned off the heating.

As he climbed the steps to the terrace he saw the heart-stopping sight of a woman's naked body floating face-down. Her arms were outstretched and her legs straight making a cruciform. She was not moving except to slowly sink.

Jes-us!

His long legs took the rest of the steps in a stride. He raced to the edge of the pool, fear causing the blackberries to rise with bile and burn his throat. In one movement, he ripped off his boots and aimed his dive. As he went to push off the side, he glimpsed a movement. As her feet touched bottom, she bunched her muscles and thrust herself upwards. His dive went haywire and he toppled. As he met the water in an awkward, crashing dive he saw her surface, erupting into the turbulence he had caused.

It is difficult to say which of them was the more astonished: Kuan-Yin seeing a blur of a fully clothed figure hurtling towards her as she surfaced, or Jake. She gasped, and choked, paddling water, bobbing in the surge of his crash-dive, watching him flounder about as, hampered by the weight of his soaked clothes, he awkwardly tried to regain his balance. Pushing his hair from his eyes, he waded towards her.

'Jesus Christ! Don't you ever, ever do that to anybody ever again.' She was wearing her most exotic make-up, the upper lids of her eyes sparkling greenish-blue were outlined in black, extending and emphasizing their oriental shape. She was extraordinary, and as beautiful now, painted as she was with operatic exaggeration, as she had been with her pale, washed face on the morning when she rode the dragon. Her hair clung flat and gleaming, and where it reached the water, it lay in a floating cape moving about her shoulders, down her back and over her lovely breasts. He put an arm about her briefly. 'Thank Christ, you're all right. I've never moved so fast in my life.'

'Jake, honey, you've grown a beard. And you've got all your clothes on,' she said teasingly.

'I thought you were drowning, didn't I?'

'Jake, baby, I'm really, really sorry. I must get out, it's colder than I thought.' She swam to the edge where she lifted herself on to the terrace and flung a large towel around her. Jake hauled himself up and stood looking down at the water running out of his heavy cord trousers and Aran sweater. 'Oh, Jake, just look at you.' Her bright red mouth worked and began to form a smile.

'You can laugh. It's bloody cold, you know.'

'There are plenty of towels in the changing place: come, take your things off and I'll fetch you one.'

'It's OK, I'll manage.'

He heard her humming contentedly as he struggled to remove his stiff and heavy clothes. She brought him a towel and a robe.

'The colour suits you, matches your eyes.' The robe, with 'T' worked on the breast, was one of several Myrr had ordered for the Old Man from a colour supplement. Jake was not to know that when she had last seen the robe, Nat had been wearing it.

'Come on, let's go up to the house. Mrs Pack's been baking. I'll make you some tea. Or should you be the one inviting me?'

'That's what I've come to find out, Jake.'

NINE

And the end of all our exploring
Will be to arrive where we started . . .

T. S. ELIOT, Four Quartets

The habitués of the Green Man were not surprised when Jake and Kuan-Yin returned from a weekend in London and announced in the bar that they had married. Several regulars said that of course they knew all along that Jake would get her in the end, remember that they said as much as soon as she came in with him?

The midwife was not surprised that the child delivered to the primigravida geriatric oriental and her blond bearded husband inherited her father's red-gold hair and her mother's beautiful nose and almond-shaped eyes. And the nurses, knowing the strange names people think up for their children, weren't surprised that this baby was named Lady Natalie. Her parents had intended that she should be Natalie, but once the nurses had started calling her Lady, it stuck. The day would come when she would be furious to be named for her great-grandmother Lady Yin.

Certainly Rex Farenbach wasn't surprised when, within days of Lady Natalie's birth, the eight Yins and Heavenly's baby checked in at the Green Man. He felt that he knew them quite well by now. Since the wedding party had been held in his restaurant, there always seemed to be one or other of the Yin family visiting Childencombe. Everybody in the village knew that they had invested money in Sunbarrow, and had been surprised at how much money there was in Chinese restaurants.

As Jez Carter said, 'You never know who your neighbours are going to be these days. Just wait till the Hong Kong ones get their British passports, we'll have Geisha girls in all the leisure centres.' But people weren't so keen on Jez Carter's jokes these days. Somebody had spray-painted 'Dirty old man' on his plate-glass shop-front and signed it 'G.A.G'. Chrissie Pack said she reckoned it could be Girls Against Gropers. It was surprising how many young women and girls said that she was probably right. No . . . probably it wasn't at all surprising.

Rex wondered whether the Yins might be interested in starting a chain of restaurants in England. The Green Man was ready to go on the market and Rex ready to settle down in a place that had no cold weather.

Lizz and Mike were surprised at meeting by chance in a bar in Boston. Mike turned out to be one of those men who seem to loosen up when they are well away from home shores. They were in an odd position when Jake and Kuan-Yin married: Surplus to requirements, Mike said. Come and spend Christmas with me at Loxwood. No strings? Lizz queried. No strings.

Daisy was surprised. Not so much surprised that Jake had decided that he wanted to keep Sunbarrow, nor that he had wanted to settle down, but she hadn't expected that Jake would be one to make such a fool of himself over a baby. She and Poppy often had long phone calls and Poppy said that she liked the idea of Jake being a New Man, and did Daisy intend making Mimm Carter into one? A question Daisy, the suddenly wealthy Marxist-feminist, had problems with; it was bad enough finding herself in bed with a Marxist entrepreneur.

From Lady's first days at home Jake had bathed and changed and dressed her. He would come back from Winchester loaded with the latest baby gear and toys. He loved to sit opposite Kuan-Yin and watch the amazing scene of his beautiful wife suckling the miracle that had knocked him sideways when he had held her hands as she came sliding into the world. He had seen scores of animal births, but a human baby . . . he couldn't get over her. She had looked so vulnerable, so fragile, so bare and in need of care, that he found it difficult to believe that she could thrive. As for Kuan-Yin, she loved to hand over the baby to Jake and watch his large hand rubbing her back, then resting her on his shoulder. She felt so tenderly towards him when he cradled the kicking baby on his knees as he cleaned and powdered her, as she did when she saw him take her off over the Downs slung on his back.

The Childencombrians would make no effort to get their tongues round such a daft name, so once she stopped being a visitor they took to calling her Mrs Jake, which, Kuan-Yin being her own woman and proud of her professional title, didn't please her at all. Chrissie knew what it was like trying to keep your identity in the village, so she started straight off calling her Dr Tallentire. Not that the villagers cared much. If she was going to be Jake's wife up at Sunbarrow, then she'd have to get used to their ways.

Wanting no surprises, Rin and Mary had prepared themselves for any eventuality in Mary's latest pregnancy test – it showed positive. Rin kept his own counsel and hardly ever allowed the thought that Lady Natalie was his half-sister to enter his head. He and Mary were engrossed in finding a large house with plenty of rooms for nursery nurses and au pairs.

Myrr met the Yins in the neutral territory of Rex's restaurant at the time of the wedding. They were nice people and it was obvious that they adored . . . Alison. Alison and Heavenly had ensured the continuance of their line. Neither produced sons, but there was time. Myrr took to Heavenly; she was like Roz – one of those intelligent women who are always underestimated because they are so openly voluptuous.

The Yins were surprised that Alison had taken to this strange, inconvenient place. It was beyond their comprehension that anyone would choose to live not only where there were no sidewalks but only a few dim streetlights.

The gathering in England to view their investment in Alison did Lady Yin a lot of good. After a great deal of anguish she allowed her sons to take her to the Immigration Department. Nobody there was inclined to lock her up or send her back to China. In fact people seemed fascinated to discover that the chairman of the Park House chain was not a large boardroom American with gold links. Many people came to talk to her, smiling and talking slow and loud and they gave her papers so that she could leave the States and get back in again. After she had tested them by going to Alison's marriage party, and found that her papers worked, she surprised Lee Han in the same way as he had surprised her. Louis and Henry tagged along, not because there was any suggestion that Lady Yin wasn't perfectly able to get herself back the way she had once come: no, Louis and Henry wanted to see whether there was room for Blossom Park to expand into Hong Kong.

Roz came to the wedding party dressed in an uncluttered power suit but with her copper hair tumbling about her shoulders in a disturbingly feminine way. With her contradictory signals, she was so confusing to men. She was impressive.

Rex Farenbach hardly left her side. He confided, 'I shan't want for a pound or two when I've sold this place, Roz. How's about you and me looking for a nice condo on some sunny island?'

'You mean one of those nice isolated beaches where you idle around until your brain softens and bits of you wither and drop off for lack of use, Rex?' Which started Rex wondering whether maybe he should keep the pub and maybe bring in a manager for the restaurant and invest in some time-share place.

At the time of the party at the Green Man, Poppy was getting the Stylianopoulous children through chicken-pox. She had a Greek boyfriend now. Not serious. Emma and Chrissie had promised to spend their holiday in Greece.

Poppy had plans to persuade Emma to do a year nannying out there.

Only Jake and Kuan-Yin knew for sure that the marriage they were all expensively celebrating was a kind of business arrangement, a marriage of convenience so that the baby should bear its rightful name of Tallentire and so that Jake should not remain on Sunbarrow as an associate but as part-owner.

By the time Christmas came the sensibly arranged, business-like arrangement looked doomed – they hadn't counted on love. There was a shared bedroom and each had another which was their own territory, though from the first night, being of the last generation to grow up used to being able to freely and safely indulge their love lives, they had as often as not found themselves in one another's arms in the shared room.

Jake thought her more beautiful than ever when Kuan-Yin began to take on her pregnant shape, and when in bed one night he felt the baby move against his back, he knew for sure that he was in love with her. He decided not to disturb the present peacefulness of their lives by saying anything, but he no longer had any desire for the company of another woman or for the atmosphere of the Green Man bar. The memory of Roz on that powerfully erotic night faded and eventually Lizz too.

Without being aware that they were doing so, they began planning like any two newly-weds. They discussed the suitability of the house for a large family and where to put a nursery. Began to tell one another about their past. Began to think as a couple, to think of the future of the farm, to plan the withdrawal of agri-chemicals from the land, consult arborists about the possibility of making a spinney? Or a small wood?

One Sunday morning when Jake had at last got round

to drawing the winter cover over the swimming-pool, she came out on to the terrace.

'Jake, honey, there's a painting hanging in my bedroom.'

He nodded. 'I thought if you didn't want it, then the Bump might.' He held her kimono-clad mound possessively. 'It's a bit unusual as a family portrait, but that's what it is. I don't think anyone else should own it, do you?'

She held out a hand which he took. 'How much do you really mind, Jake?'

'About the Old Man? I don't know, I don't think that I mind at all. I find it pretty difficult to believe. It just seems to be my bump . . . our bump.'

'It was Tallentire. He was the only one. Mike was too soon and Rin too late.'

He continued holding and caressing the silk curve. 'And Jake not at all.'

'Do you remember the day when you found me floating in the pool?'

He twisted his brows and gave her an odd smile. 'You don't think I'm ever likely to forget, do you?'

'When I arrived at the house, it was empty and there was not one thing I could find as evidence that what happened between me and Tallentire had ever really happened. I sat on the terrace and thought: It's as if I've had a dream, or remembered a film, the set was there but no people, no things to tell me that my bump wasn't a phantom pregnancy, all in the mind.'

Jake idly fished out one or two leaves.

'We made love there the first time. Can I tell you?'

Jake wasn't sure that he wanted to know, but he had felt the baby move so he steeled himself to know its history and nodded.

'When you found me floating I was searching for something real. I had lost an earring . . . we were searching for it . . . and then it happened. I wasn't actually looking for

464

it that day, and it was gone anyhow, but I was trying somehow to make it real.' She smiled briefly. 'It's a technique we shrinks use sometimes. Back home I had come to think that it had only been a summer affair – the kind of thing that used to be called a shipboard romance, people got married on the strength of them. Tallentire might have followed me to the States – anything might have happened. And yet, when I wanted a memory powerful enough to hold on to, I couldn't find one.' She smiled at something going on behind her eyes. 'And then as I came up from the bottom as I had that night, you came hurling yourself into the water, and for a second you were your father, and I knew that it had happened.'

He felt a kind of power he had not experienced before surge through him, he wanted to pick her up and carry her into the house, to tell her not to worry, that he would look after her. She was not wearing her cosmetic face which was the thing that always made her appear strong and confident. He put his arms about her and she seemed to relax into them. 'And was that enough to reassure you? That second of thinking I was the Old Man.'

'Not was the Old Man in that sense, but the image was vivid enough to jolt my mind into driving gear.'

She certainly puzzled him at times.

'You think I'm nuts,' she said.

'No, I don't . . . a touch fanciful maybe?'

'I'm entitled, in my condition.'

'That's true.'

'I found my real memory just afterwards, in the changing room. You put on Tallentire's bathrobe, and there it was, a real thing with his initials and everything. It was what I needed to make me decide that I must keep the bump. As soon as I did that, I felt all my mixed-up bits and pieces fly back into their proper places then, and they've stayed there. It makes me feel very good, you know. Come on, what's so funny?'

'Not funny really. But, I mean, you're what ... a Jungian? an analytical psychologist? and here you are talking about your mixed-up bits and pieces flying back in their proper places?'

She grinned at him. 'We're human too, you know.'

'Oh yes? You'll be telling me next that your name is Frailty.'

She pulled his face down to her level and kissed him. 'Oh, Jake honey, to think that we might never . . .' But she did not put that thought into words.

Back in her bedroom, she stood looking again at the huge picture that entirely filled one wall. It was a room full of picture, of action, power and eroticism. The presence of it entirely changed the nature of the room. Uncle Han would probably say that it had done something to the *ch'i*: at some time she would look into that.

She reflected on what one day she might tell the child about the painting:

For a while there, we were the figures in the picture. We were not Alison and Nathaniel. It began with Tallentire telling me about ancient customs, and I had talked a lot about the state of mind of priests and priestesses who believe they become gods or goddesses and the state of mind of people who believe in them.

I said, 'Did I ever tell you that I'm named for a goddess, Tallentire?'

And he replied, 'It wouldn't surprise me.'

So I told him, 'The original Kuan-Yin is the goddess of mercy and compassion.'

I guess we can persuade ourselves of most things if we set out to do it – y'know, suggestion. We were great candidates to become deities. At the time I had the impression of being able to stay under water for a long time. We had been out in the sun all day, I guess it fried our brains a little. Anyhow, that's the man who put some magic into me to make you grow and become a person.

Mommy? If that's the one who put the magic in you . . .
what did Daddy do to get me?

There might not be an answer to that. Perhaps this family
portrait might go to a gallery.

> And all shall be well and
> All manner of thing shall be well
> When the tongues of flame are in-folded
> Into the crowned knot of fire
> And the fire and the rose are one.

T.S. ELIOT, *Four Quartets*

CHILDREN IN HIGH APPLE-TREES

The long, hot summer of 1990 was not repeated the following year; the hot days came late. Abundant spring rain fell
on Sunbarrow. The flocks on the Downs and herds in the
meadows cropped plentiful grass. Jake began the slow
process of weaning the soil from its intensive feeds of
phosphate and nitrates and on to waste products from the
chicken barns, the slaughter-house and their many and
varied horticultural harvests. It was an enormous under-
taking on a scale as huge as was necessary to change
Sunbarrow. It would take years. But for Jake the scheme
exerted a powerful pull. It kept him in, on and around Sunbarrow for all the daylight hours.

People said: He's going to be the Old Man all over again.

But they were wrong, he would not be. For one thing
nobody ever addressed him as anything but Jake. And he
was not, as Nat had been, thrust into adult responsibility
before he was an adult. And he had sown his wild oats at
the best age to enjoy doing so. He had gone into manhood

with the security that money and good fortune gives, plus a mother who loved him and siblings he liked and respected and who could live their lives without his help. And he had gone into marriage with security and a wealthy wife in partnership. Now, he had a splendid roof over his head, an intelligent, beautiful wife and a wanted child. Jake Tallentire had had a youth as golden as the thousands of acres of corn that surrounded his life.

As the summer of 1991 waned into the hot days of late July and August, farm after farm in the ancient Hampshire-Wessex triangle announced or tried to keep secret the locations of pictograms of ever more complexity. Jake was for ever being asked to make statements to the press and always used the occasion to say something about his increasing opposition to modern farming methods: 'I have only one theory and that is that they will cease appearing once the land is no longer force-fed to produce grain, much of which goes to fatten beef for burger bars, or to store in silos.'

He had no grounds for such a belief, but Kuan-Yin supported the probability that he was right. When Tallentire had inherited Sunbarrow, his land was dying of starvation so he had fed it with what was available – junk food in quantity. Jake believed that the land had become satiated and in need of a nutritious diet.

In late July and August new pictograms of high complexity appeared on every warm, dry night, making Sunbarrow a Mecca for film-makers, news-gatherers, scientists, tourists and knowledgeable lay people. Jake, still holding to his philosophy that no one should ever lay claim to the vast symbols, opened his fields to anyone who wanted to come and look. However, once they began coming in their many hundreds, he saw the sense of letting Mimm Carter organize sightseers so long as he didn't rip them off.

'No more than a pound, Mimm, and no charge for kids.'

'OK, as long as you agree to a strawberry and Coke stall, and a few mementoes.'

It was agreed, and all through weeks of the ripening and harvesting of the corn, Mimm and his helpers were in the fields for twelve hours a day ensuring that nobody desecrated Sunbarrow and that the tangible memories – books, charts, picture postcards, pencils and keyrings – essentials of tourism, were available to take home. Although he did a good trade in all this, most people who came to Butter, Clump, Fatt and Other Fields, and saw a pictogram for the first time, wanted no memento of the occasion: it was lodged for ever in the eye of their mind.

In mid-August, after three consecutive hot, dry days and nights, Mimm, helmetless on his pristine Norton bike, rode one morning at dawn into the Sunbarrow yard just as Jake was leaving the house eating his usual chunks of toast.

'You're about early, Mimm.'

'Have you seen your field up by the old Roman Road? You know the one, next to the one with barley ... used to be the Thomases' old farm before your dad bought it?'

'Butter Field? Not since last week.'

Mimm gave a wry smile. 'Didn't reckon you had.'

'I'll probably be over there today. The combines should go in this week.'

The brief look that flashed across Mimm's face seemed to be one of a kind of distress. 'You won't want to do that, Jakey.'

'What's over there, then, Mimm?'

Mimm jerked his head in the direction where the old Thomas farm lay. 'Come and have a look. Hop on.'

Butter Field was one of the prairie fields that Nat had created by grubbing up the hedges between a number of small fields that had once made up the two farms of the Thomas and the Butt families. It was the largest field on Sunbarrow and, like many others on this terrain, lay on a

469

slope. The slope of this wide prairie was upwards away from the old Roman Road. Mimm hiked his motor-bike on to its stand off the road and led the way up the gradient verge and over the field-gate.

The field held three new patterns, two similar to others on Sunbarrow land, but at the bottom of the slope, the eye was at once drawn to the largest and most beautiful.

'Well, Jakey, what do you make of them?'

Jake shook his head, not knowing what to answer.

The finely drawn ring enclosed a circle of equally finely executed 'petals' composed of perfect arcs joined tip to tip around a central core, as though created by a giant draughtsman. A stylized flower, it was Kuan-Yin's predicted Golden flower.

'What do you reckon then, Mimm? Is it a flower or is it a flower?'

'Yeah, bloody clever too. The corn's gone down like the big ones you had on Clump Field, you know sort of bent and woven, not just pushed down all the same way. Beats me how they do it.'

Which was more or less what Jake said later that same day when he spoke to Soo Batty, one of the more serious radio interviewers who had come to Butter Field with an almost open mind.

When Soo asked sightseers, 'What do you make of it?', most did their best to articulate their feelings, answering with short laughs, not wanting to be ridiculed in the way that some people who claimed to have seen UFOs in this same neck of the woods had been.

'I don't know, what can you make of a thing like that? Ha, ha. It makes you think, though. I always said it must be the winds did it . . . course, I hadn't ever seen one till now . . . but nah, ain't no winds I know could do a thing like that. Stands to reason, don't it?'

'We saw the one over Pepperbox way. We don't think this one's as good as the one at Pepperbox, do we? Of course, this one's more understandable. Well, it's a flower, isn't it?'

Soo asked, 'What do you think causes them?'

'Oh, it has to be scientific, hasn't it? Electricity or . . . plasma? . . . isn't that what it's called? I don't know much about it myself, but I don't reckon it's little green men.'

'If it is an electrical discharge or some such thing, how do you think it makes a flower?'

'Oh, I don't know, you have to leave all that to the scientists. Ha, ha. Makes you feel good, though. Don't you feel good? I do. I hope there are some more.'

She held up her mike to the salesman who had spoken to Jake back last spring. 'I've been coming to these fields for the last three years. It's not like any of the others. It's just fan-bloody-tastic. Marvellous . . . don't you reckon?'

'You've seen others, other corn circles? On this farm?'

'Oh yeah, I'm in the fitted kitchen business. This is my area. I always stop and have a look on my way back home – in the summer that is. Liverpool. Can't call them circles, can you? Triangles, ladders . . . bloody marvellous. I don't know why folks want to investigate and what-not about it? There's a couple of scientific chaps down there, both sure they're right, arguing the toss as though they had a monopoly. I read about a chap who reckons he makes them. Christ, he's got to go some to make a thing like that in the dark. I know it was in the dark because it wasn't there yesterday evening. Experts? They don't know any more than the rest of us. Ha, ha. If Jesus Christ appeared, there'd be some would say he was static electricity. That thing's bloody fantastic, though, don't you reckon? I hope they don't harvest yet. I'm going to bring my daughter down with me next trip.'

And Soo Batty asked scientists whom she introduced as experts:

'Are you any nearer the answer?'

They were not, but on tape they ploughed on. And Soo,

so like the ordinary public when faced with assured professorial tones, let them get away with half-truths and muddled answers for fear of being scorned.

'There is nothing new here. Spinning air, as I've said before, responsible for making the spiral mark that is the characteristic of these circles.'

'But these are not all composed of circles, are they? There are lines and angles and highly complex patterns. And this one's a flower . . .'

'So are frost patterns and snowflakes complex. No mystery, everything fits present scientific knowledge and with what I've been saying over the years.'

And she asked Jake. 'Mr Tallentire, you have lived with this phenomenon for several years, you farm the land and harvest the crops on which it occurs . . . you know how corn behaves. Can you think of anything at all that might cause this effect?'

'I can't.'

'No machinery that might be employed?'

'I don't know of any.'

'They're complicated and huge. It would take quite a time to produce them manually, wouldn't you say?'

'I guess it would. Especially at night. Even if you had a plan, you couldn't line up on anything . . . it's bloody dark up here, I can tell you.'

'You think it would need quite an army . . . plans, organization, lights. Time and money?'

'It would.'

'OK then, Mr Tallentire, you're a pretty down-to-earth sort of a man, you live, eat and sleep close to the phenomenon, what do you think is causing it?'

After a short pause, which was cut in the editing, Jake said, 'The more I see and learn about it, I can't get away from the thought that there's an intelligence at work here. An intelligence with a great sense of humour. A bit of a joker in fact.'

Soo Batty did not pursue the questioning, or if she did it was edited out for the programme.

Jake guessed that he'd probably be presented in the press as belonging to the lunatic fringes, the Sons of God and the End of the Worlders. On the other hand, they might wonder what he meant by 'a bit of a joker'. So what? The good opinion of people who didn't know him had never bothered him.

As he walked away from Butter Field back to the farm offices to give instructions that none of the corn close to the symbols was to be harvested, he pondered on the roundabout way he had been led into a marriage with the one woman with whom he now felt sure he could spend a lifetime. When he had told her this, she had agreed. Perhaps, she said, they had been working their way towards one another through other previous lives.

'Who knows, Jake, this may be the last level for us.'

'The last level?'

'We may not have to return to earthly bodies again.'

He was beginning to understand the sudden change that she had wrought in the Old Man. She shocked you into thinking unconventionally. She wasn't afraid of her thoughts or her instincts.

In some ways, she was as mystical and enigmatic as that flower. In comparison, other women were now unexciting. A lifetime would not be enough with Kuan-Yin. He must ask her about this last level. He wouldn't like to find himself in eternity without her.

They had spent much of their time together organizing the new Sunbarrow, starting with the planting of new hedgerows, a complete reversal of the grubbing-out operations that had gone on in the fifties and sixties, not only at Sunbarrow but in fruit orchards all over Hampshire. By the autumn he had several acres of Sunbarrow land fenced off, and before the soil cooled, he and Kuan-Yin took Lady Natalie to where Queer Stone now lay in pieces, and planted the first of a non-profit-making crop such as Sunbarrow had not known in a long time. These were not modern apple-trees grafted on to modern dwarfing stock, but trees that when full-grown would need people on ladders to pick their fruit.

> Time present and time past
> Are both perhaps present in time future,
> And time future contained in time past.
> If all time is eternally present
> All time is unredeemable.
> What might have been is an abstraction . . .

T.S. ELIOT, *Four Quartets*

Here, in this corner of England that used to be known as Wessex, there abound circles of stones, unnatural hills, wood henges, tumuli, tors and lone stones that are so familiar to us who live here that often we do not give them a second glance. Six thousand years of history whizz past on a short shopping trip. On Sunday mornings we climb St Catherine's Hill and watch our children walk dolly-steps on the coiled serpent of the unfathomable Maze where we sit on the grass. There, children who don't particularly want to know ask: How did it come here? Why? Who did it? What's Neolithic? Why did they make it?

Trying to give them an answer, something stirs deep within us and we shy away from knowing: I don't know, Justin, it was ages ago, perhaps it was some game they played.

Going home, we wind down the car window and point to a cornfield and say: Look, Johnny, look, Helen, look, there's another one of those. And for a few miles we speculate, and wonder at the vast complicated symbol that was not there when we passed by yesterday.

Then on the radio authoritative voices tell us that they know! It is the wind. It is the different temperature levels. It is men with boards strapped to their feet. It is the local cricket team, mating hedgehogs or rutting stags, the SAS, the MoD, advertising agencies. And, although we know that there is probably a grain of all of these truths in the explanations, somewhere, in that part of our minds that is like the photographer's black velvet bag, we long ago identified the authoritative voice. It is the one that gives us misinformation and plays dirty tricks.

We know what happened to our spirits when we saw for the first time, Hermes caduceus, the symbol of Gaea Hermaphrodite and the Golden Chrysanthemum carved into a cornfield.

In our weekend, unorthodox heart of hearts – when on a long leash from our logical, practical, science-imbued selves – we roam the seashore, the lakes, woods, downs and open places dreaming that Nidhoggr has gnawed its way through the roots of its tree and the Spirit is free.

In that heart of hearts we crave new myths in which northern dragons smile as the one Rin Tallentire made for his father smiles. We long for the tunnel vision of science to be found wanting and our time-level and dimension to be just one of many. We long to reunite with the mystical, other half of our whole selves. Or something!

We hope that the beautiful complicated circles and triangles, the keys, spirals and arcs, the symmetrical ship's wheel, and the Golden flower in the cornfields, might be a message to the planet; for we have screwed it up and we haven't the strength or the will to save ourselves.

But what if . . . ? We ease off the accelerator at the thought . . . what if it should be a message *from* the planet?

'Do apples grow well around here, Jake?'

'This used to be prime hard-fruit country.'

'Don't let us grow supermarket fruit. Let us specialize in rare kinds.'

'On big trees like there used to be on Sunbarrow. Big trees that will grow fast so that it won't be long before they're high enough for children to climb into the branches.'

'Is that sound business practice?'

'Not in Blossom Park or old-style Sunbarrow terms.'

'But we wouldn't go broke?'

'You can take up Mike Alexander's offer of a partnership. I wouldn't object to being a kept man. And just imagine . . . in spring Clump Field will be a fantastic sight, apple-blossom as far as the eye can see. We'll put cherry trees in the Other Field and keep bees for the pollination. We could go back to using the old-fashioned straw skeps.'

'You're a romantic at heart, Jake.'

'I wouldn't want to argue with that.'

'OK then, honey. We'll have your big tall apple-trees, and we'll have a dozen children to help with the harvest. They could sell honey by the roadside.'

'Sunbarrow will be famous for its apples and babies.'

'Oh, how wonderfully yellow-brick road. People could come and picnic here.'

'How does "Blossom Park Orchards" sound?'

'It sounds like a Chinese restaurant.'

'June and George would be pleased; so would your grandmother.'

'This place would never answer to any other name but Sunbarrow, Jake.'

'"Sunbarrow Orchards", then.'

Lady, as she did whenever she was doing anything – or

when she was doing nothing for that matter – drew their attention by banging a rattling toy with amazing skill.

'Jake, I've offered Lizz's picture on loan to my old college. You don't mind?'

'It's yours, Kuan-Yin.'

'Right, honey.'

'It does dominate that room, don't you think?'

The baby demanded their attention, which they happily gave. Some time in the future when Lady was grown, she could have the picture if she wanted it.

'If we had another baby, we could call her Blossom.'

'We could, if she wasn't a boy.'

'I'm pregnant, Jake.'

By the spring of 1992, the hawthorn hedge that had been reinstated around Butter Field the previous autumn sprouted bright, healthy green. In June, when black-haired baby George was born, the first of the Butterfield walnut trees were in leaf.

'Walnuts?' asked pregnant Heavenly, visiting with Louis who was dandling their first two children.

Kuan-Yin, carrying both the Tallentire babies, yet still looking as exotic and lovely as when she first came to Sunbarrow, was supervising the building of a child-proof wall around the swimming-pool. 'We're trying to stop screwing the land.'

Heavenly was good with accounts and investment reports. 'The projected figures look good.'

Jake liked his sister-in-law, voluptuous and long-legged; he had never seen her when she was not pregnant. 'Apples you plant for yourself, cherries for your children, walnuts for your grandchildren. In forty years, they'll be glad we planted walnuts.'

'Well, you can't put it all down in dollars and cents,' Louis said.

Jake thought: You can't put *any* of that down to dollars and cents.

BETTY BURTON
SOUTHSEA
HAMPSHIRE
FEBRUARY 1991